SKANDALON

ARSENAL PULP PRESS
Suite 202–211 East Georgia St.
Vancouver, BC V6A 1Z6
Canada
arsenalpulp.com

Cet ouvrage a bénéficié du soutien des Programmes d'aide à la publication de l'Institut français.

This is a work of fiction. Any resemblance of characters to persons either living or deceased is purely coincidental.

Printed and bound in the Republic of Korea

Library and Archives Canada Cataloguing in Publication:

Maroh, Julie, 1985–
[Skandalon. English]
Skandalon / Julie Maroh ; translated by David Homel.

Translation of French book with same title.
Issued in print and electronic formats.
ISBN 978-1-55152-552-5 (pbk.).—ISBN 978-1-55152-553-2 (epub)

1. Graphic novels. I. Homel, David, translator II. Title.
III. Title: Skandalon. English.

PN6747.M36S5313 2014   741.5'944   C2014-904385-6
                                                 C2014-904386-4

JULIE MAROH

SKANDALON

translated by DAVID HOMEL

ARSENAL PULP PRESS VANCOUVER

"There is more difference betwixt such and such a man than there is betwixt such a man and such a beast."

—Montaigne

"Society prohibits only what it provokes."

—Claude Lévi-Strauss

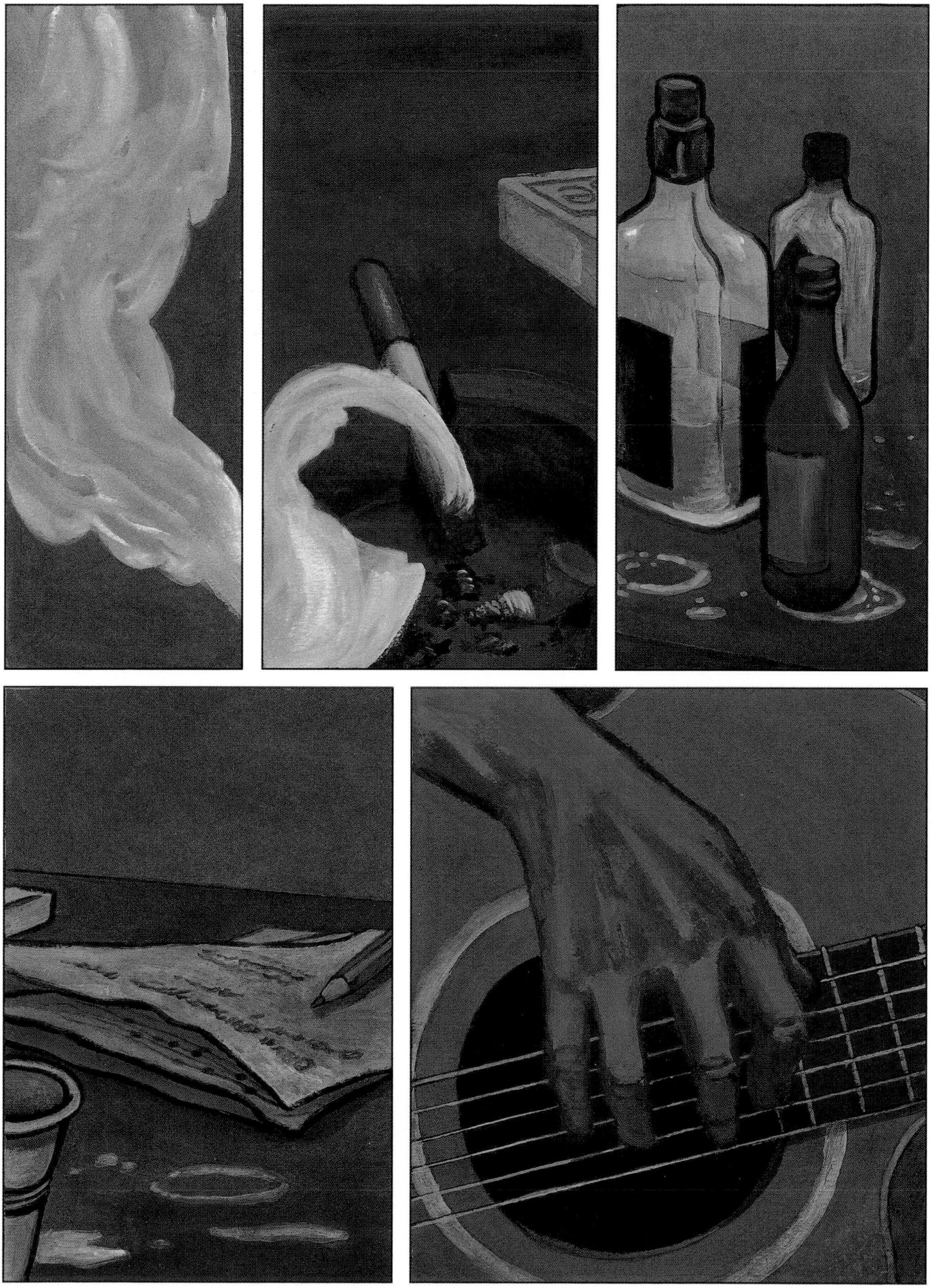

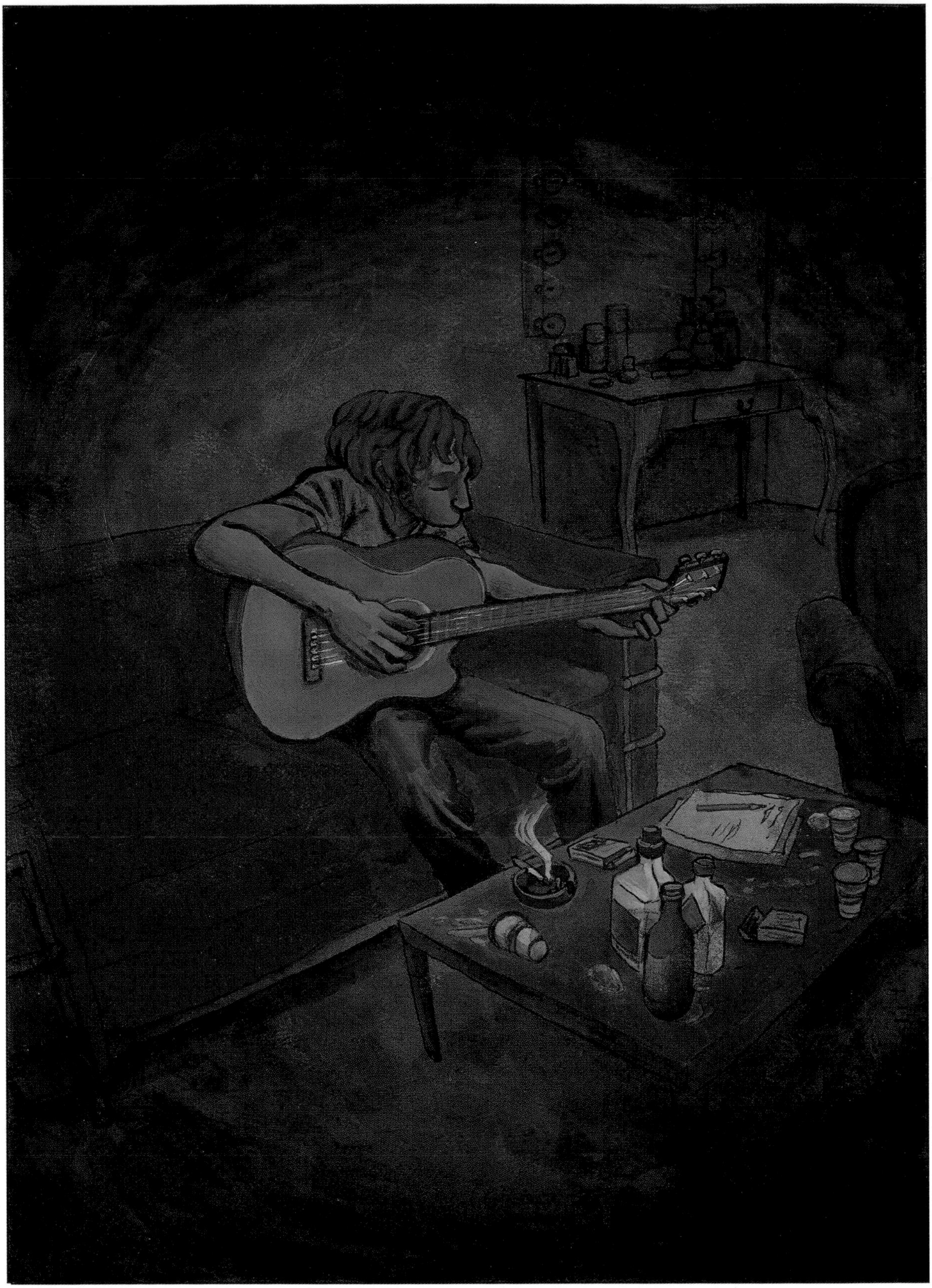

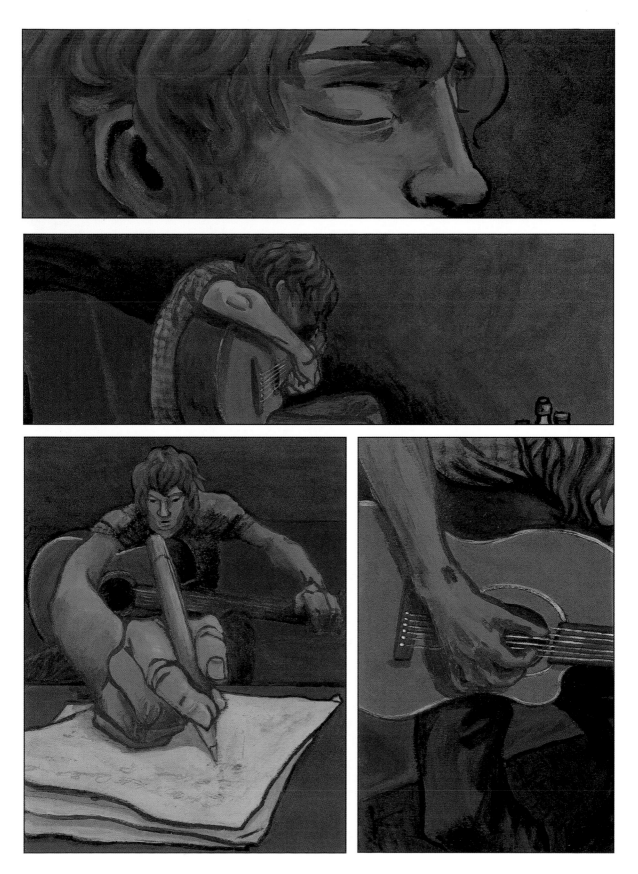

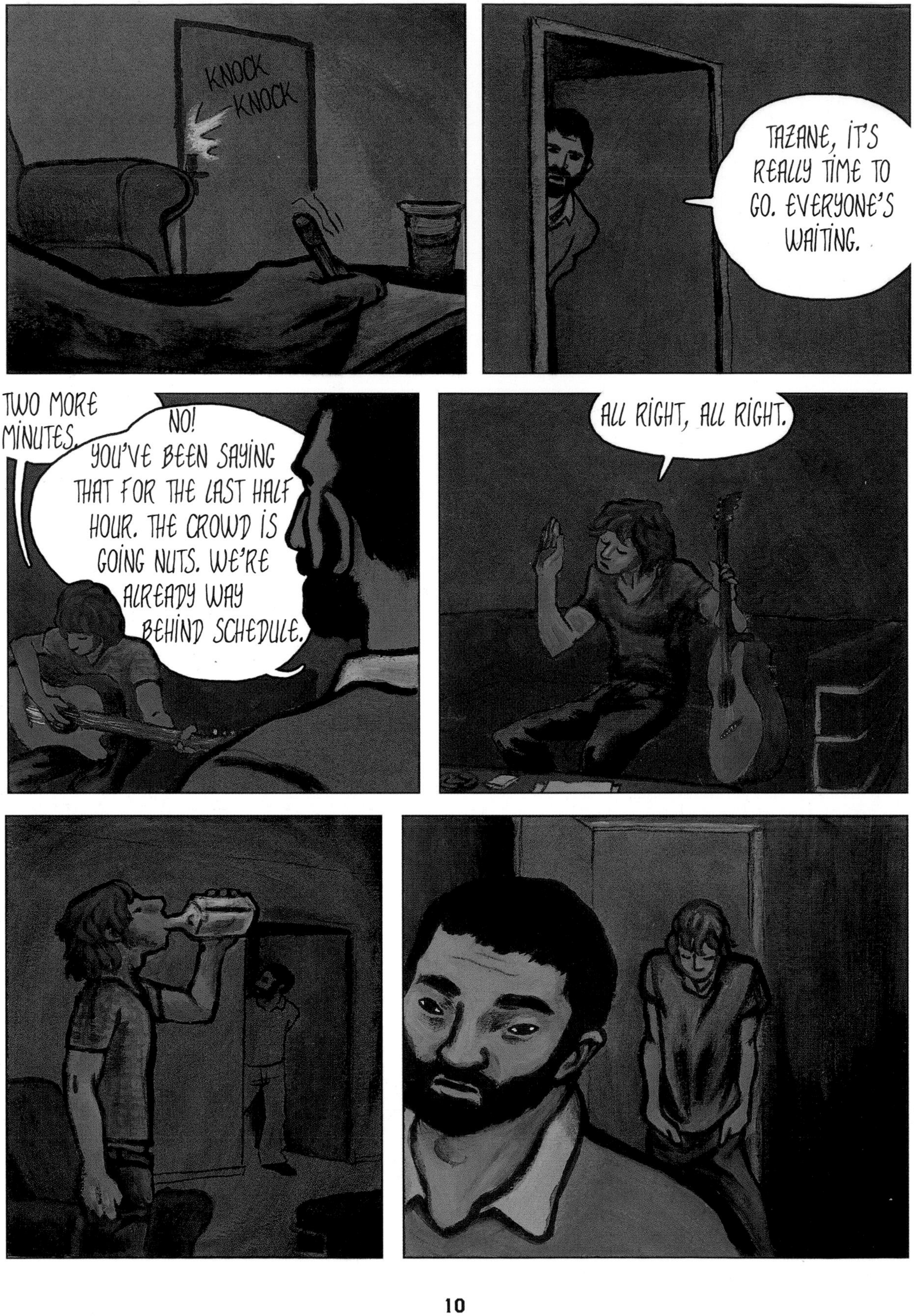
KNOCK KNOCK
TAZANE, IT'S REALLY TIME TO GO. EVERYONE'S WAITING.
TWO MORE MINUTES.
NO! YOU'VE BEEN SAYING THAT FOR THE LAST HALF HOUR. THE CROWD IS GOING NUTS. WE'RE ALREADY WAY BEHIND SCHEDULE.
ALL RIGHT, ALL RIGHT.

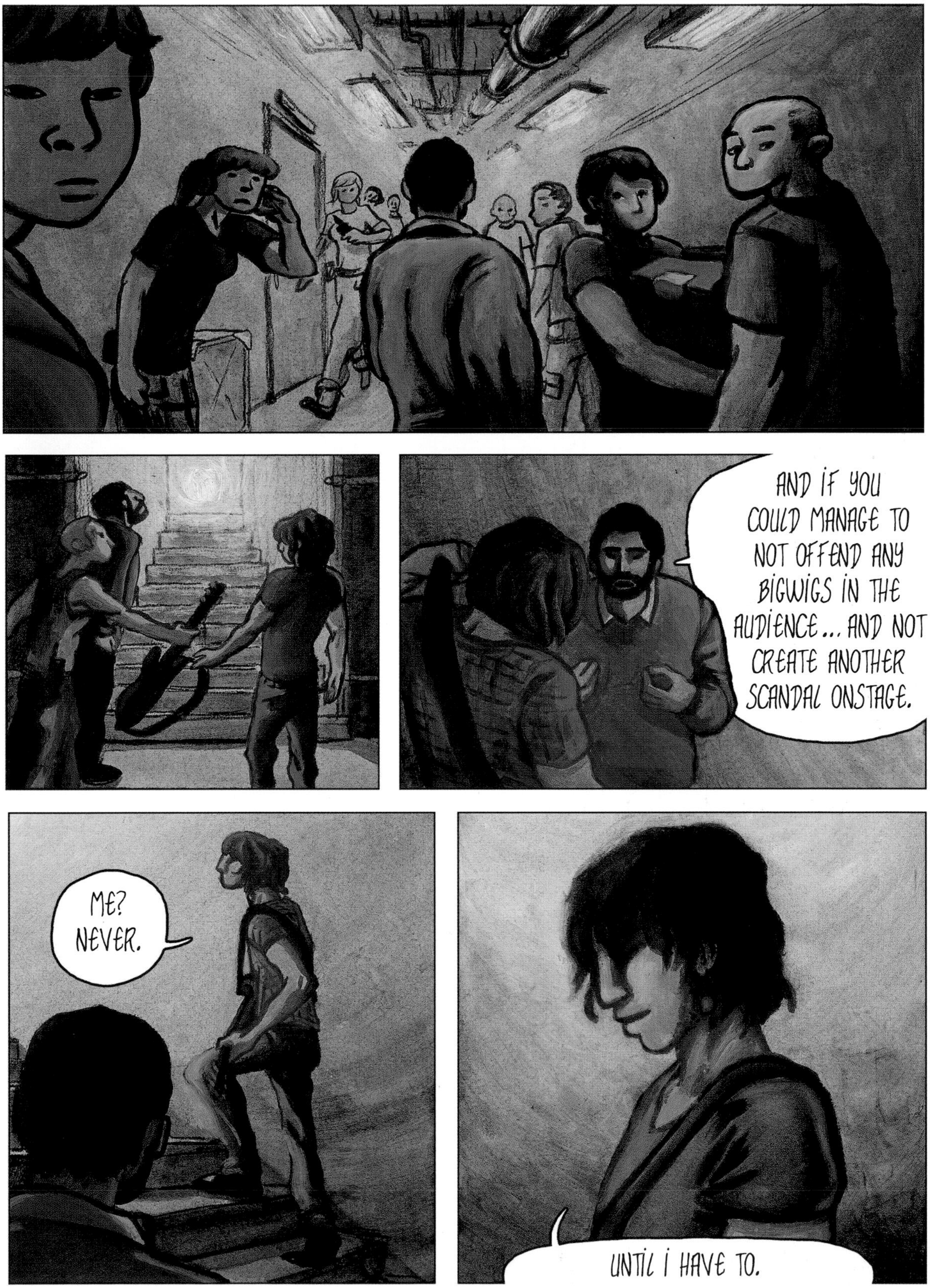
AND IF YOU COULD MANAGE TO NOT OFFEND ANY BIGWIGS IN THE AUDIENCE... AND NOT CREATE ANOTHER SCANDAL ONSTAGE.
ME? NEVER.
UNTIL I HAVE TO.

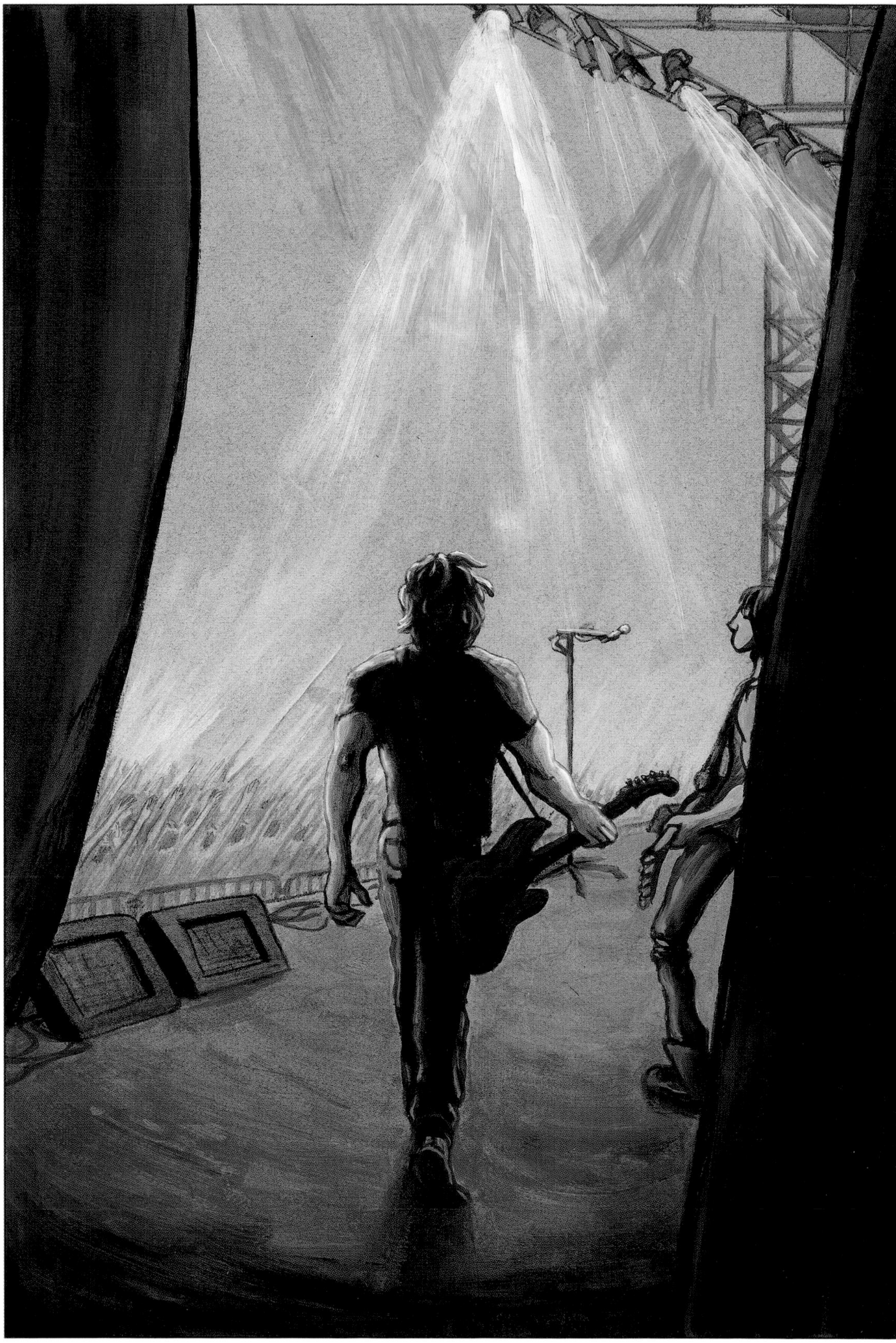

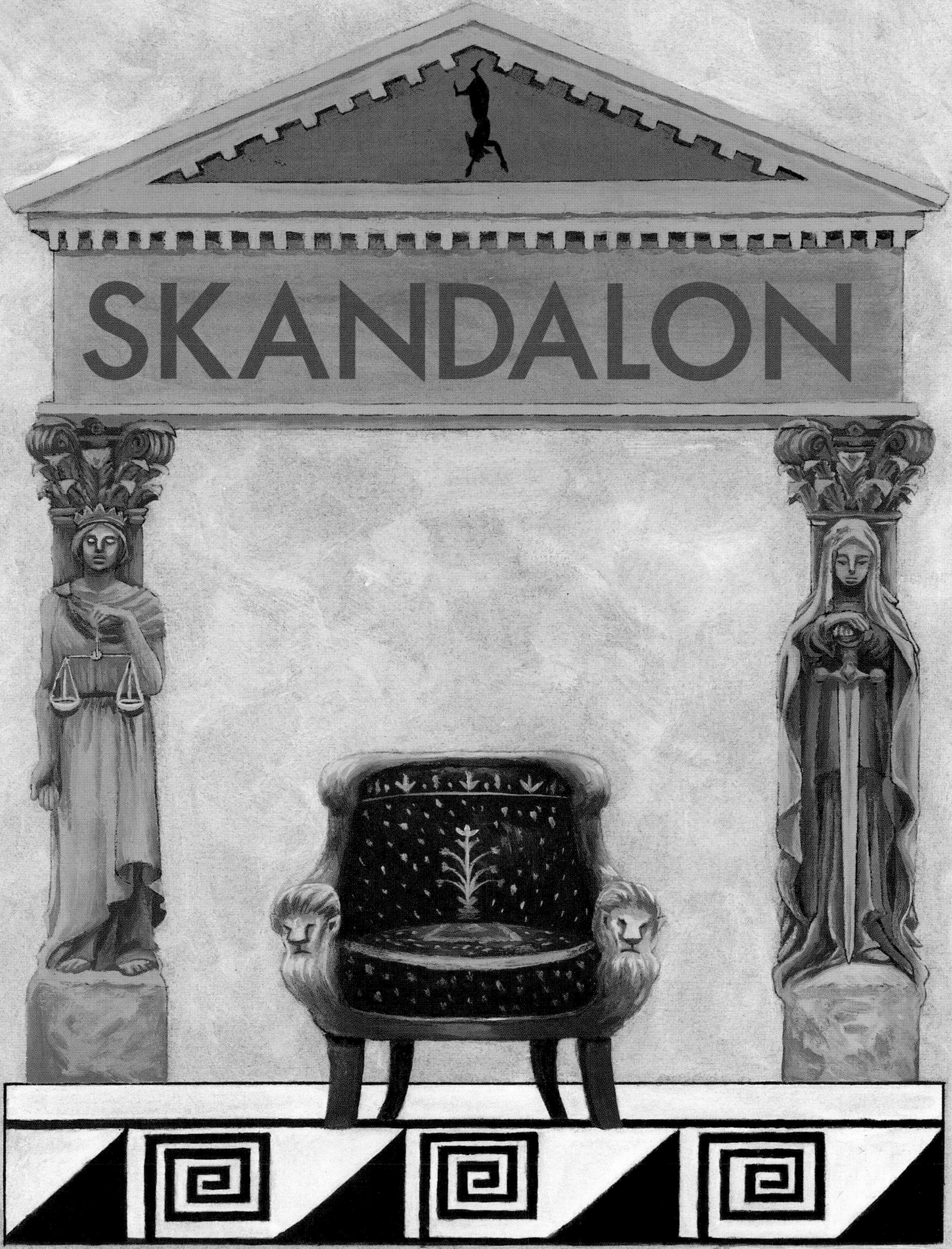
SKANDALON

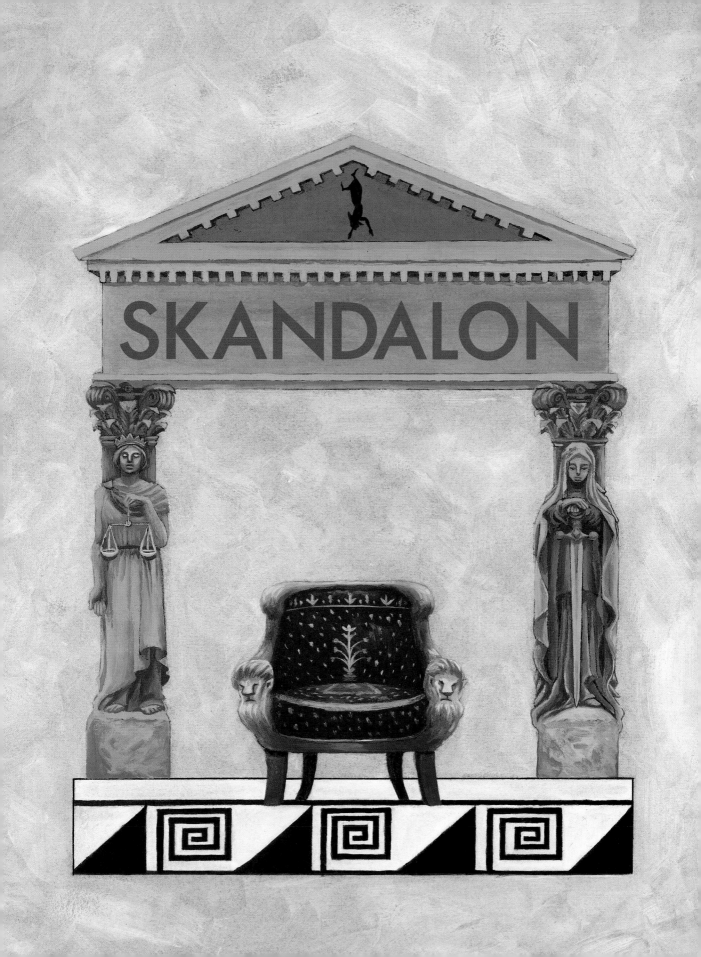

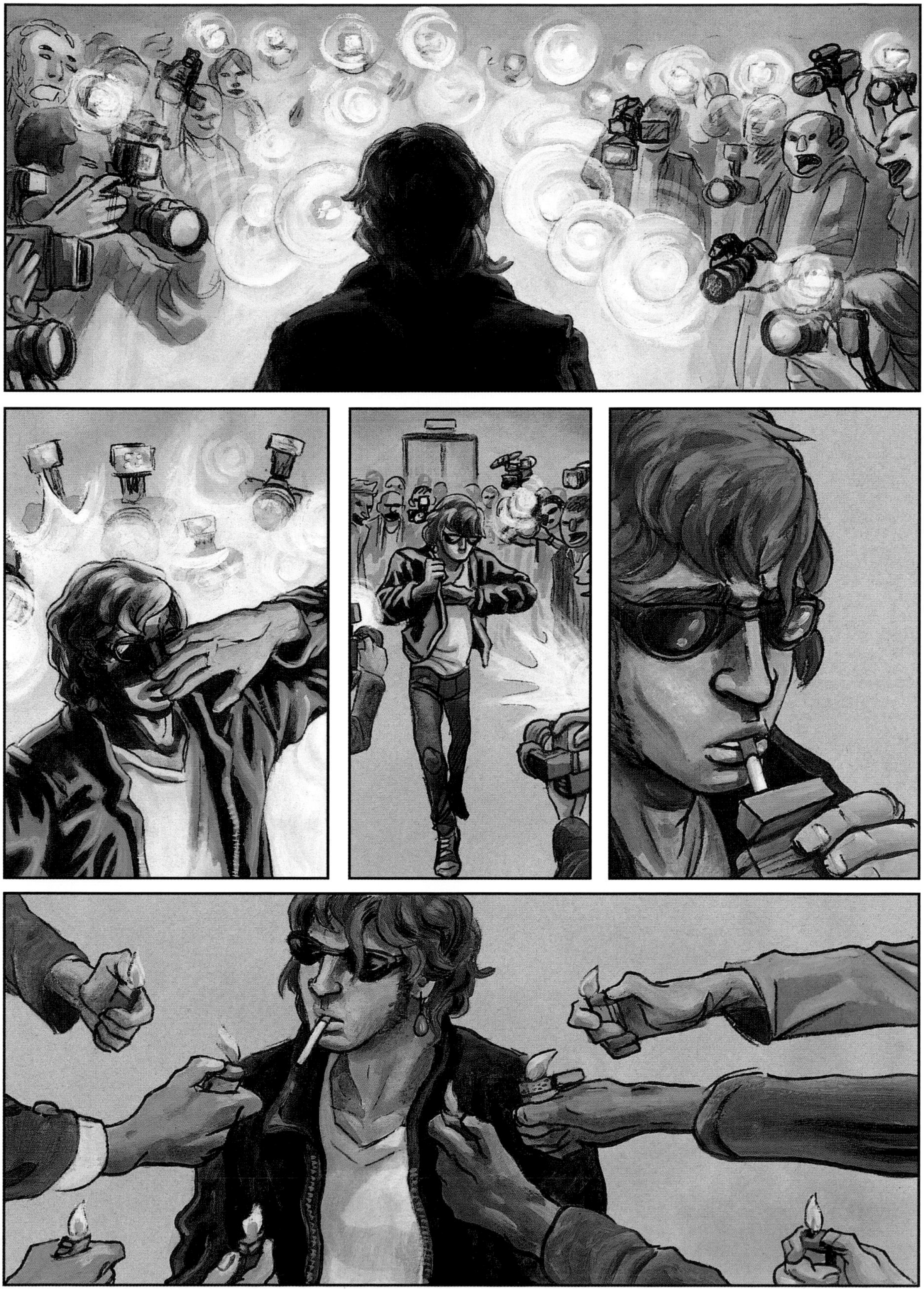

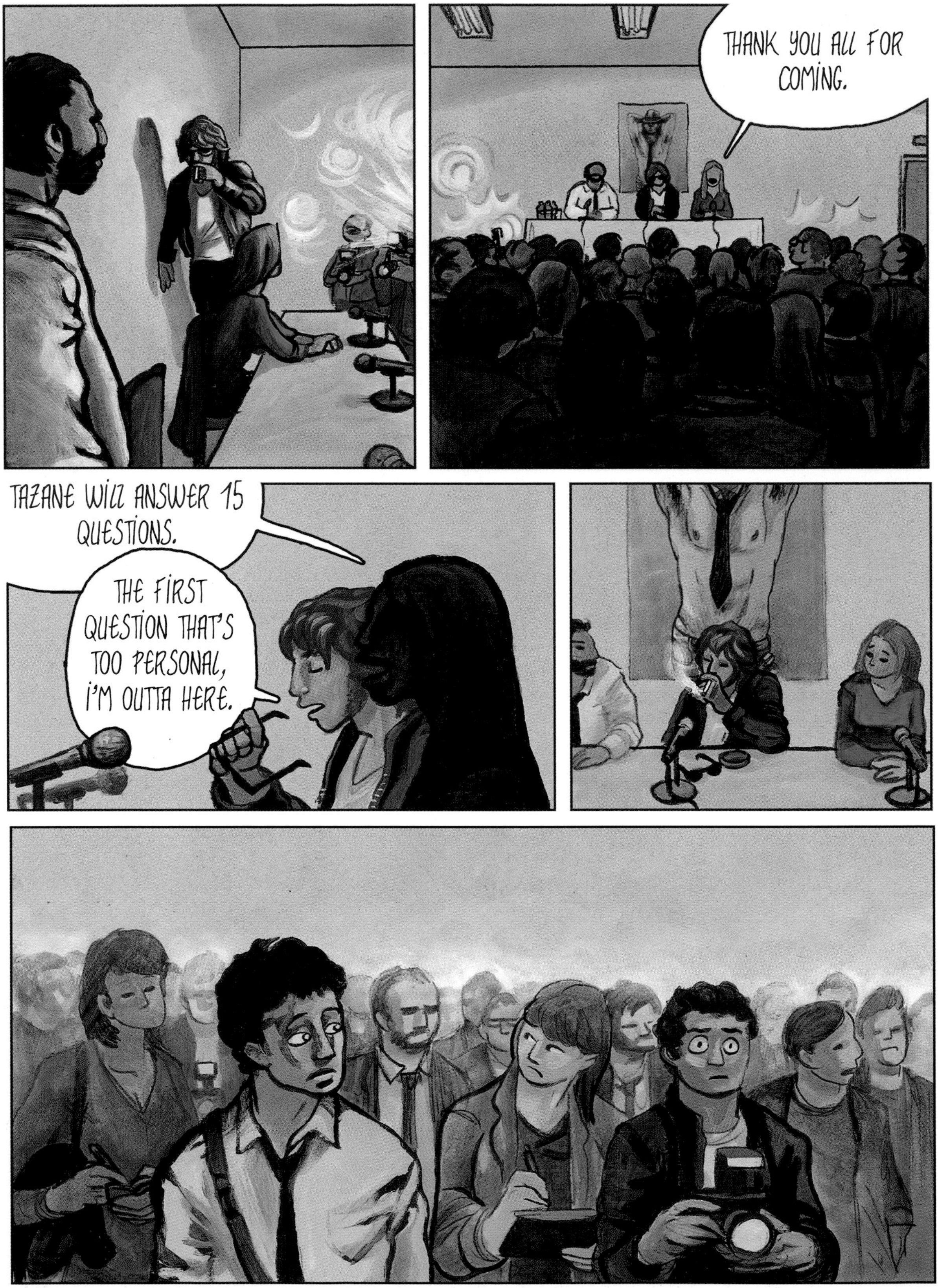
THANK YOU ALL FOR COMING.
TAZANE WILL ANSWER 15 QUESTIONS.
THE FIRST QUESTION THAT'S TOO PERSONAL, I'M OUTTA HERE.

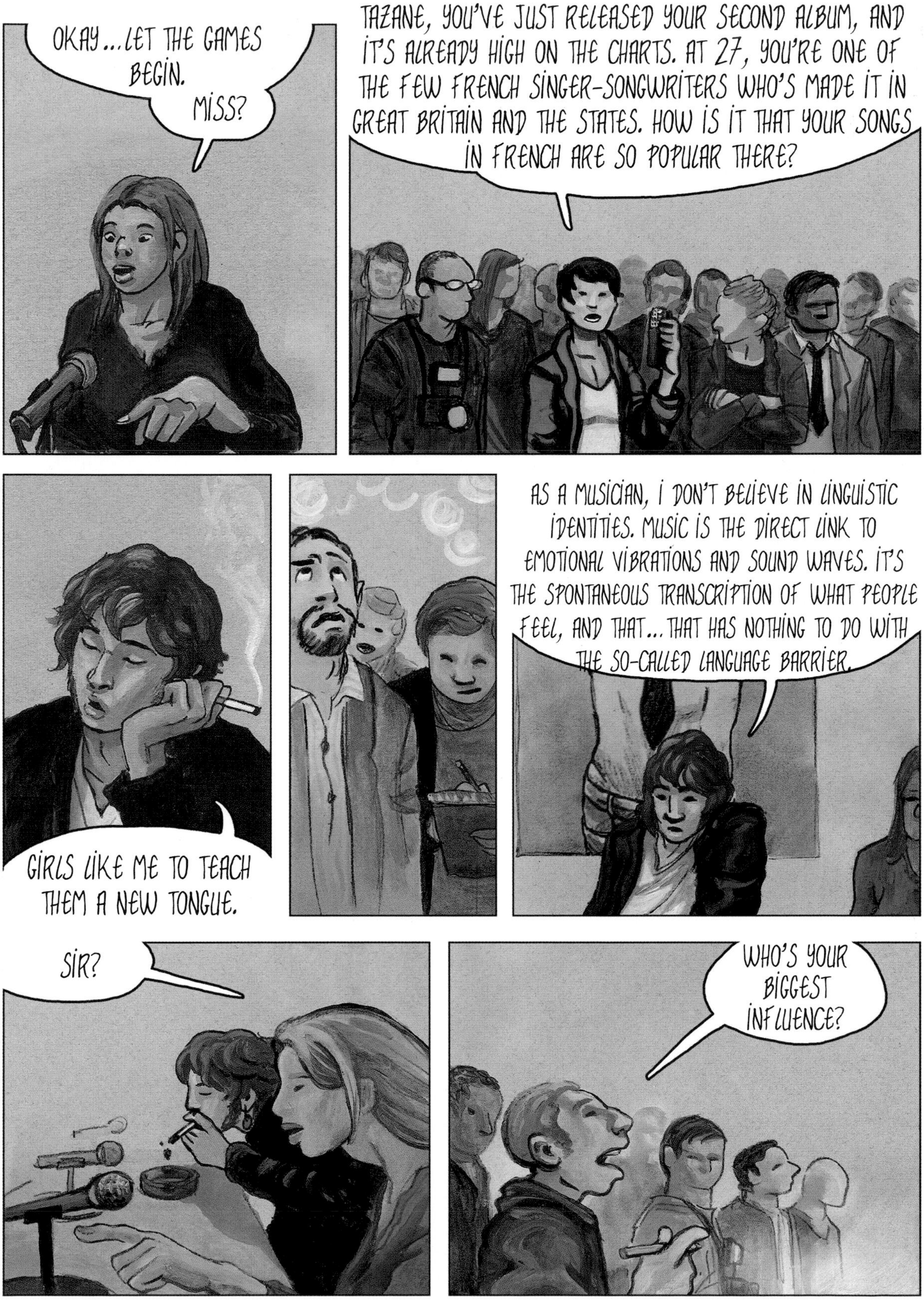
OKAY...LET THE GAMES BEGIN.
MISS?
TAZANE, YOU'VE JUST RELEASED YOUR SECOND ALBUM, AND IT'S ALREADY HIGH ON THE CHARTS. AT 27, YOU'RE ONE OF THE FEW FRENCH SINGER-SONGWRITERS WHO'S MADE IT IN GREAT BRITAIN AND THE STATES. HOW IS IT THAT YOUR SONGS IN FRENCH ARE SO POPULAR THERE?
GIRLS LIKE ME TO TEACH THEM A NEW TONGUE.
AS A MUSICIAN, I DON'T BELIEVE IN LINGUISTIC IDENTITIES. MUSIC IS THE DIRECT LINK TO EMOTIONAL VIBRATIONS AND SOUND WAVES. IT'S THE SPONTANEOUS TRANSCRIPTION OF WHAT PEOPLE FEEL, AND THAT... THAT HAS NOTHING TO DO WITH THE SO-CALLED LANGUAGE BARRIER.
SIR?
WHO'S YOUR BIGGEST INFLUENCE?

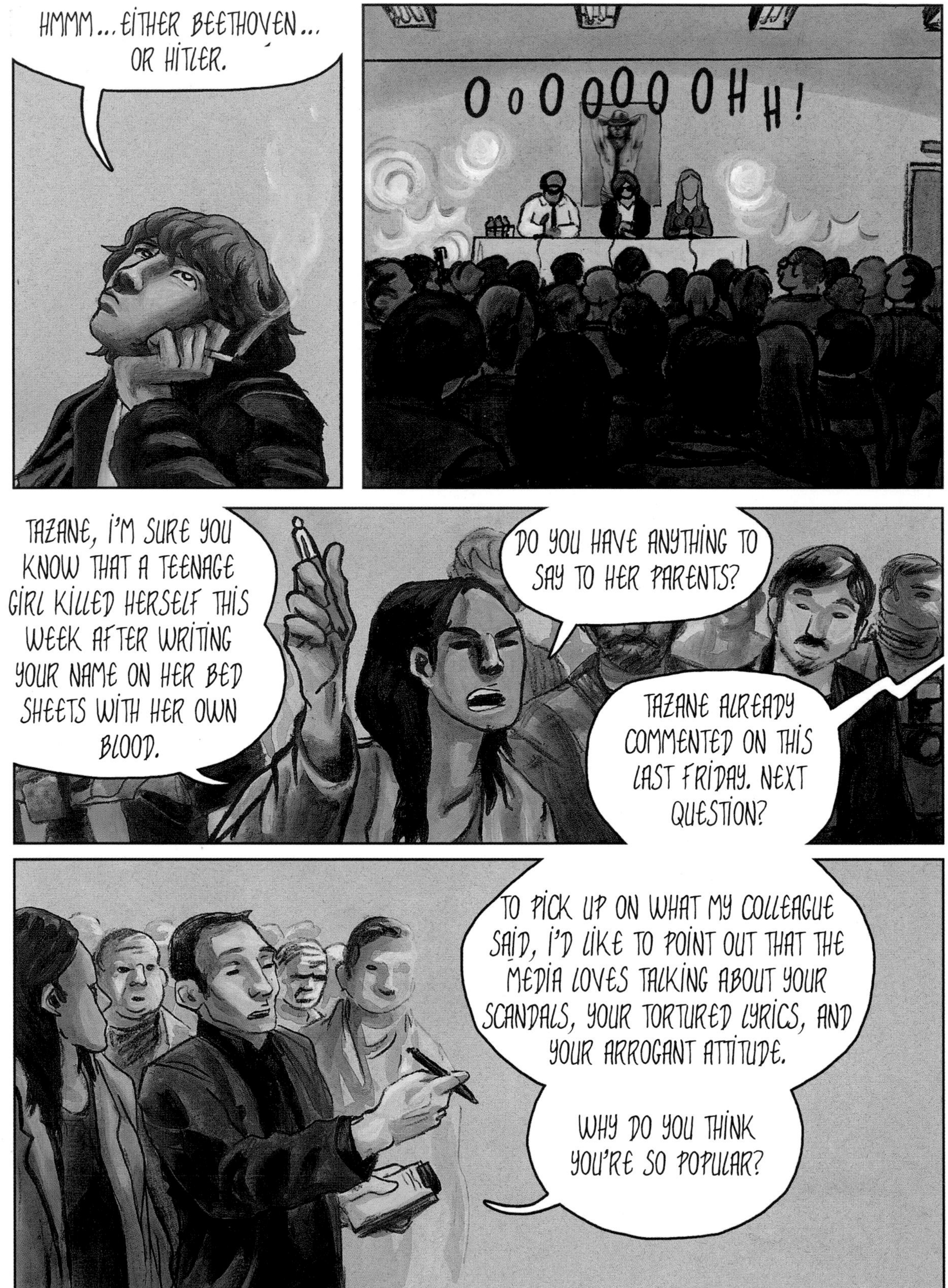
HMMM... EITHER BEETHOVEN... OR HITLER.
OOOOOOOHH!
TAZANE, I'M SURE YOU KNOW THAT A TEENAGE GIRL KILLED HERSELF THIS WEEK AFTER WRITING YOUR NAME ON HER BED SHEETS WITH HER OWN BLOOD.
DO YOU HAVE ANYTHING TO SAY TO HER PARENTS?
TAZANE ALREADY COMMENTED ON THIS LAST FRIDAY. NEXT QUESTION?
TO PICK UP ON WHAT MY COLLEAGUE SAID, I'D LIKE TO POINT OUT THAT THE MEDIA LOVES TALKING ABOUT YOUR SCANDALS, YOUR TORTURED LYRICS, AND YOUR ARROGANT ATTITUDE.
WHY DO YOU THINK YOU'RE SO POPULAR?

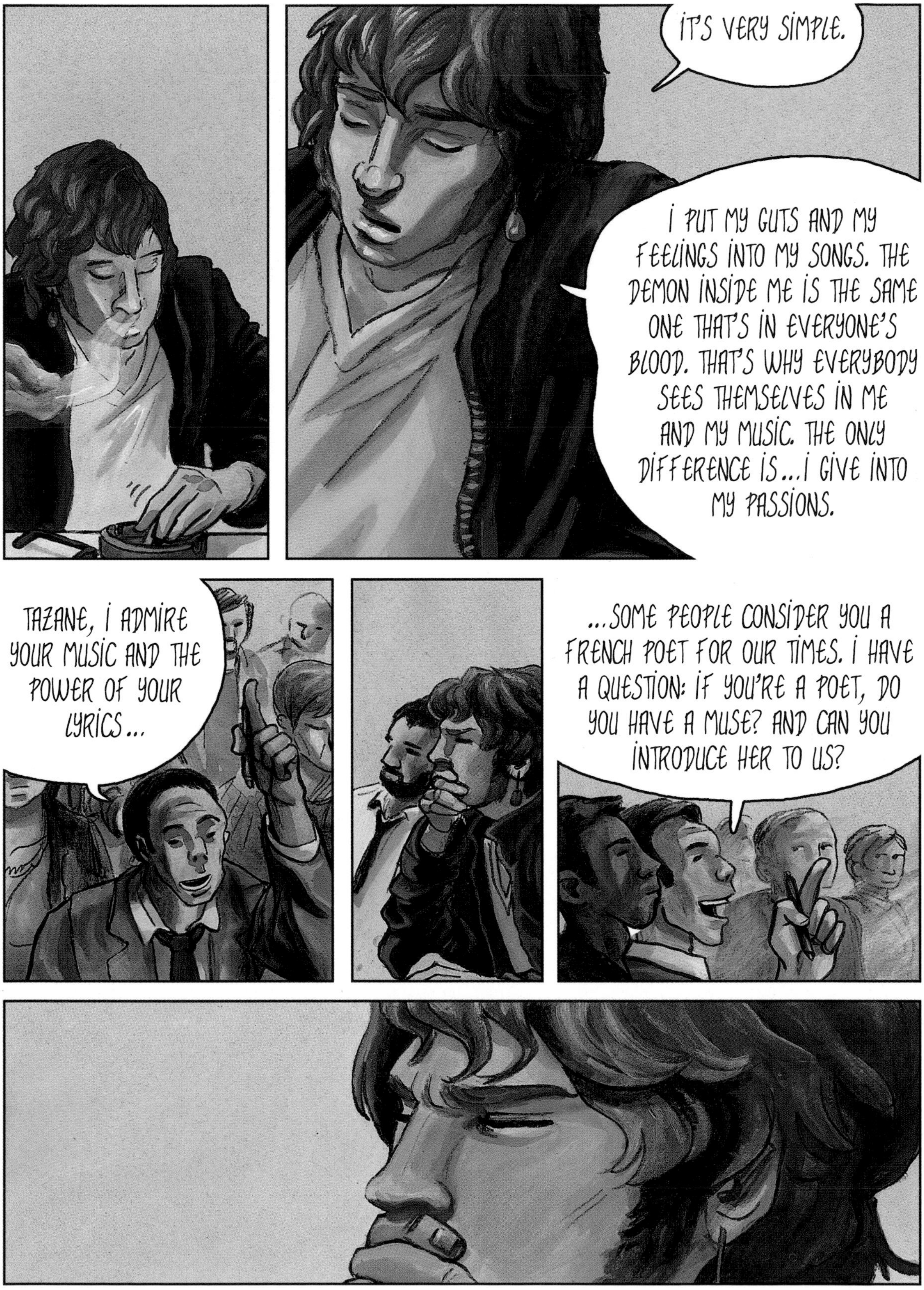
IT'S VERY SIMPLE.
I PUT MY GUTS AND MY FEELINGS INTO MY SONGS. THE DEMON INSIDE ME IS THE SAME ONE THAT'S IN EVERYONE'S BLOOD. THAT'S WHY EVERYBODY SEES THEMSELVES IN ME AND MY MUSIC. THE ONLY DIFFERENCE IS...I GIVE INTO MY PASSIONS.
TAZANE, I ADMIRE YOUR MUSIC AND THE POWER OF YOUR LYRICS...
...SOME PEOPLE CONSIDER YOU A FRENCH POET FOR OUR TIMES. I HAVE A QUESTION: IF YOU'RE A POET, DO YOU HAVE A MUSE? AND CAN YOU INTRODUCE HER TO US?

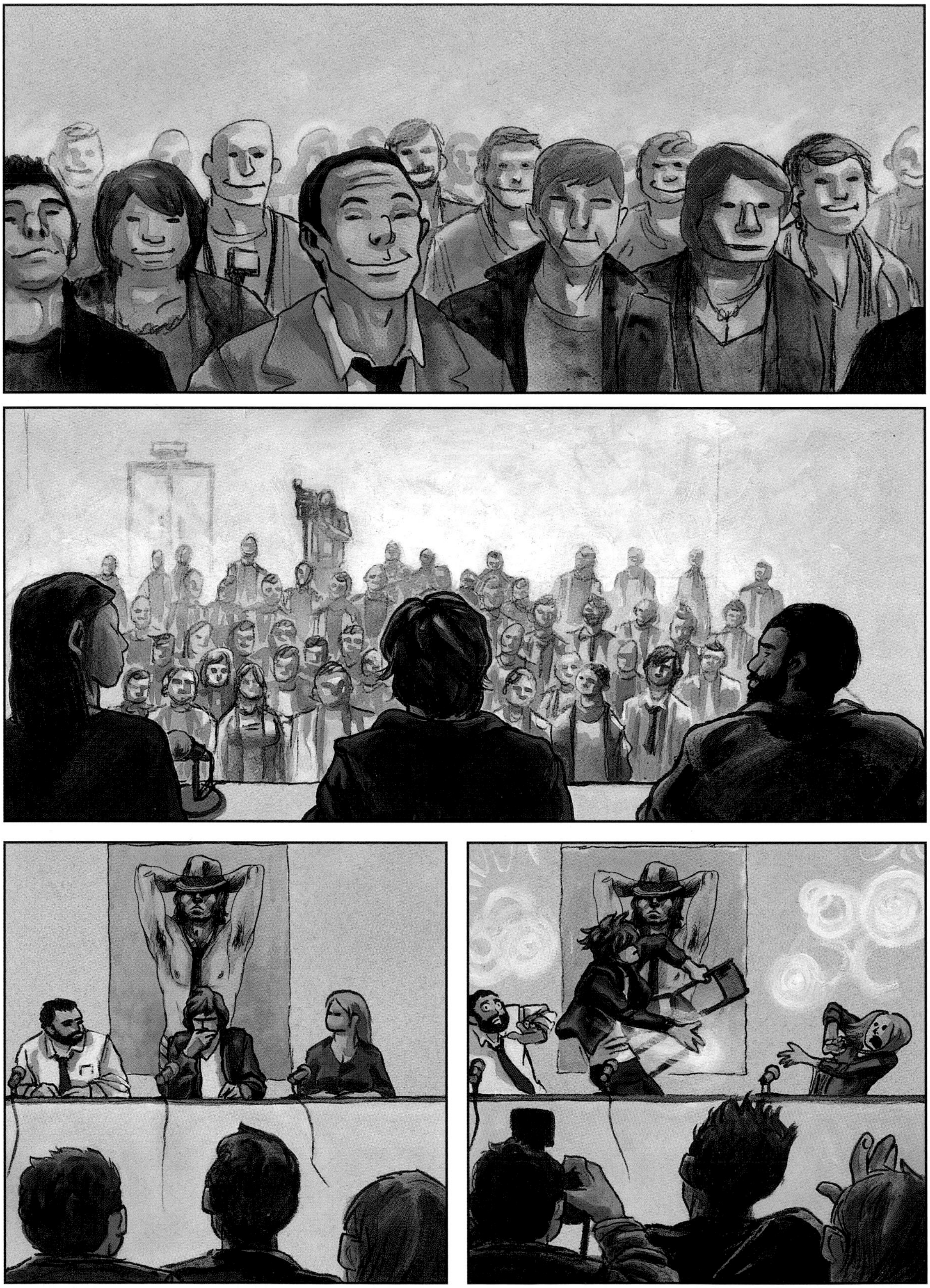

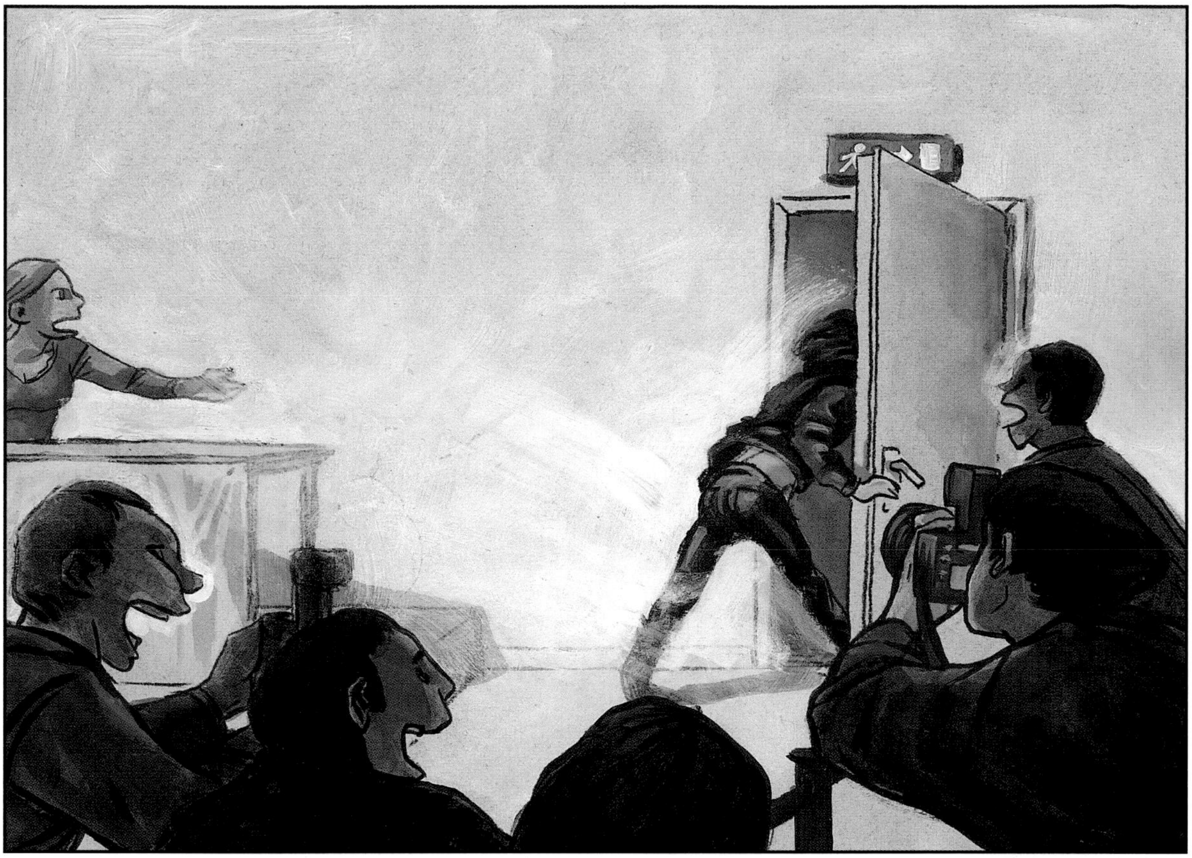
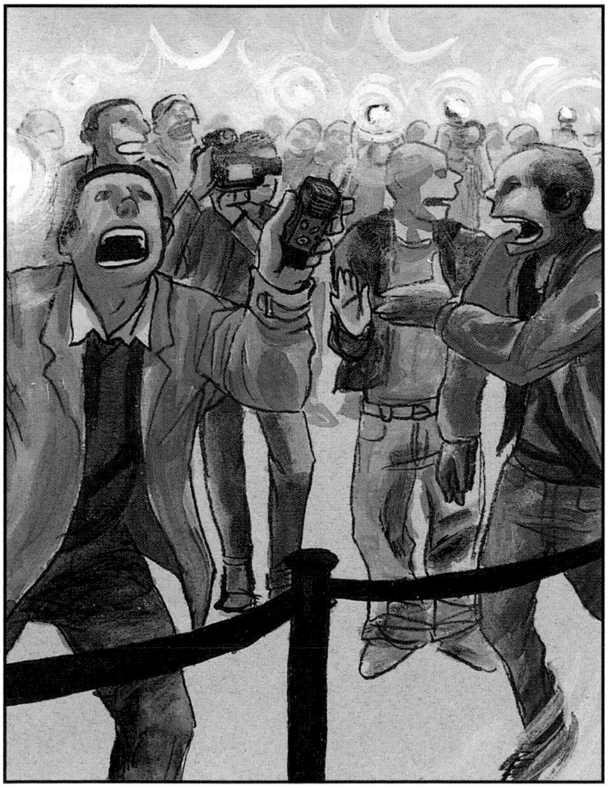
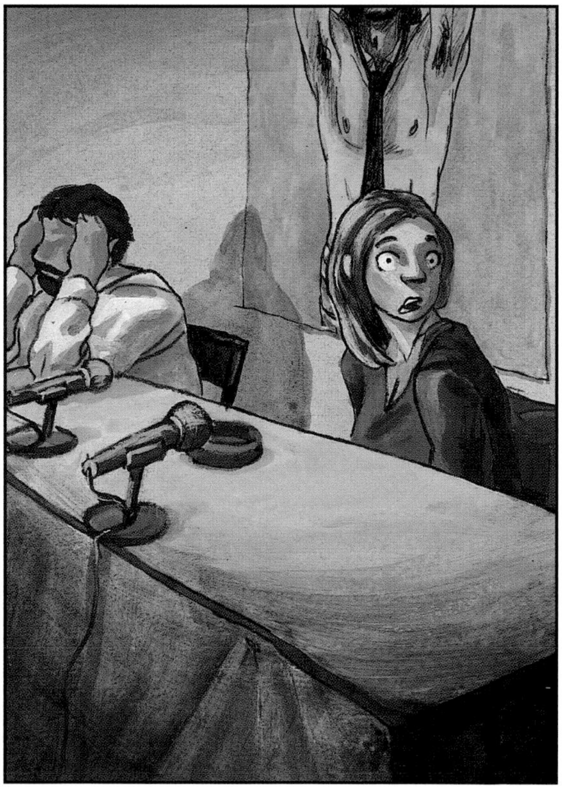

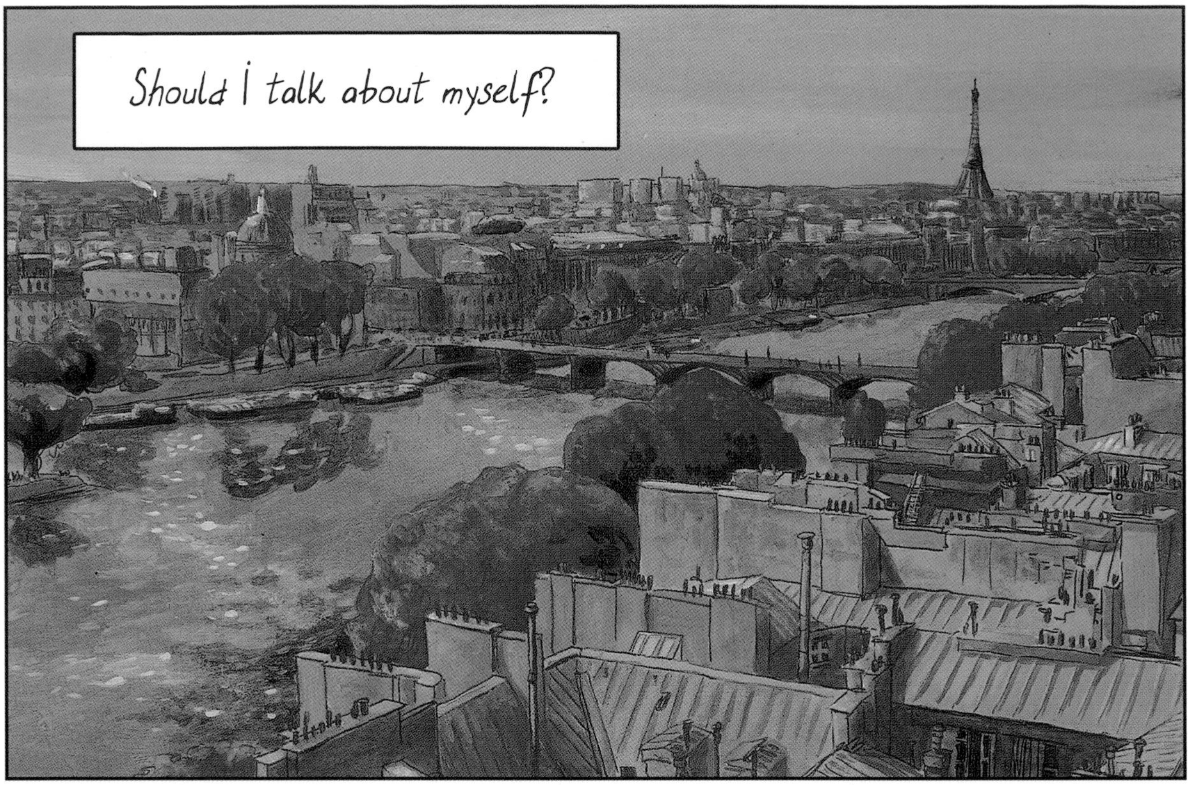
Should I talk about myself?

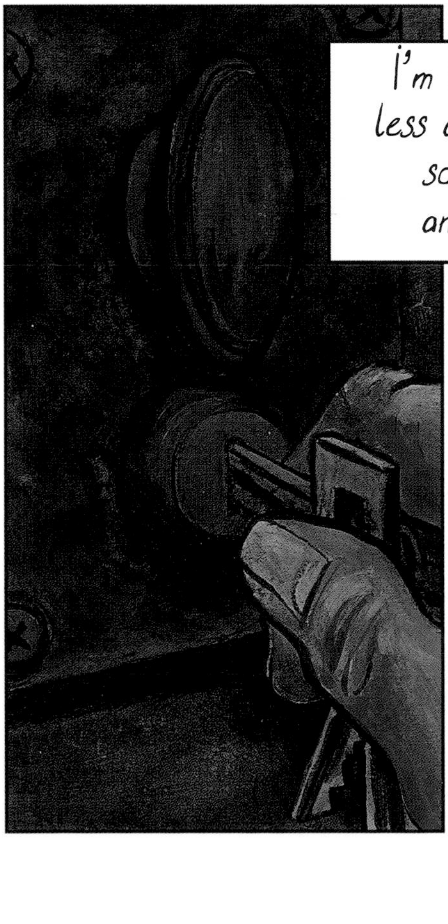

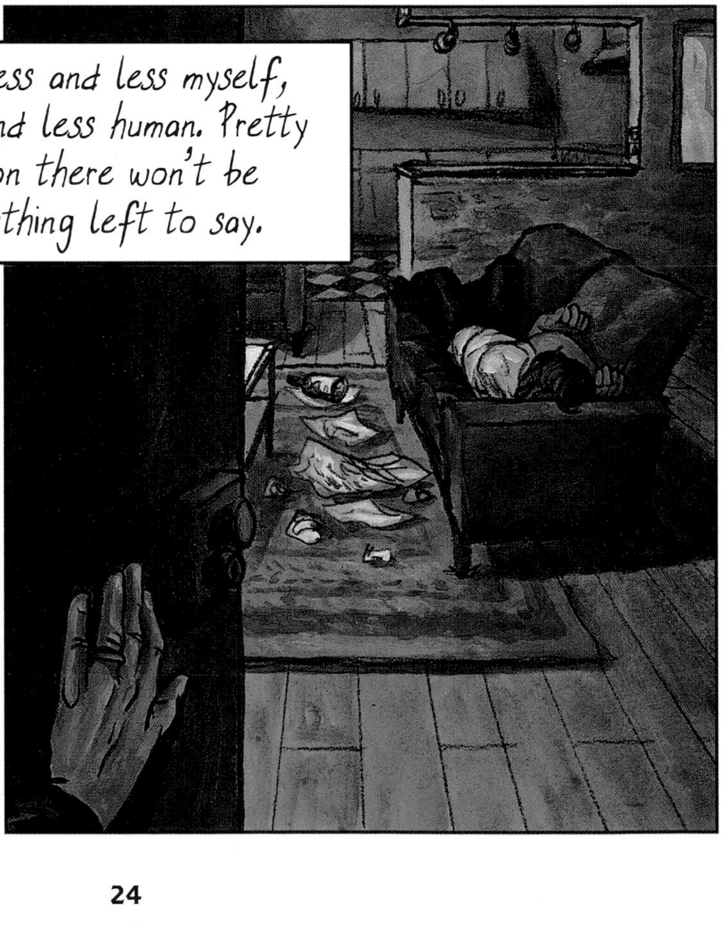
I'm less and less myself, less and less human. Pretty soon there won't be anything left to say.

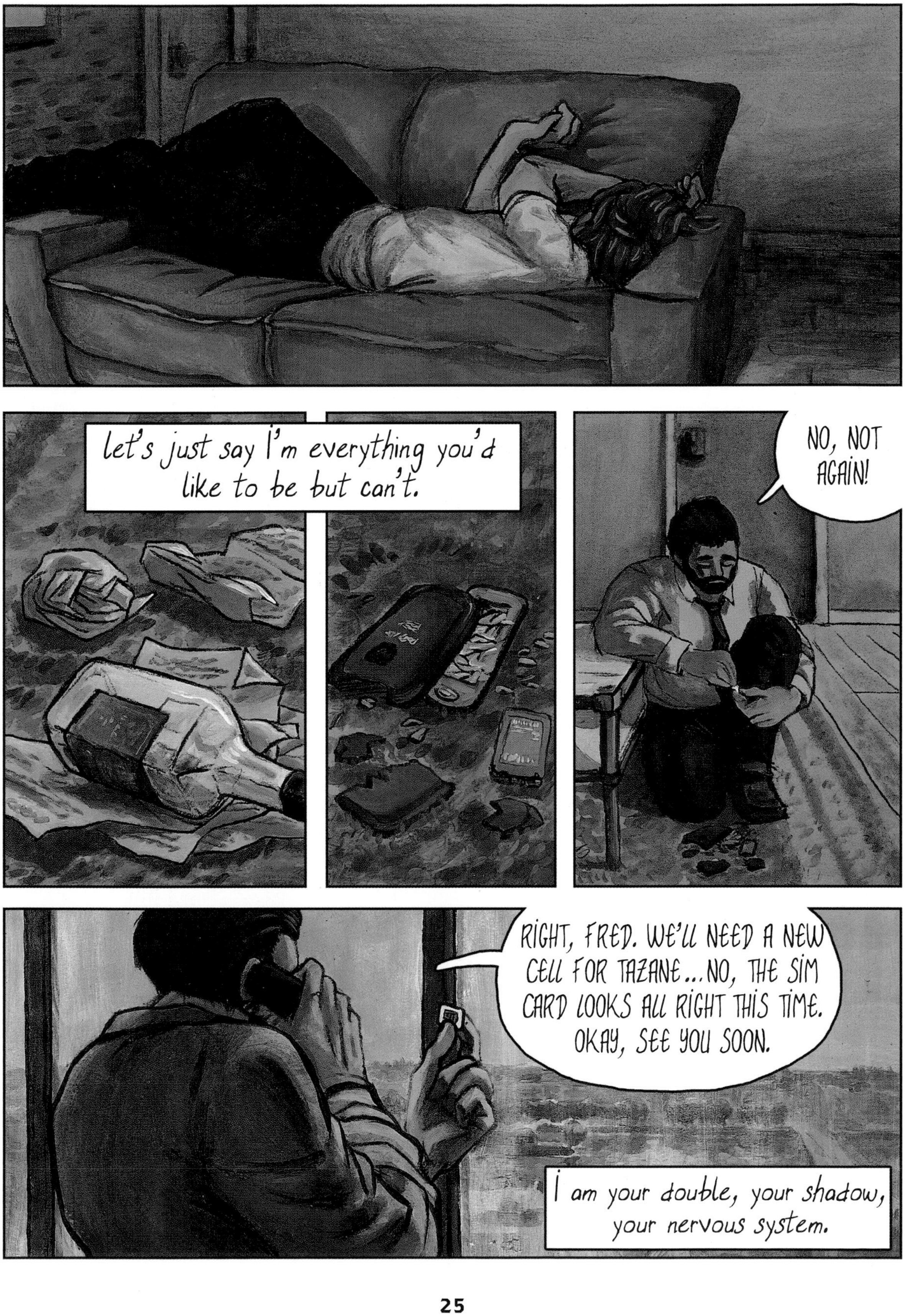
let's just say I'm everything you'd like to be but can't.
NO, NOT AGAIN!
RIGHT, FRED. WE'LL NEED A NEW CELL FOR TAZANE...NO, THE SIM CARD LOOKS ALL RIGHT THIS TIME. OKAY, SEE YOU SOON.
I am your double, your shadow, your nervous system.

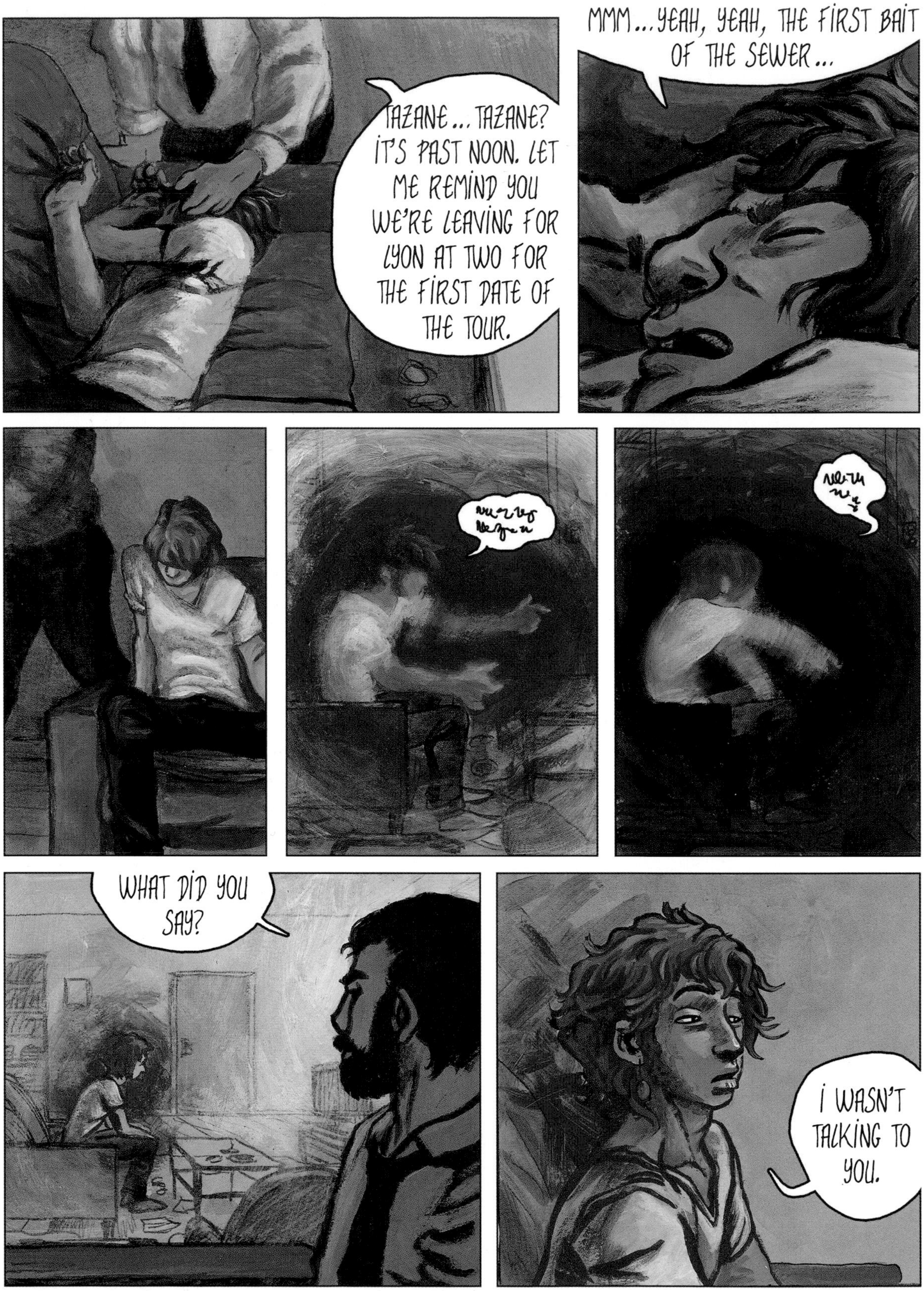
TAZANE... TAZANE? IT'S PAST NOON. LET ME REMIND YOU WE'RE LEAVING FOR LYON AT TWO FOR THE FIRST DATE OF THE TOUR.
MMM... YEAH, YEAH, THE FIRST BAIT OF THE SEWER...
WHAT DID YOU SAY?
I WASN'T TALKING TO YOU.

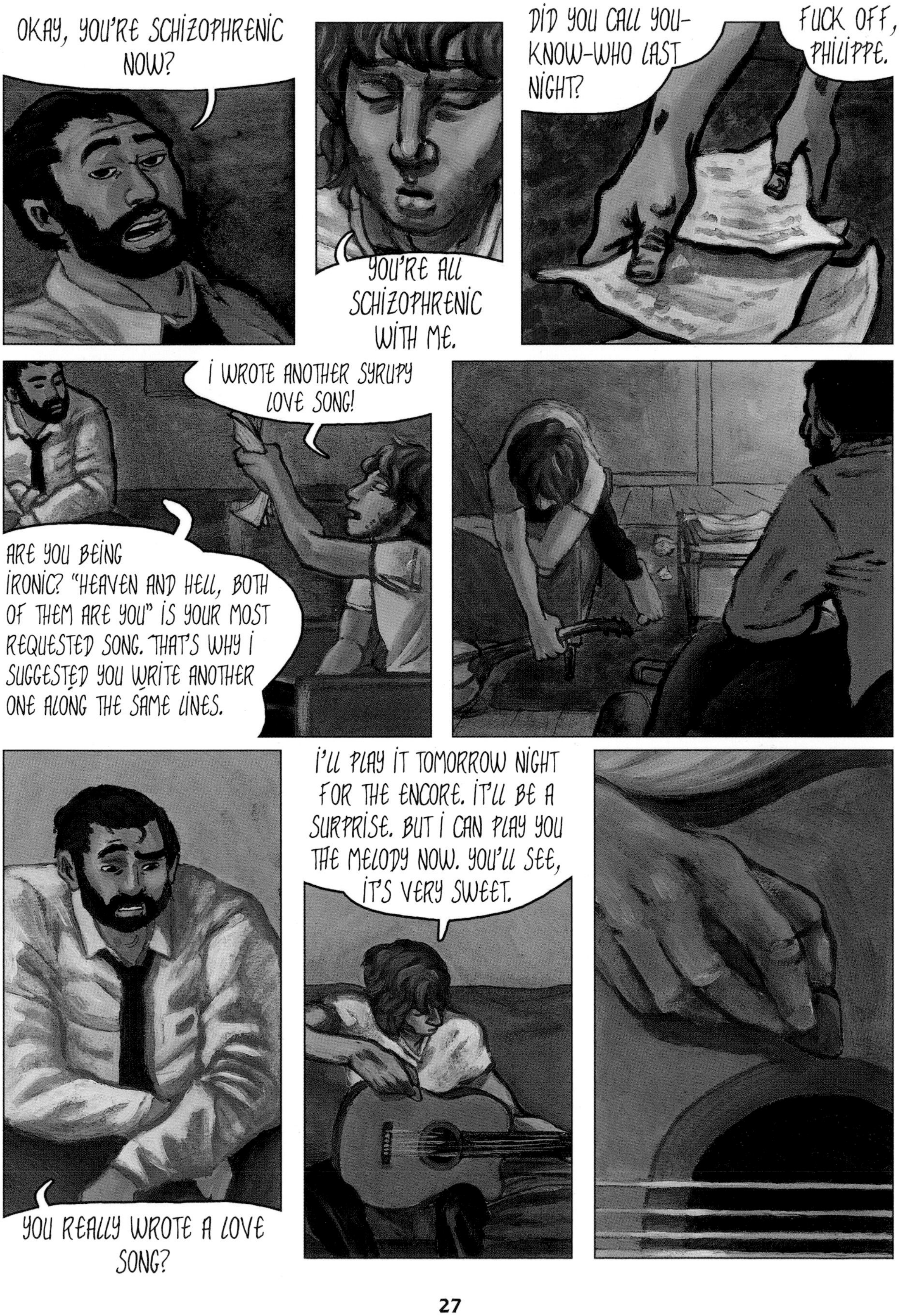
OKAY, YOU'RE SCHIZOPHRENIC NOW?
YOU'RE ALL SCHIZOPHRENIC WITH ME.
DID YOU CALL YOU-KNOW-WHO LAST NIGHT?
FUCK OFF, PHILIPPE.
I WROTE ANOTHER SYRUPY LOVE SONG!
ARE YOU BEING IRONIC? "HEAVEN AND HELL, BOTH OF THEM ARE YOU" IS YOUR MOST REQUESTED SONG. THAT'S WHY I SUGGESTED YOU WRITE ANOTHER ONE ALONG THE SAME LINES.
YOU REALLY WROTE A LOVE SONG?
I'LL PLAY IT TOMORROW NIGHT FOR THE ENCORE. IT'LL BE A SURPRISE. BUT I CAN PLAY YOU THE MELODY NOW. YOU'LL SEE, IT'S VERY SWEET.

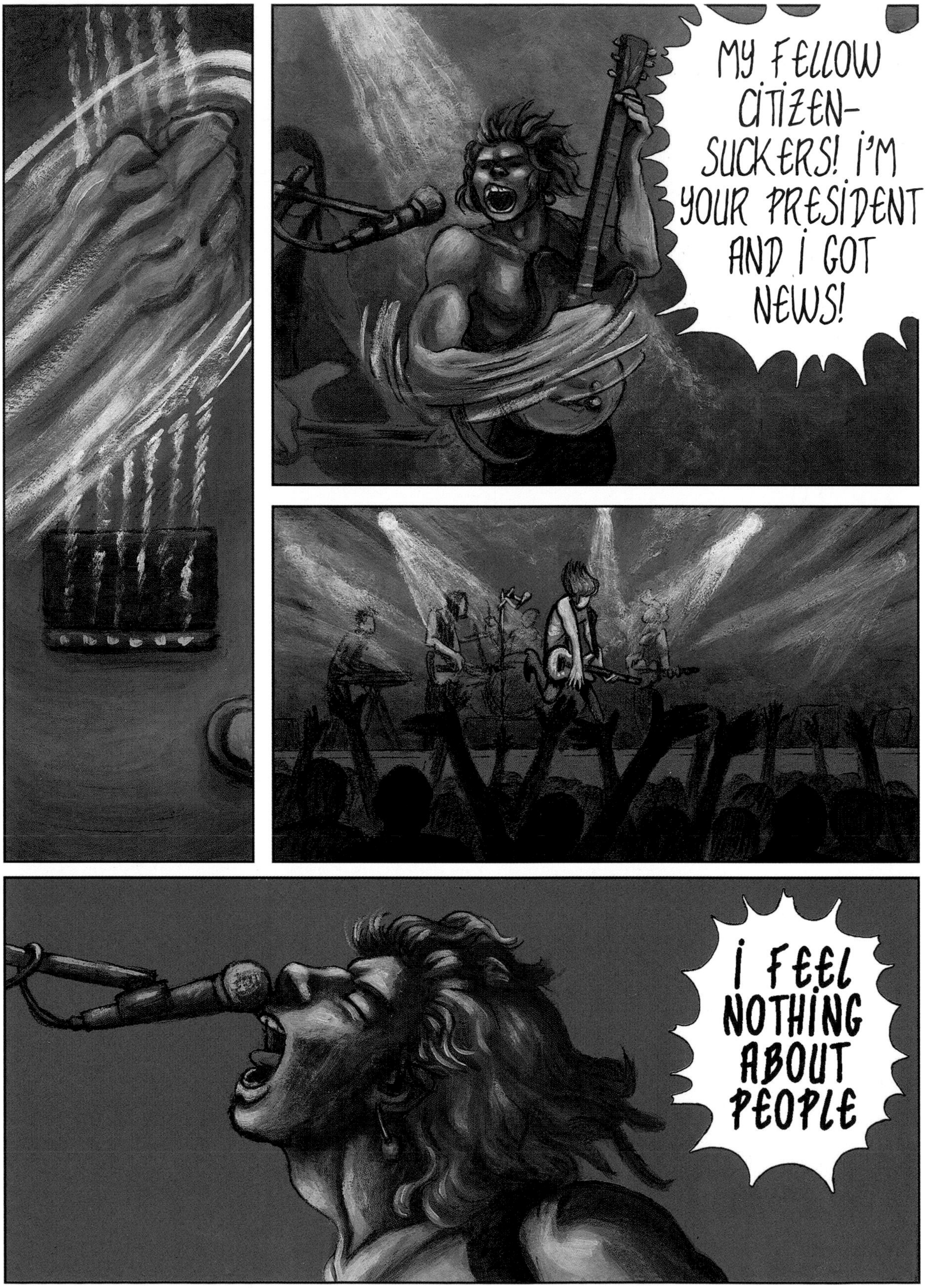
MY FELLOW CITIZEN-SUCKERS! I'M YOUR PRESIDENT AND I GOT NEWS!
I FEEL NOTHING ABOUT PEOPLE

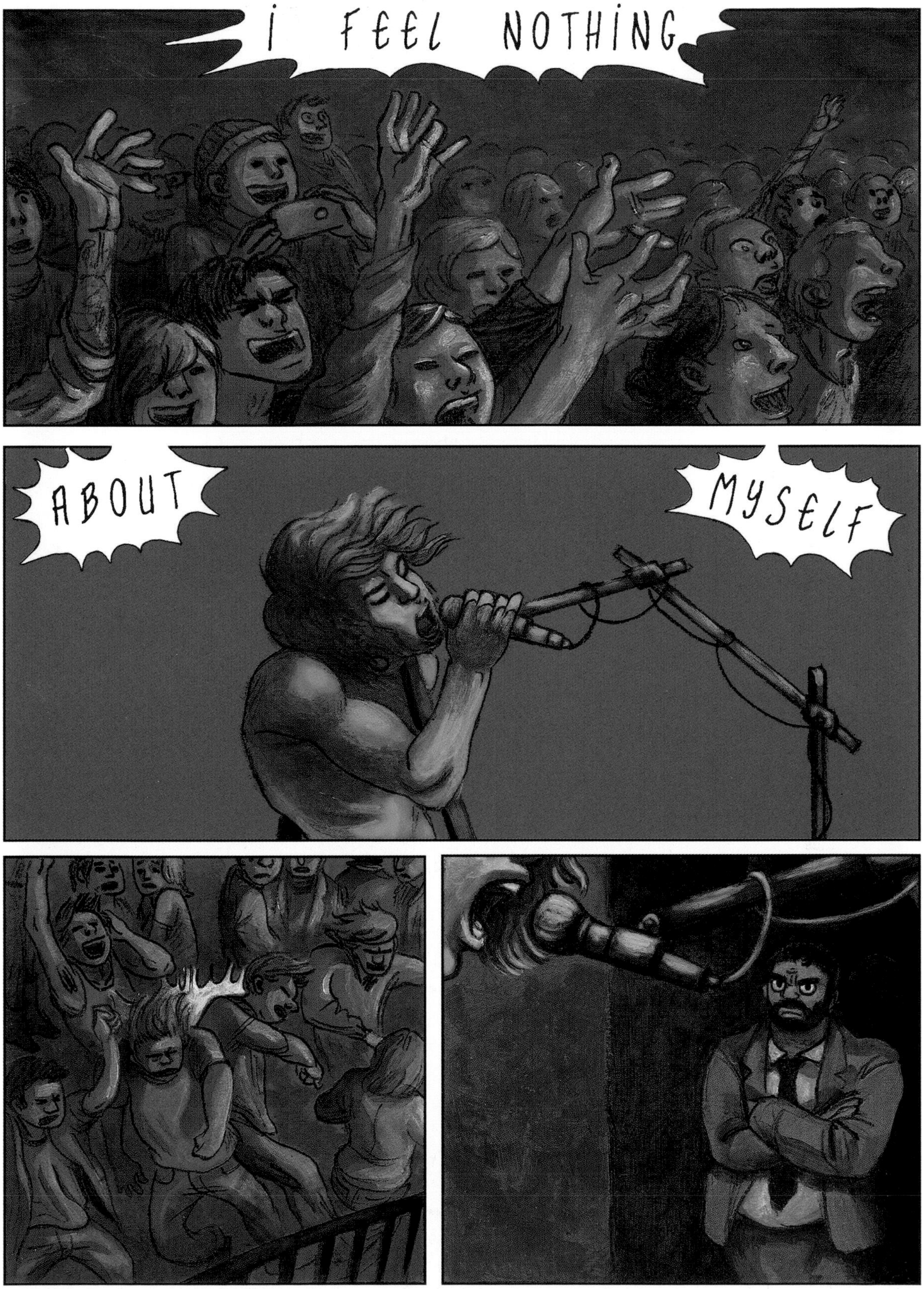
I FEEL NOTHING
ABOUT
MYSELF

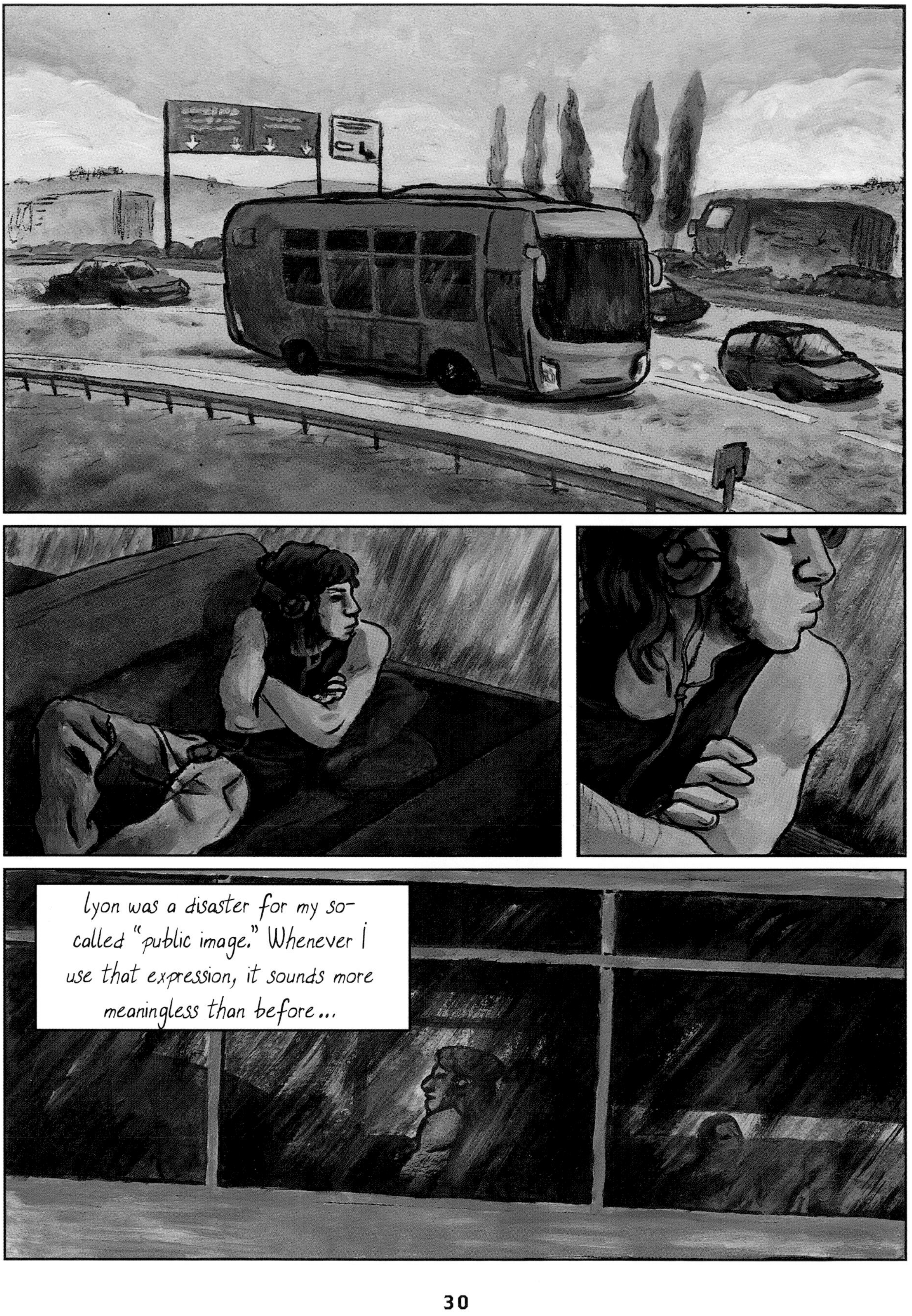
Lyon was a disaster for my so-called "public image." Whenever I use that expression, it sounds more meaningless than before...

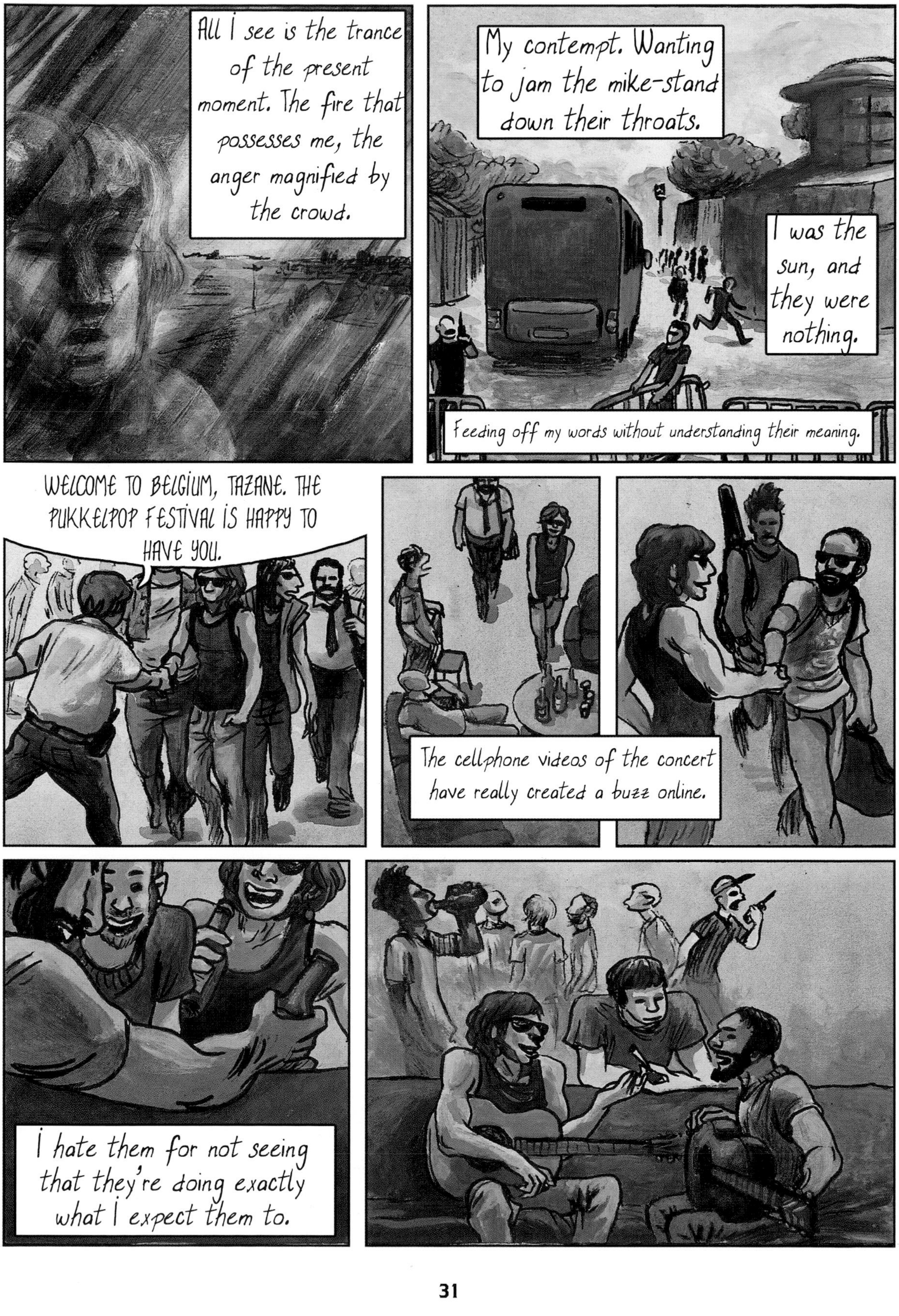
All I see is the trance of the present moment. The fire that possesses me, the anger magnified by the crowd.
My contempt. Wanting to jam the mike-stand down their throats.
I was the sun, and they were nothing.
Feeding off my words without understanding their meaning.
WELCOME TO BELGIUM, TAZANE. THE PUKKELPOP FESTIVAL IS HAPPY TO HAVE YOU.
The cellphone videos of the concert have really created a buzz online.
I hate them for not seeing that they're doing exactly what I expect them to.

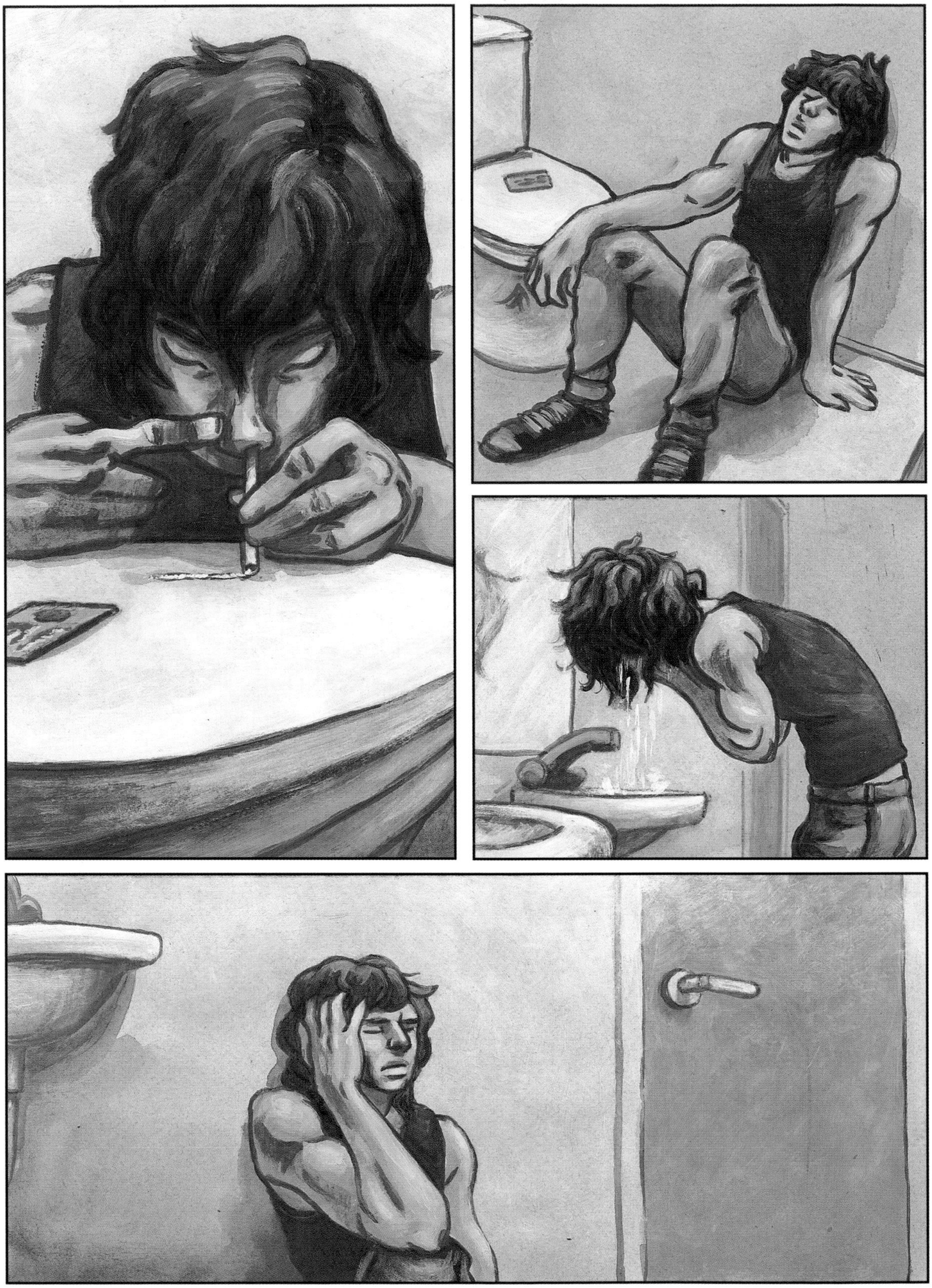

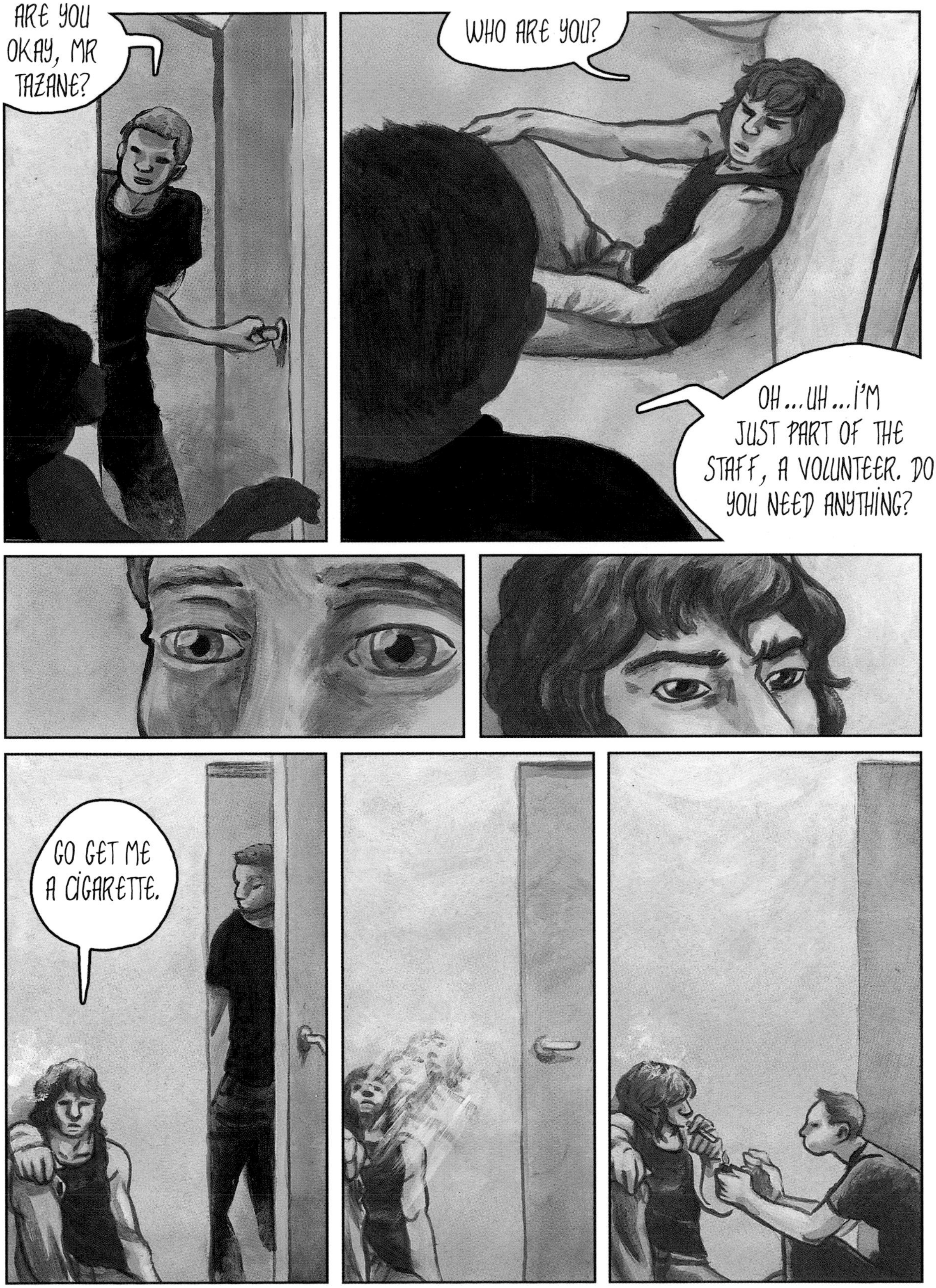
ARE YOU OKAY, MR TAZANE?
WHO ARE YOU?
OH...UH...I'M JUST PART OF THE STAFF, A VOLUNTEER. DO YOU NEED ANYTHING?
GO GET ME A CIGARETTE.

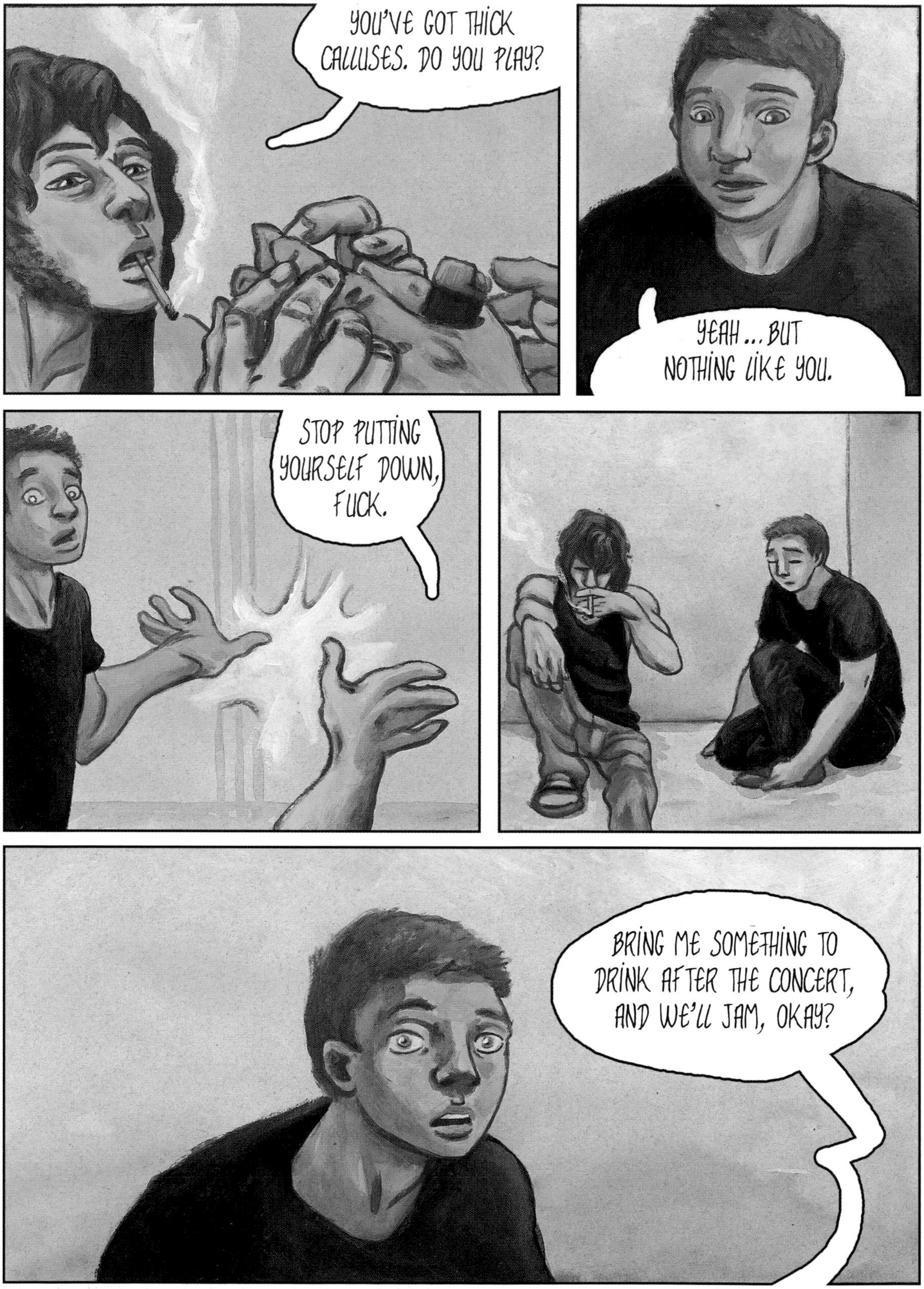
YOU'VE GOT THICK CALLUSES. DO YOU PLAY?
YEAH... BUT NOTHING LIKE YOU.
STOP PUTTING YOURSELF DOWN, FUCK.
BRING ME SOMETHING TO DRINK AFTER THE CONCERT, AND WE'LL JAM, OKAY?

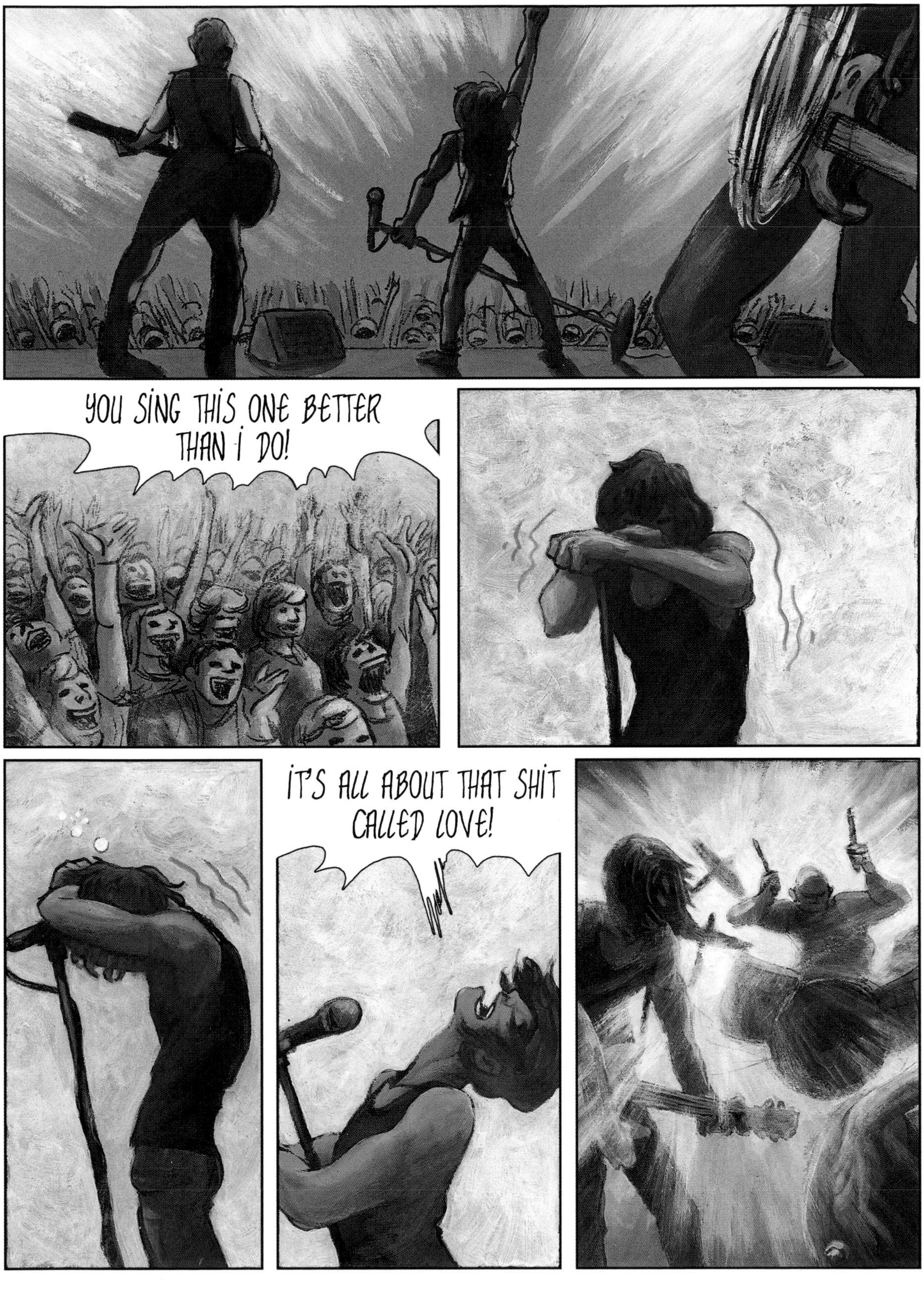
YOU SING THIS ONE BETTER THAN I DO!
IT'S ALL ABOUT THAT SHIT CALLED LOVE!

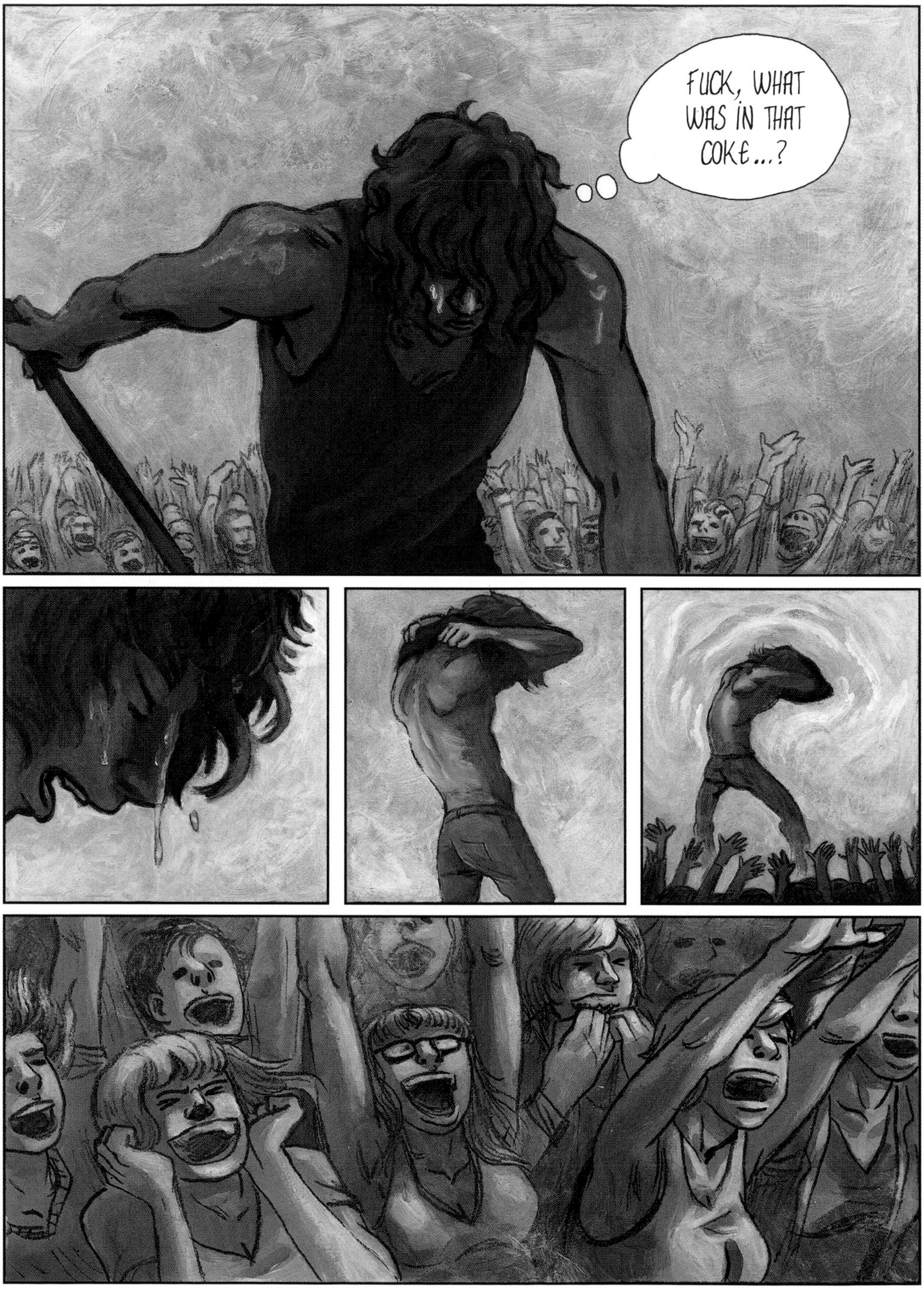
FUCK, WHAT WAS IN THAT COKE...?

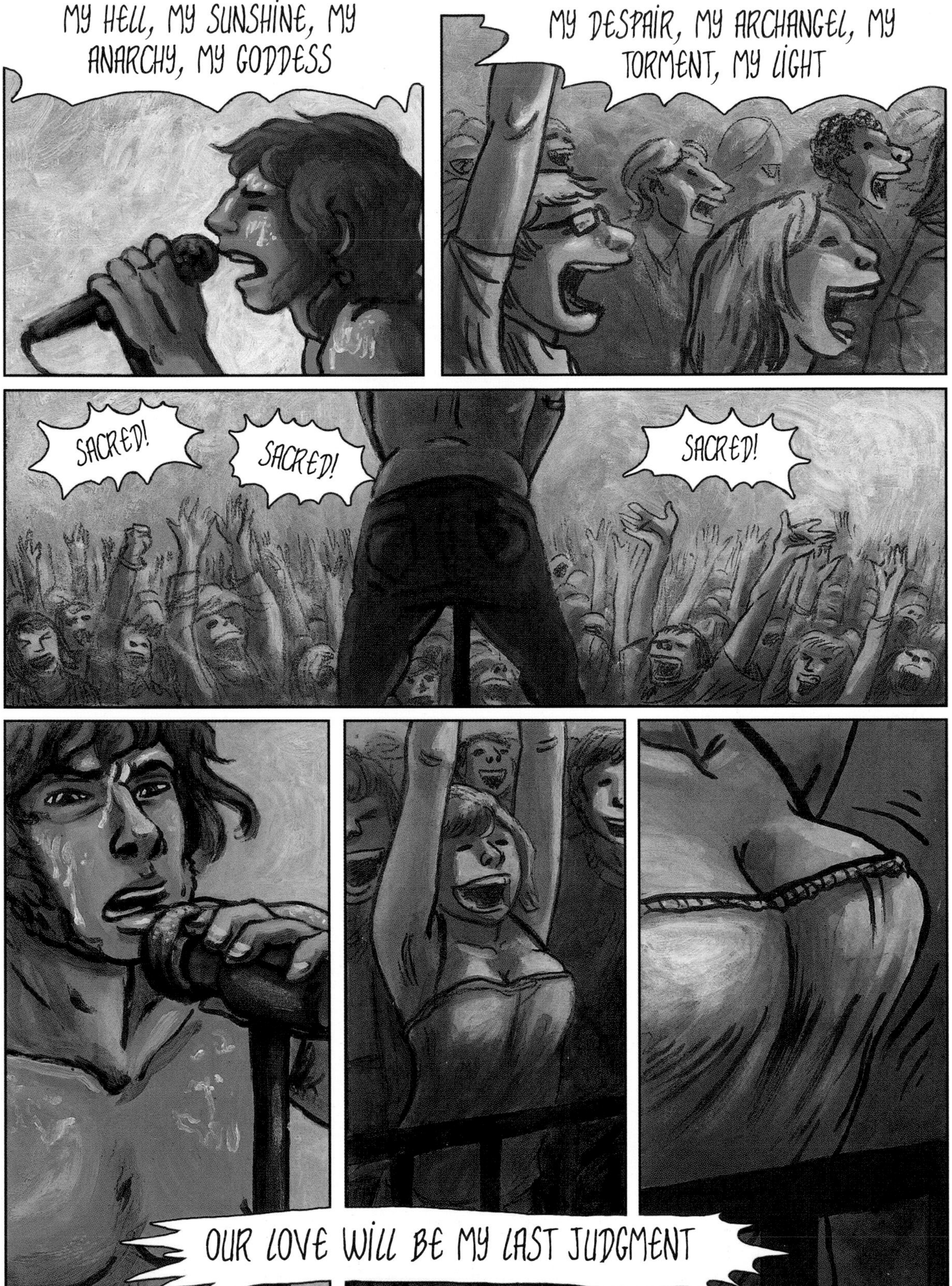
MY HELL, MY SUNSHINE, MY ANARCHY, MY GODDESS
MY DESPAIR, MY ARCHANGEL, MY TORMENT, MY LIGHT
SACRED!
SACRED!
SACRED!
OUR LOVE WILL BE MY LAST JUDGMENT

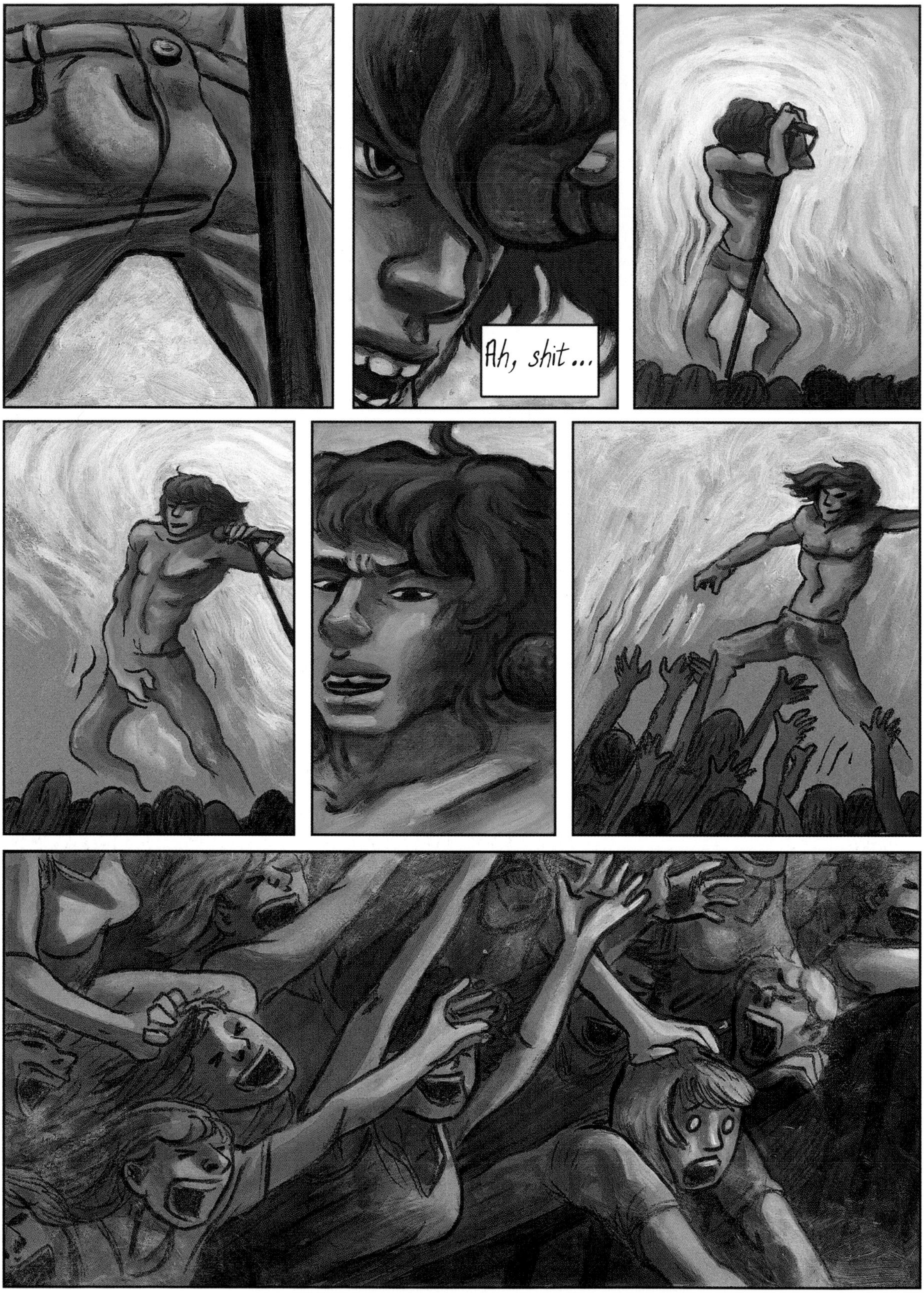
Ah, shit...

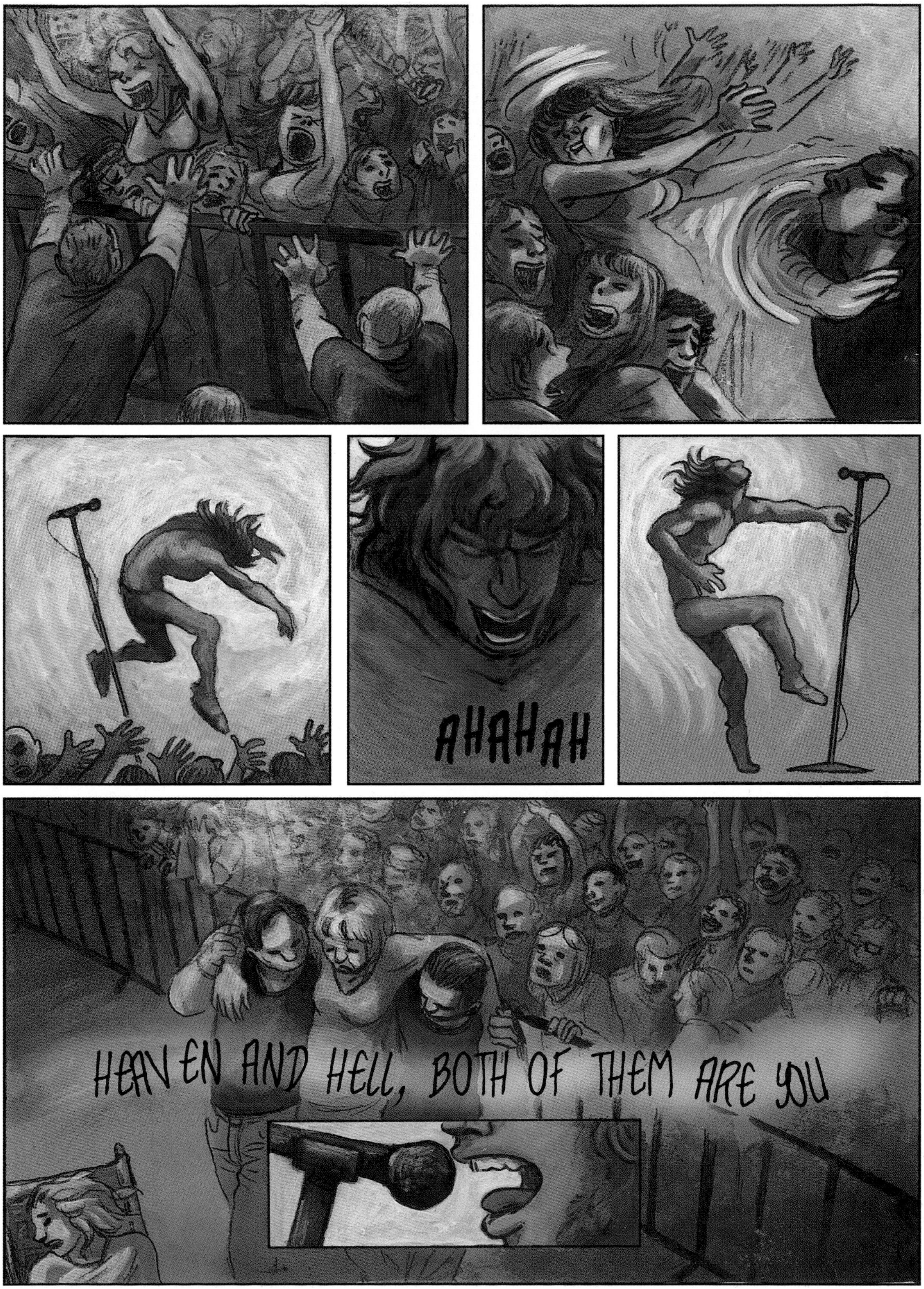
AHAHAH
HEAVEN AND HELL, BOTH OF THEM ARE YOU

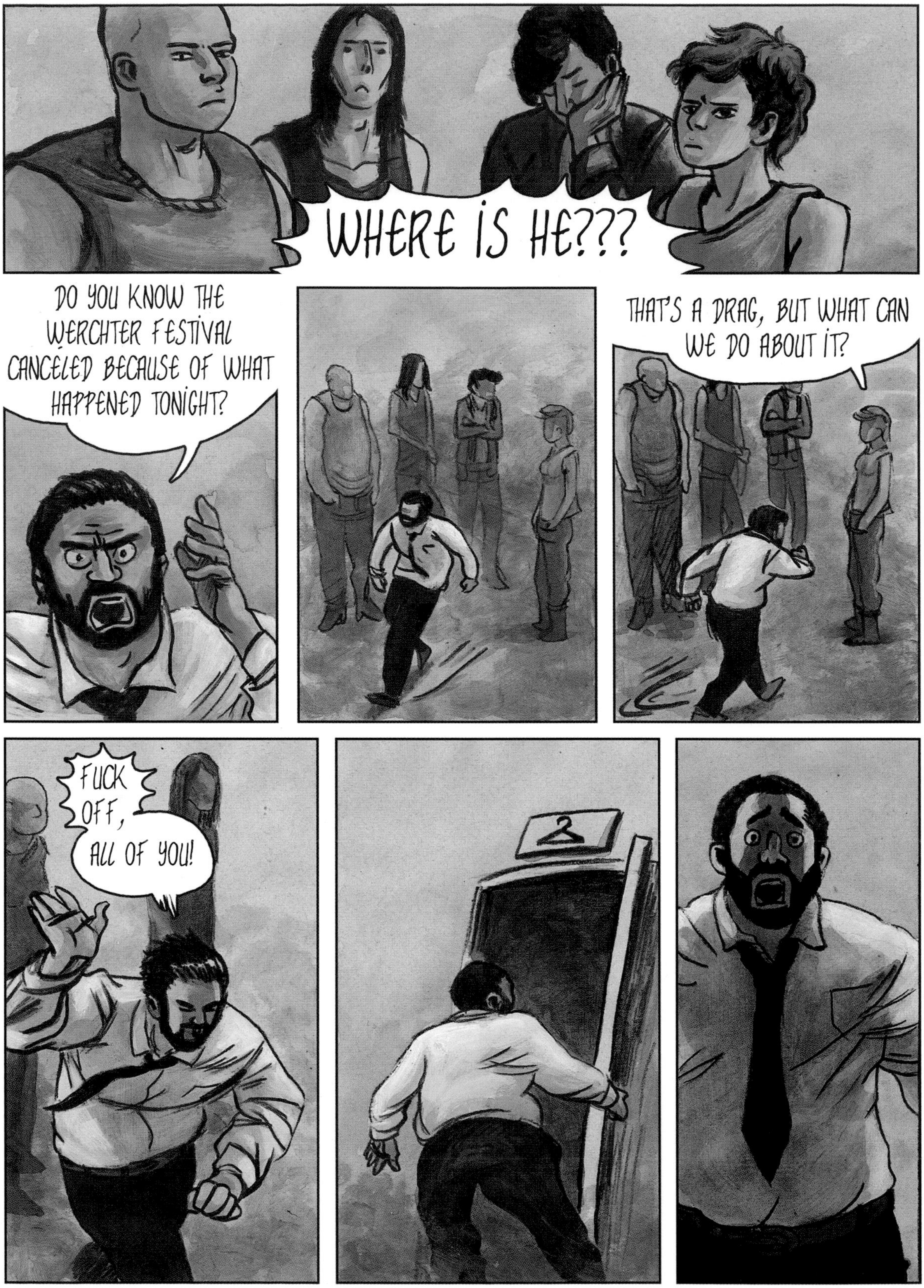
WHERE IS HE???
DO YOU KNOW THE WERCHTER FESTIVAL CANCELED BECAUSE OF WHAT HAPPENED TONIGHT?
THAT'S A DRAG, BUT WHAT CAN WE DO ABOUT IT?
FUCK OFF, ALL OF YOU!

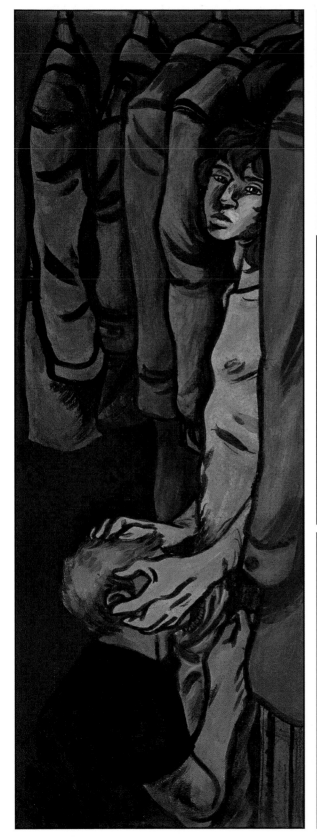

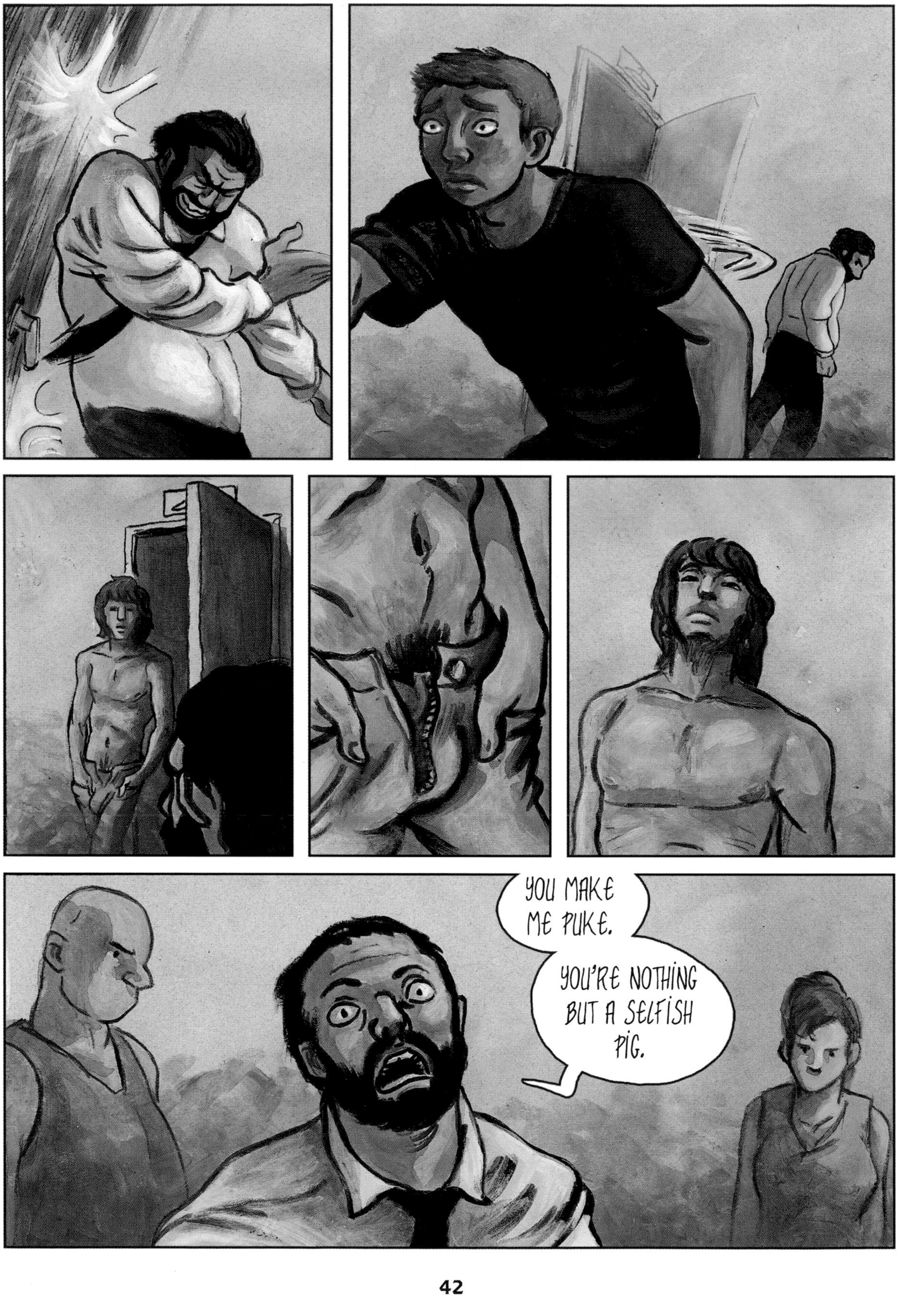
YOU MAKE ME PUKE.
YOU'RE NOTHING BUT A SELFISH PIG.

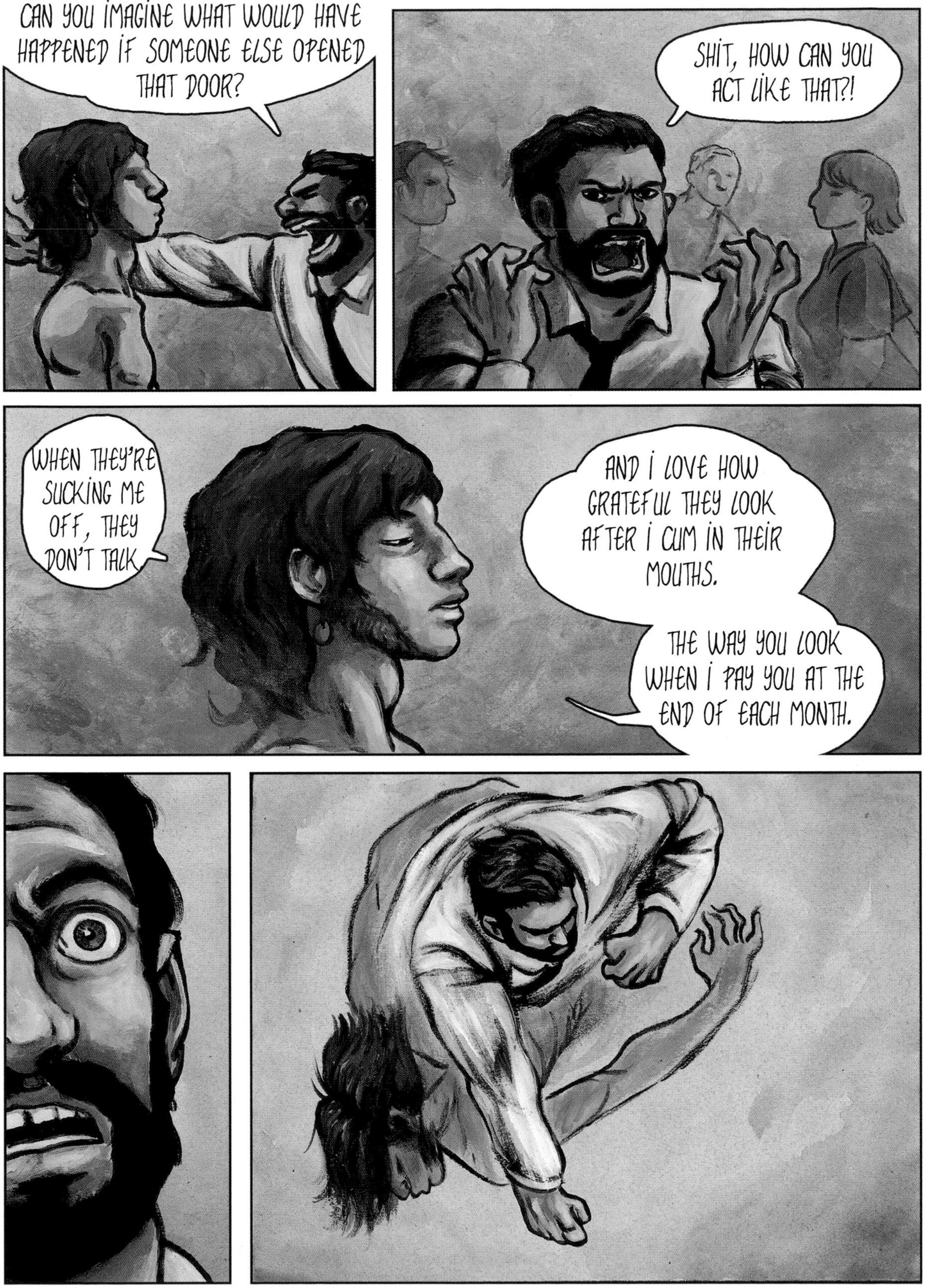
CAN YOU IMAGINE WHAT WOULD HAVE HAPPENED IF SOMEONE ELSE OPENED THAT DOOR?
SHIT, HOW CAN YOU ACT LIKE THAT?!
WHEN THEY'RE SUCKING ME OFF, THEY DON'T TALK.
AND I LOVE HOW GRATEFUL THEY LOOK AFTER I CUM IN THEIR MOUTHS.
THE WAY YOU LOOK WHEN I PAY YOU AT THE END OF EACH MONTH.

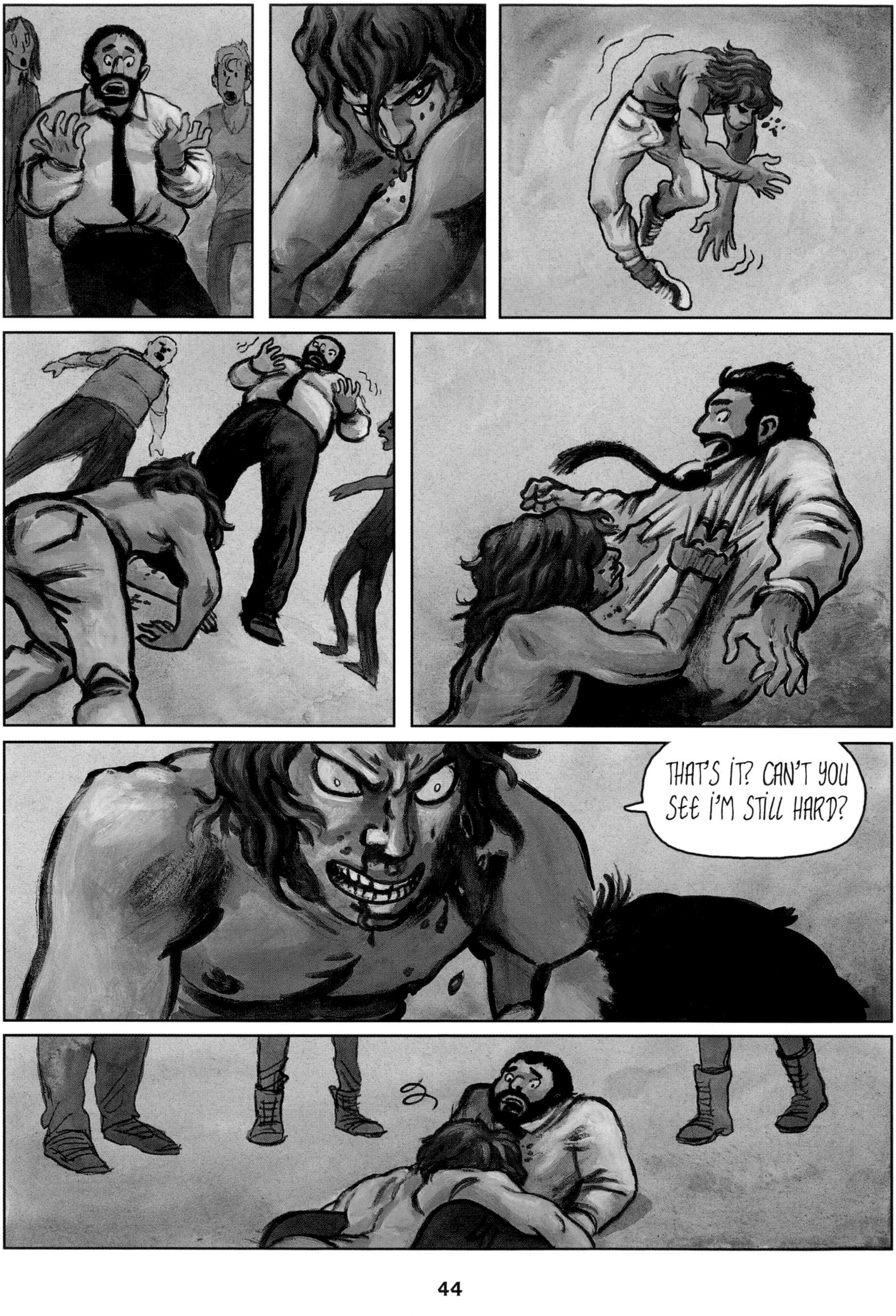
THAT'S IT? CAN'T YOU SEE I'M STILL HARD?

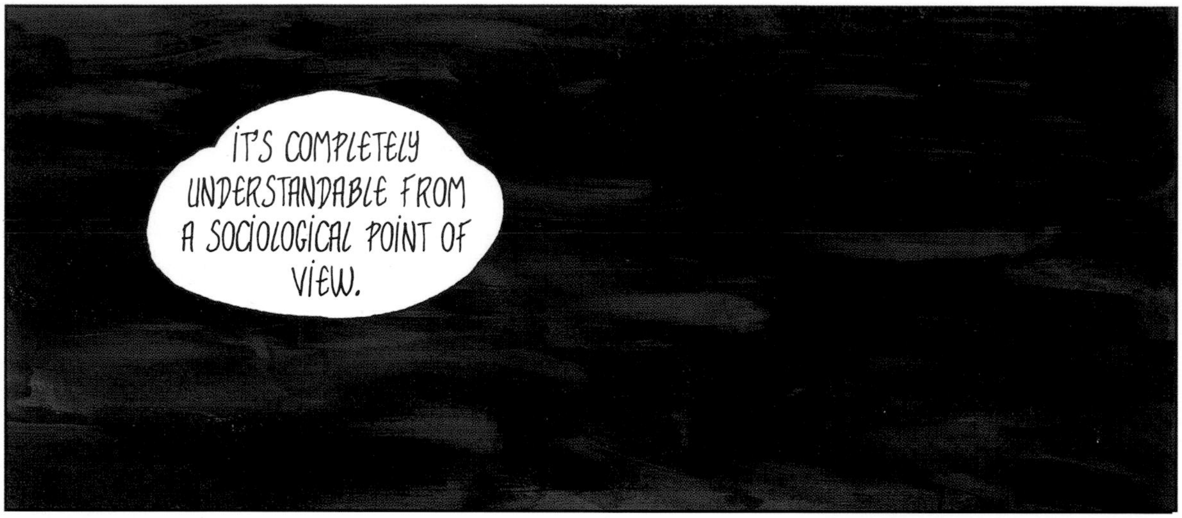
IT'S COMPLETELY UNDERSTANDABLE FROM A SOCIOLOGICAL POINT OF VIEW.

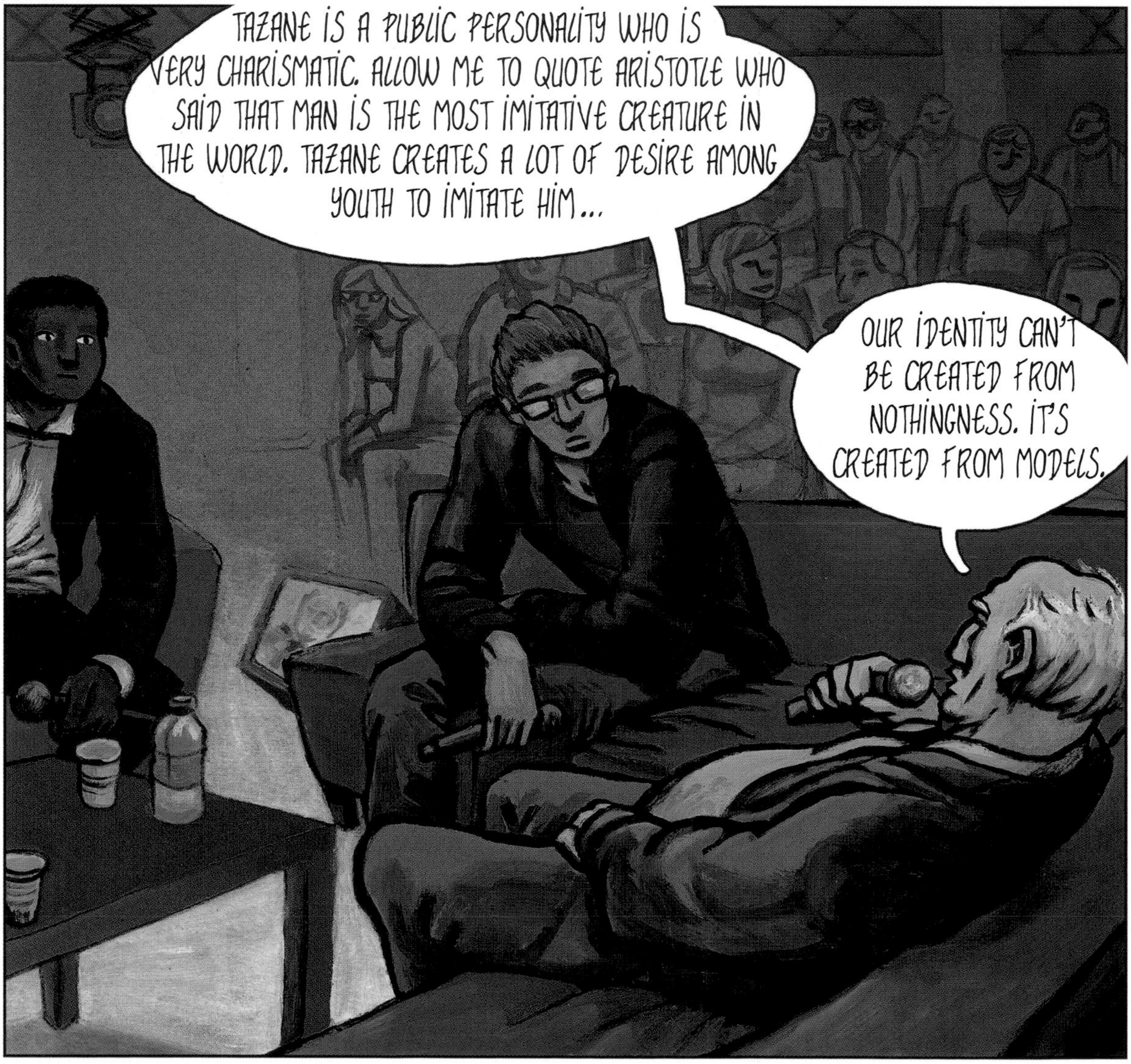
TAZANE IS A PUBLIC PERSONALITY WHO IS VERY CHARISMATIC. ALLOW ME TO QUOTE ARISTOTLE WHO SAID THAT MAN IS THE MOST IMITATIVE CREATURE IN THE WORLD. TAZANE CREATES A LOT OF DESIRE AMONG YOUTH TO IMITATE HIM...
OUR IDENTITY CAN'T BE CREATED FROM NOTHINGNESS. IT'S CREATED FROM MODELS.

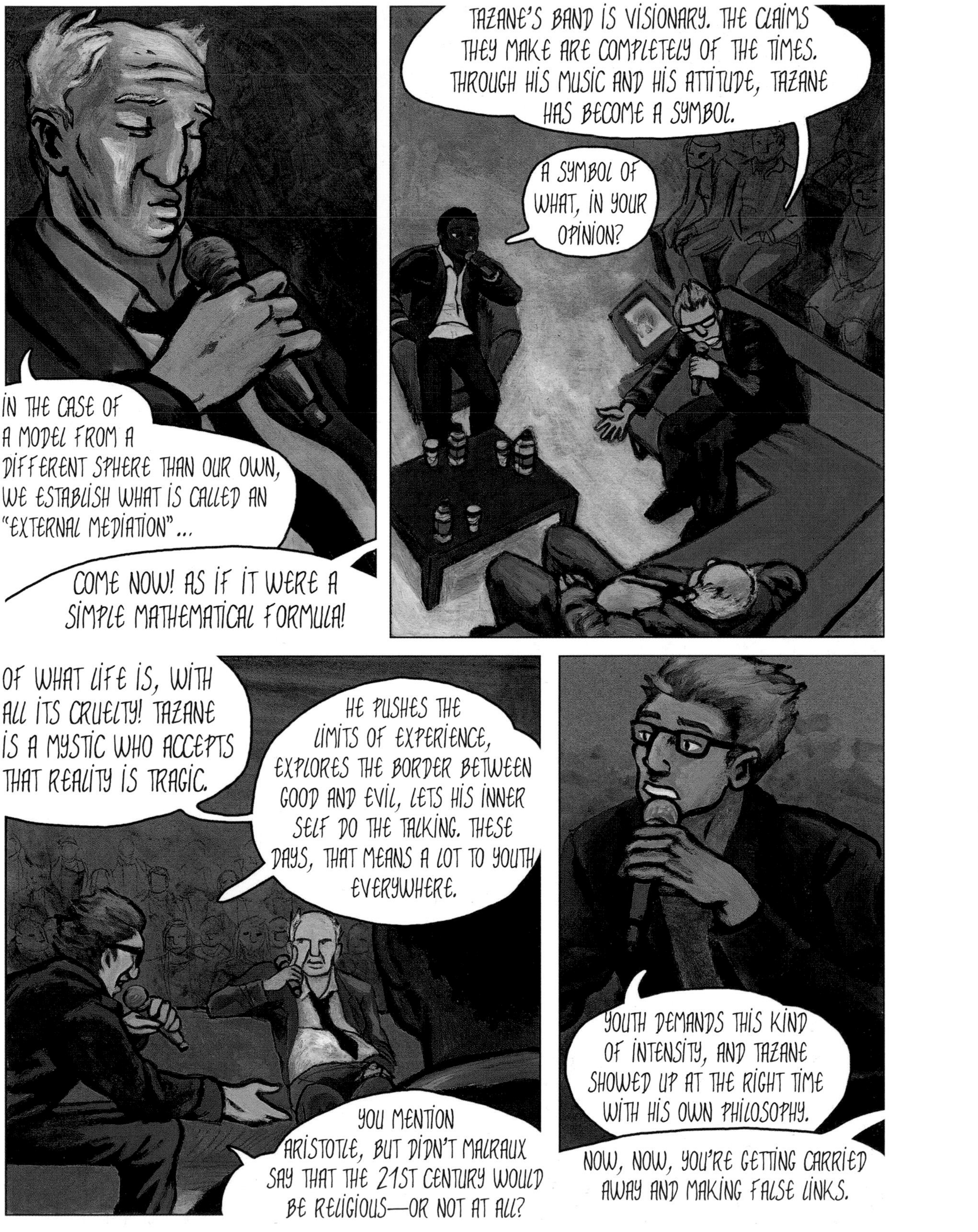
IN THE CASE OF A MODEL FROM A DIFFERENT SPHERE THAN OUR OWN, WE ESTABLISH WHAT IS CALLED AN "EXTERNAL MEDIATION"...
COME NOW! AS IF IT WERE A SIMPLE MATHEMATICAL FORMULA!
TAZANE'S BAND IS VISIONARY. THE CLAIMS THEY MAKE ARE COMPLETELY OF THE TIMES. THROUGH HIS MUSIC AND HIS ATTITUDE, TAZANE HAS BECOME A SYMBOL.
A SYMBOL OF WHAT, IN YOUR OPINION?
OF WHAT LIFE IS, WITH ALL ITS CRUELTY! TAZANE IS A MYSTIC WHO ACCEPTS THAT REALITY IS TRAGIC.
HE PUSHES THE LIMITS OF EXPERIENCE, EXPLORES THE BORDER BETWEEN GOOD AND EVIL, LETS HIS INNER SELF DO THE TALKING. THESE DAYS, THAT MEANS A LOT TO YOUTH EVERYWHERE.
YOU MENTION ARISTOTLE, BUT DIDN'T MALRAUX SAY THAT THE 21ST CENTURY WOULD BE RELIGIOUS—OR NOT AT ALL?
YOUTH DEMANDS THIS KIND OF INTENSITY, AND TAZANE SHOWED UP AT THE RIGHT TIME WITH HIS OWN PHILOSOPHY.
NOW, NOW, YOU'RE GETTING CARRIED AWAY AND MAKING FALSE LINKS.

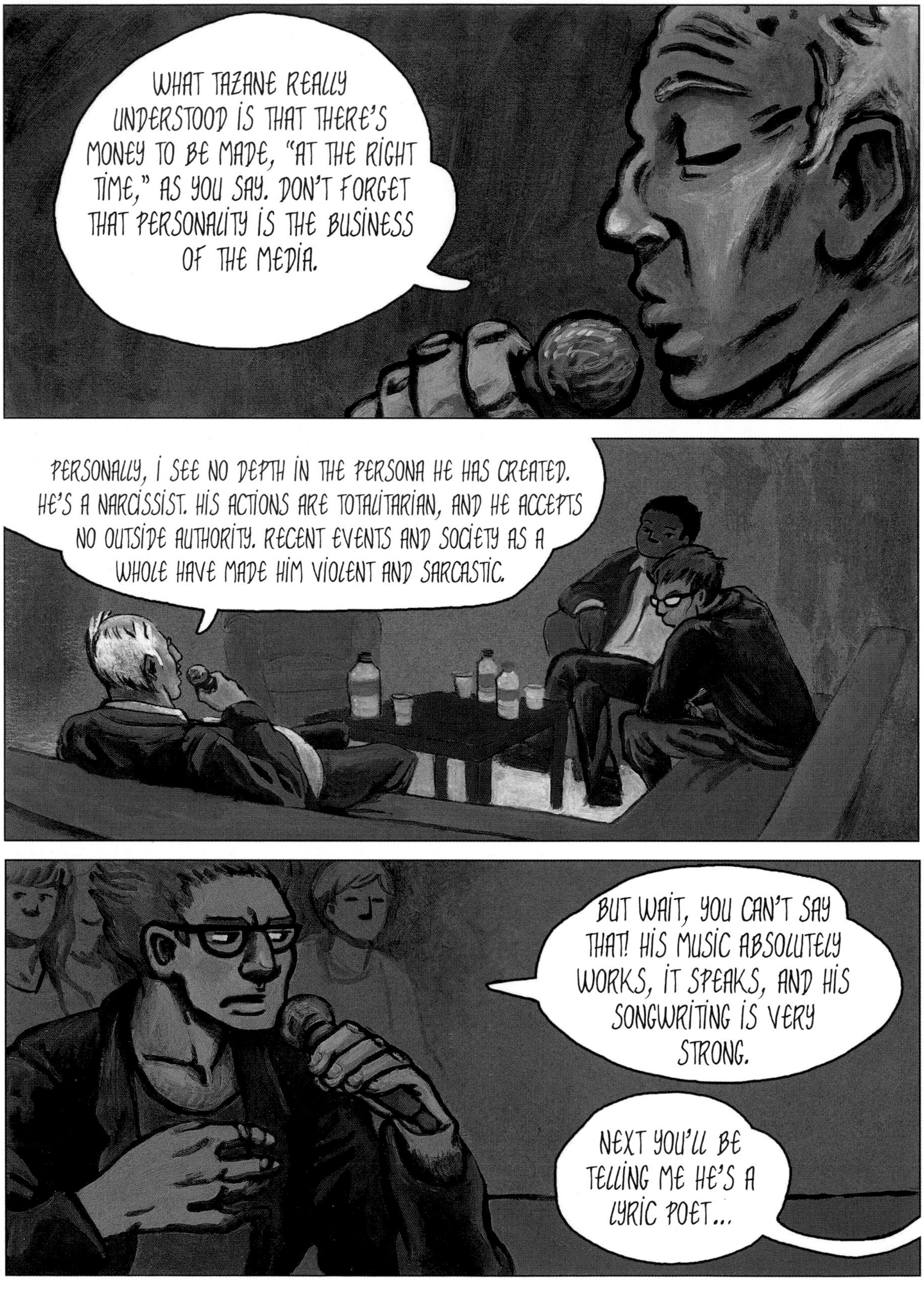
WHAT TAZANE REALLY UNDERSTOOD IS THAT THERE'S MONEY TO BE MADE, "AT THE RIGHT TIME," AS YOU SAY. DON'T FORGET THAT PERSONALITY IS THE BUSINESS OF THE MEDIA.
PERSONALLY, I SEE NO DEPTH IN THE PERSONA HE HAS CREATED. HE'S A NARCISSIST. HIS ACTIONS ARE TOTALITARIAN, AND HE ACCEPTS NO OUTSIDE AUTHORITY. RECENT EVENTS AND SOCIETY AS A WHOLE HAVE MADE HIM VIOLENT AND SARCASTIC.
BUT WAIT, YOU CAN'T SAY THAT! HIS MUSIC ABSOLUTELY WORKS, IT SPEAKS, AND HIS SONGWRITING IS VERY STRONG.
NEXT YOU'LL BE TELLING ME HE'S A LYRIC POET...

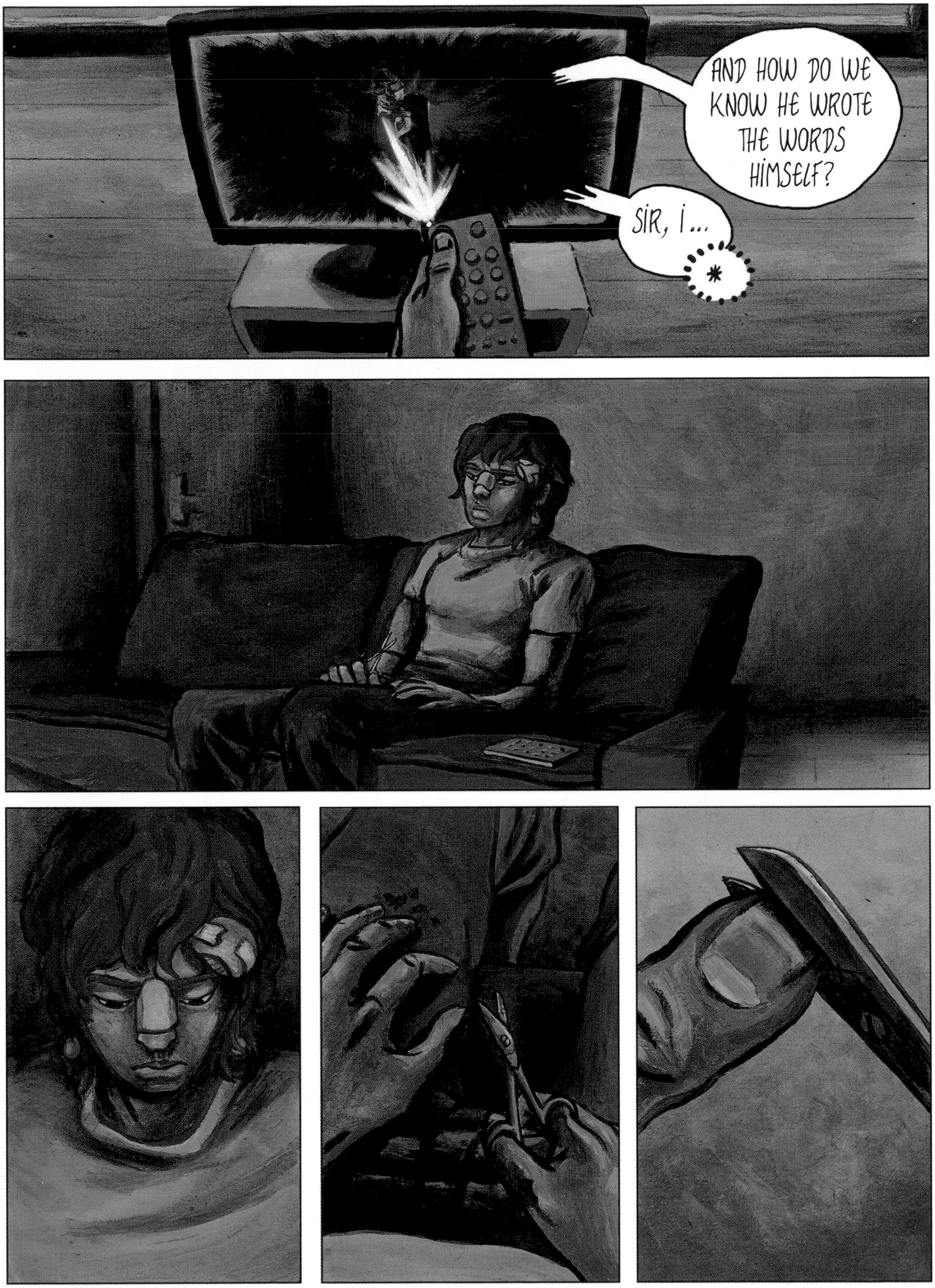
AND HOW DO WE KNOW HE WROTE THE WORDS HIMSELF?
SIR, I...

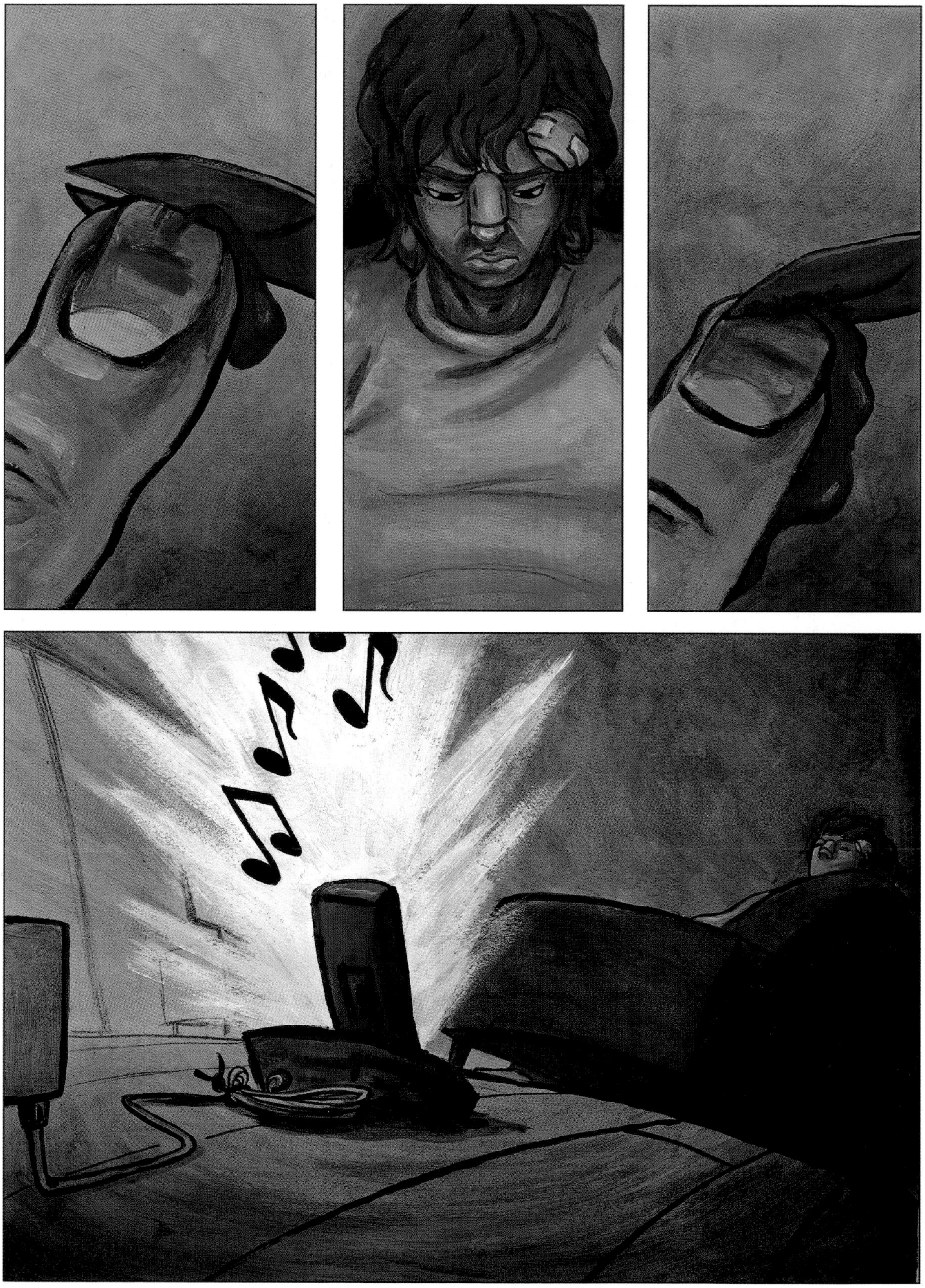

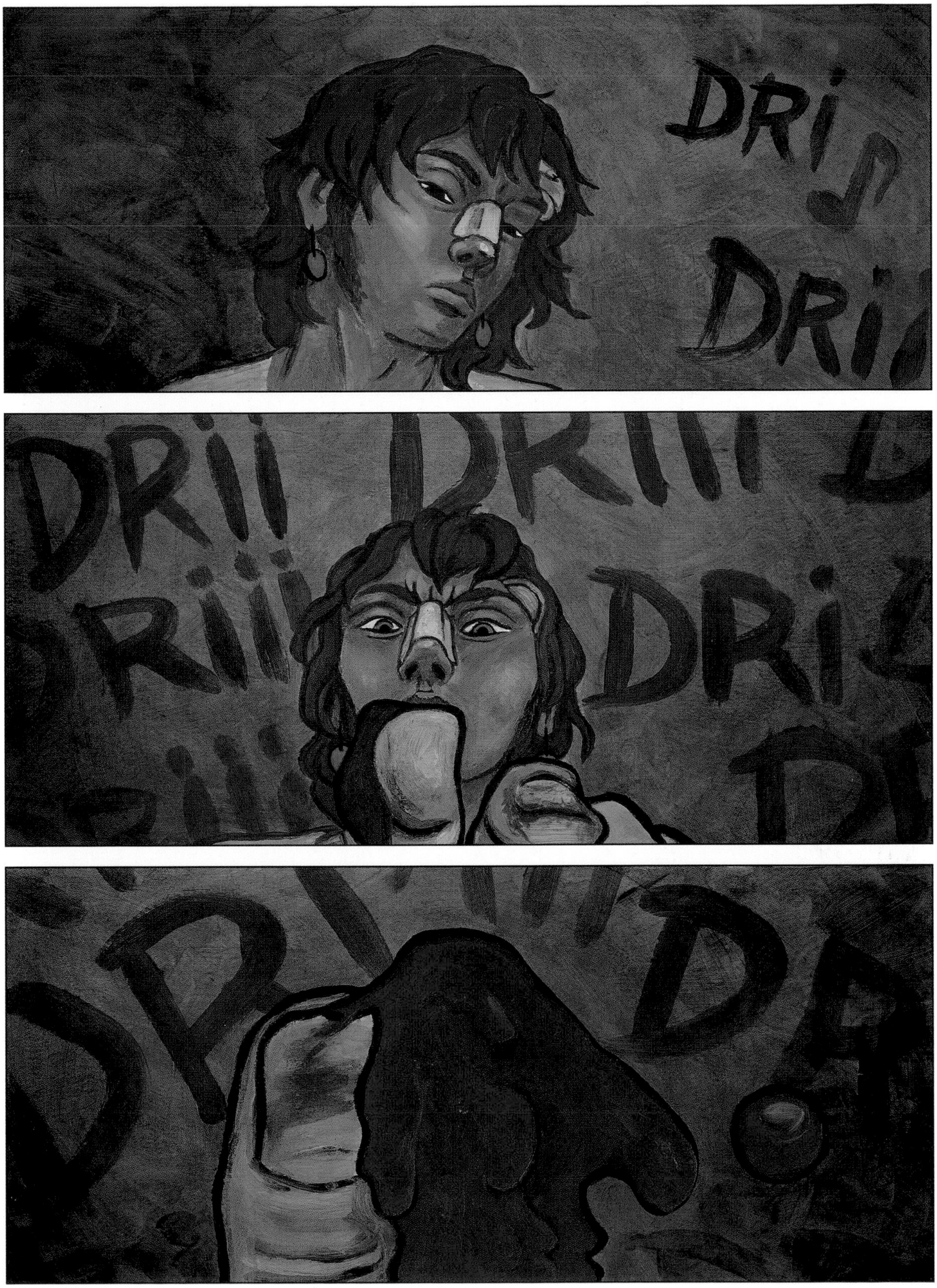
DRi
DRi
DRii
DRiii
DRiii
DRi

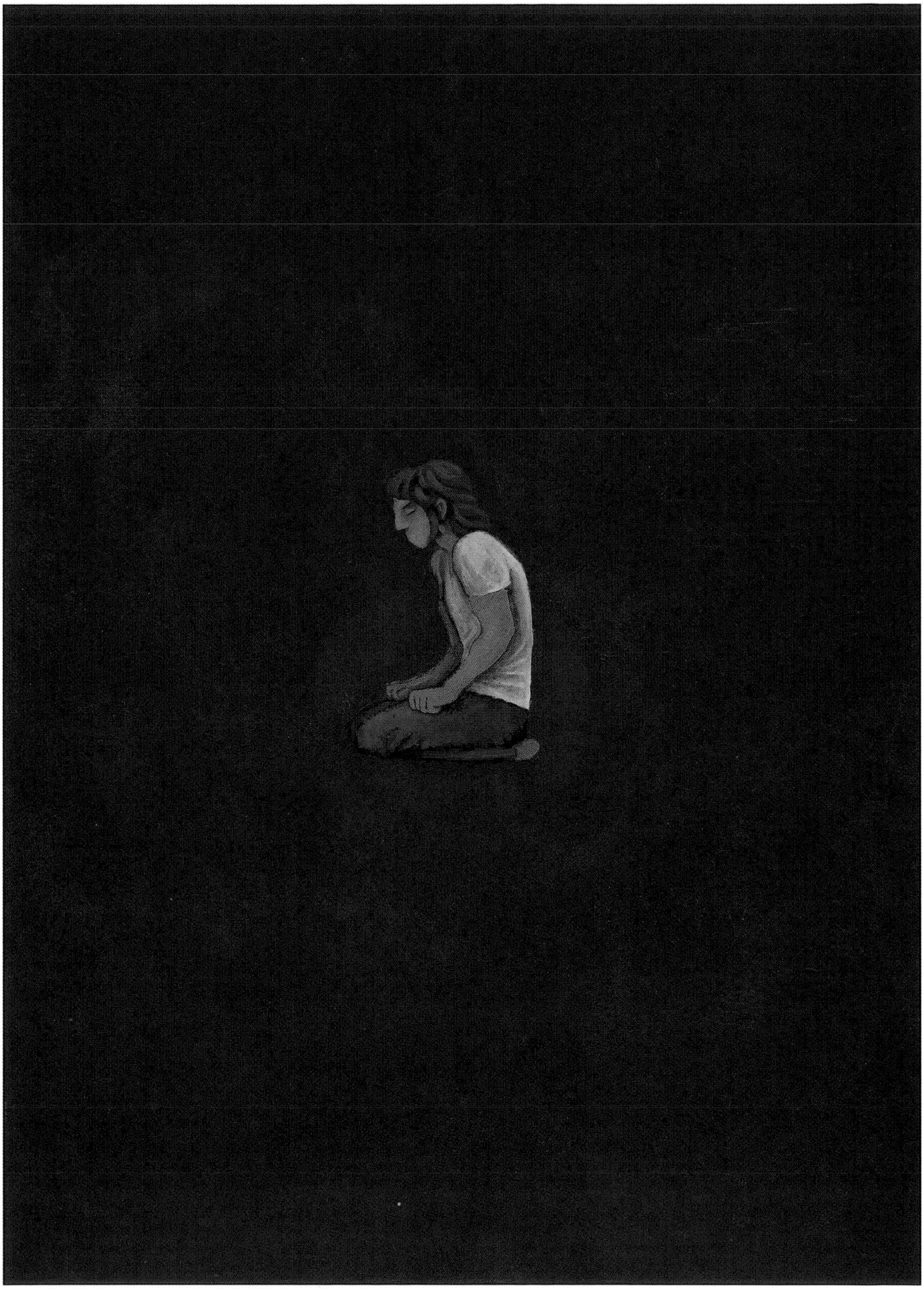

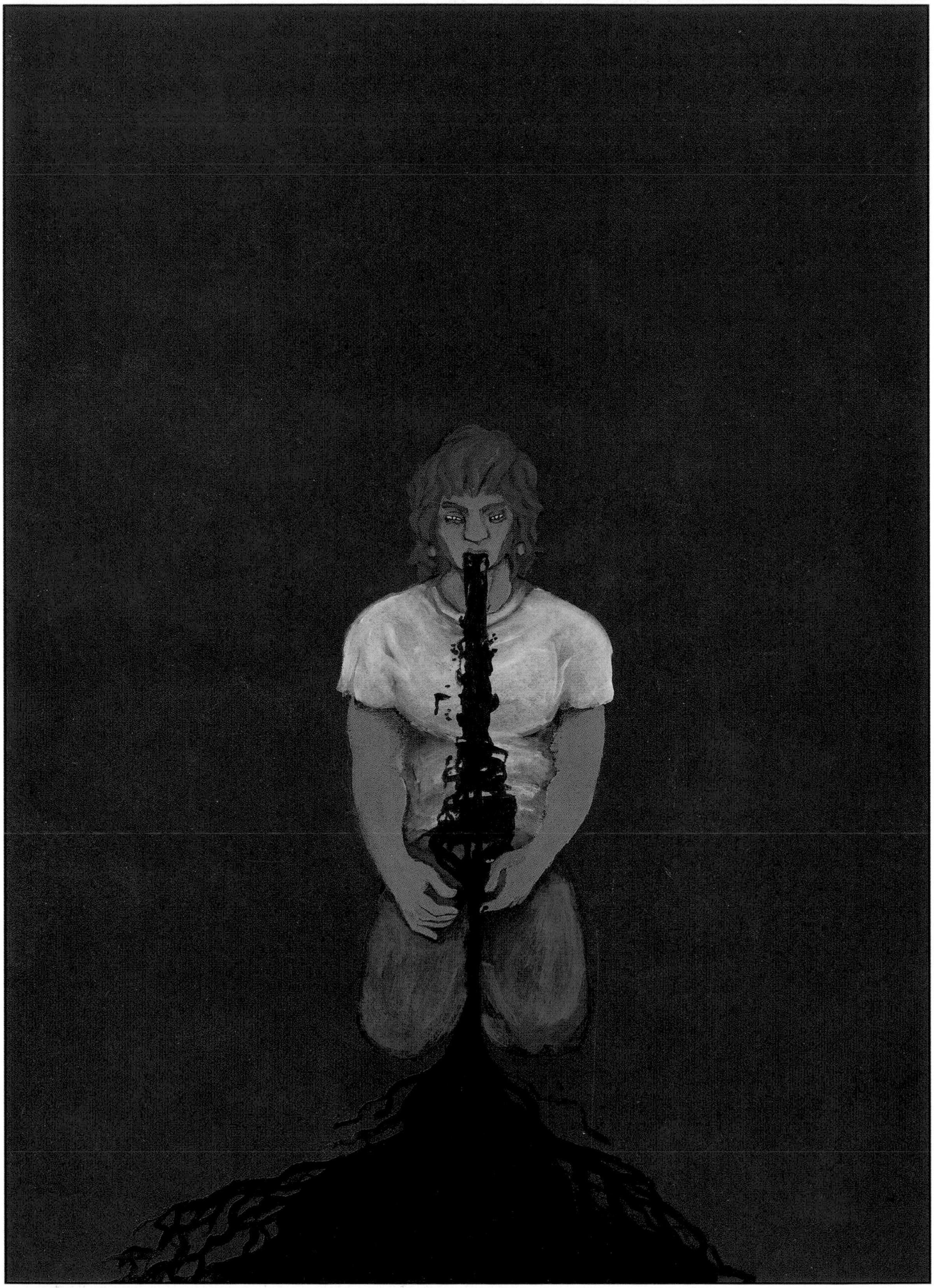

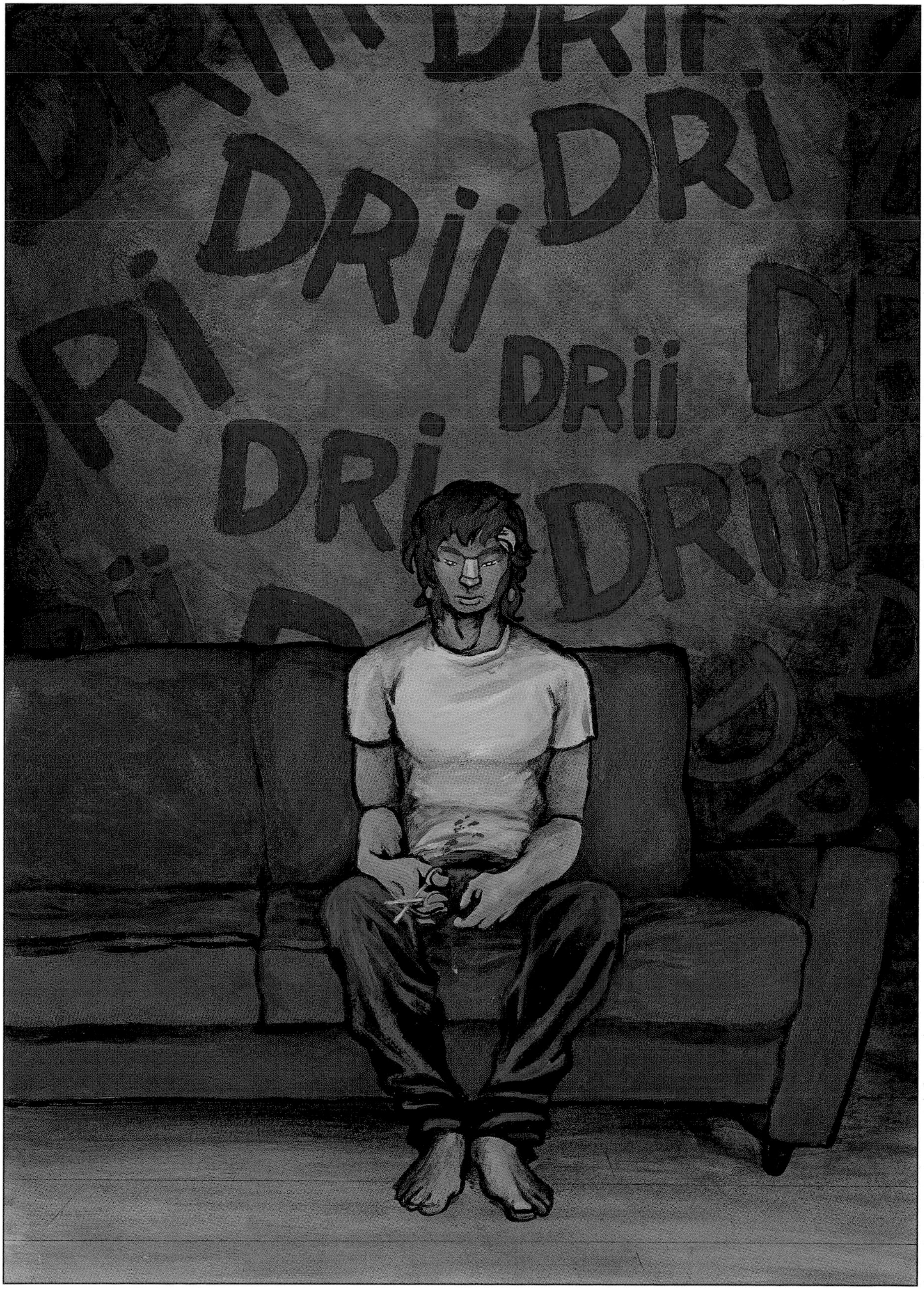
DRi
DRii
DRi
DRii
DRi
DRiii

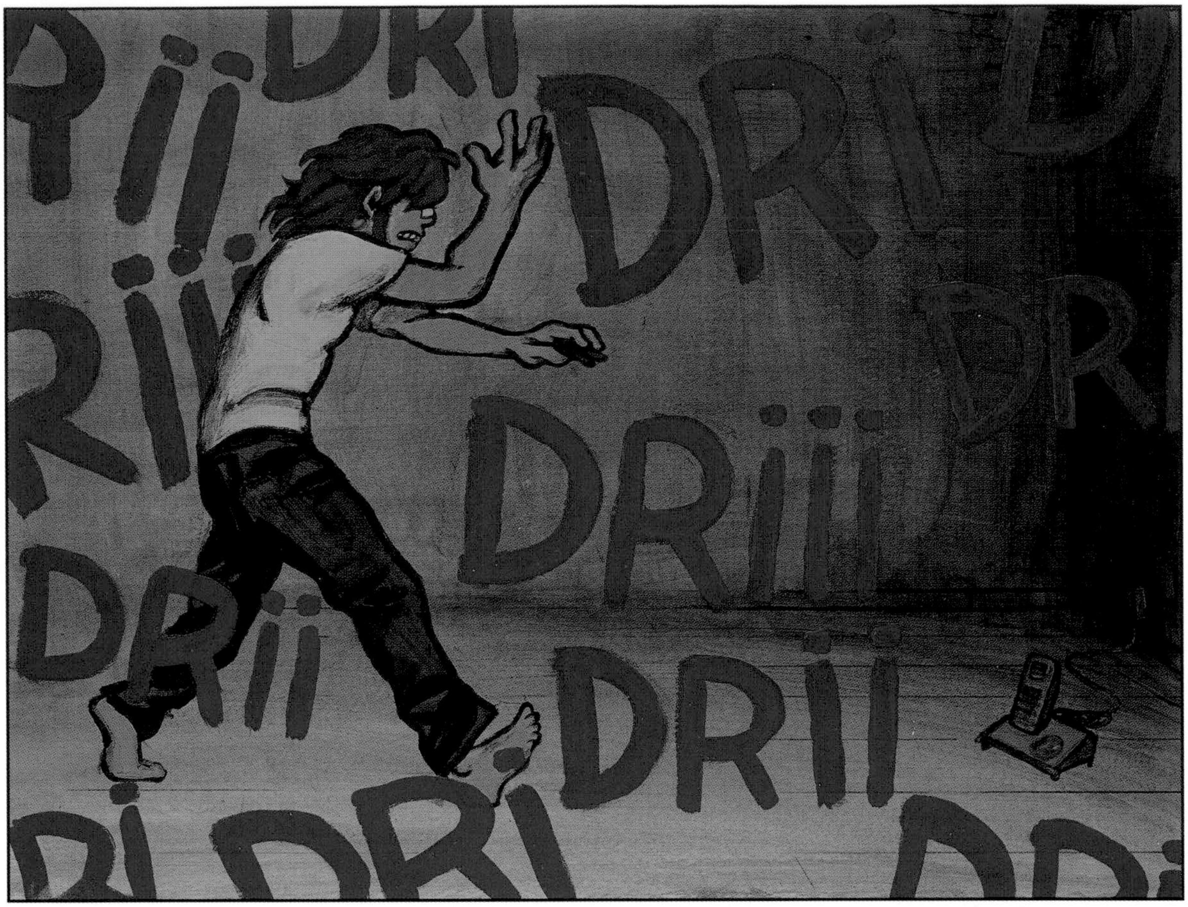
DRI
DRI
DRii
DRii
DRii
DRii
DRI

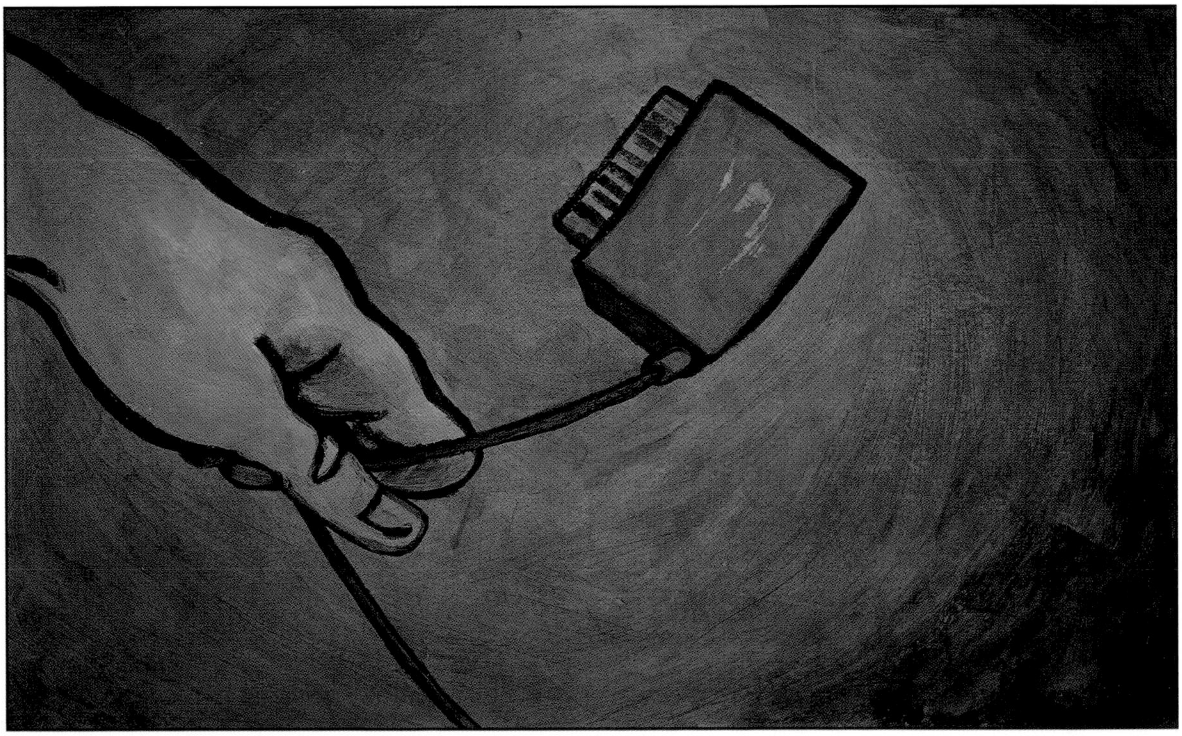

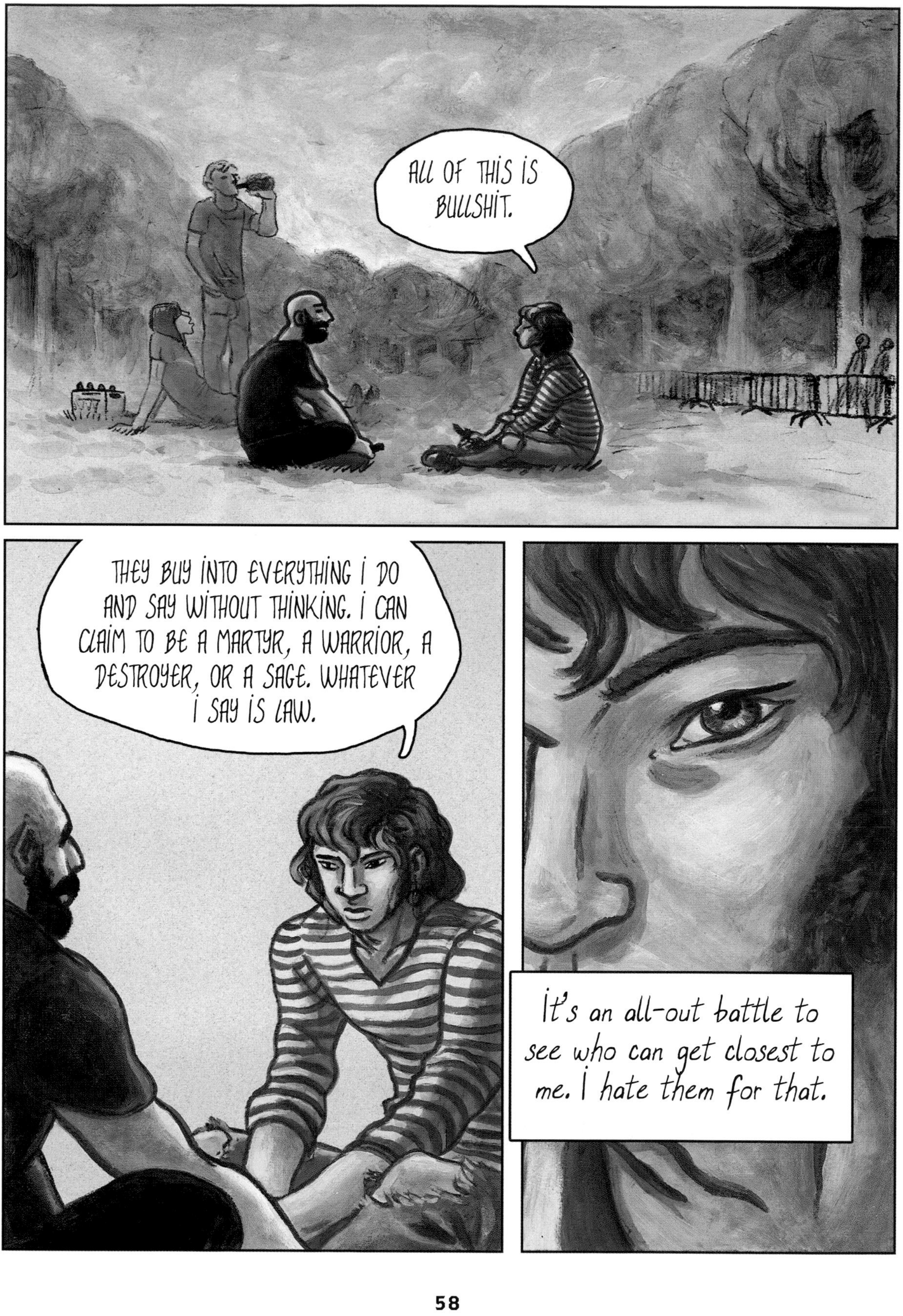
ALL OF THIS IS BULLSHIT.
THEY BUY INTO EVERYTHING I DO AND SAY WITHOUT THINKING. I CAN CLAIM TO BE A MARTYR, A WARRIOR, A DESTROYER, OR A SAGE. WHATEVER I SAY IS LAW.
It's an all-out battle to see who can get closest to me. I hate them for that.

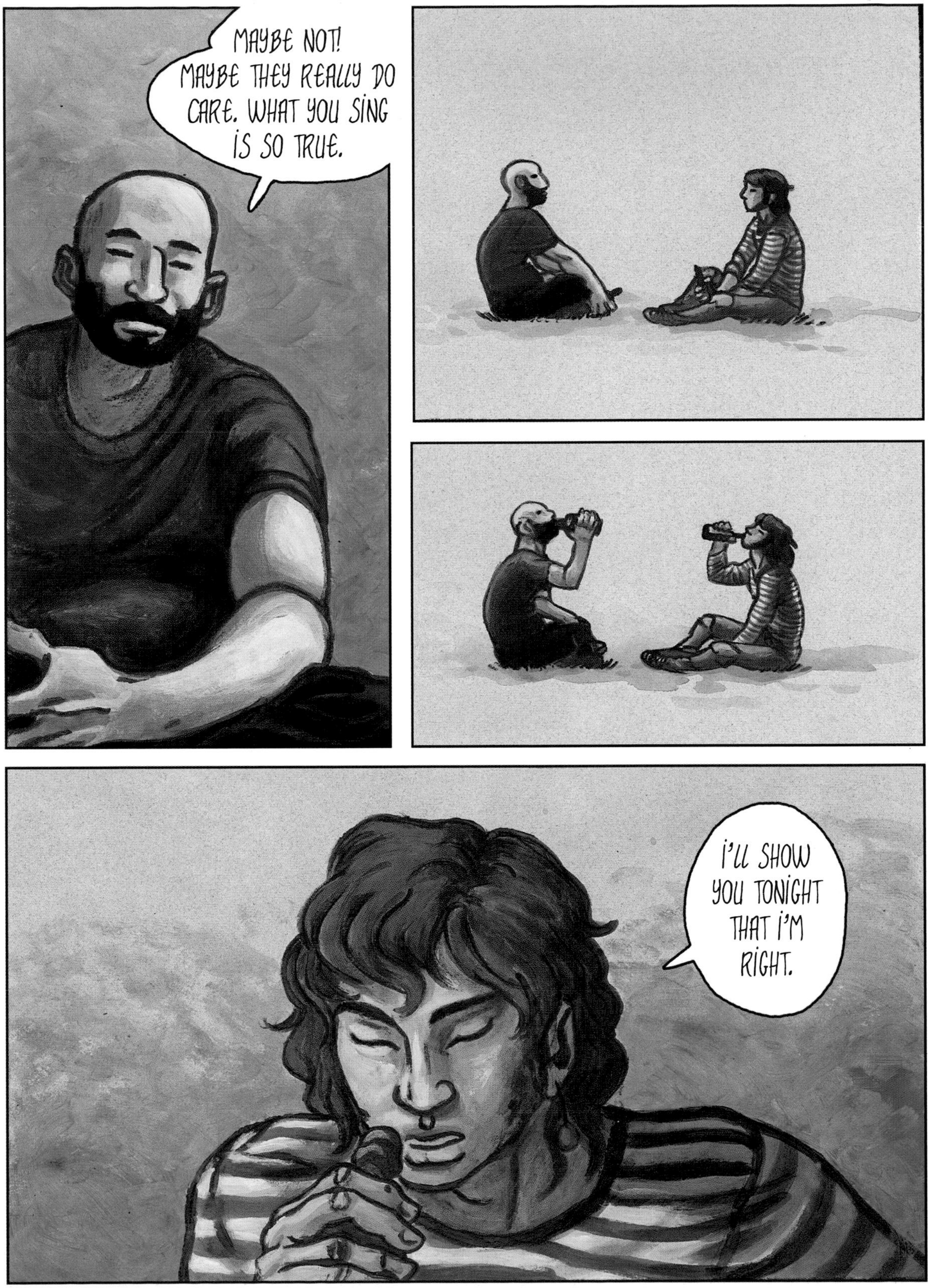
MAYBE NOT! MAYBE THEY REALLY DO CARE. WHAT YOU SING IS SO TRUE.
I'LL SHOW YOU TONIGHT THAT I'M RIGHT.

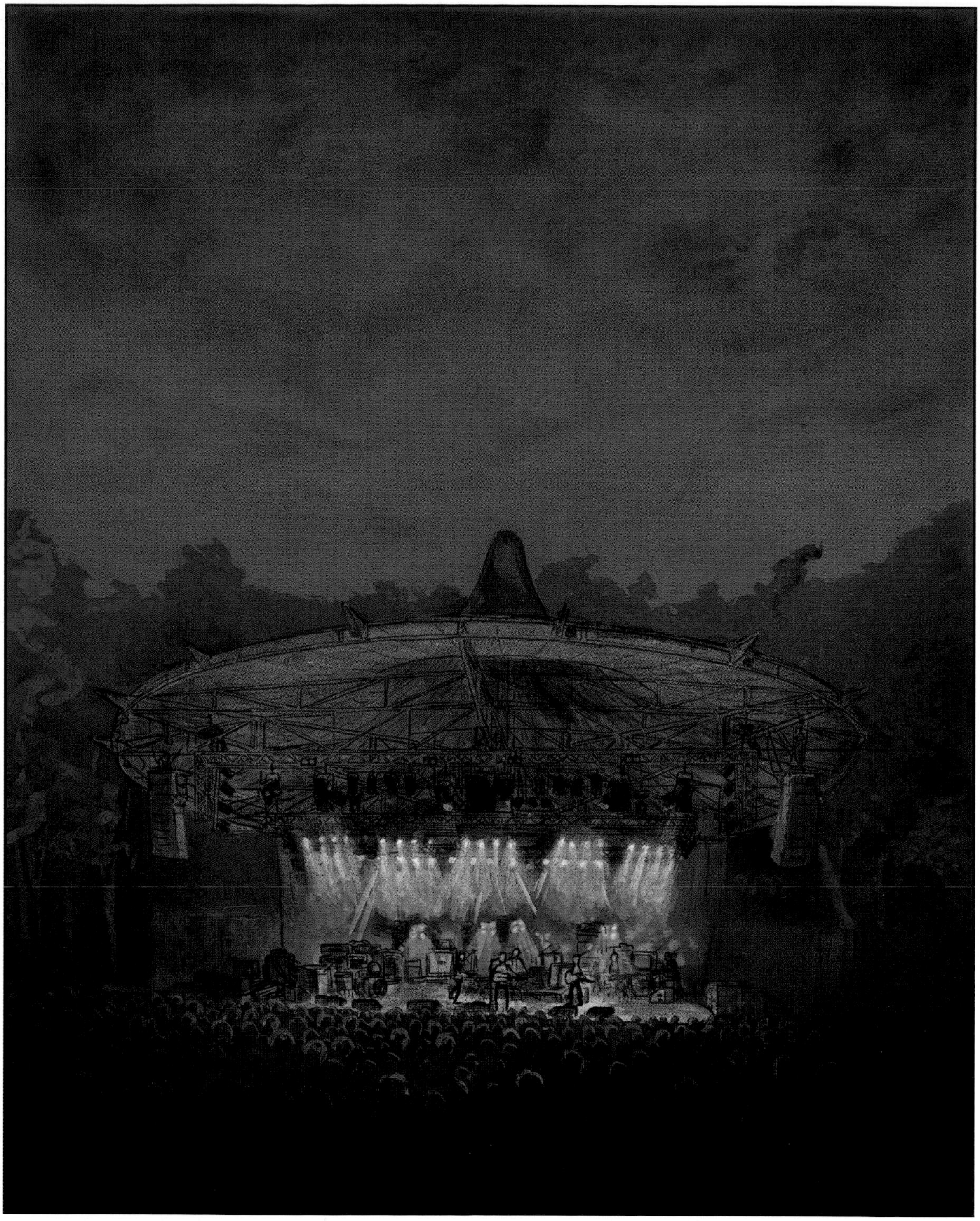

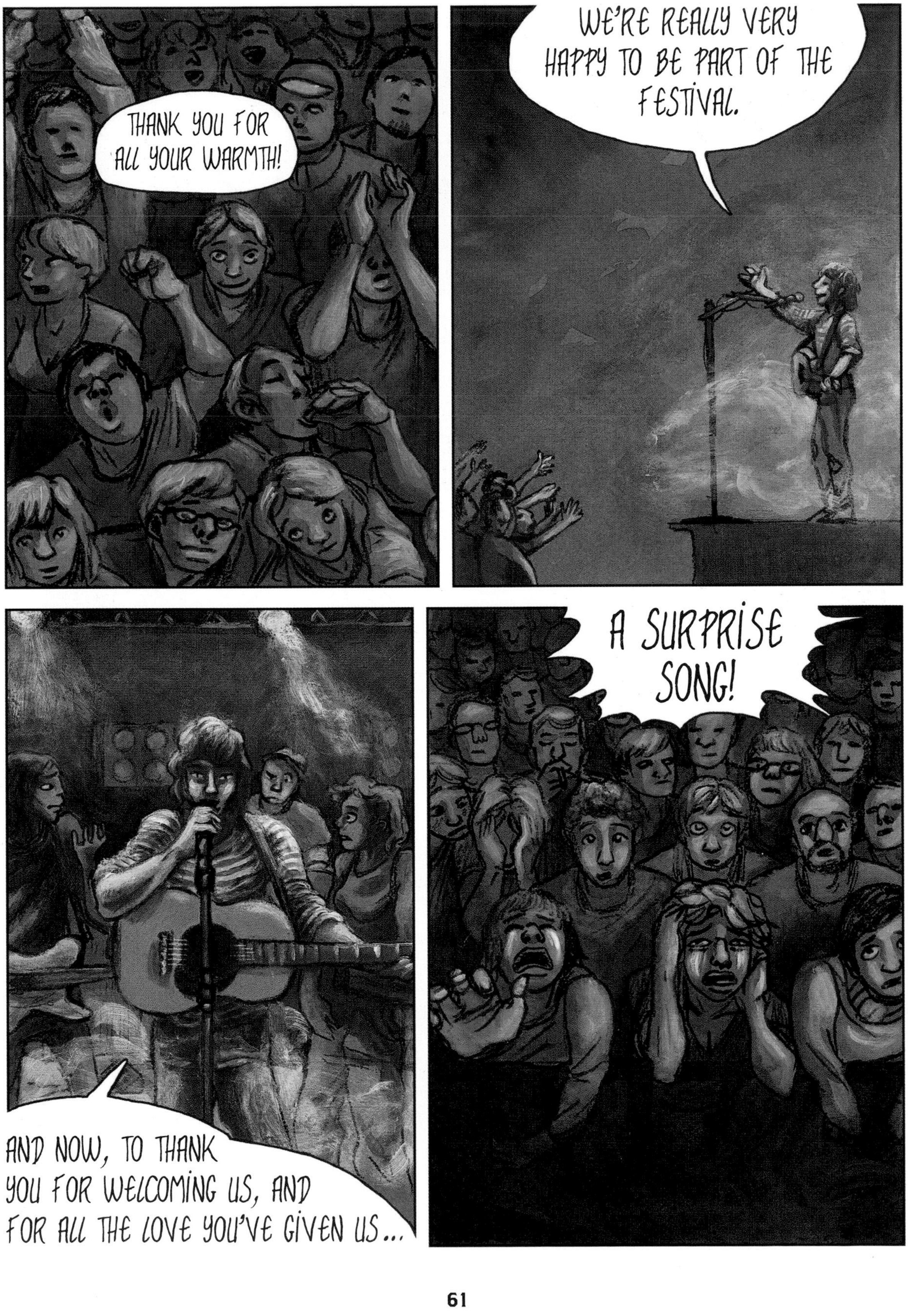
THANK YOU FOR ALL YOUR WARMTH!
WE'RE REALLY VERY HAPPY TO BE PART OF THE FESTIVAL.
AND NOW, TO THANK YOU FOR WELCOMING US, AND FOR ALL THE LOVE YOU'VE GIVEN US...
A SURPRISE SONG!

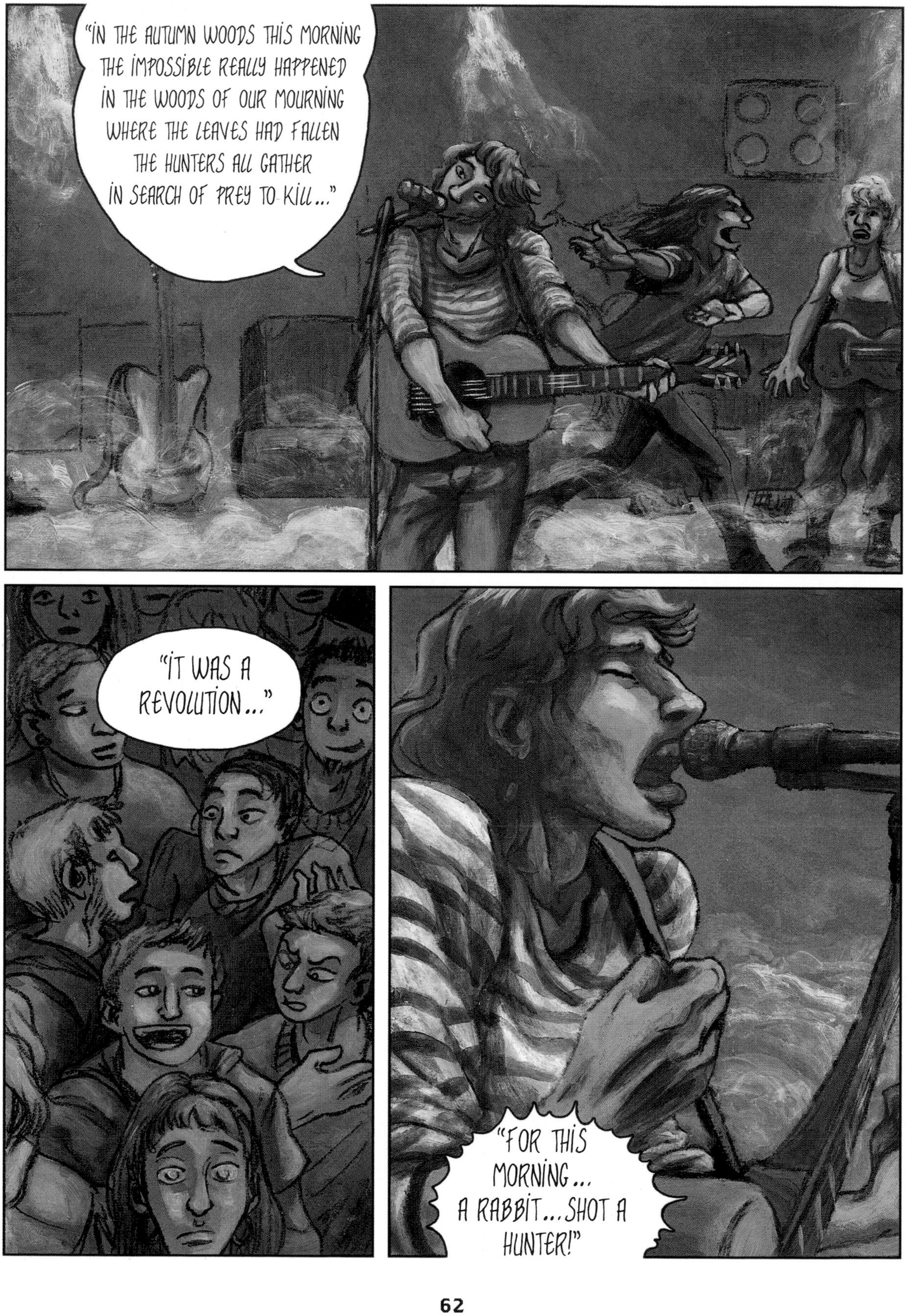
"IN THE AUTUMN WOODS THIS MORNING THE IMPOSSIBLE REALLY HAPPENED IN THE WOODS OF OUR MOURNING WHERE THE LEAVES HAD FALLEN THE HUNTERS ALL GATHER IN SEARCH OF PREY TO KILL..."
"IT WAS A REVOLUTION..."
"FOR THIS MORNING... A RABBIT...SHOT A HUNTER!"

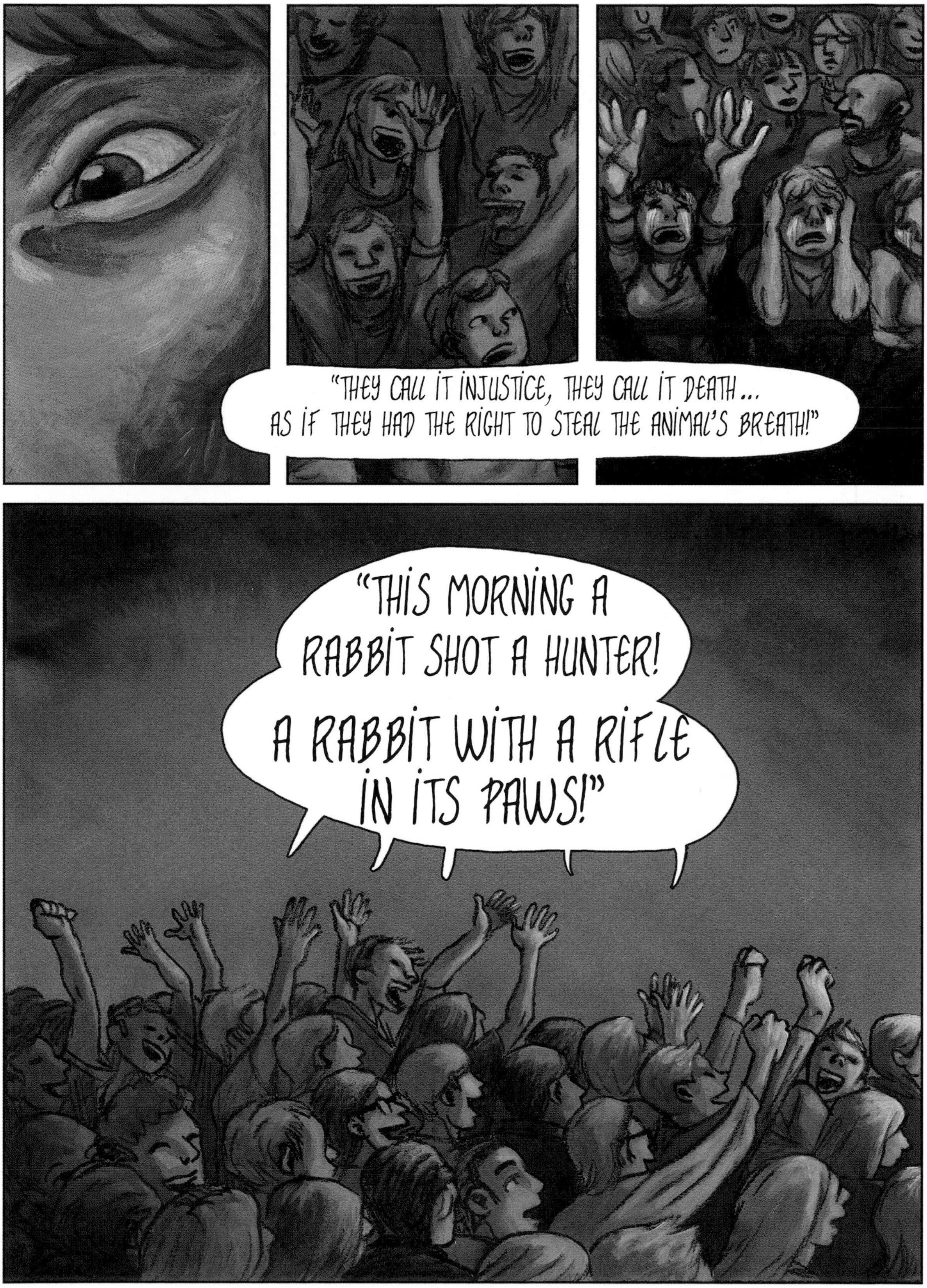
"THEY CALL IT INJUSTICE, THEY CALL IT DEATH...
AS IF THEY HAD THE RIGHT TO STEAL THE ANIMAL'S BREATH!"
"THIS MORNING A RABBIT SHOT A HUNTER!
A RABBIT WITH A RIFLE IN ITS PAWS!"

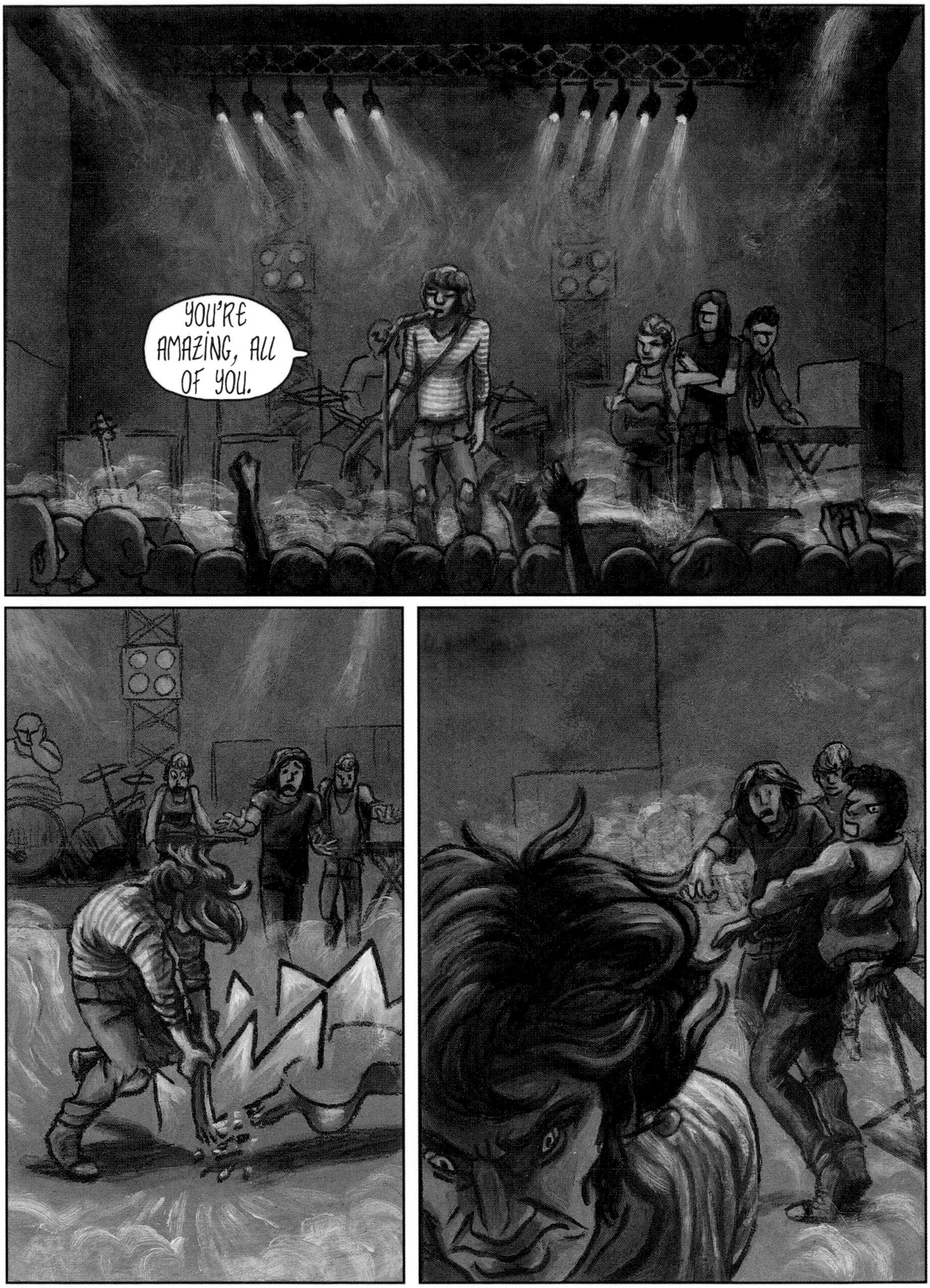
YOU'RE AMAZING, ALL OF YOU.

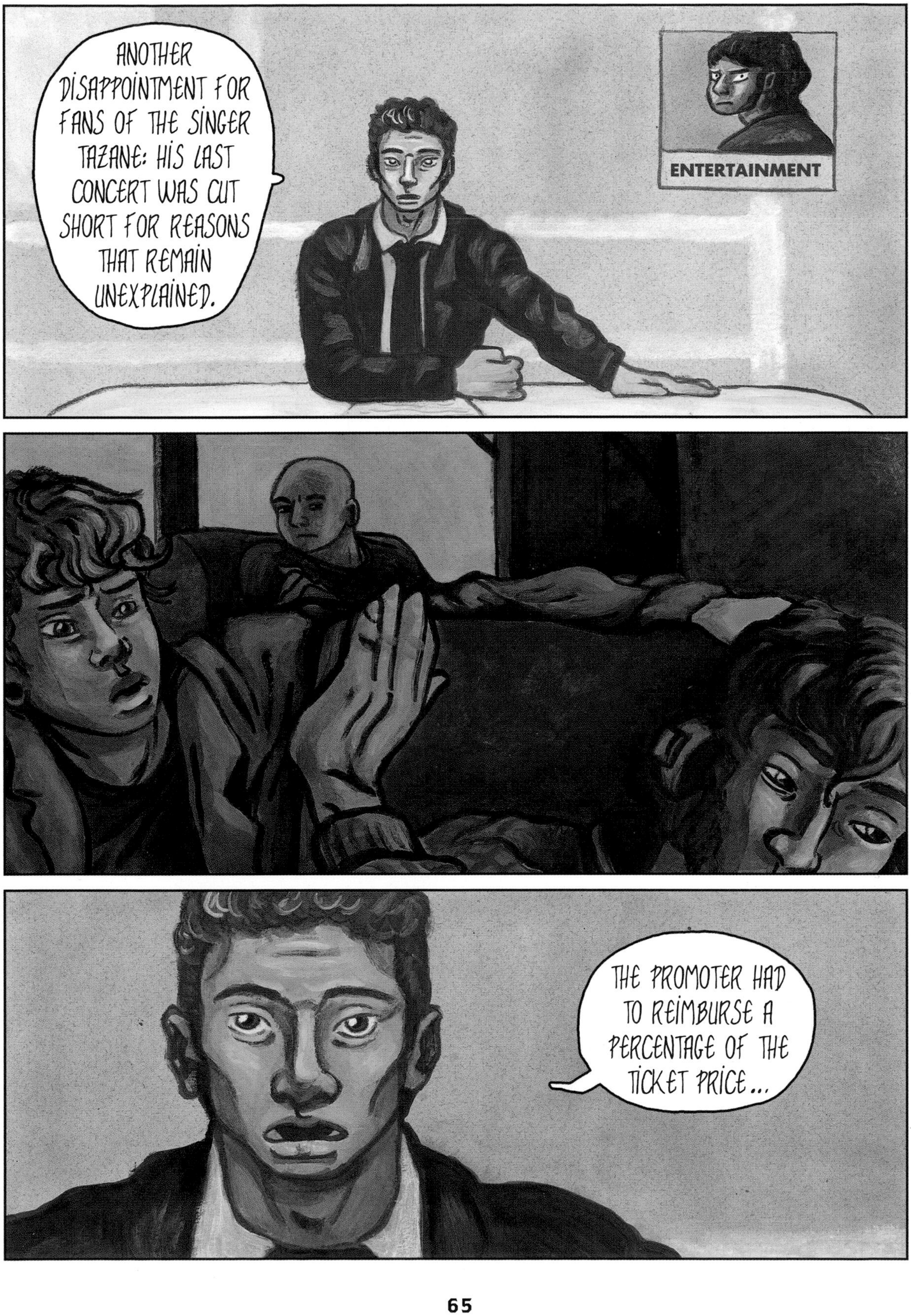
ANOTHER DISAPPOINTMENT FOR FANS OF THE SINGER TAZANE: HIS LAST CONCERT WAS CUT SHORT FOR REASONS THAT REMAIN UNEXPLAINED.
ENTERTAINMENT
THE PROMOTER HAD TO REIMBURSE A PERCENTAGE OF THE TICKET PRICE...

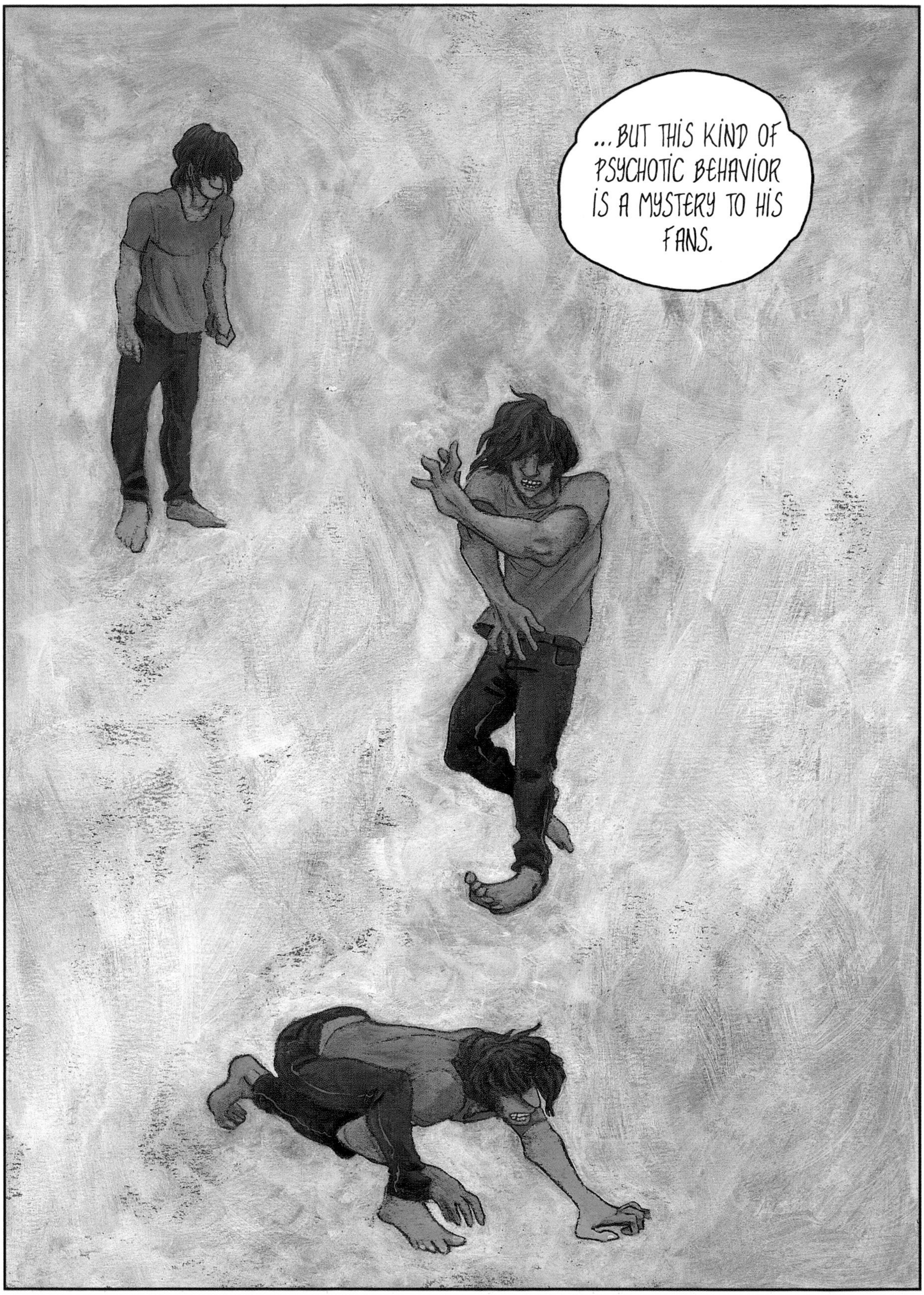
...BUT THIS KIND OF PSYCHOTIC BEHAVIOR IS A MYSTERY TO HIS FANS.

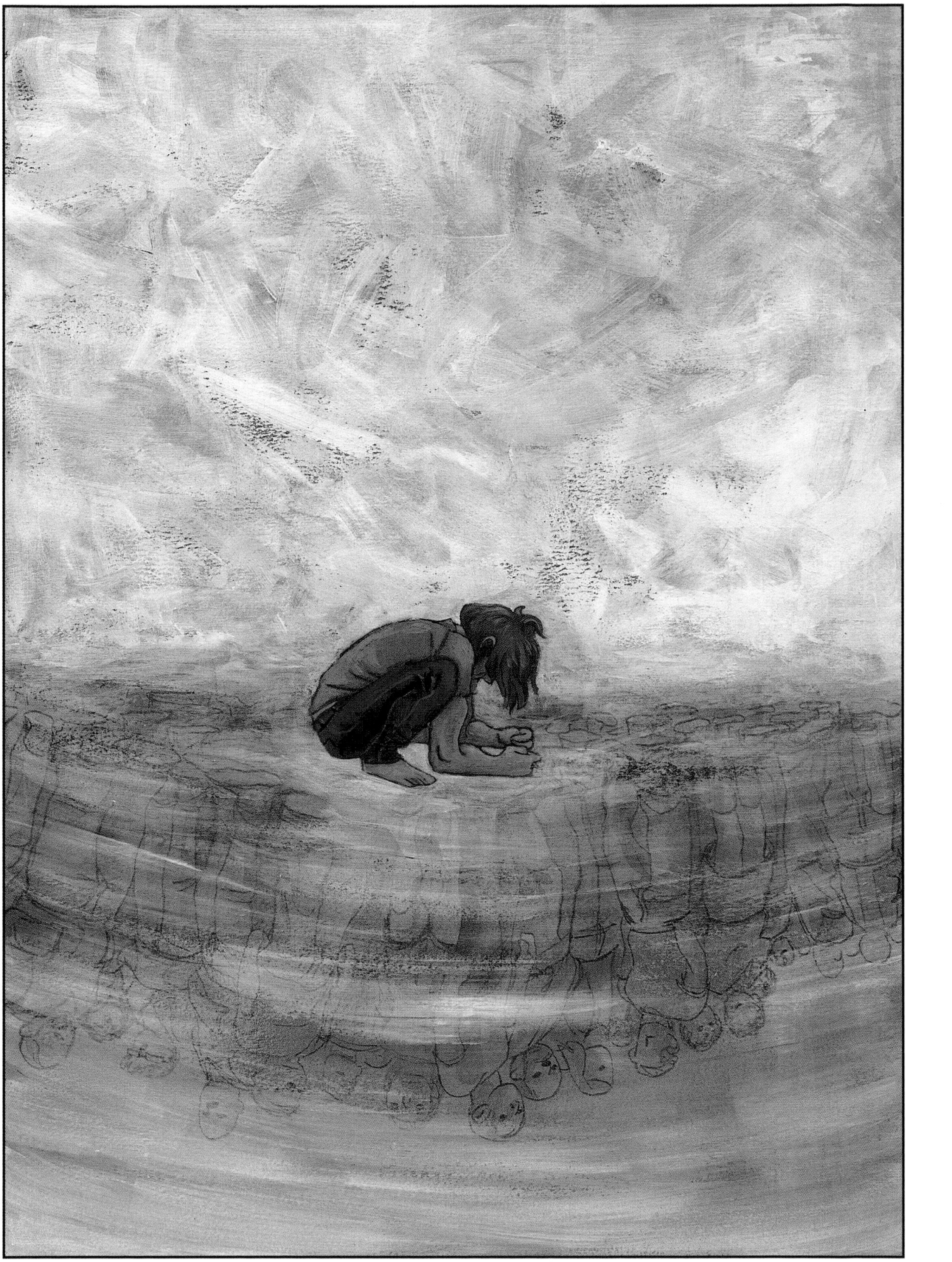

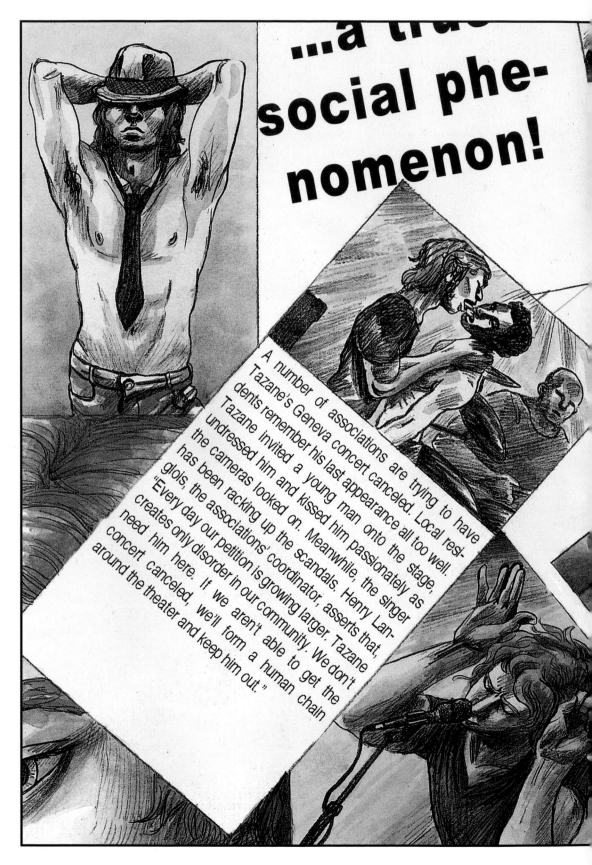

...a true social phenomenon!

A number of associations are trying to have Tazane's Geneva concert canceled. Local residents remember his last appearance all too well. Tazane invited a young man onto the stage, undressed him and kissed him passionately as the cameras looked on. Meanwhile, the singer has been racking up the scandals. Henry Langlois, the associations' coordinator, asserts that, "Every day our petition is growing larger. Tazane creates only disorder in our community. We don't need him here. If we aren't able to get the concert canceled, we'll form a human chain around the theater and keep him out."

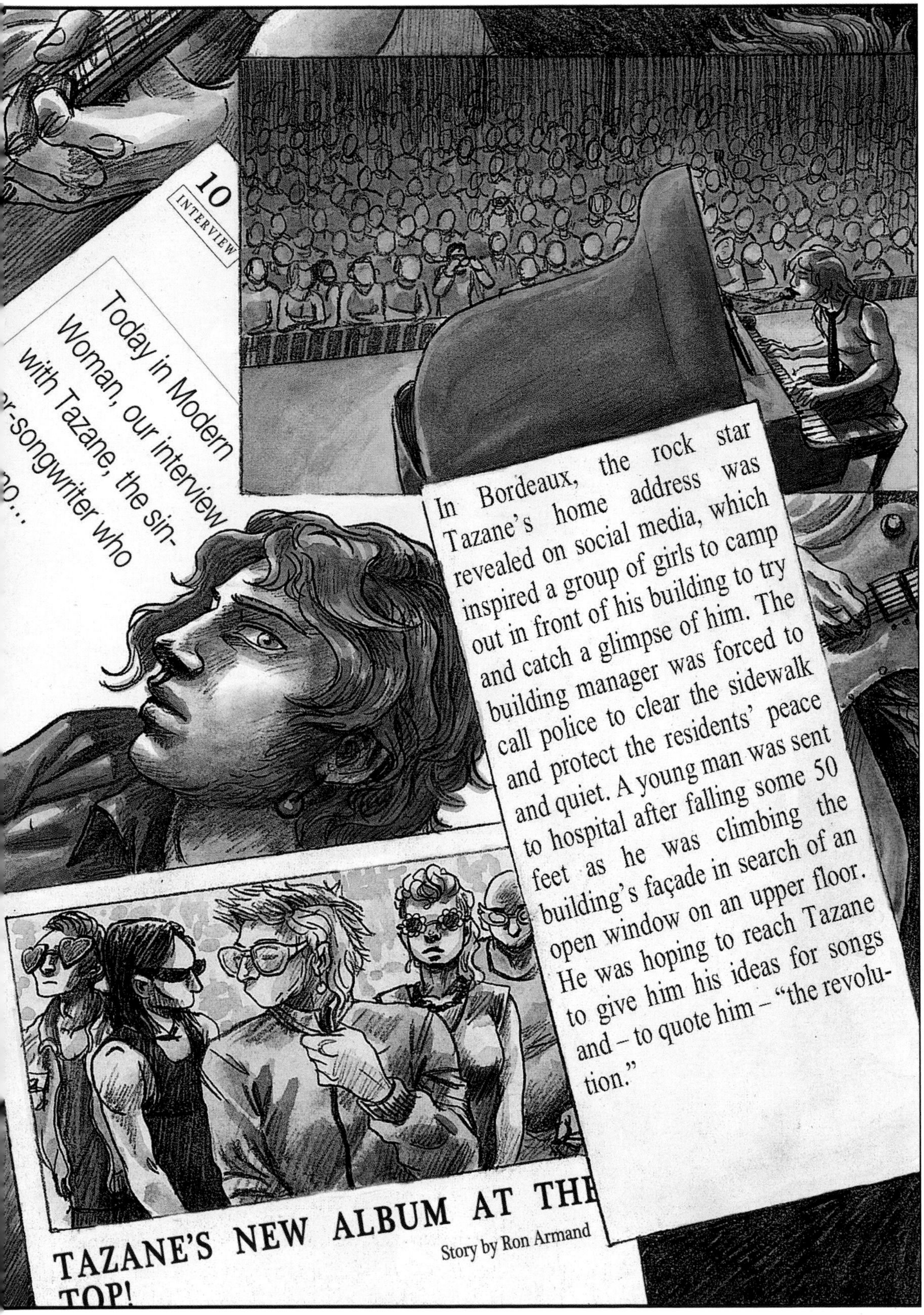

10
INTERVIEW
Today in Modern
Woman, our interview
with Tazane, the sin-
-songwriter who
In Bordeaux, the rock star Tazane's home address was revealed on social media, which inspired a group of girls to camp out in front of his building to try and catch a glimpse of him. The building manager was forced to call police to clear the sidewalk and protect the residents' peace and quiet. A young man was sent to hospital after falling some 50 feet as he was climbing the building's façade in search of an open window on an upper floor. He was hoping to reach Tazane to give him his ideas for songs and – to quote him – "the revolution."
TAZANE'S NEW ALBUM AT TH
TOP!
Story by Ron Armand

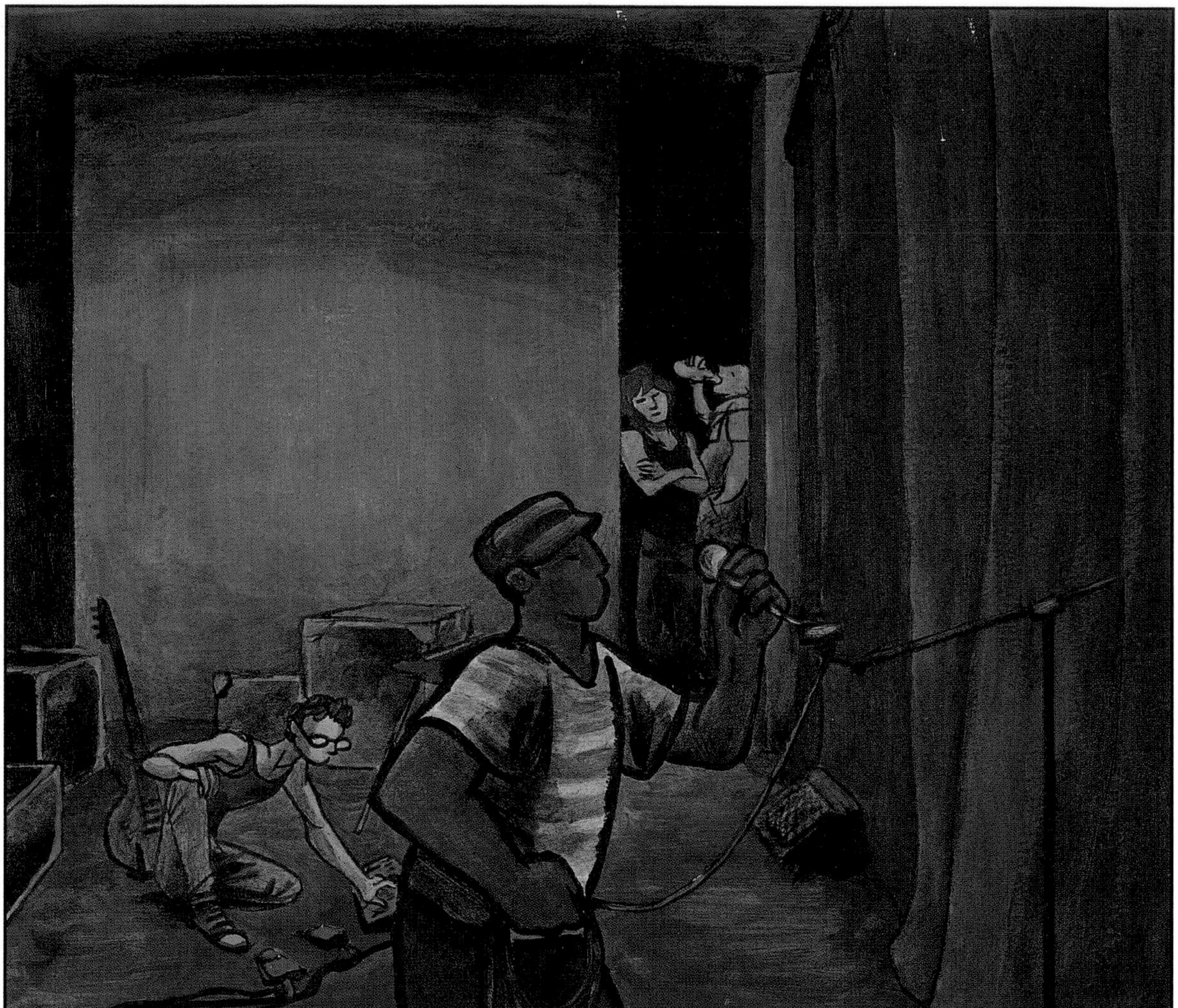
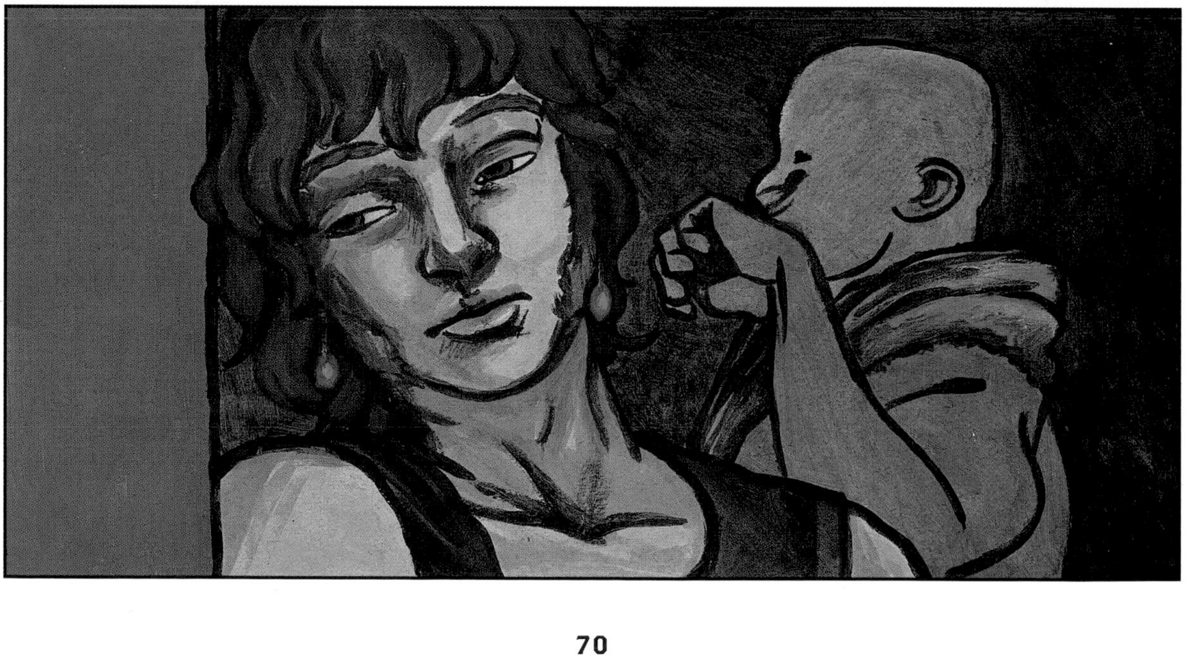

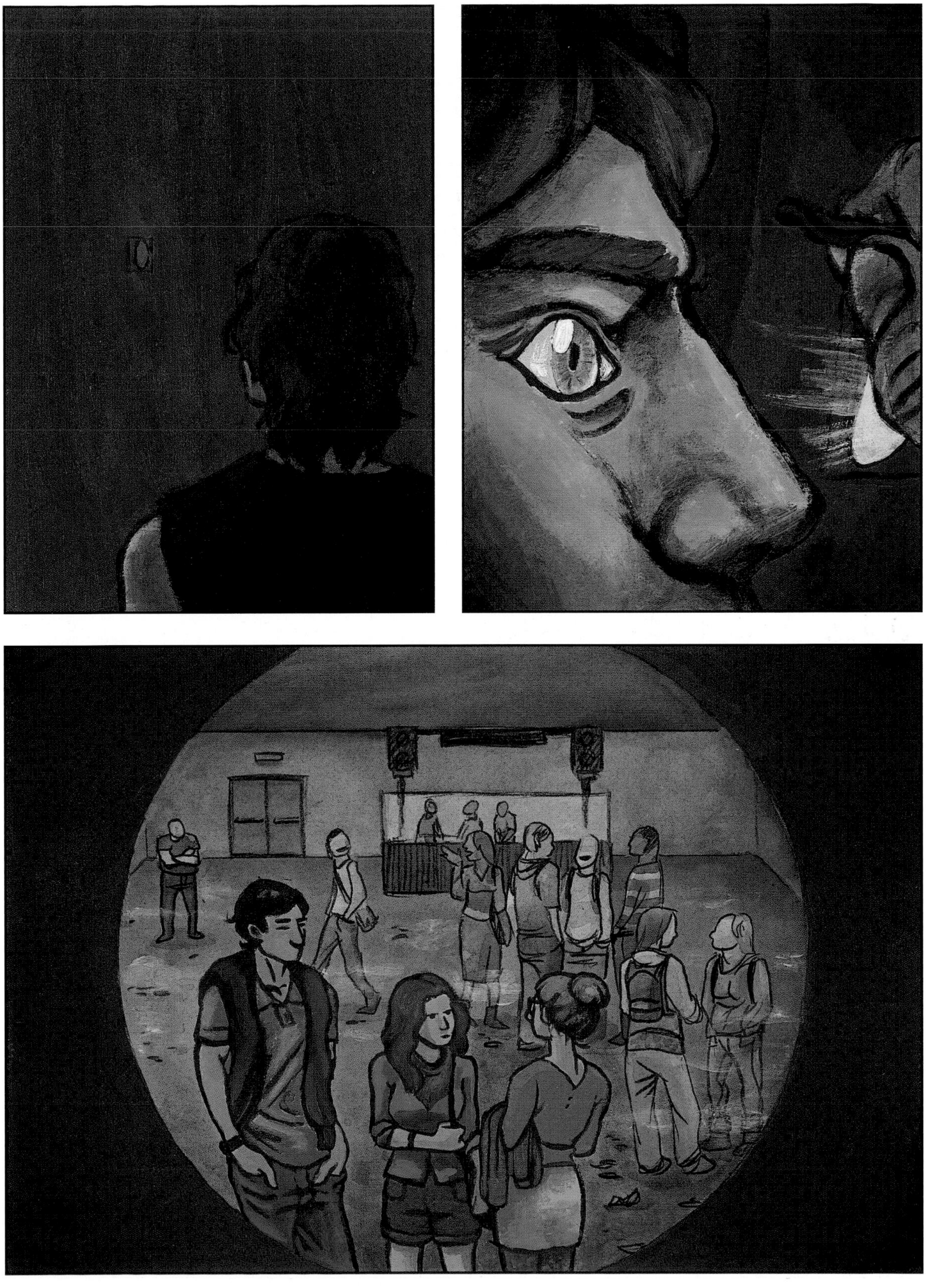

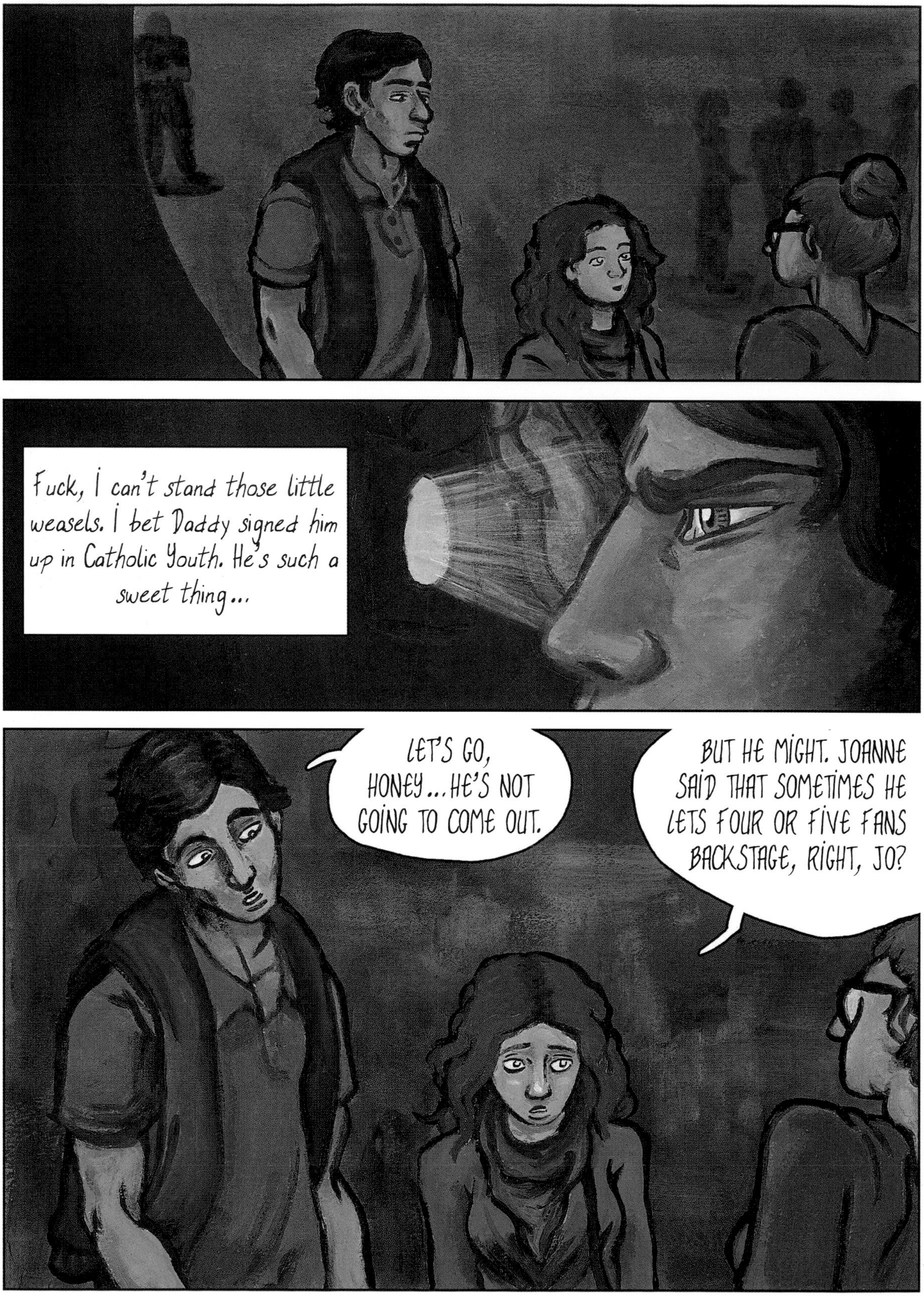
Fuck, I can't stand those little weasels. I bet Daddy signed him up in Catholic Youth. He's such a sweet thing...
LET'S GO, HONEY...HE'S NOT GOING TO COME OUT.
BUT HE MIGHT. JOANNE SAID THAT SOMETIMES HE LETS FOUR OR FIVE FANS BACKSTAGE, RIGHT, JO?

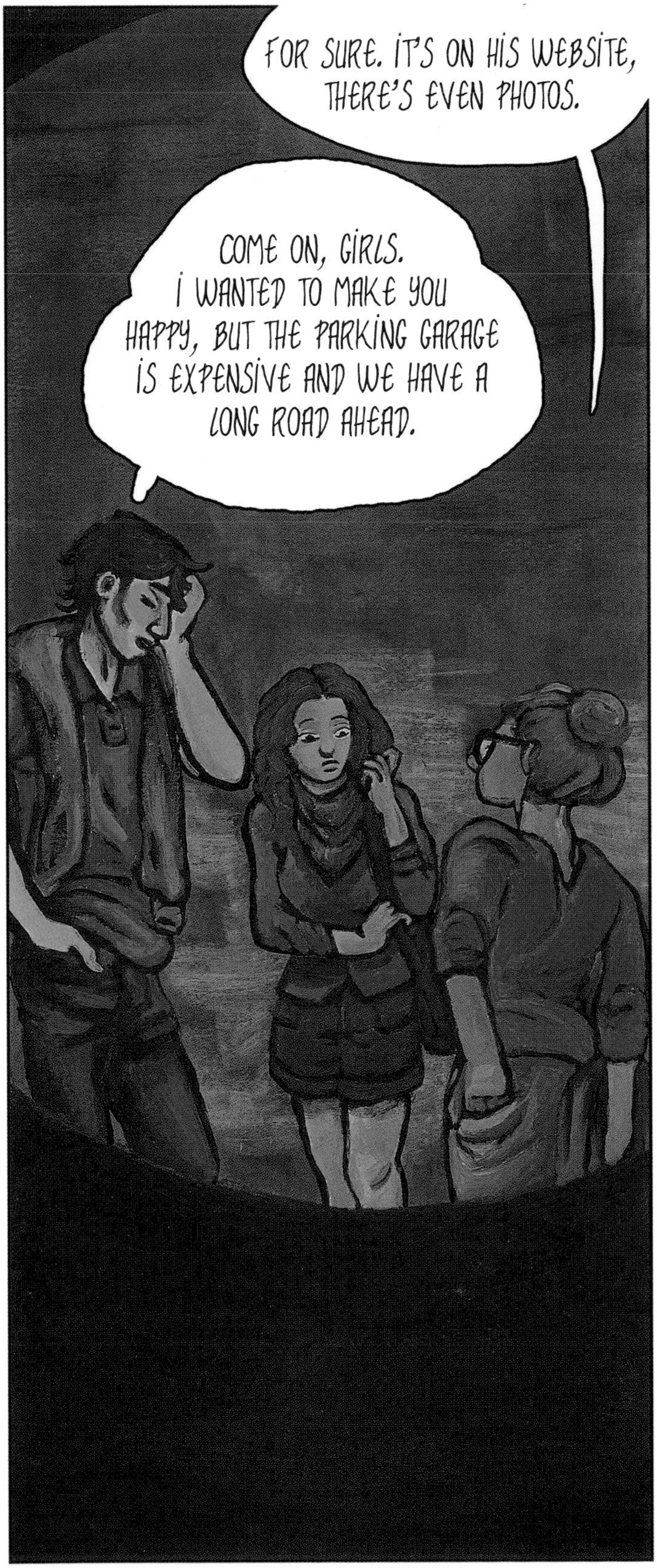
For sure. It's on his website, there's even photos.
Come on, girls. I wanted to make you happy, but the parking garage is expensive and we have a long road ahead.

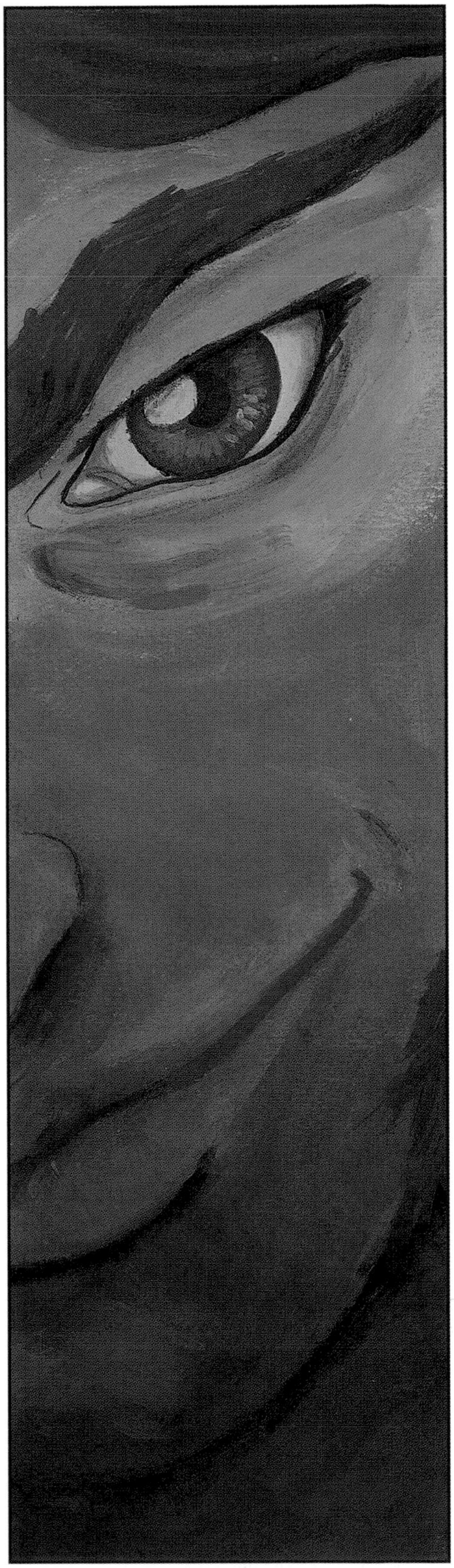

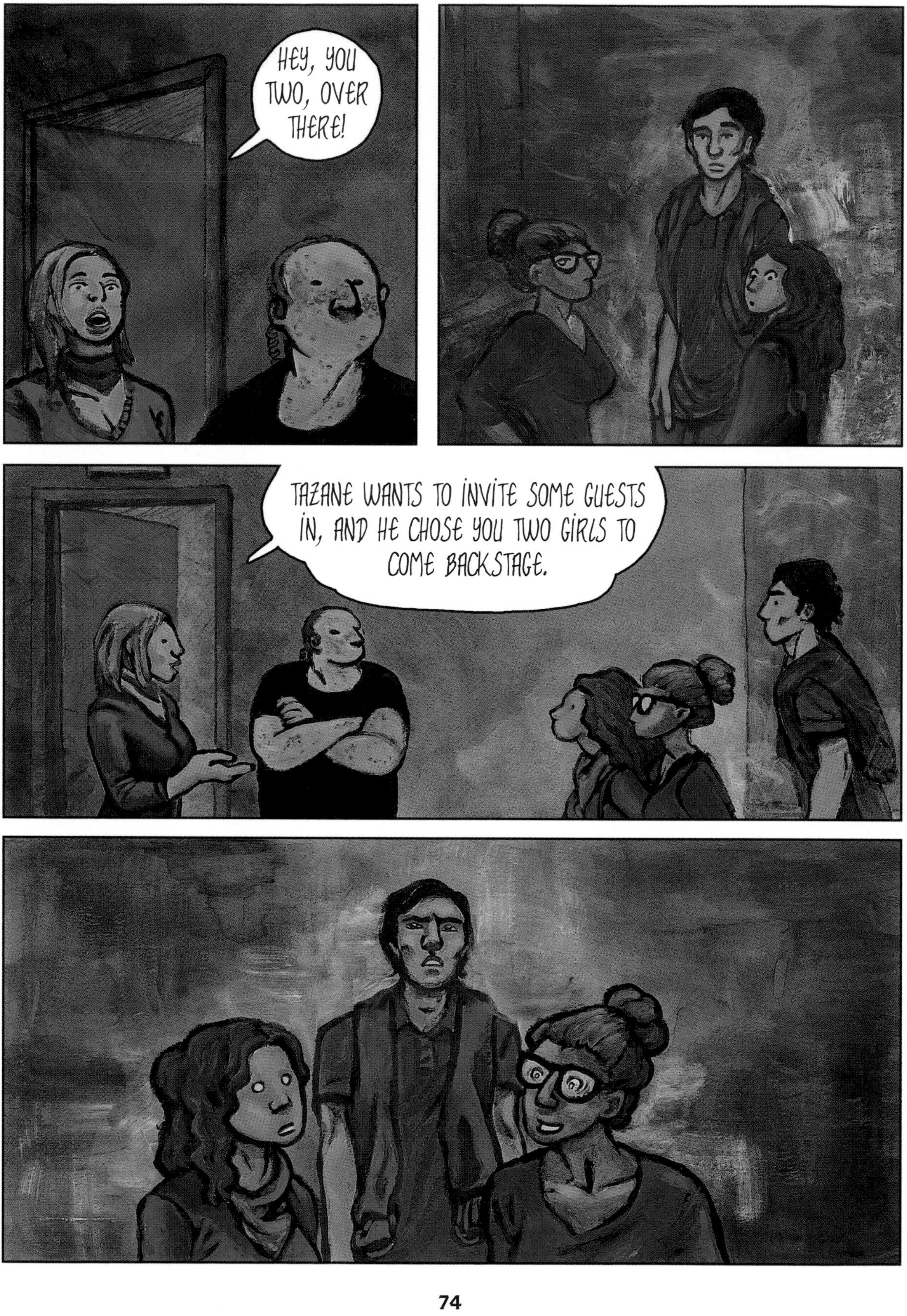
HEY, YOU TWO, OVER THERE!
TAZANE WANTS TO INVITE SOME GUESTS IN, AND HE CHOSE YOU TWO GIRLS TO COME BACKSTAGE.

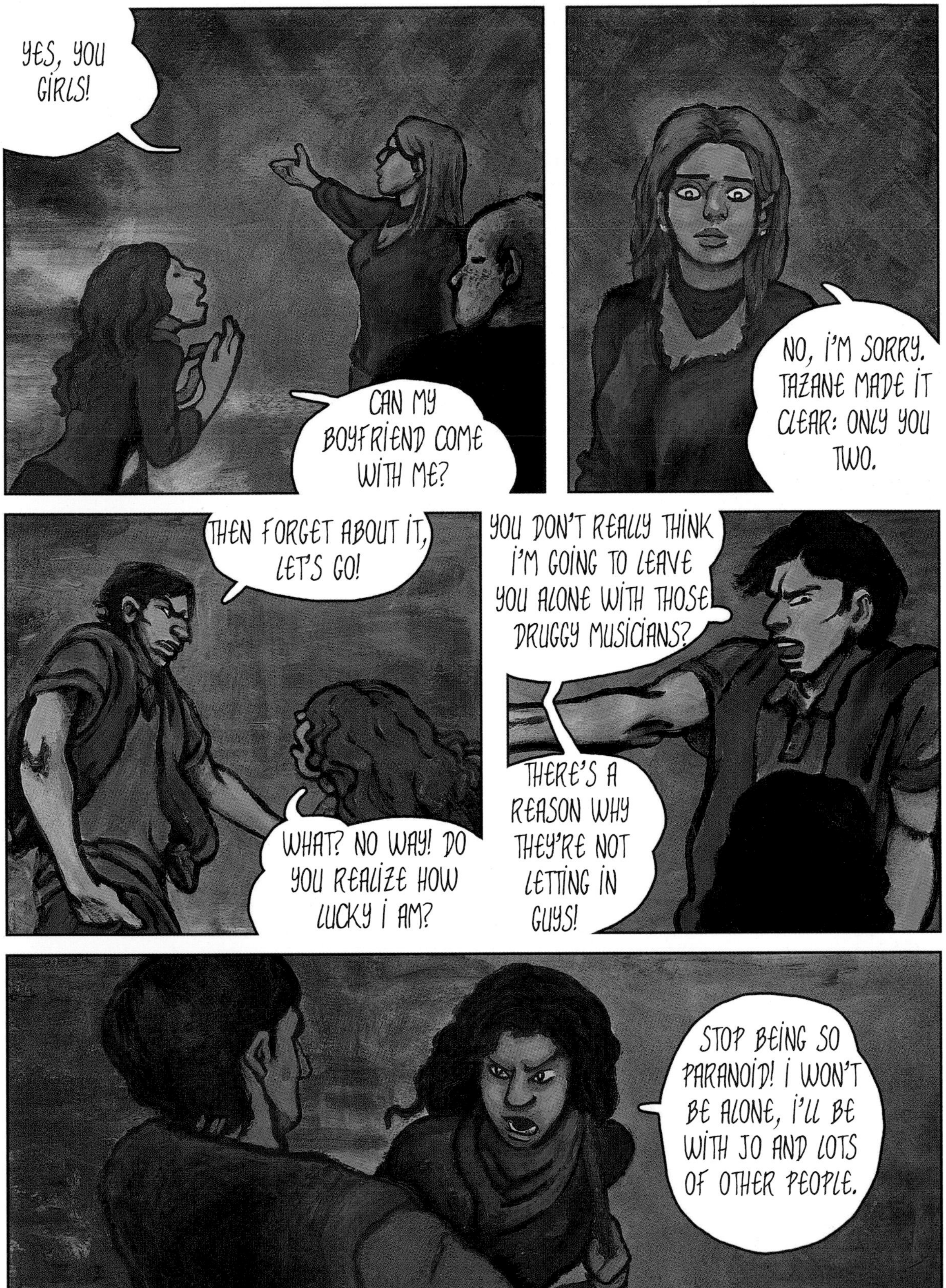
YES, YOU GIRLS!
CAN MY BOYFRIEND COME WITH ME?
NO, I'M SORRY. TAZANE MADE IT CLEAR: ONLY YOU TWO.
THEN FORGET ABOUT IT, LET'S GO!
WHAT? NO WAY! DO YOU REALIZE HOW LUCKY I AM?
YOU DON'T REALLY THINK I'M GOING TO LEAVE YOU ALONE WITH THOSE DRUGGY MUSICIANS?
THERE'S A REASON WHY THEY'RE NOT LETTING IN GUYS!
STOP BEING SO PARANOID! I WON'T BE ALONE, I'LL BE WITH JO AND LOTS OF OTHER PEOPLE.

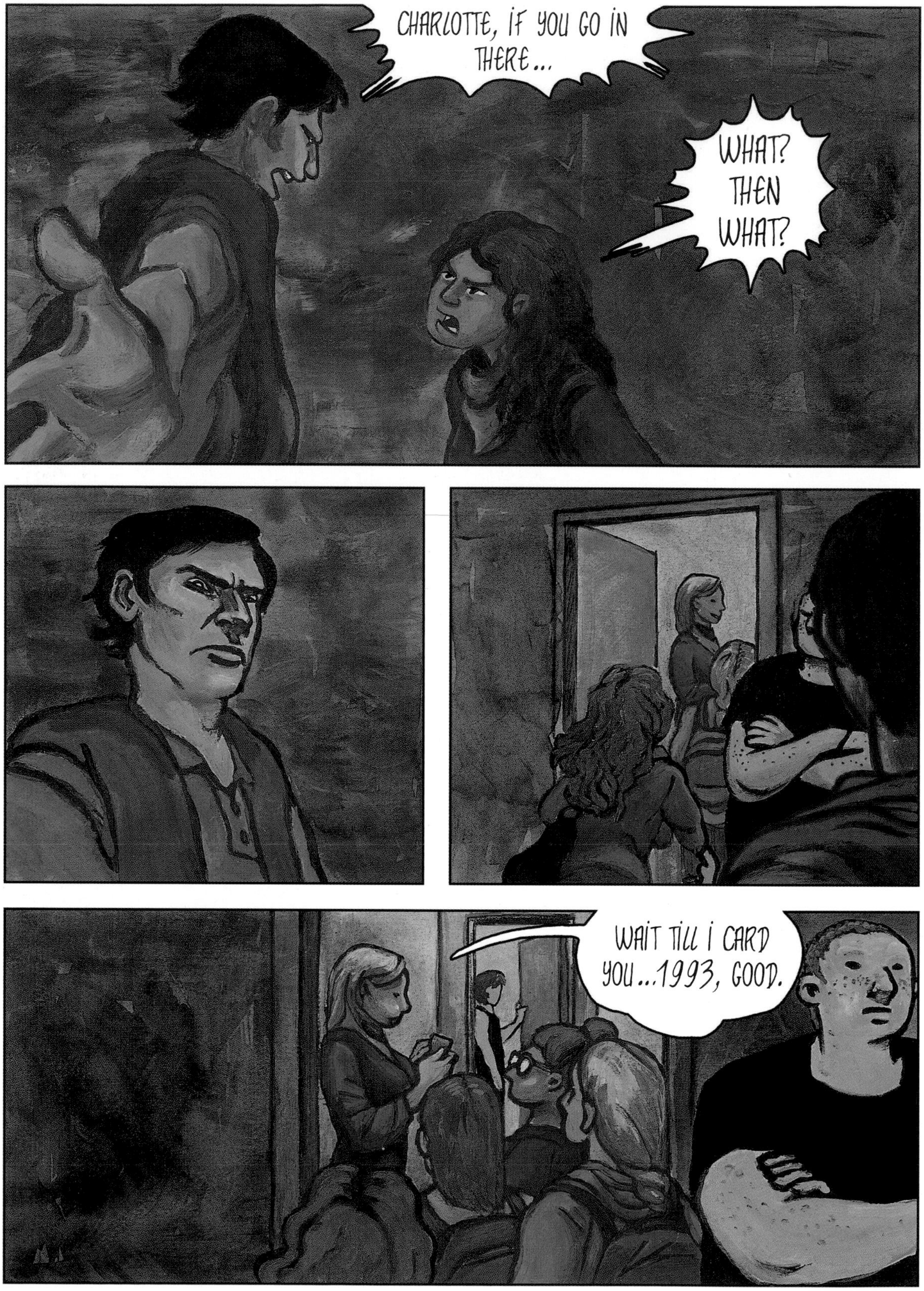
CHARLOTTE, IF YOU GO IN THERE...
WHAT? THEN WHAT?
WAIT TILL I CARD YOU...1993, GOOD.

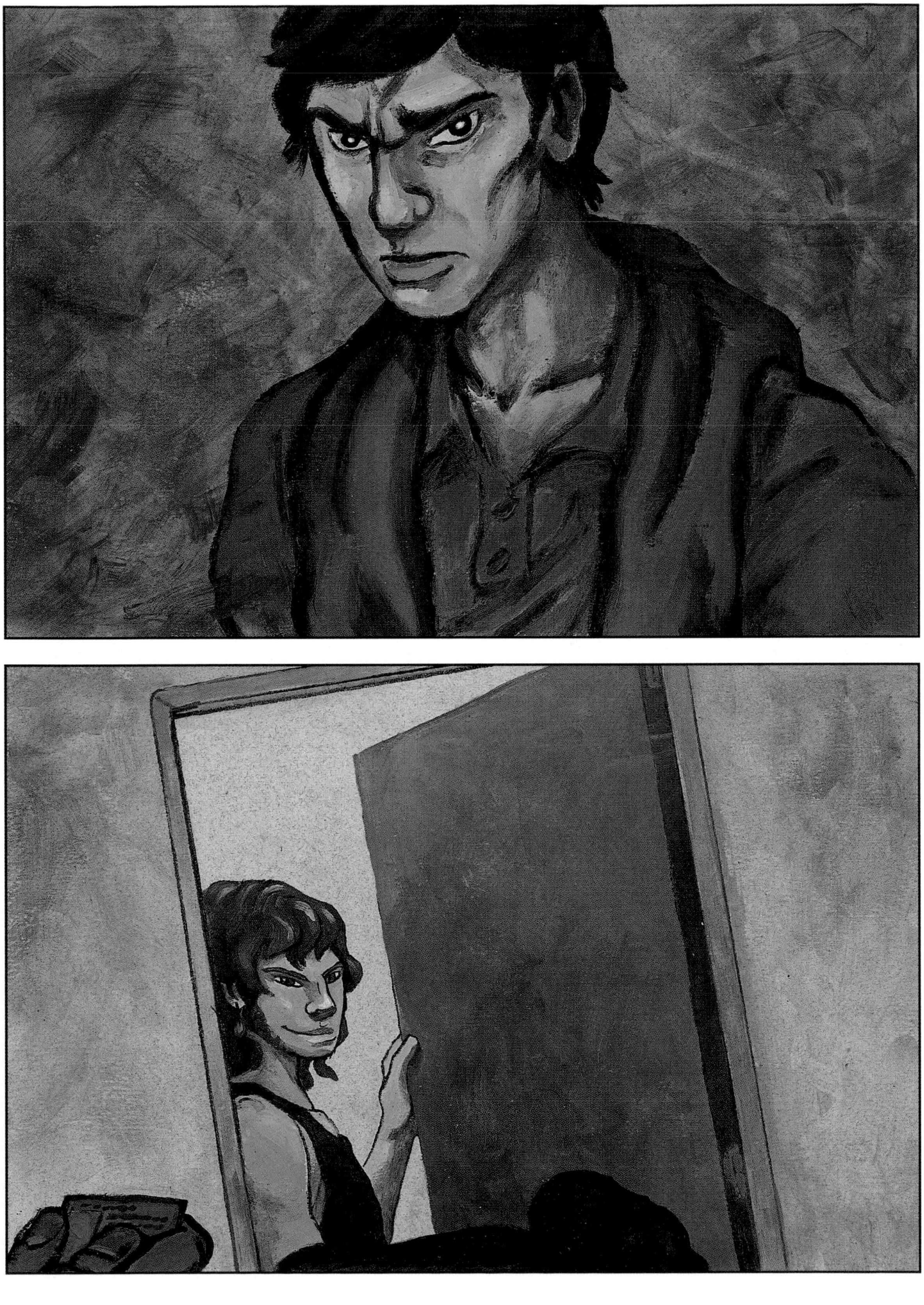

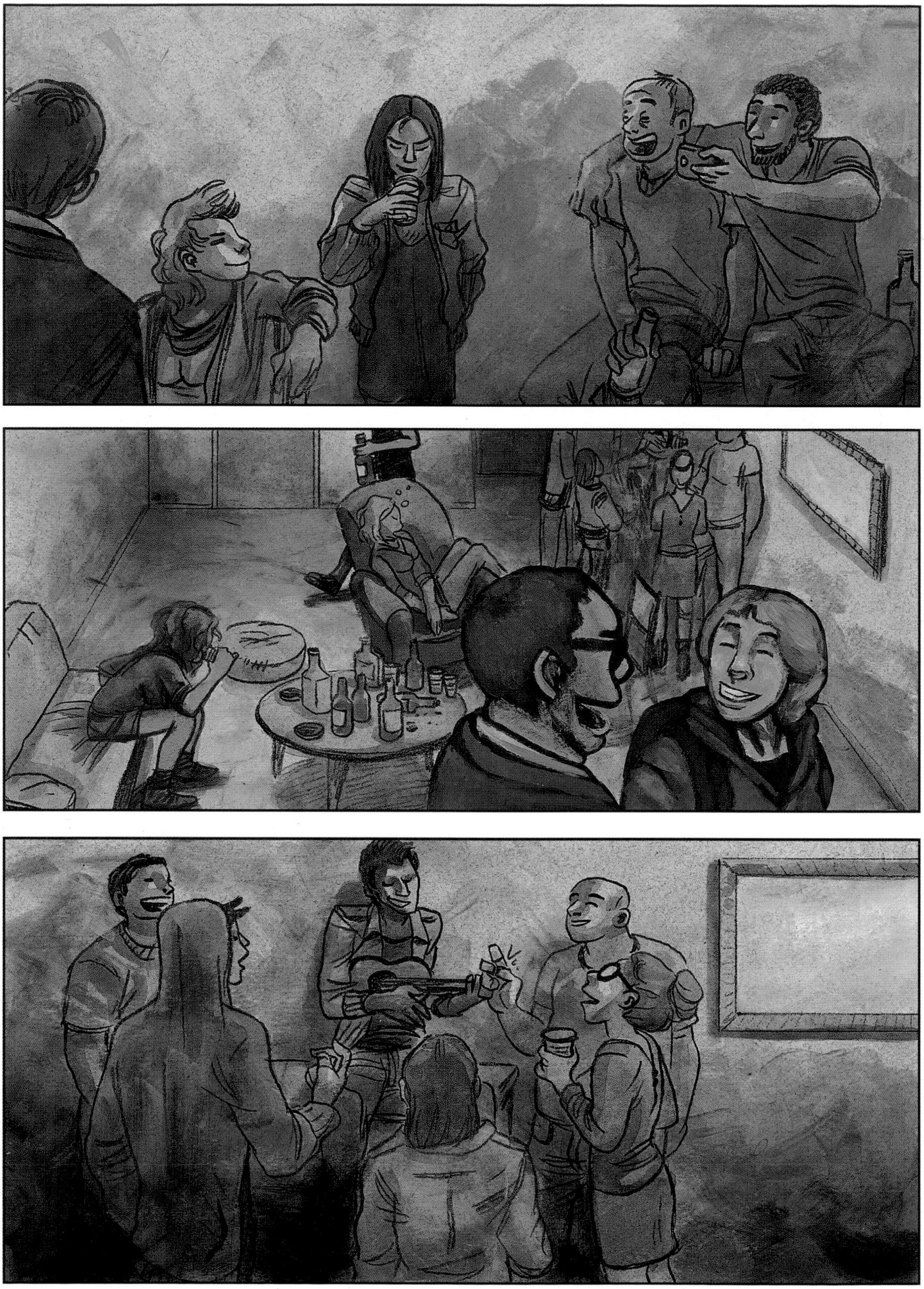

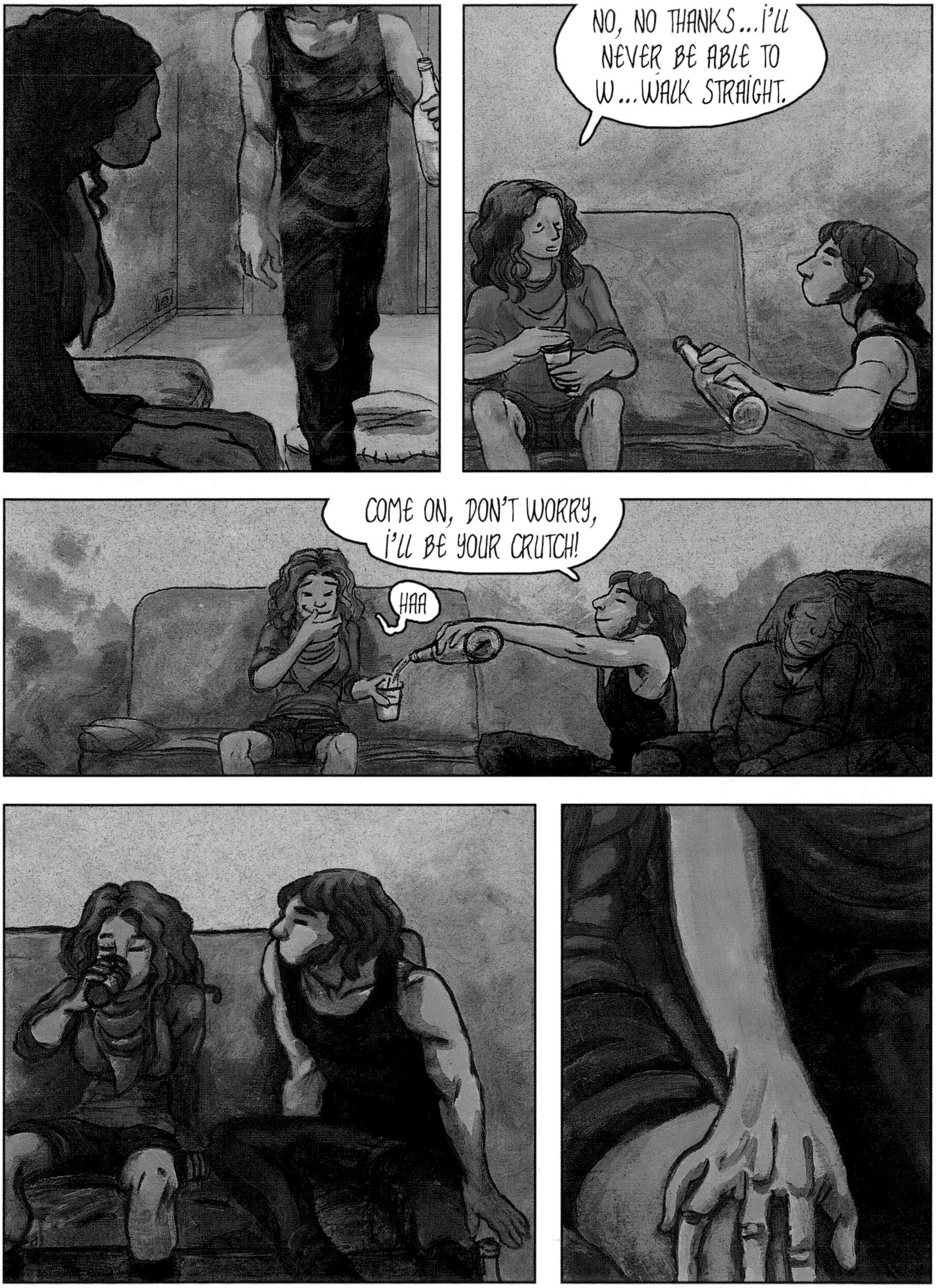
NO, NO THANKS...I'LL NEVER BE ABLE TO W...WALK STRAIGHT.
COME ON, DON'T WORRY, I'LL BE YOUR CRUTCH!
HAA

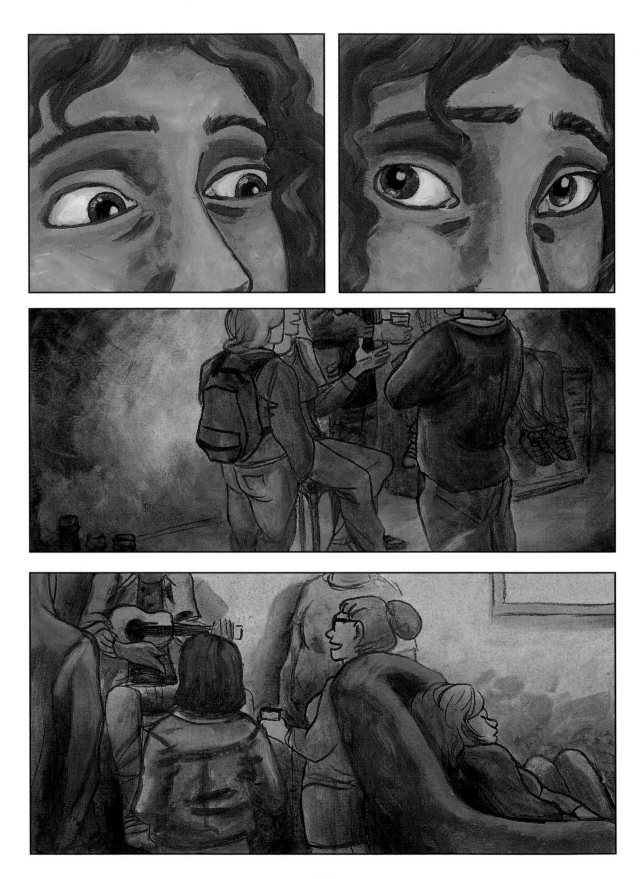

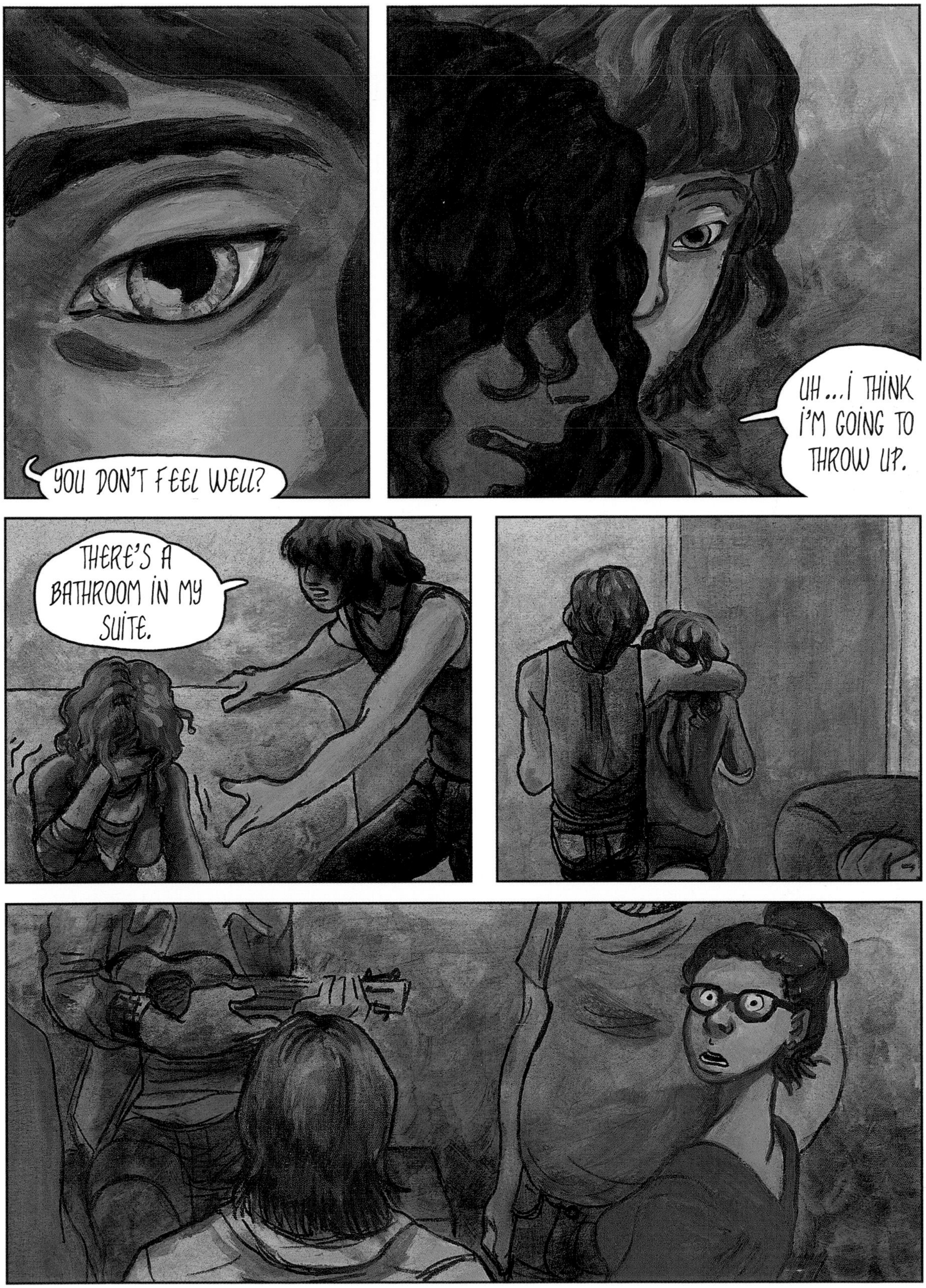
YOU DON'T FEEL WELL?
UH...I THINK I'M GOING TO THROW UP.
THERE'S A BATHROOM IN MY SUITE.

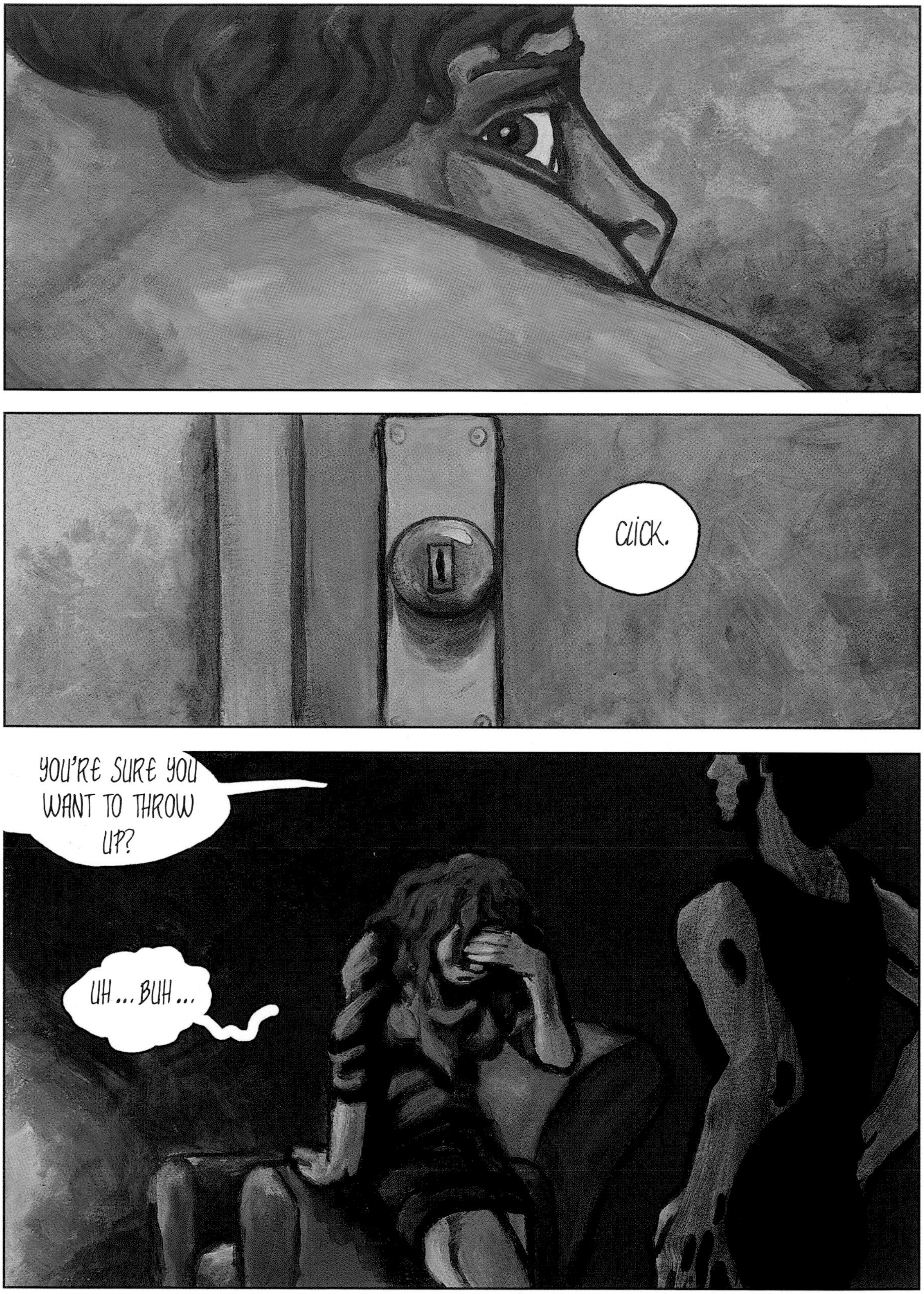
CLICK.
YOU'RE SURE YOU WANT TO THROW UP?
UH ... BUH ...

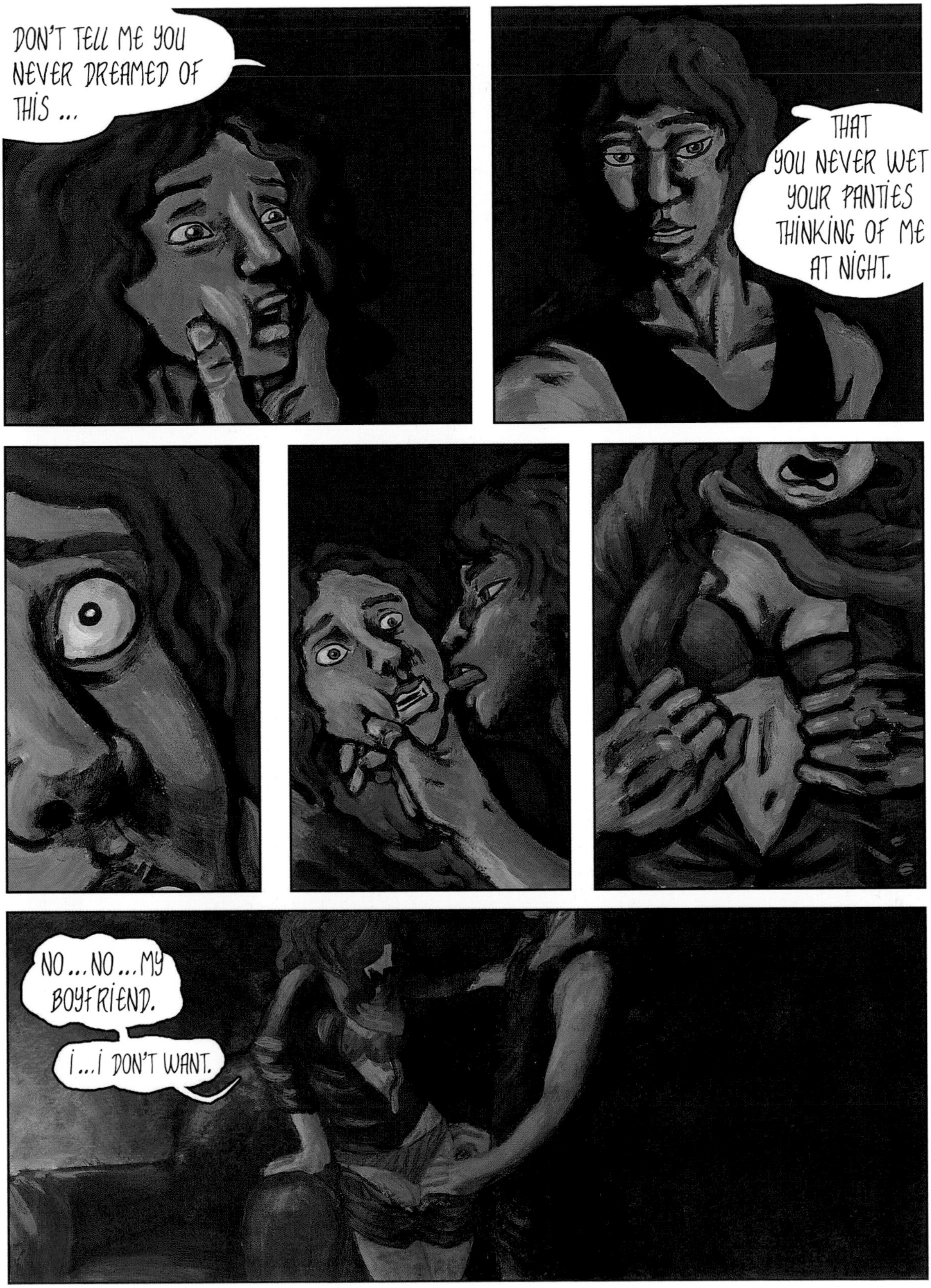
DON'T TELL ME YOU NEVER DREAMED OF THIS ...
THAT YOU NEVER WET YOUR PANTIES THINKING OF ME AT NIGHT.
NO ... NO ... MY BOYFRIEND.
I ... I DON'T WANT.

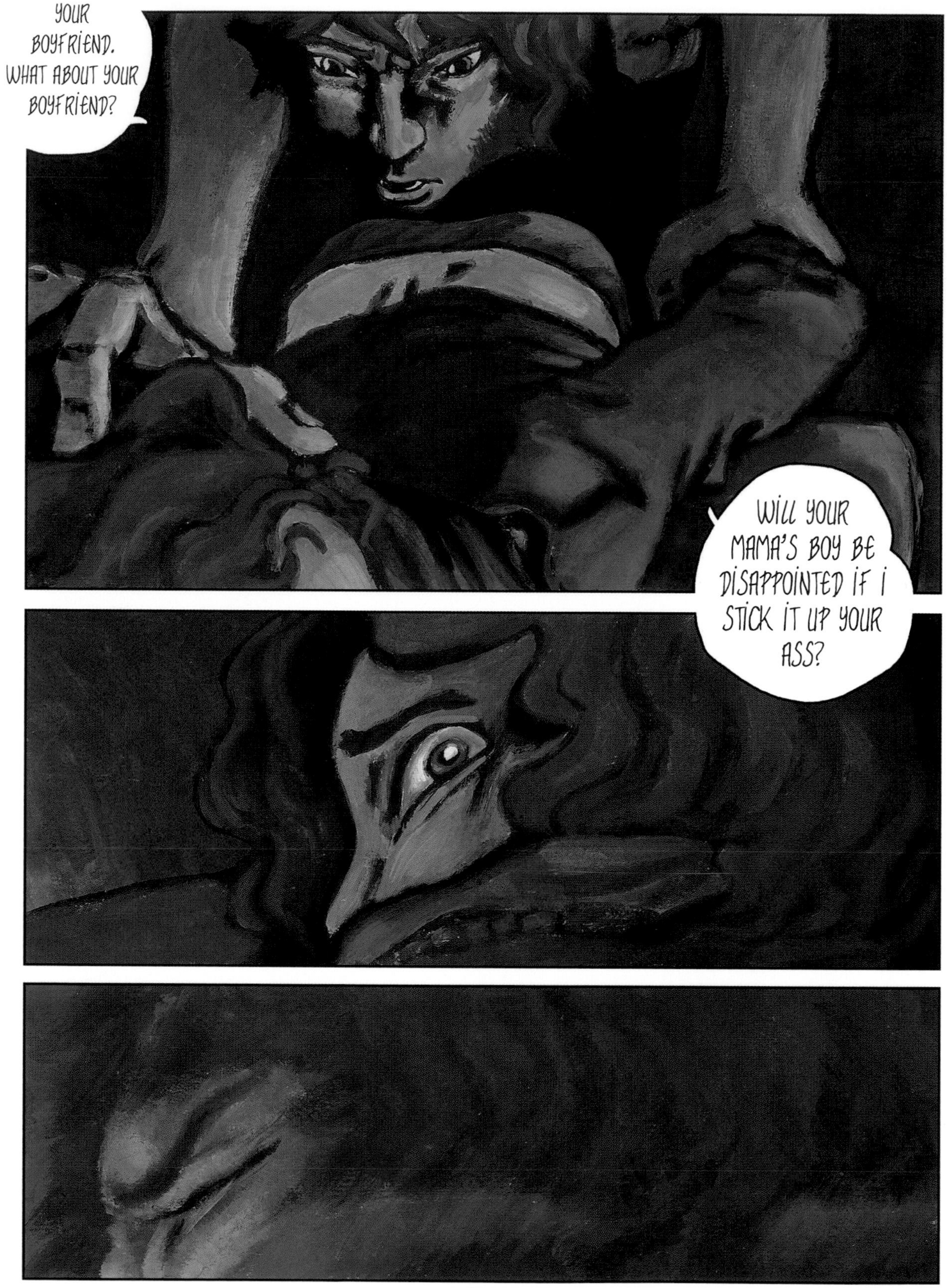
YOUR BOYFRIEND. WHAT ABOUT YOUR BOYFRIEND?
WILL YOUR MAMA'S BOY BE DISAPPOINTED IF I STICK IT UP YOUR ASS?

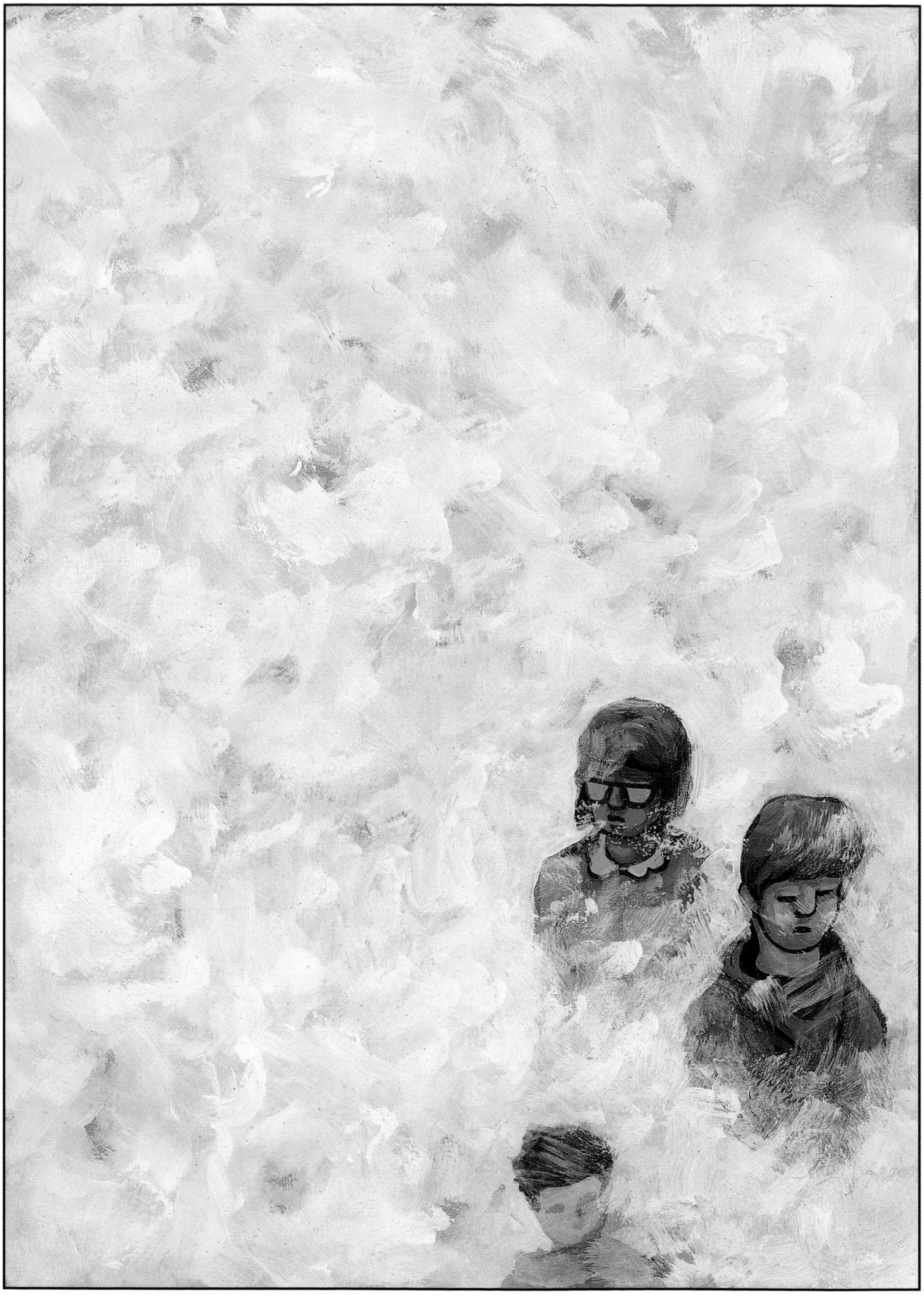

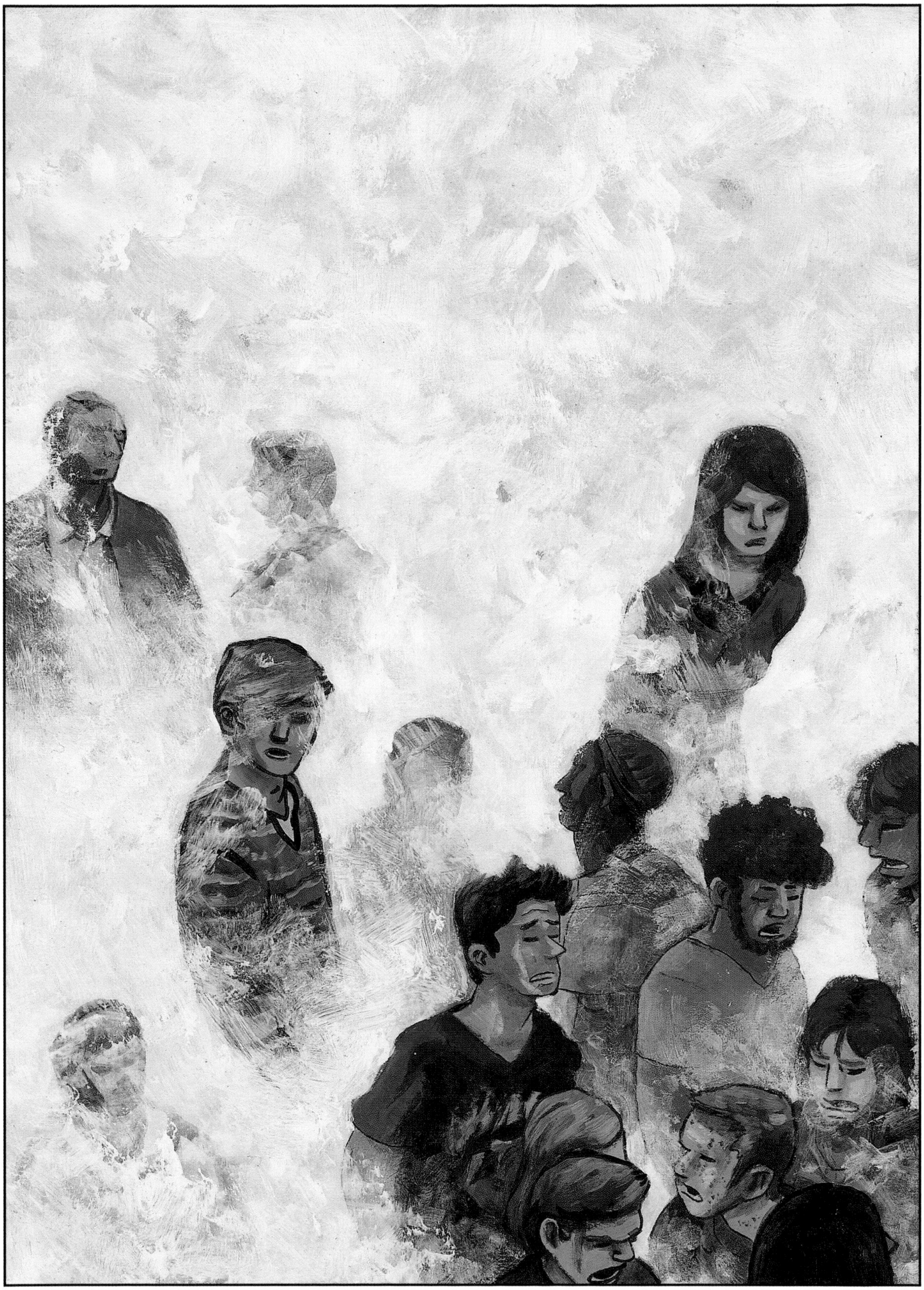

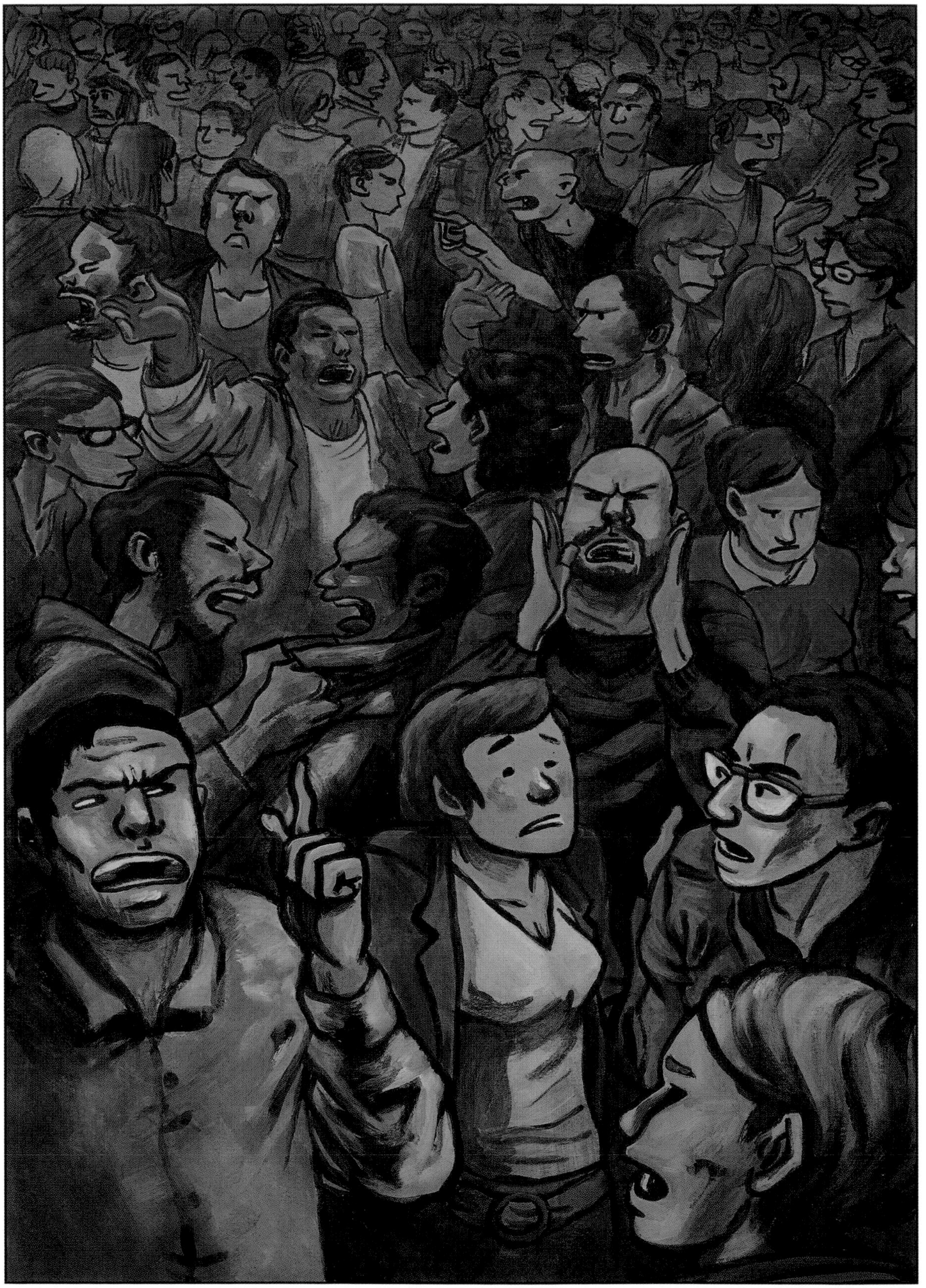

THIS IS TRULY A SPONTANEOUS AND EXTRAORDINARY EVENT TAKING PLACE IN PLACE DE LA NATION IN PARIS, AFTER THE ANNOUNCEMENT LATE LAST NIGHT OF THE ARREST OF THE FAMOUS SINGER-SONGWRITER TAZANE FOR THE ALLEGED RAPE OF A YOUNG WOMAN.

TAZANE INNOCENT

ALTHOUGH PROOF OF SEXUAL RELATIONS HAS BEEN CONFIRMED, NOTHING YET INDICATES THAT TAZANE IS GUILTY OF THE CHARGES BROUGHT AGAINST HIM.

LA JUSTICE VAINCRA LES PRÉJUGES!

TAZAN EN PALESTINE

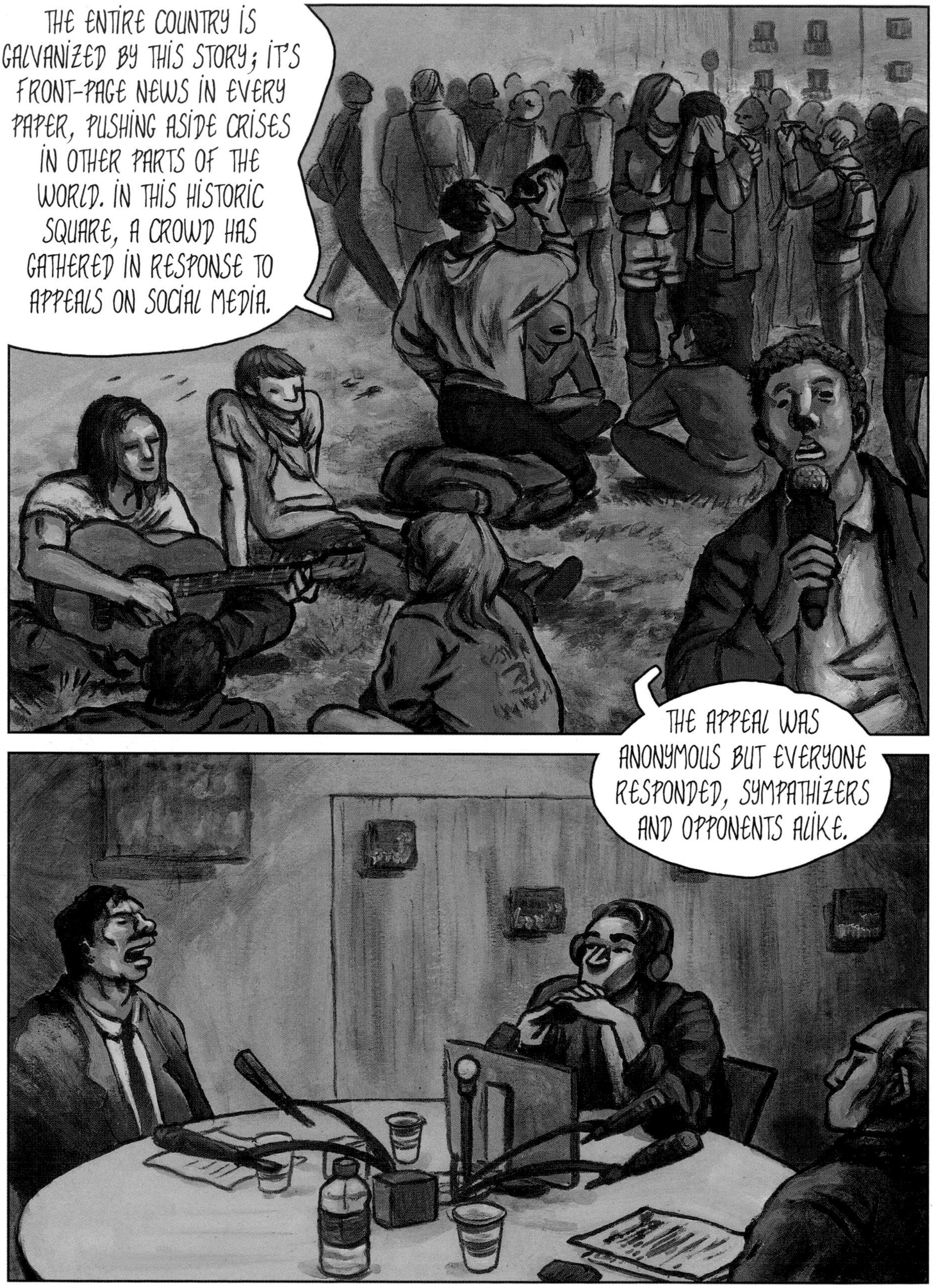
THE ENTIRE COUNTRY IS GALVANIZED BY THIS STORY; IT'S FRONT-PAGE NEWS IN EVERY PAPER, PUSHING ASIDE CRISES IN OTHER PARTS OF THE WORLD. IN THIS HISTORIC SQUARE, A CROWD HAS GATHERED IN RESPONSE TO APPEALS ON SOCIAL MEDIA.
THE APPEAL WAS ANONYMOUS BUT EVERYONE RESPONDED, SYMPATHIZERS AND OPPONENTS ALIKE.

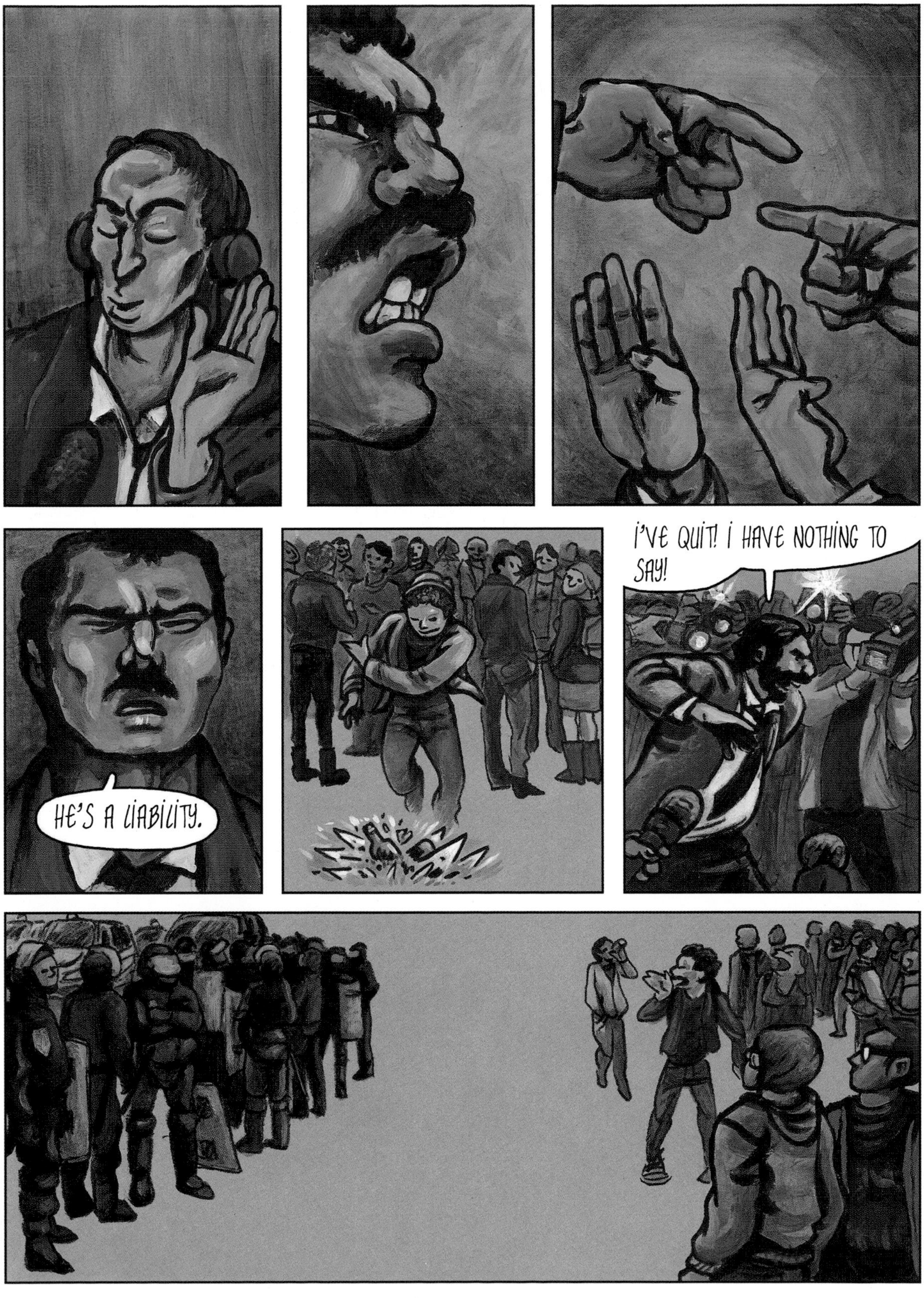
HE'S A LIABILITY.
I'VE QUIT! I HAVE NOTHING TO SAY!

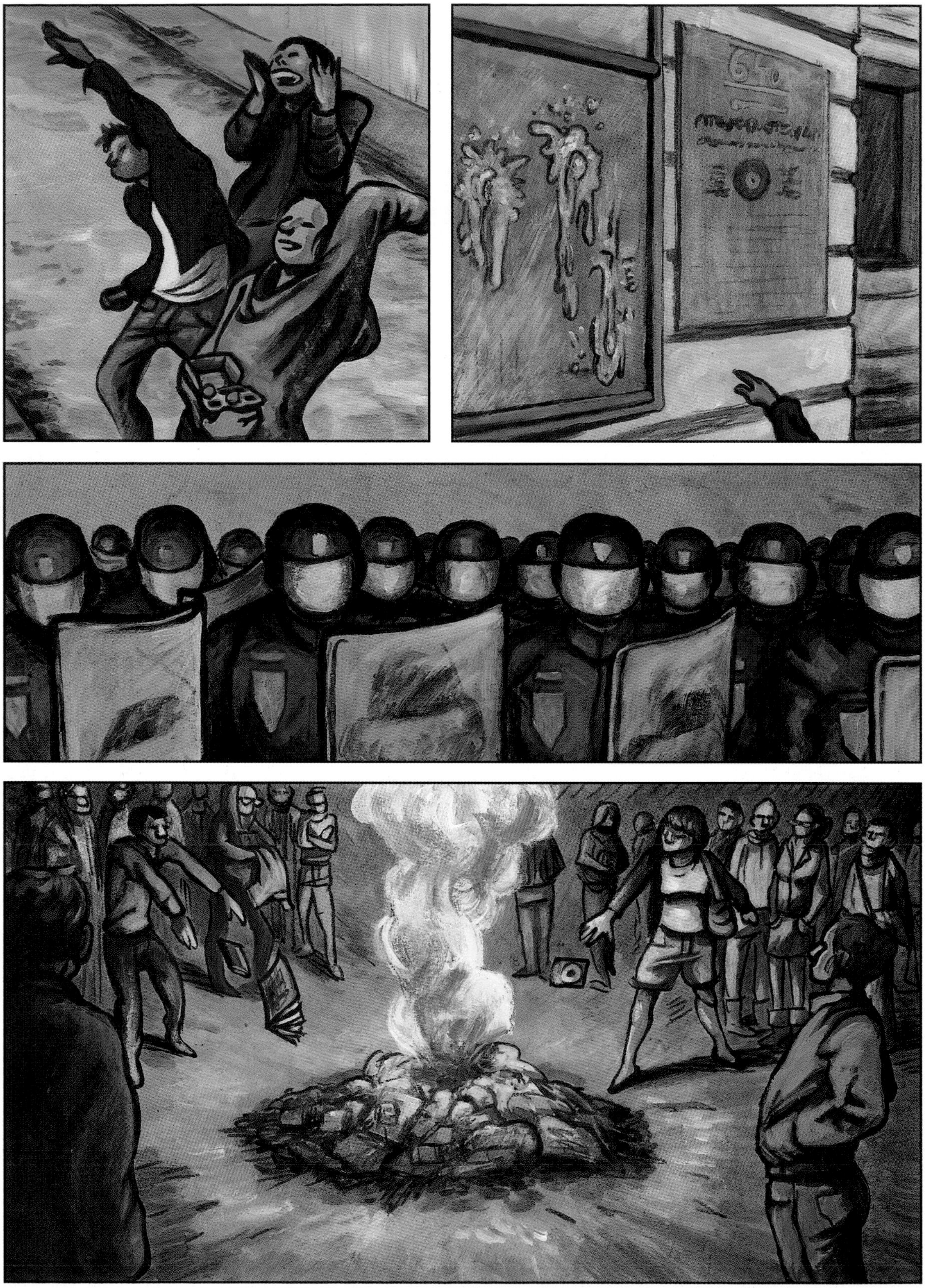

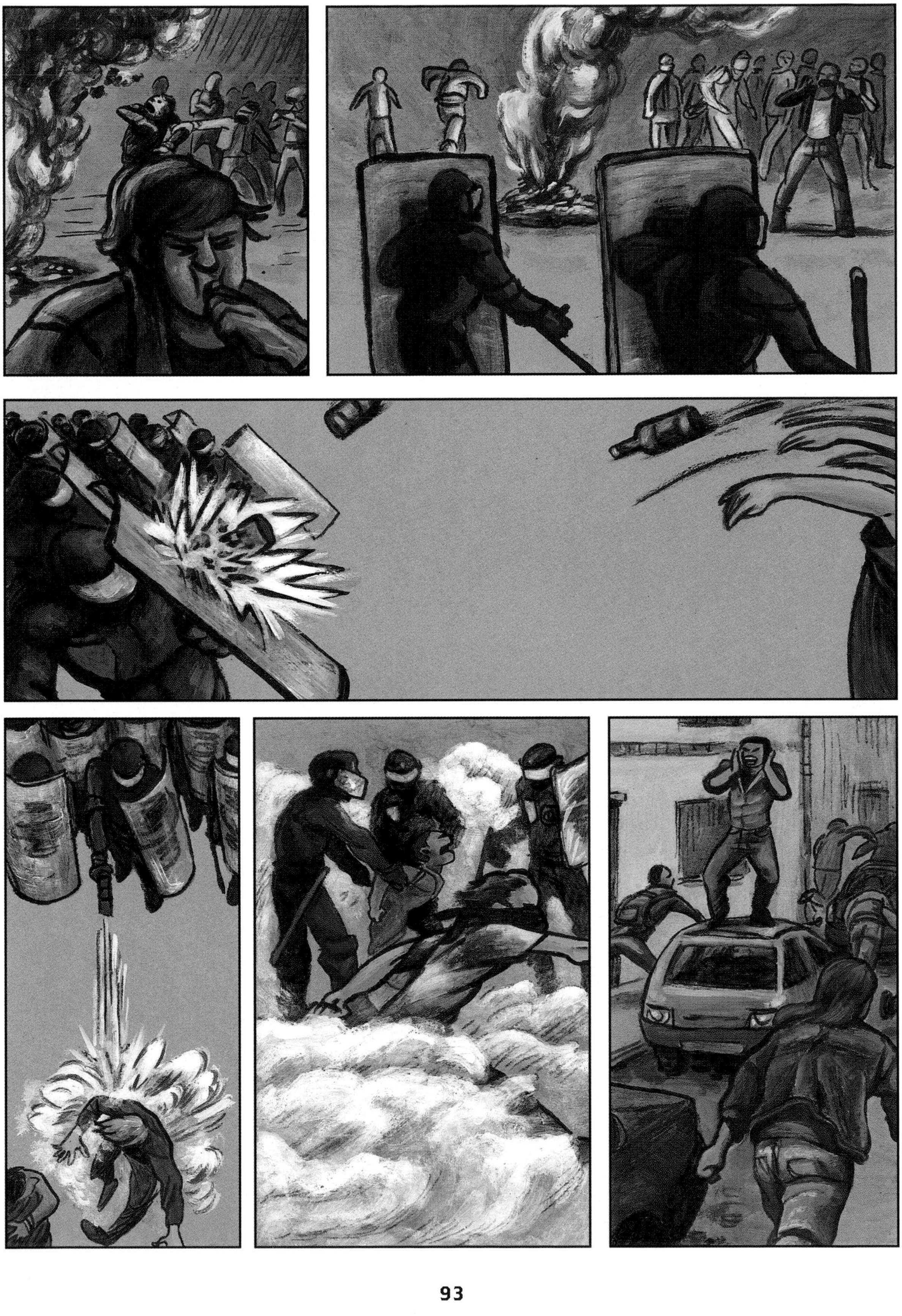

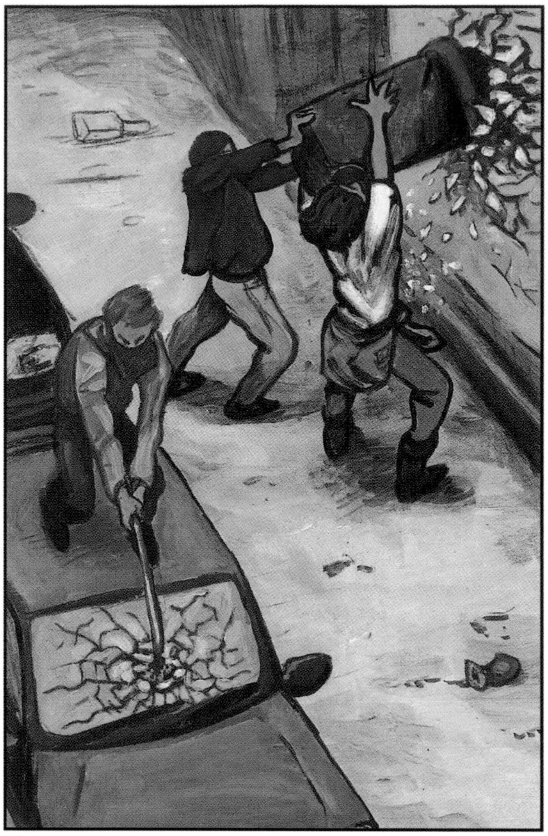

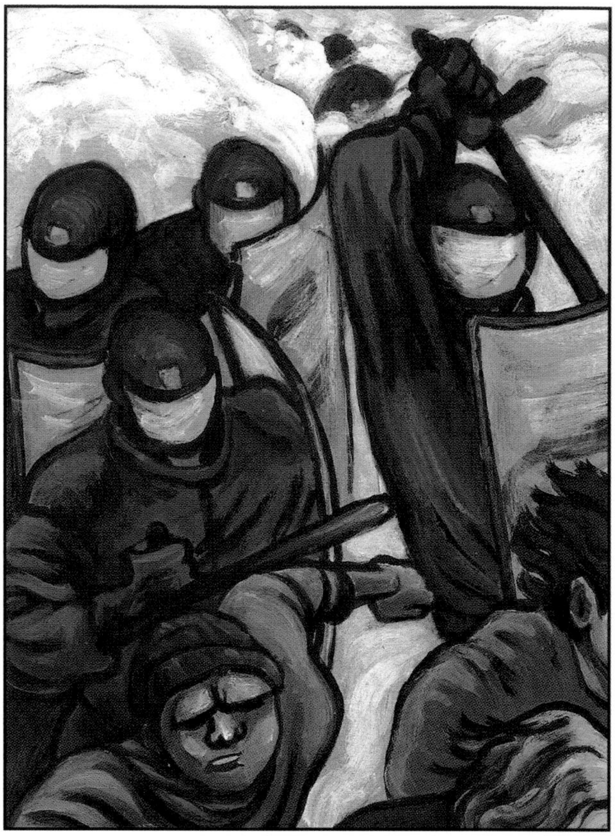

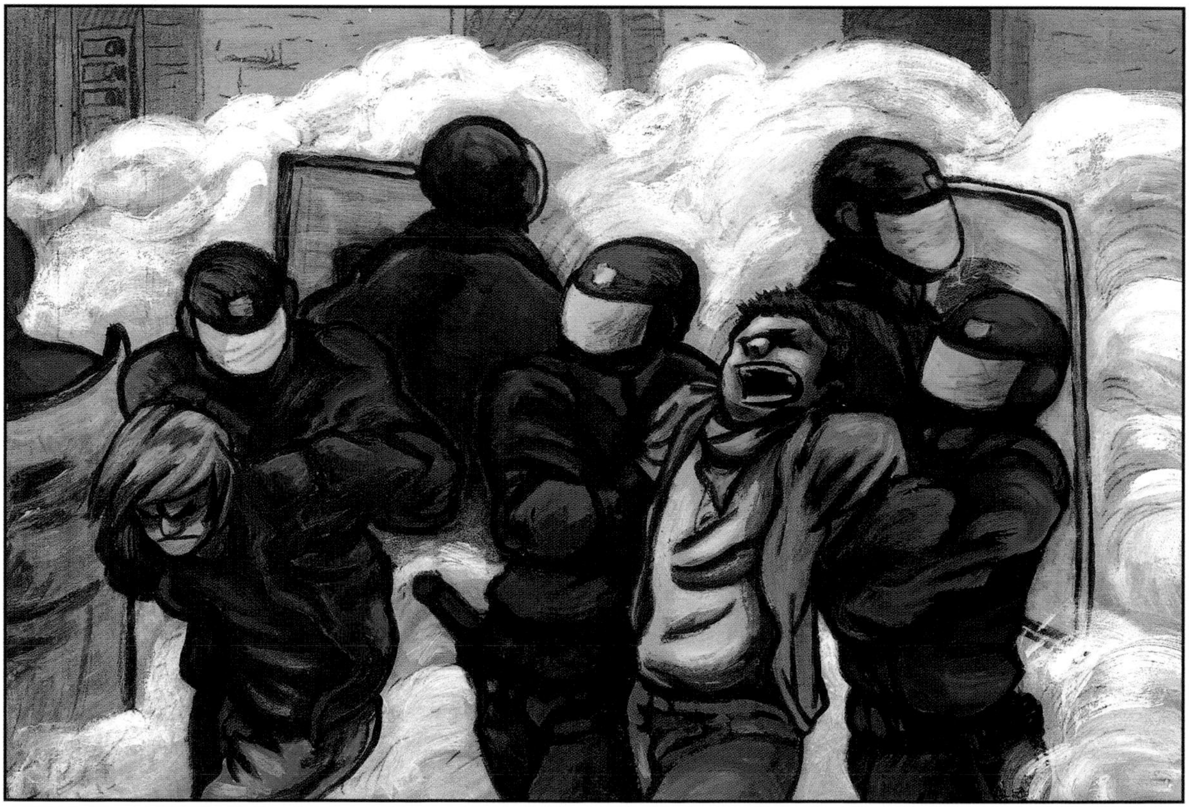

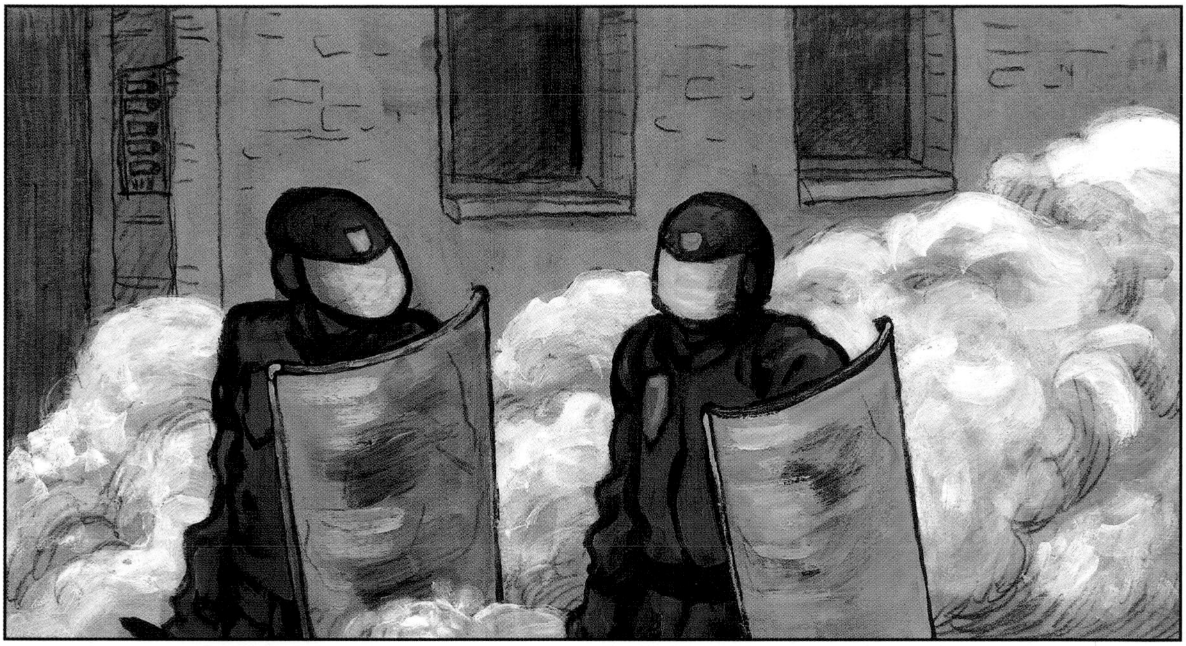

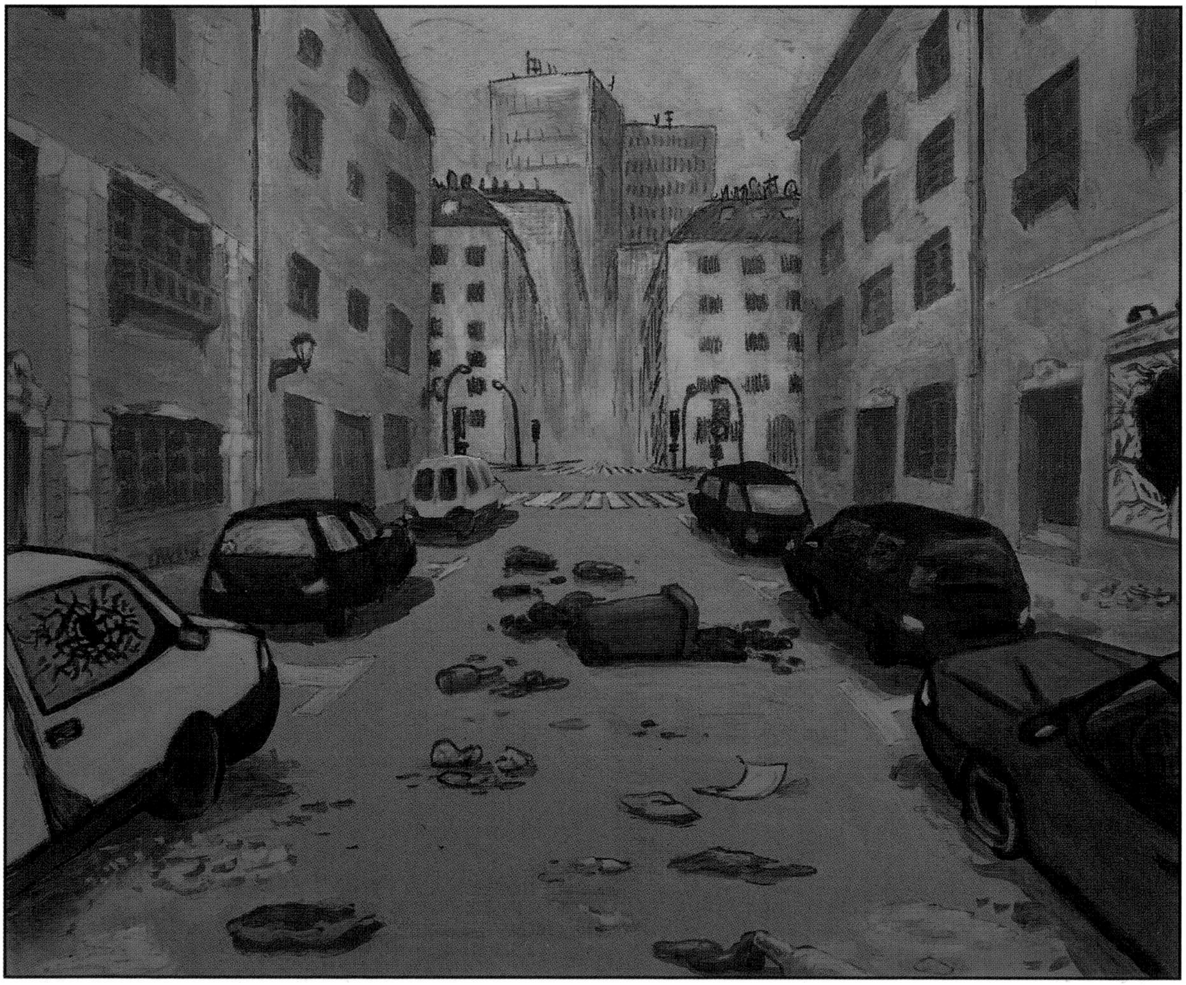

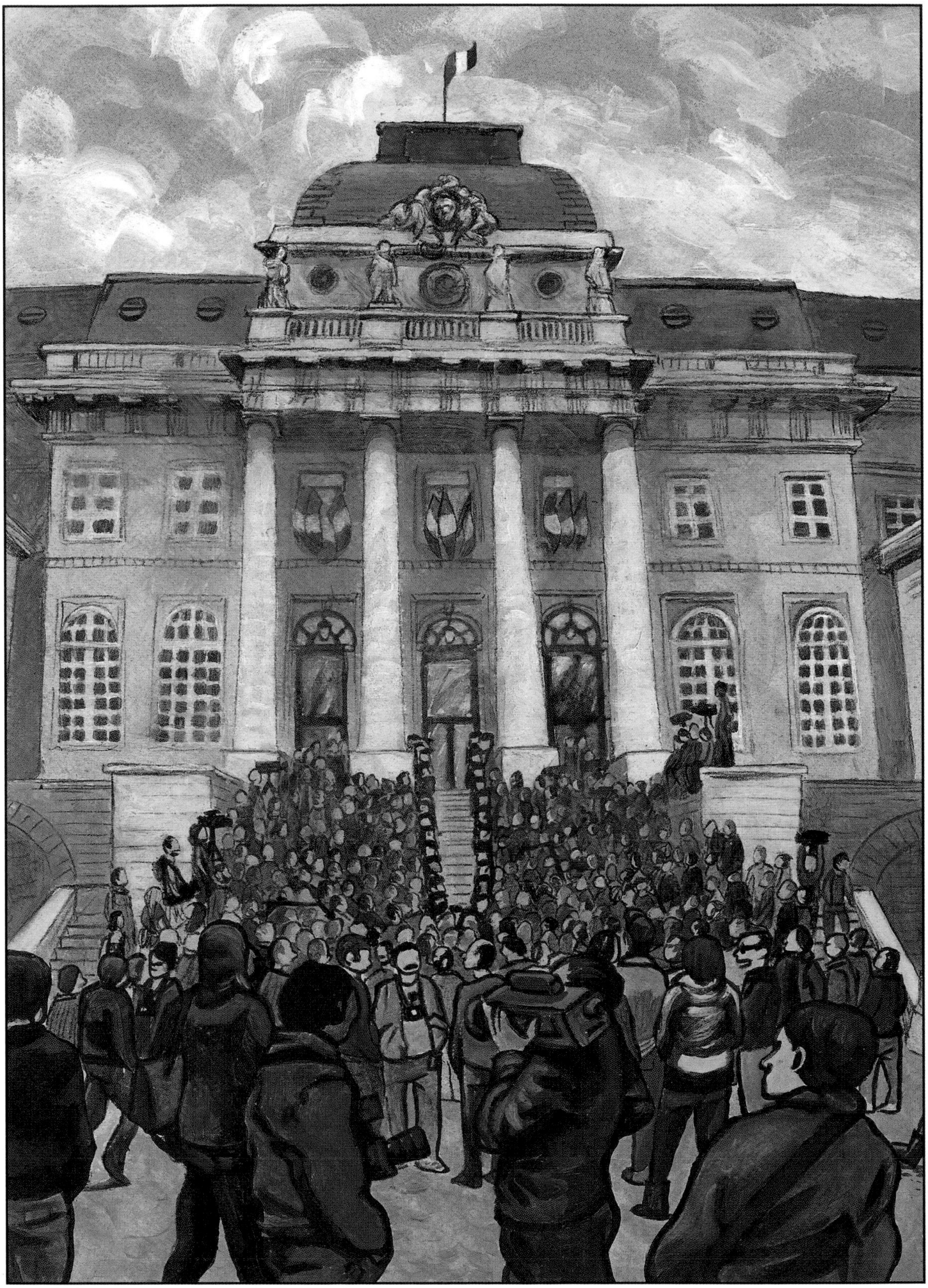

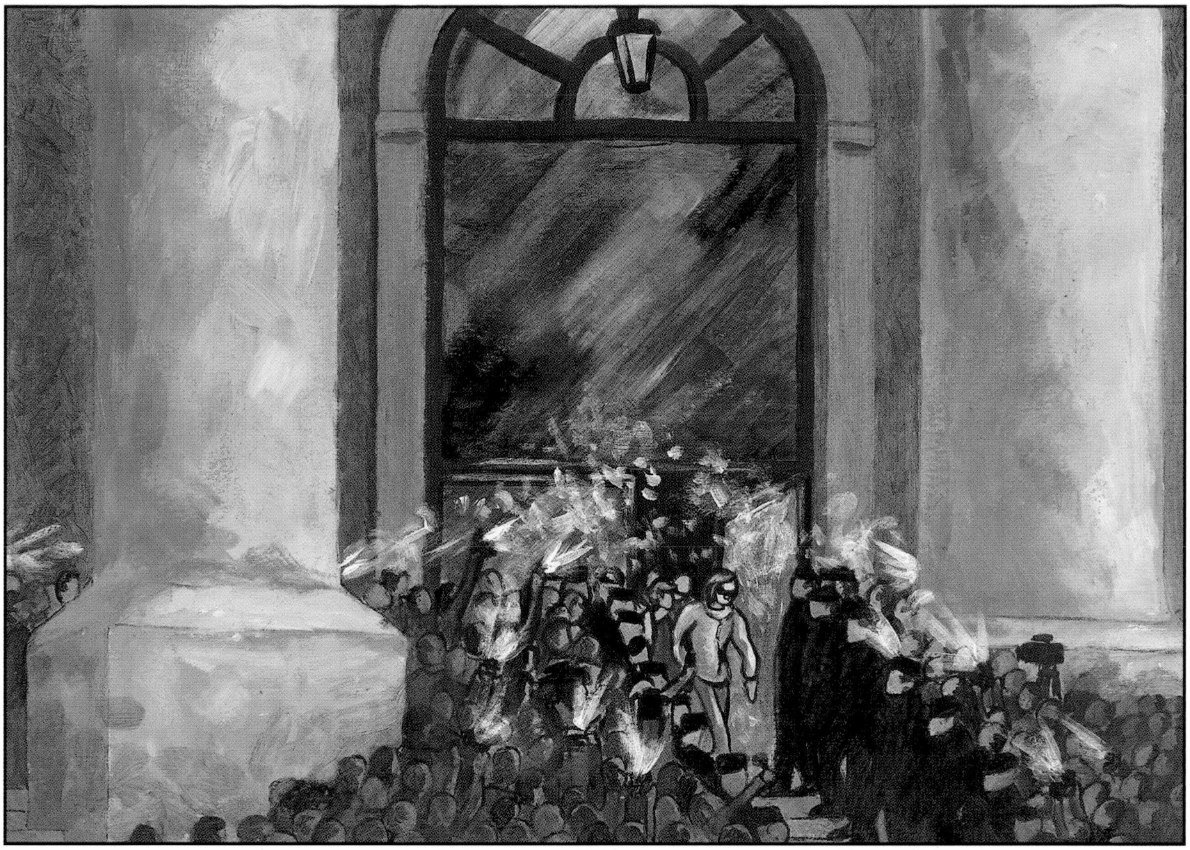

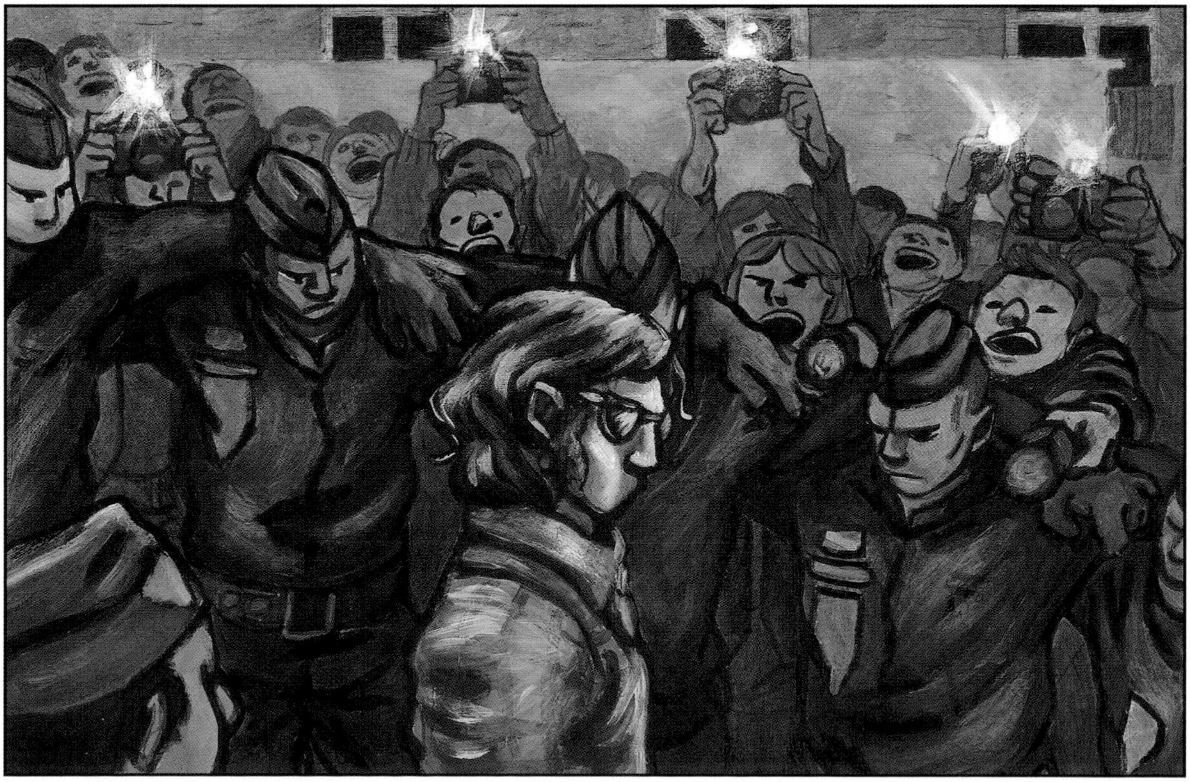

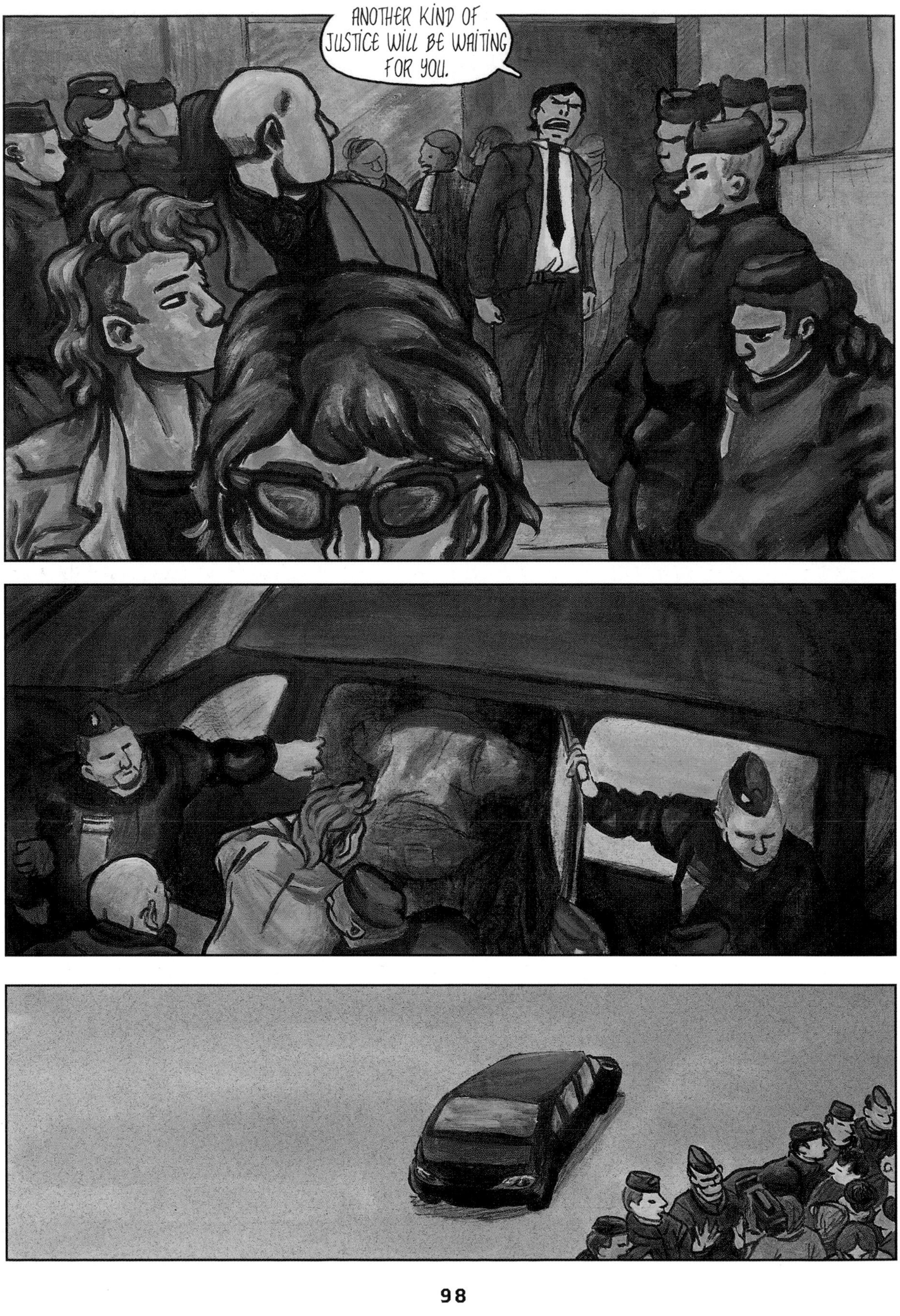
ANOTHER KIND OF JUSTICE WILL BE WAITING FOR YOU.

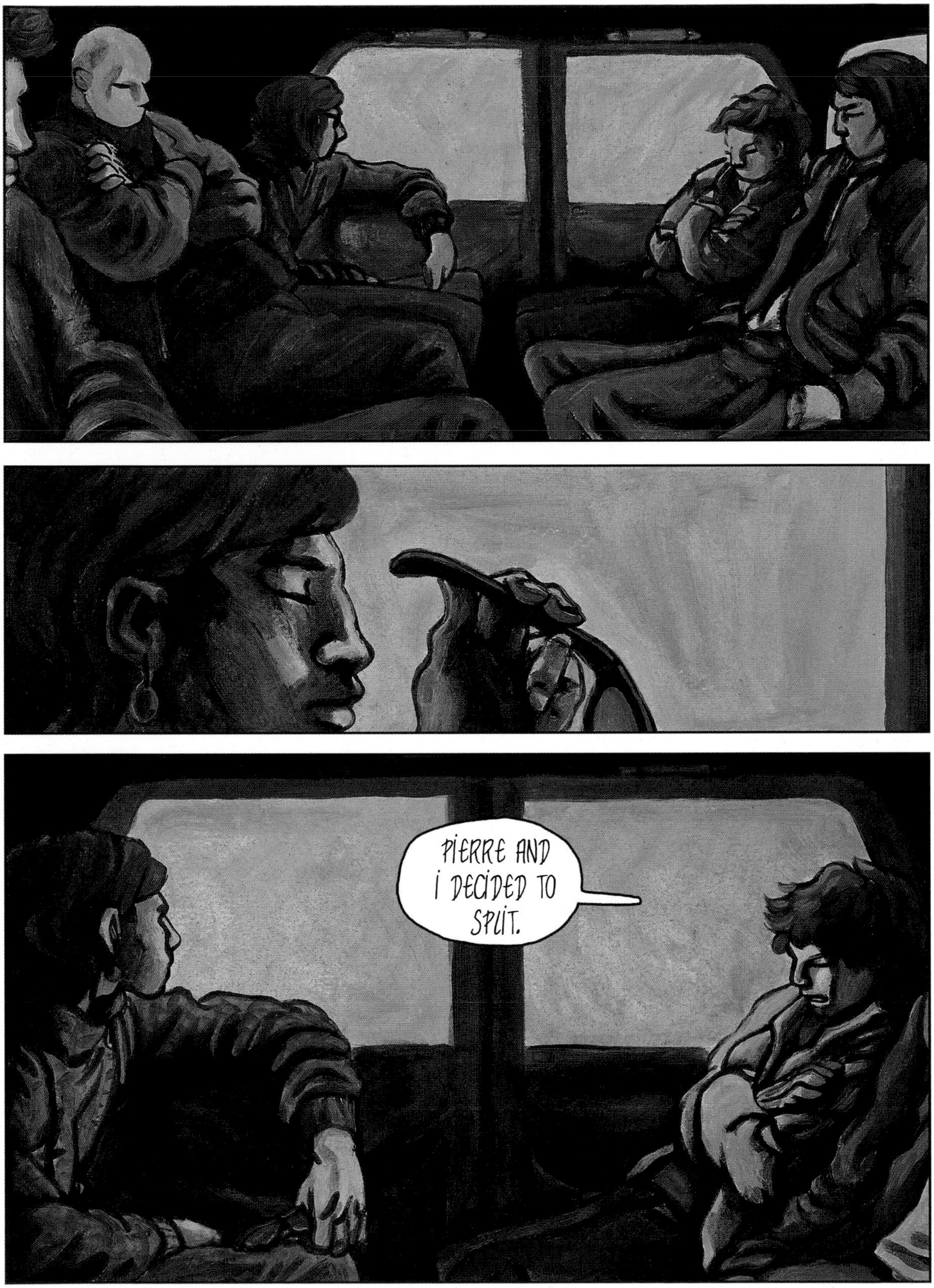
PIERRE AND I DECIDED TO SPLIT.

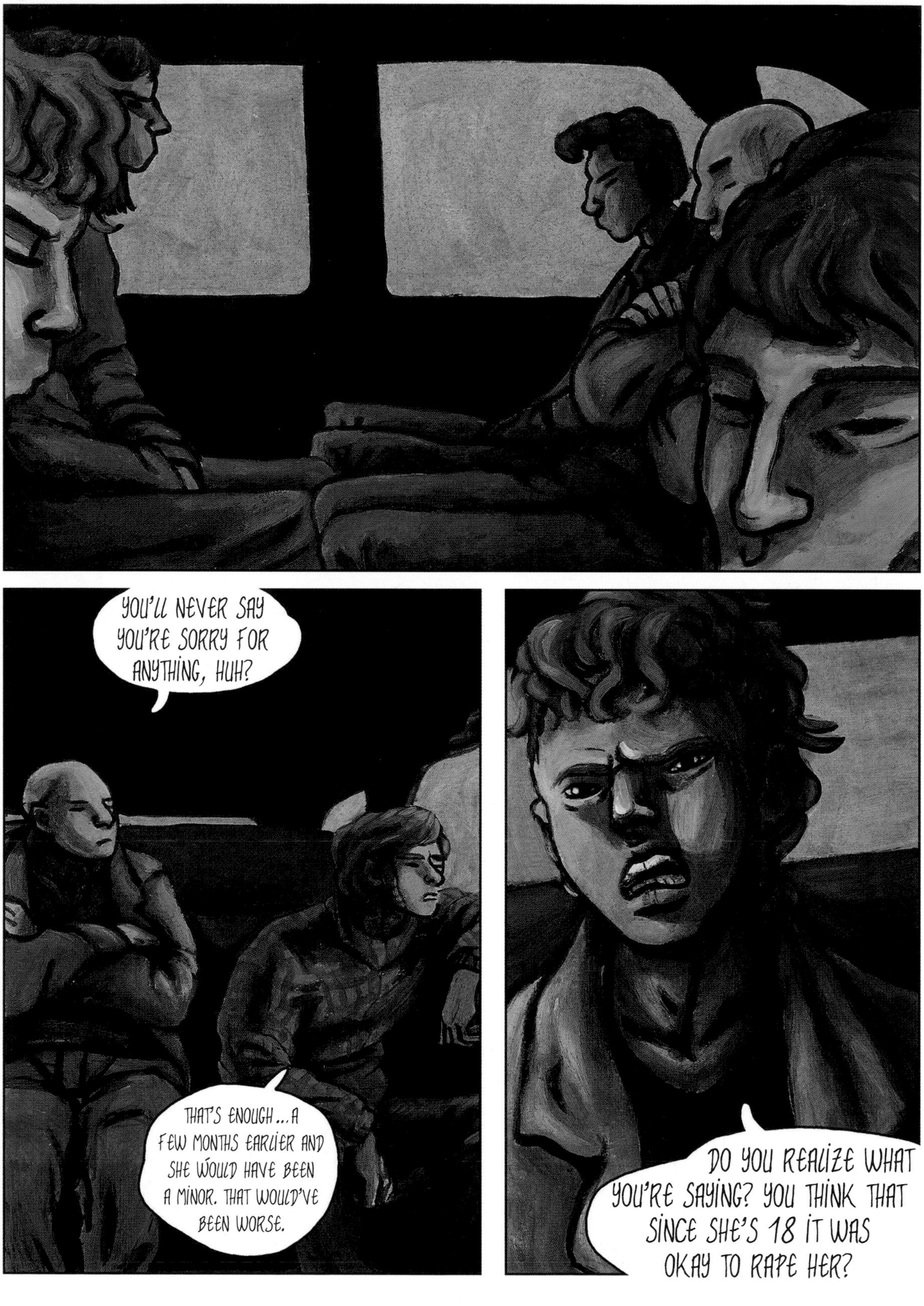
YOU'LL NEVER SAY YOU'RE SORRY FOR ANYTHING, HUH?
THAT'S ENOUGH... A FEW MONTHS EARLIER AND SHE WOULD HAVE BEEN A MINOR. THAT WOULD'VE BEEN WORSE.
DO YOU REALIZE WHAT YOU'RE SAYING? YOU THINK THAT SINCE SHE'S 18 IT WAS OKAY TO RAPE HER?

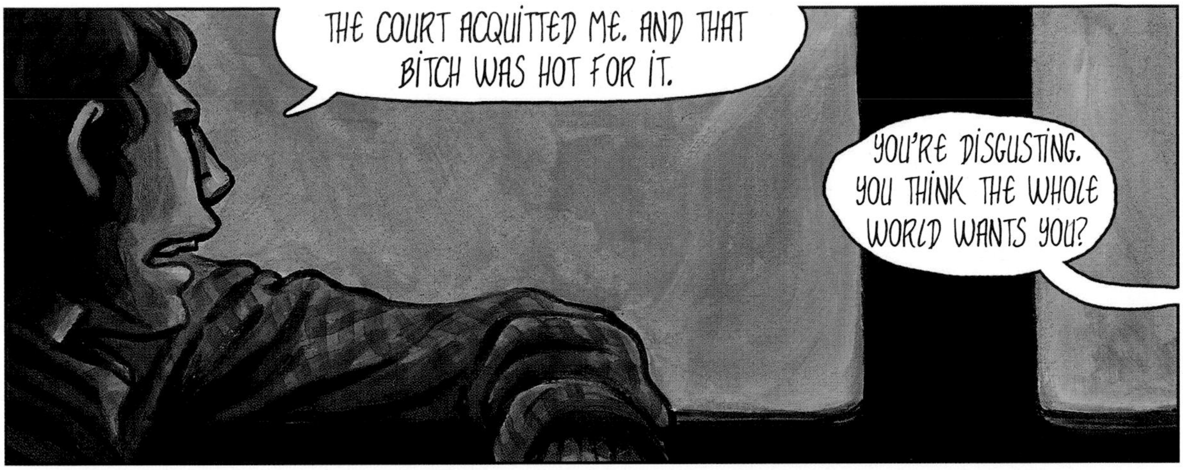
THE COURT ACQUITTED ME. AND THAT BITCH WAS HOT FOR IT.
YOU'RE DISGUSTING. YOU THINK THE WHOLE WORLD WANTS YOU?

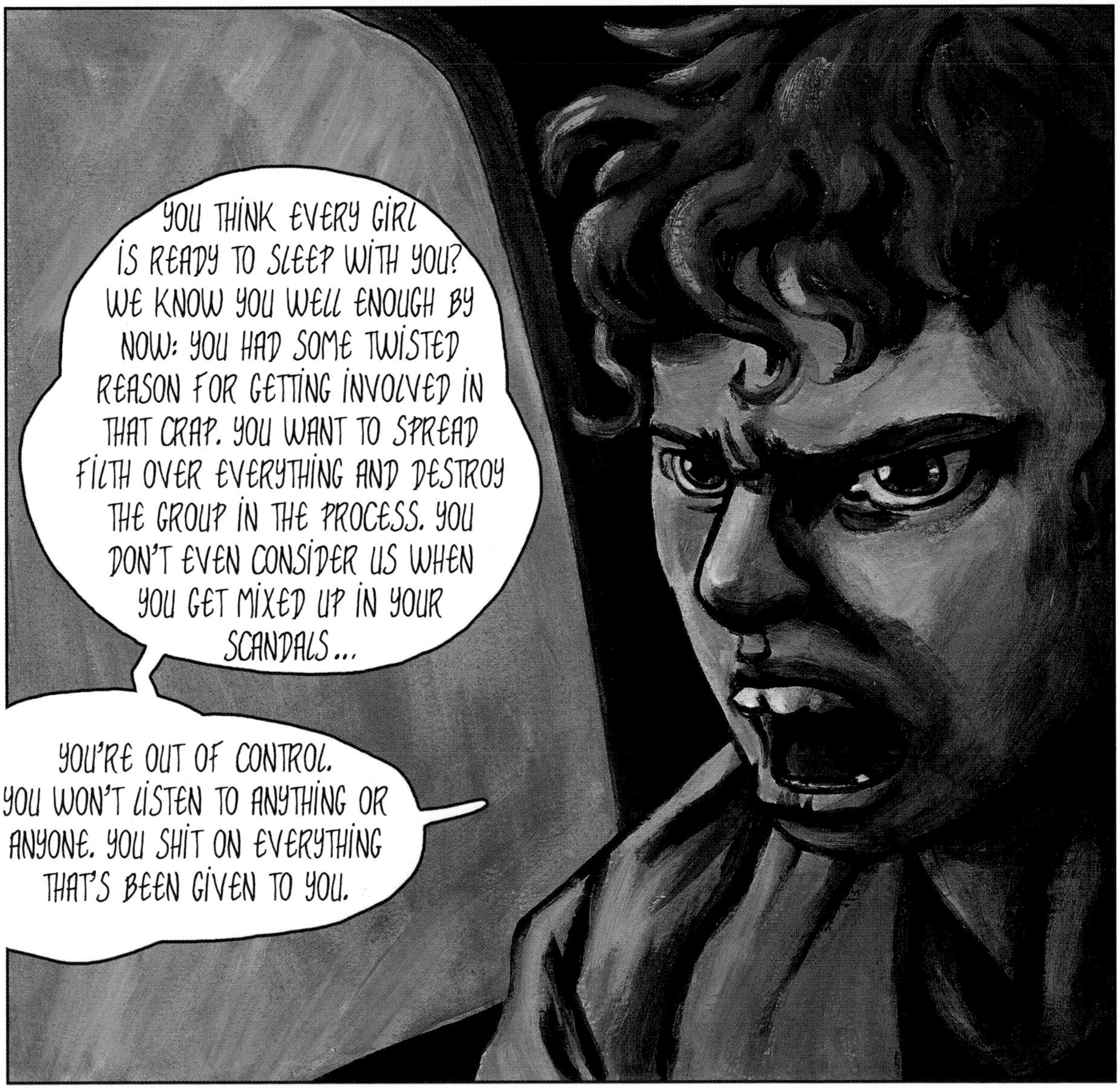
YOU THINK EVERY GIRL IS READY TO SLEEP WITH YOU? WE KNOW YOU WELL ENOUGH BY NOW: YOU HAD SOME TWISTED REASON FOR GETTING INVOLVED IN THAT CRAP. YOU WANT TO SPREAD FILTH OVER EVERYTHING AND DESTROY THE GROUP IN THE PROCESS. YOU DON'T EVEN CONSIDER US WHEN YOU GET MIXED UP IN YOUR SCANDALS...
YOU'RE OUT OF CONTROL. YOU WON'T LISTEN TO ANYTHING OR ANYONE. YOU SHIT ON EVERYTHING THAT'S BEEN GIVEN TO YOU.

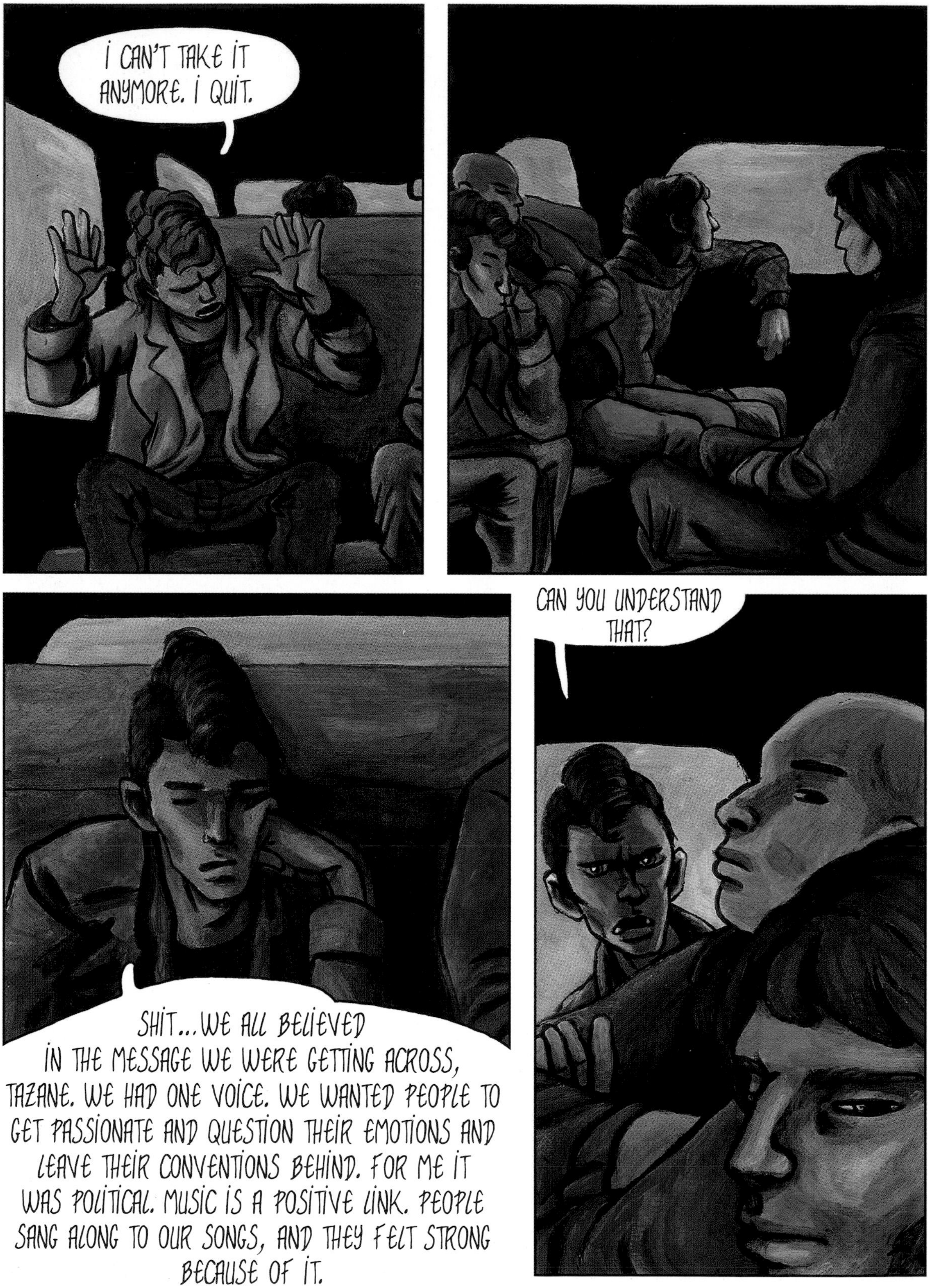
I CAN'T TAKE IT ANYMORE. I QUIT.
CAN YOU UNDERSTAND THAT?
SHIT... WE ALL BELIEVED IN THE MESSAGE WE WERE GETTING ACROSS, TAZANE. WE HAD ONE VOICE. WE WANTED PEOPLE TO GET PASSIONATE AND QUESTION THEIR EMOTIONS AND LEAVE THEIR CONVENTIONS BEHIND. FOR ME IT WAS POLITICAL. MUSIC IS A POSITIVE LINK. PEOPLE SANG ALONG TO OUR SONGS, AND THEY FELT STRONG BECAUSE OF IT.

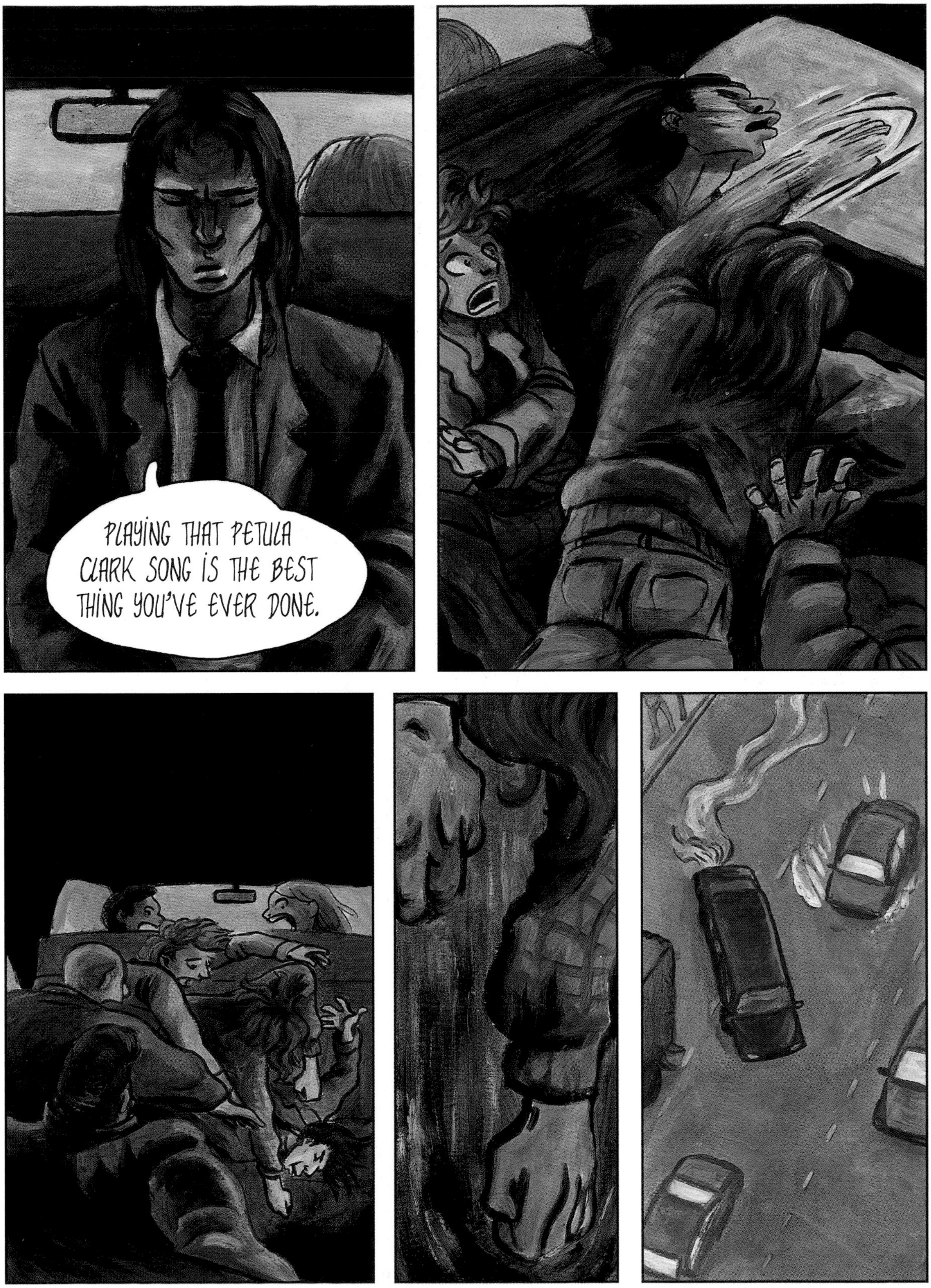
PLAYING THAT PETULA CLARK SONG IS THE BEST THING YOU'VE EVER DONE.

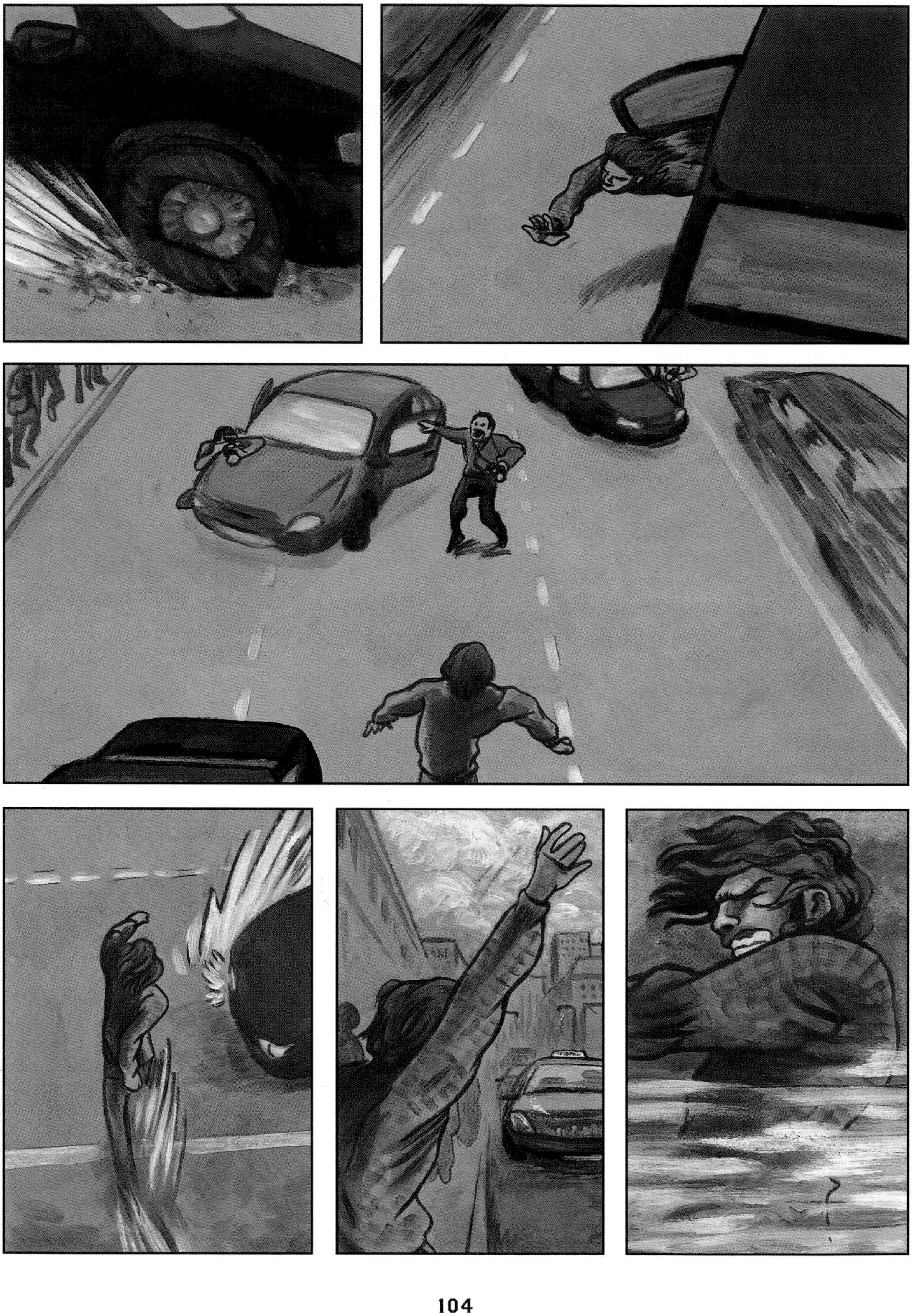

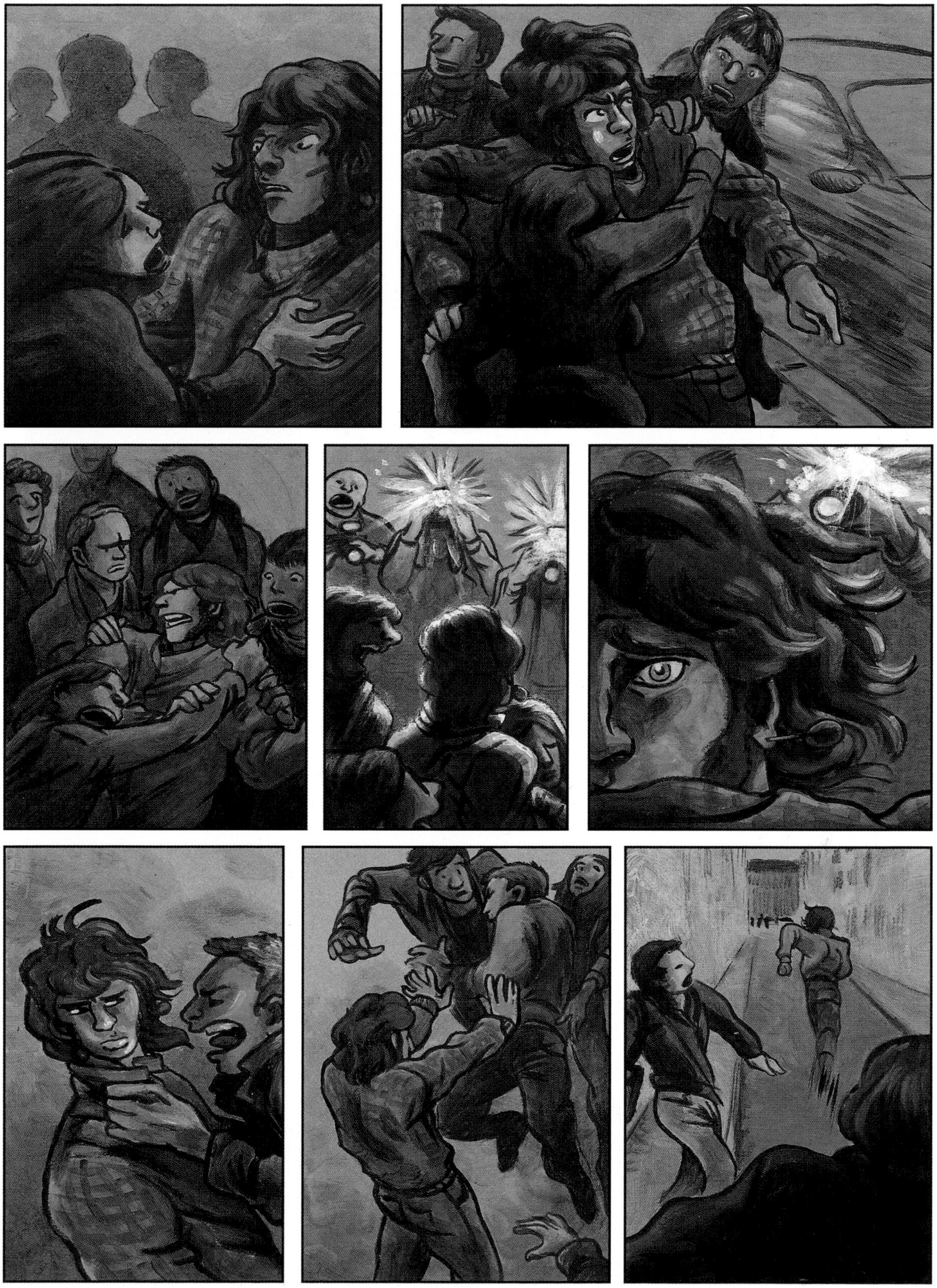

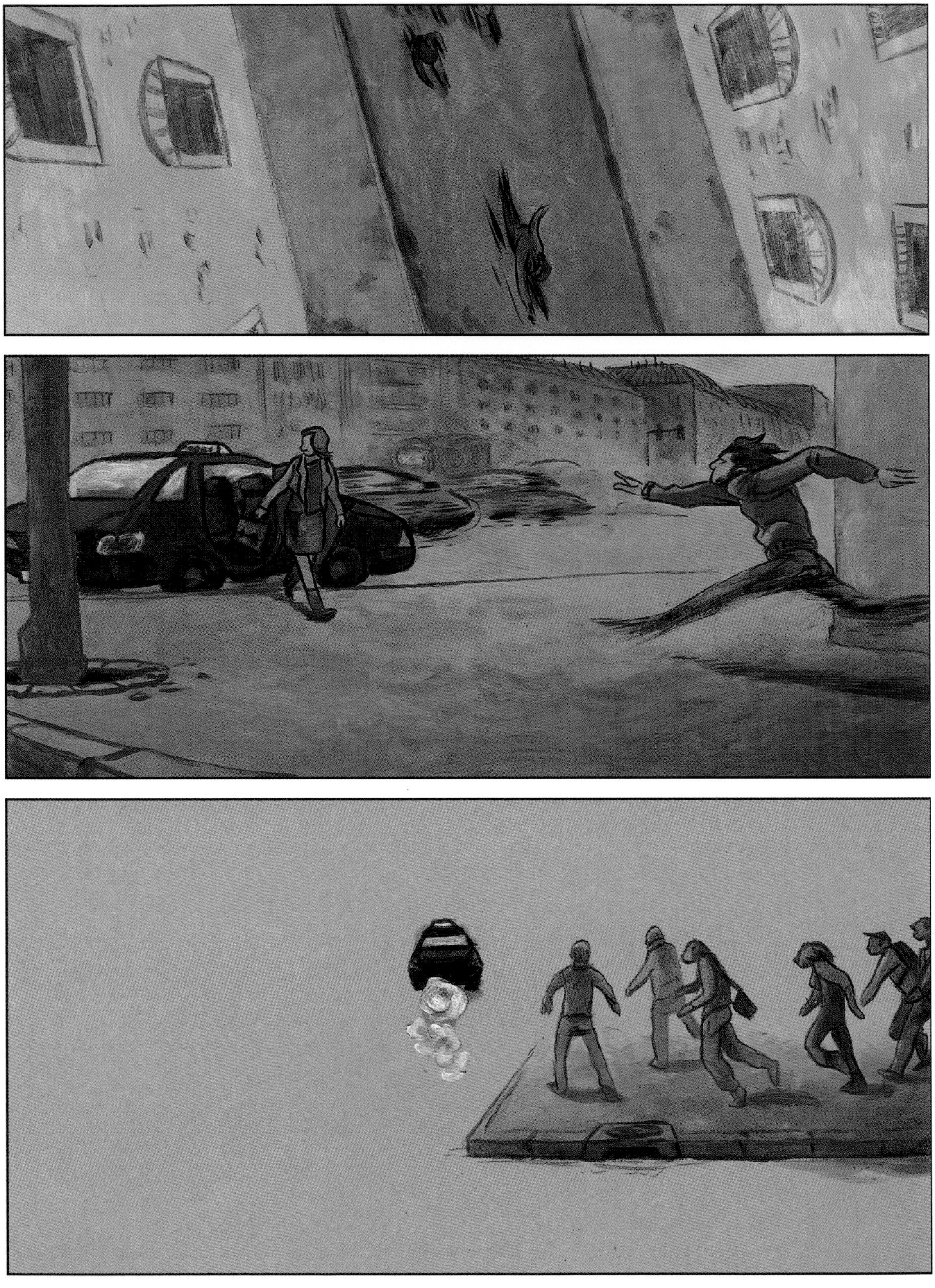

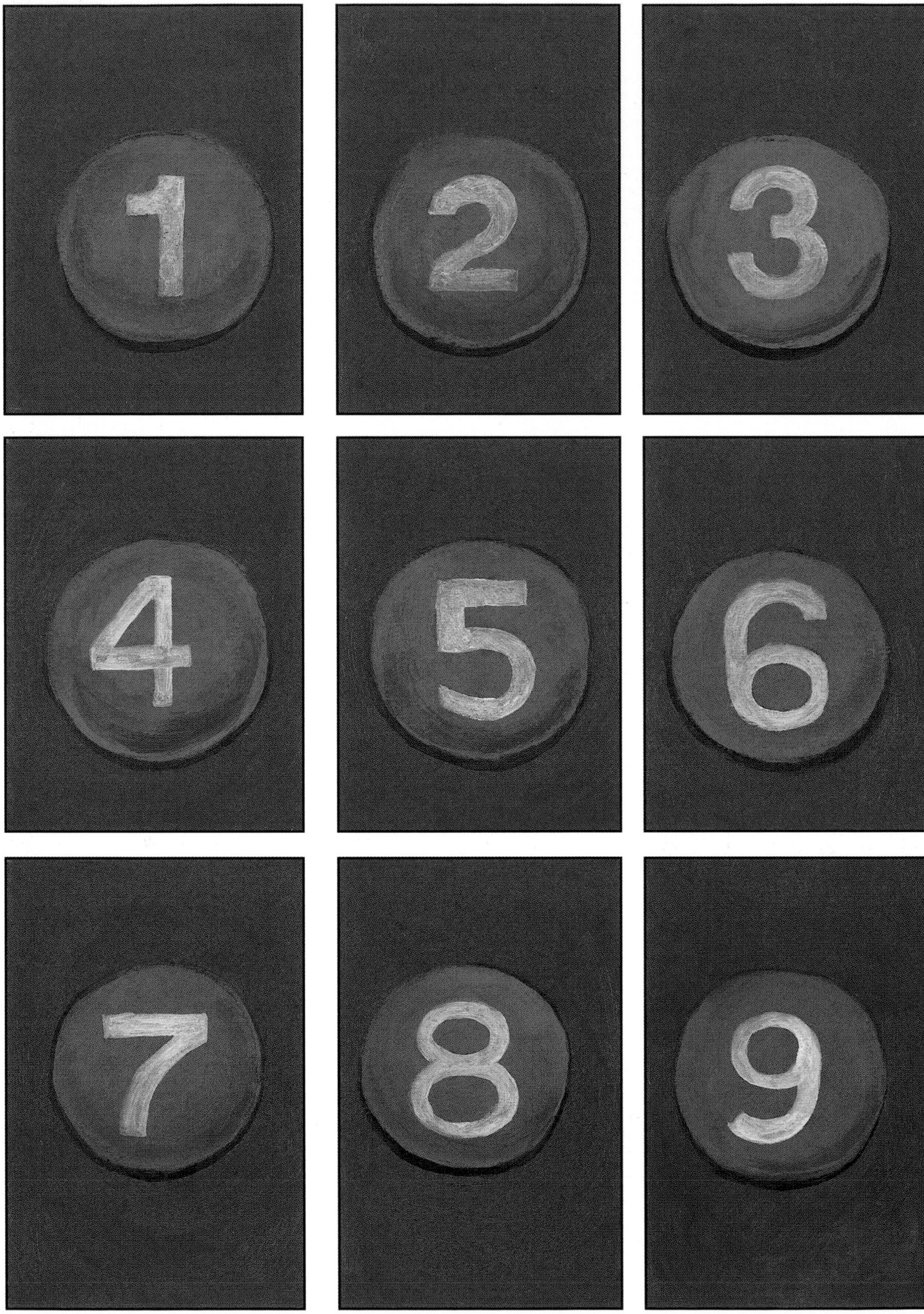
1
2
3
4
5
6
7
8
9

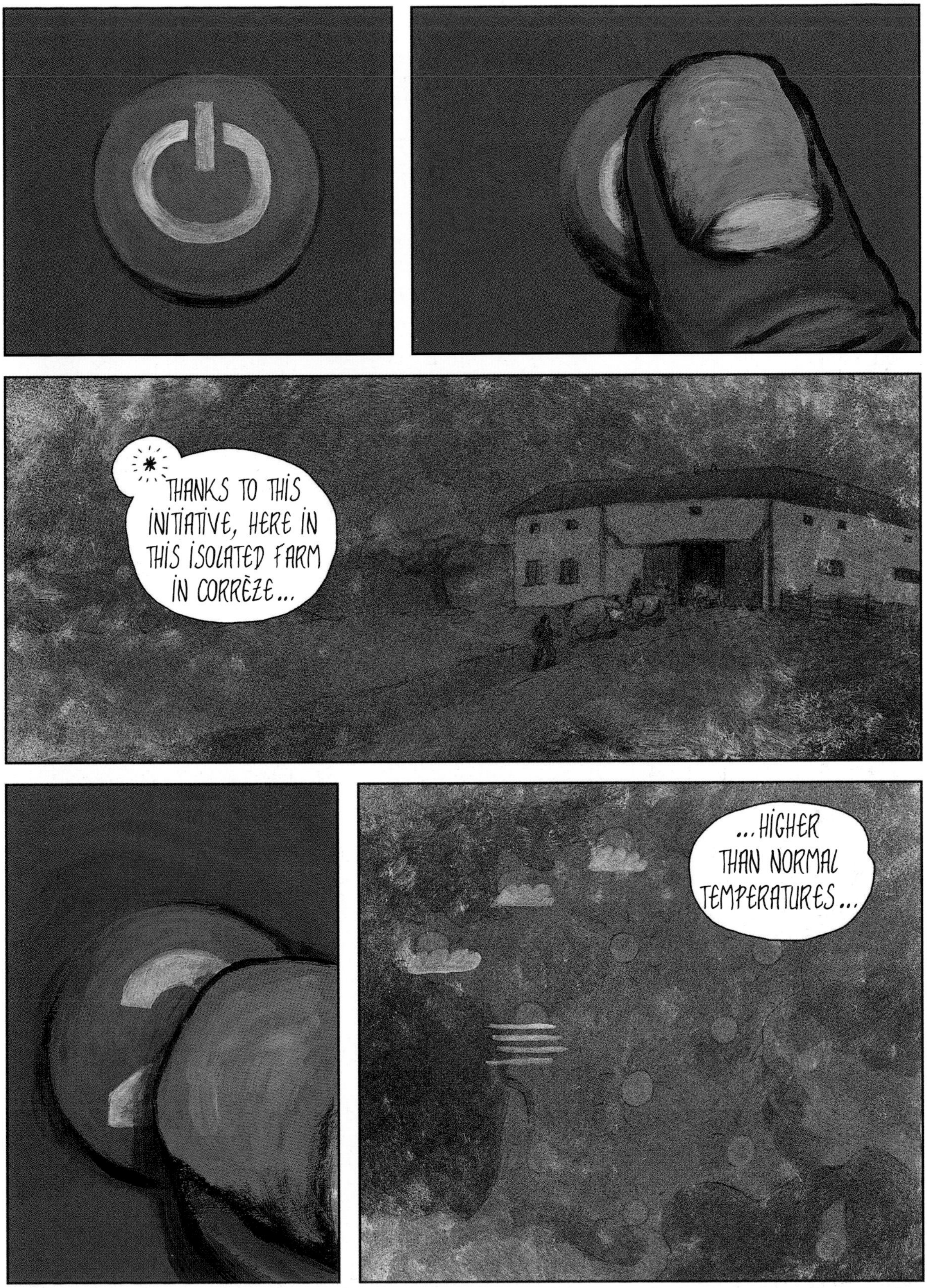
THANKS TO THIS INITIATIVE, HERE IN THIS ISOLATED FARM IN CORRÈZE...
...HIGHER THAN NORMAL TEMPERATURES...

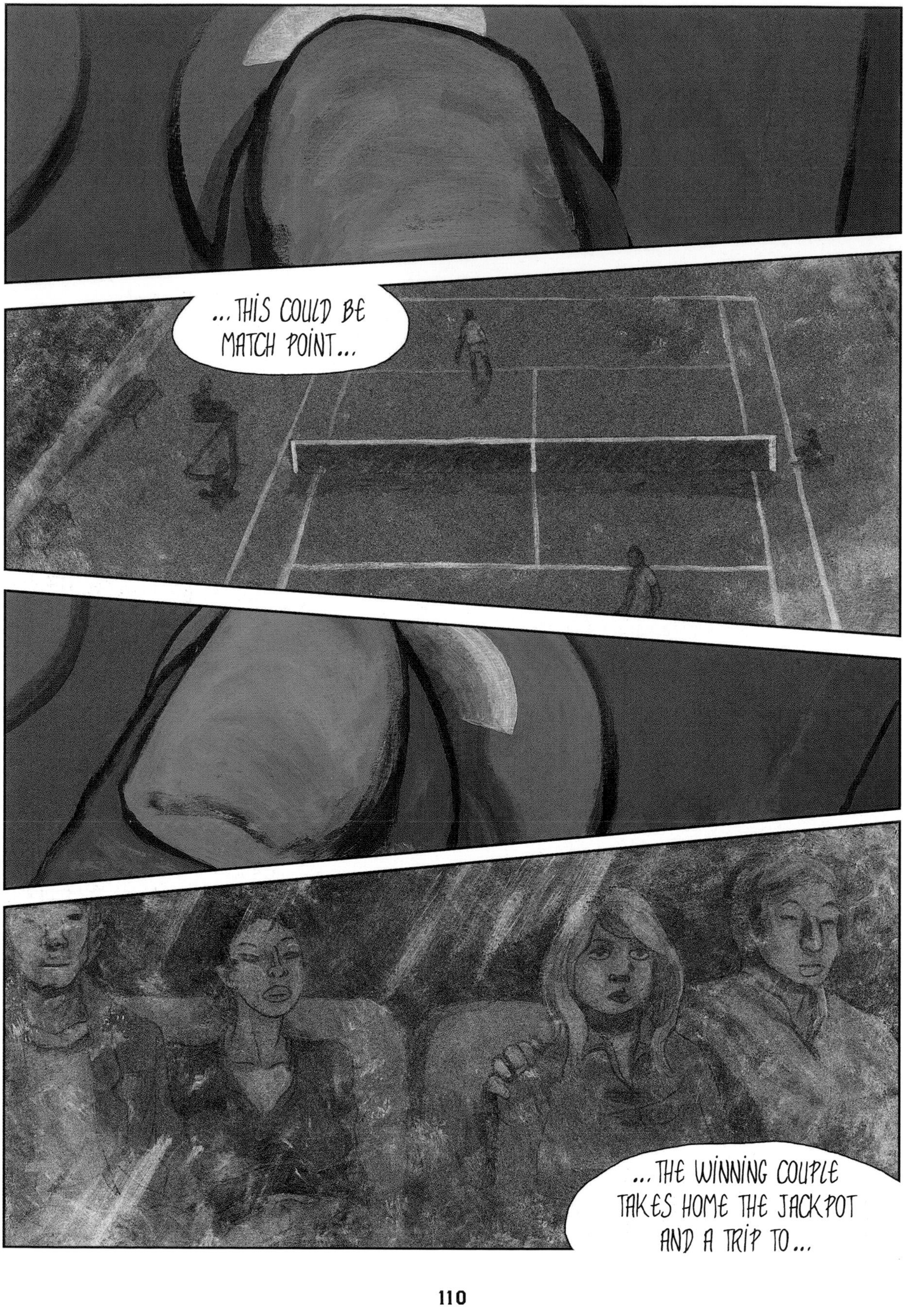
...THIS COULD BE MATCH POINT...
...THE WINNING COUPLE TAKES HOME THE JACKPOT AND A TRIP TO...

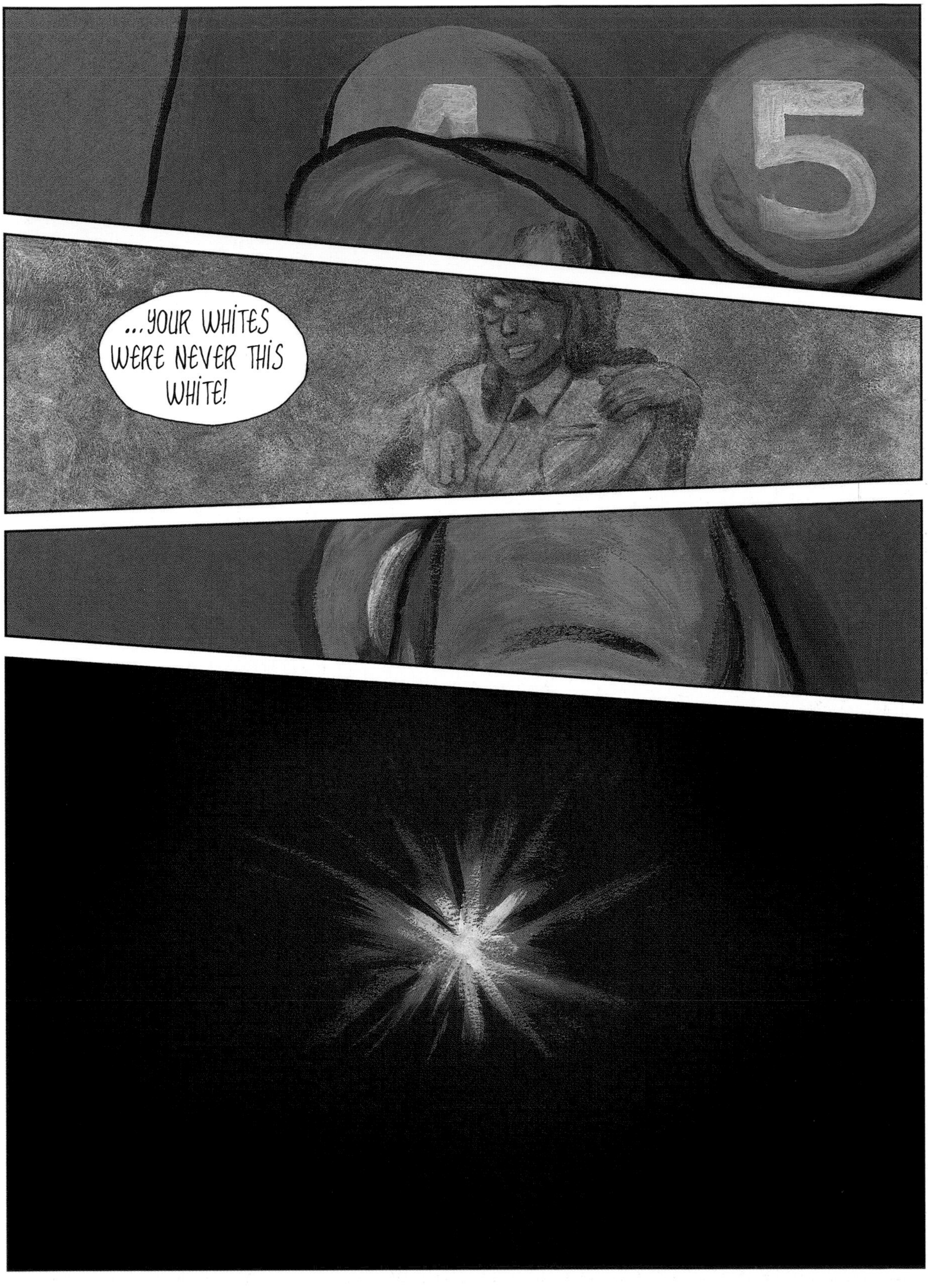
...YOUR WHITES WERE NEVER THIS WHITE!

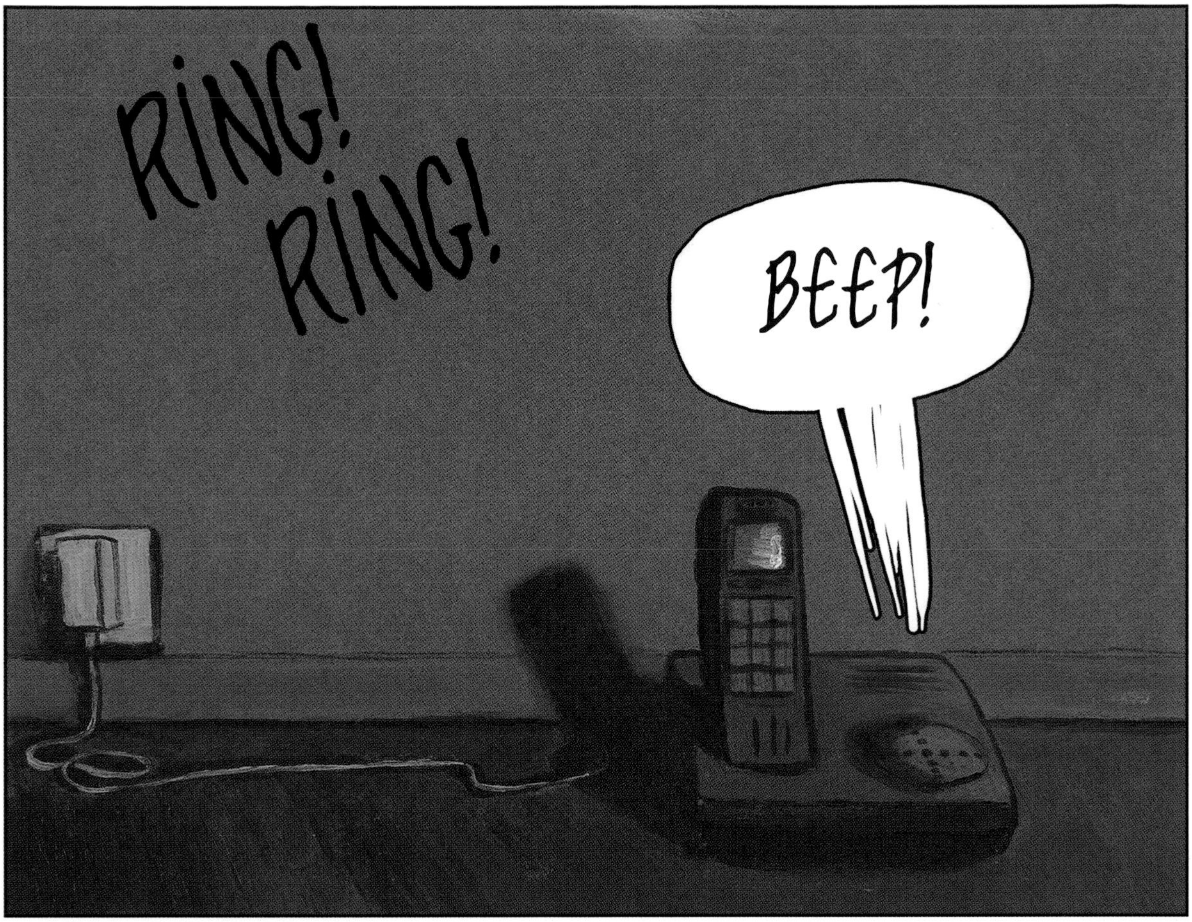
RING! RING!
BEEP!

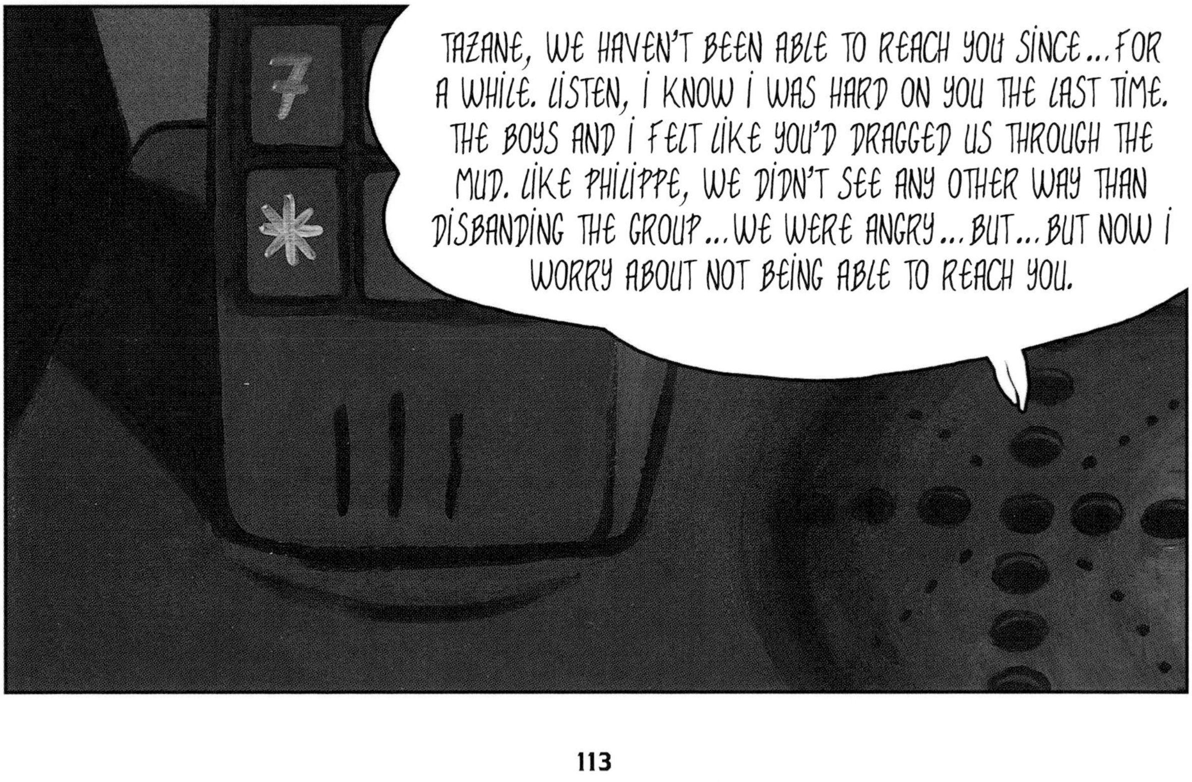
TAZANE, WE HAVEN'T BEEN ABLE TO REACH YOU SINCE... FOR A WHILE. LISTEN, I KNOW I WAS HARD ON YOU THE LAST TIME. THE BOYS AND I FELT LIKE YOU'D DRAGGED US THROUGH THE MUD. LIKE PHILIPPE, WE DIDN'T SEE ANY OTHER WAY THAN DISBANDING THE GROUP... WE WERE ANGRY... BUT... BUT NOW I WORRY ABOUT NOT BEING ABLE TO REACH YOU.

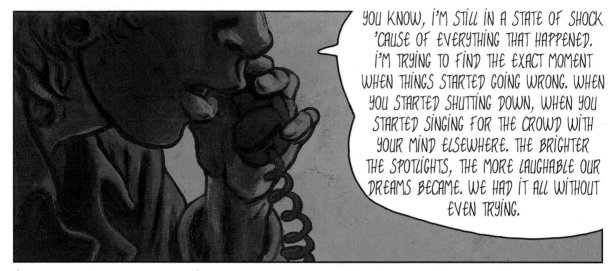

YOU KNOW, I'M STILL IN A STATE OF SHOCK 'CAUSE OF EVERYTHING THAT HAPPENED. I'M TRYING TO FIND THE EXACT MOMENT WHEN THINGS STARTED GOING WRONG. WHEN YOU STARTED SHUTTING DOWN, WHEN YOU STARTED SINGING FOR THE CROWD WITH YOUR MIND ELSEWHERE. THE BRIGHTER THE SPOTLIGHTS, THE MORE LAUGHABLE OUR DREAMS BECAME. WE HAD IT ALL WITHOUT EVEN TRYING.

I UNDERSTAND THAT YOU GOT DISGUSTED HOW THE CROWDS ADORED YOU NO MATTER WHAT, BUT THE WAY YOU WENT...I MEAN, I DON'T THINK THAT...

≡ SIGH ≡

SORRY, I DIDN'T CALL TO BLAME YOU ALL OVER AGAIN. JUST TO TELL YOU I'M SORRY, THINGS GOT OUT OF CONTROL ... YOU SHOULD FIND YOURSELF. I BET THAT'LL MAKE YOU LAUGH, BUT I THINK YOU LEFT YOUR HUMANITY BACKSTAGE.

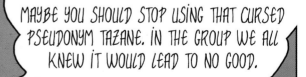

MAYBE YOU SHOULD STOP USING THAT CURSED PSEUDONYM TAZANE. IN THE GROUP WE ALL KNEW IT WOULD LEAD TO NO GOOD.

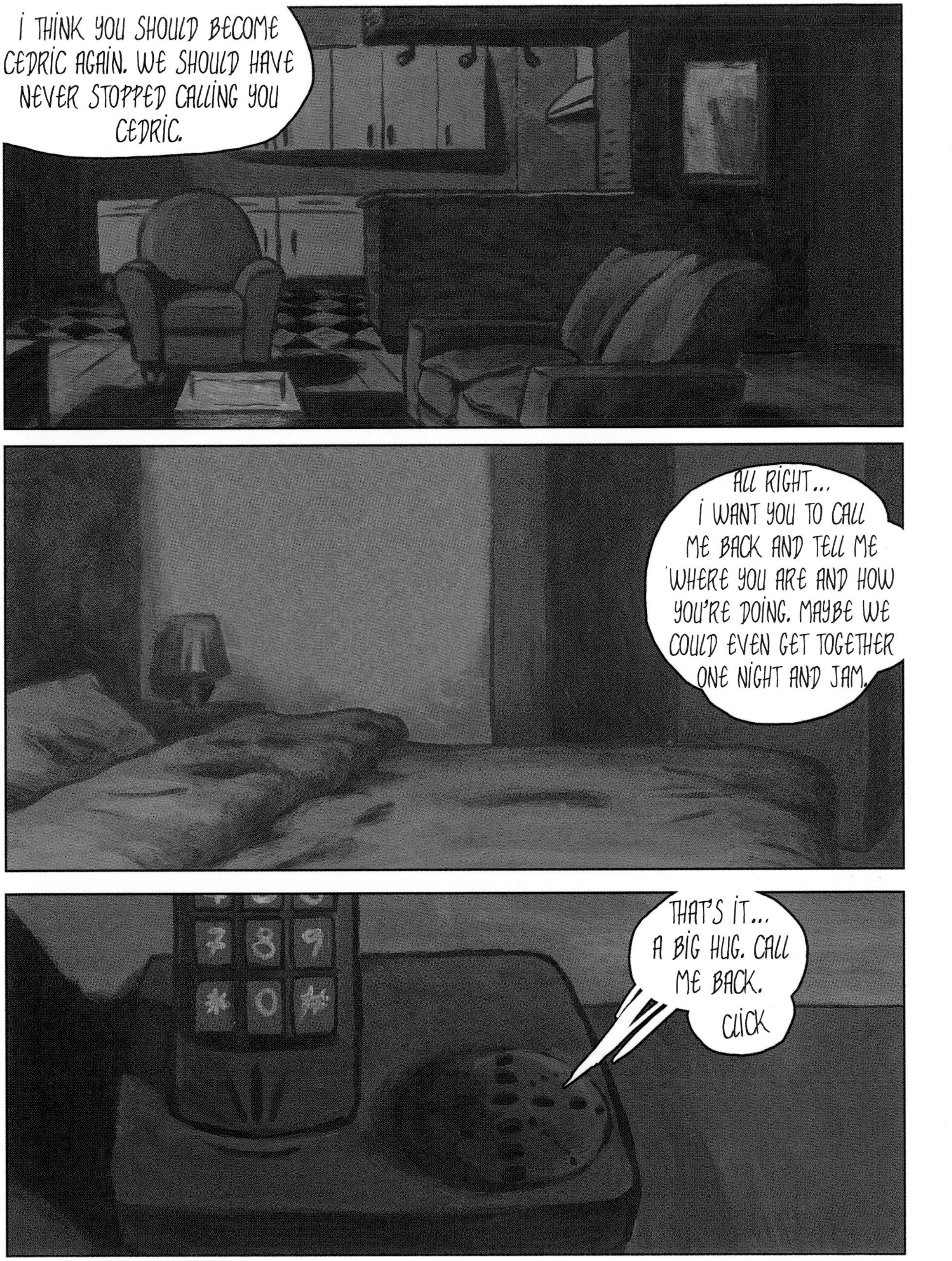
I THINK YOU SHOULD BECOME CEDRIC AGAIN. WE SHOULD HAVE NEVER STOPPED CALLING YOU CEDRIC.
ALL RIGHT... I WANT YOU TO CALL ME BACK AND TELL ME WHERE YOU ARE AND HOW YOU'RE DOING. MAYBE WE COULD EVEN GET TOGETHER ONE NIGHT AND JAM.
THAT'S IT... A BIG HUG. CALL ME BACK.
CLICK
7 8 9
* 0 #

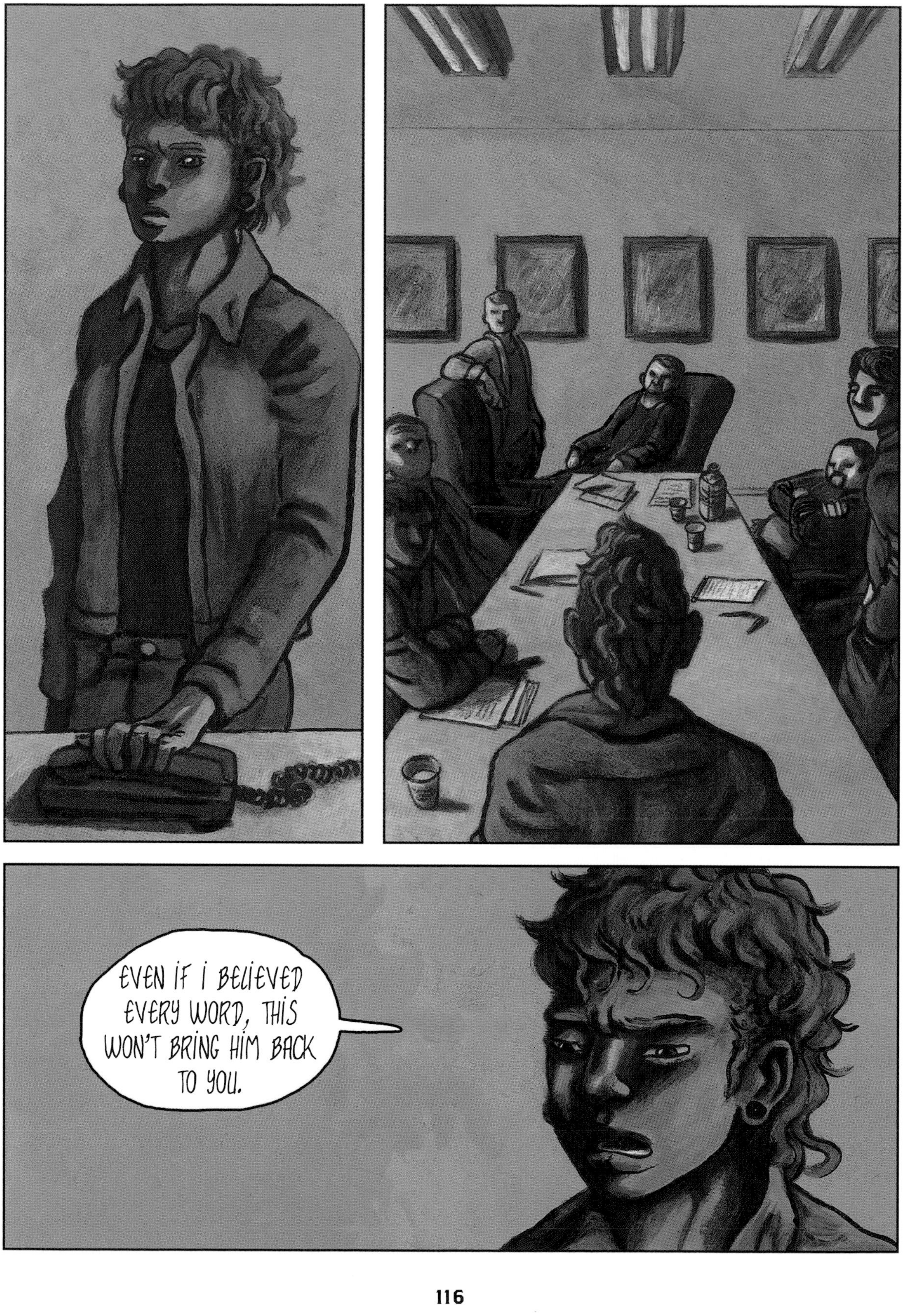
EVEN IF I BELIEVED EVERY WORD, THIS WON'T BRING HIM BACK TO YOU.

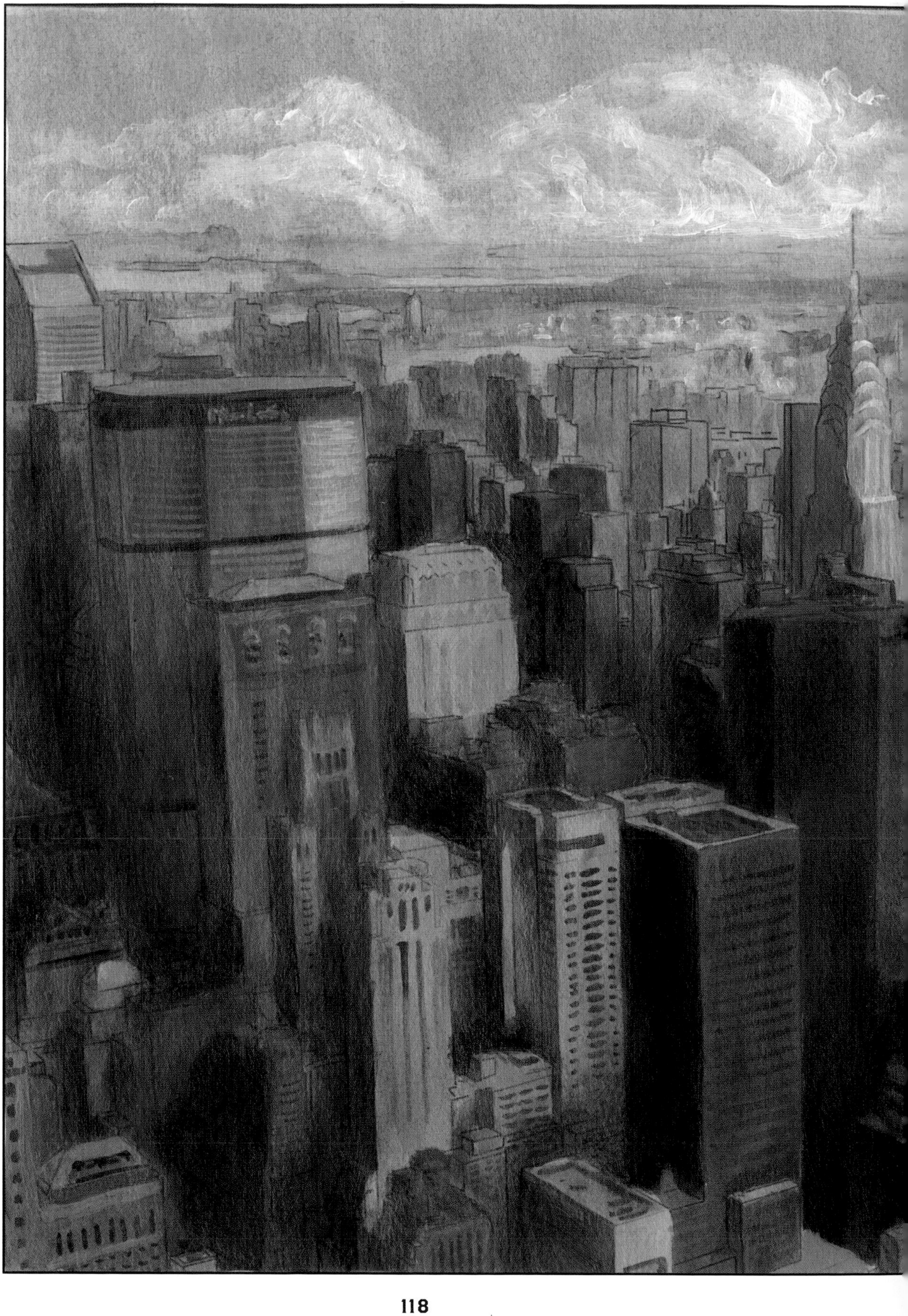

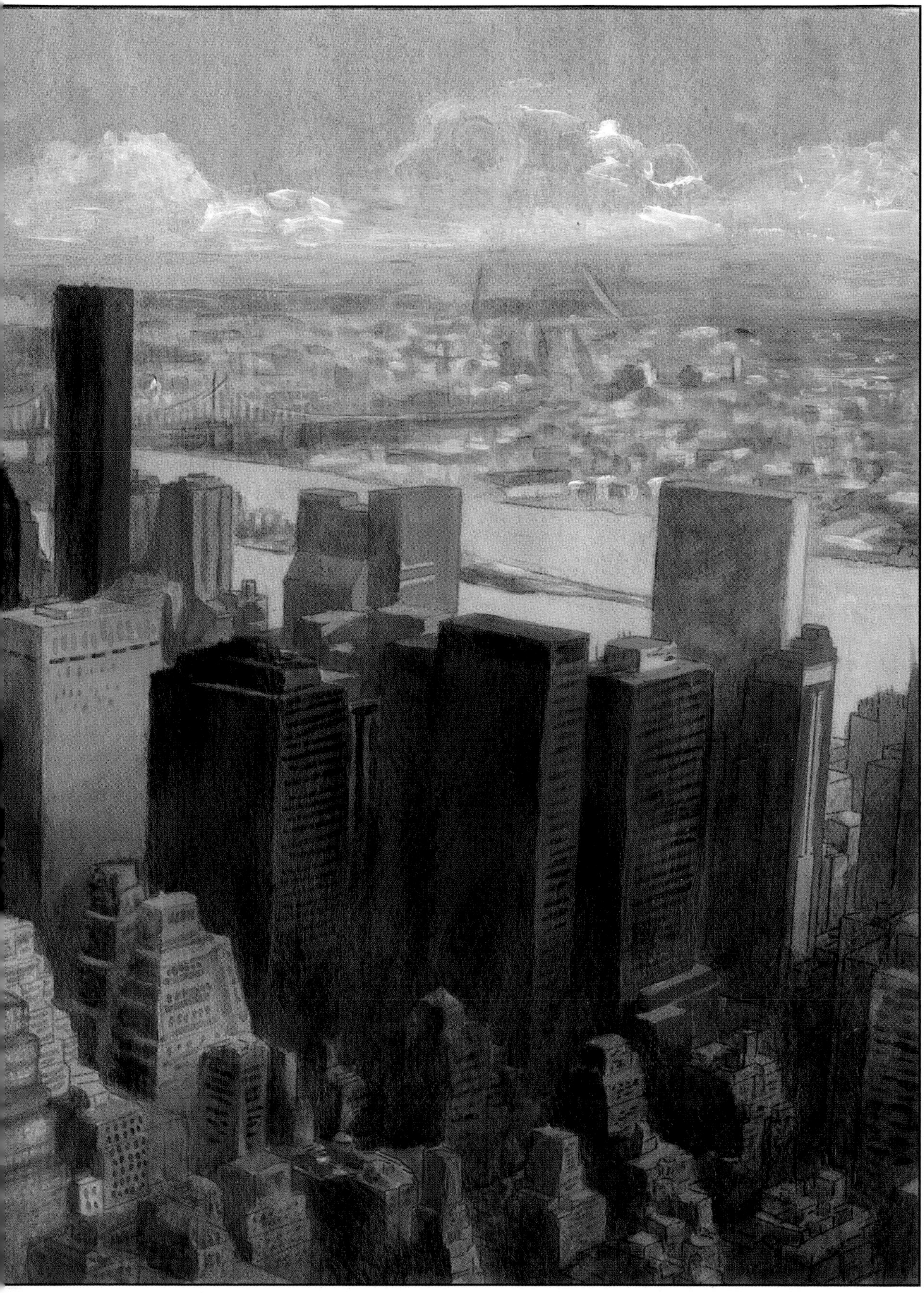

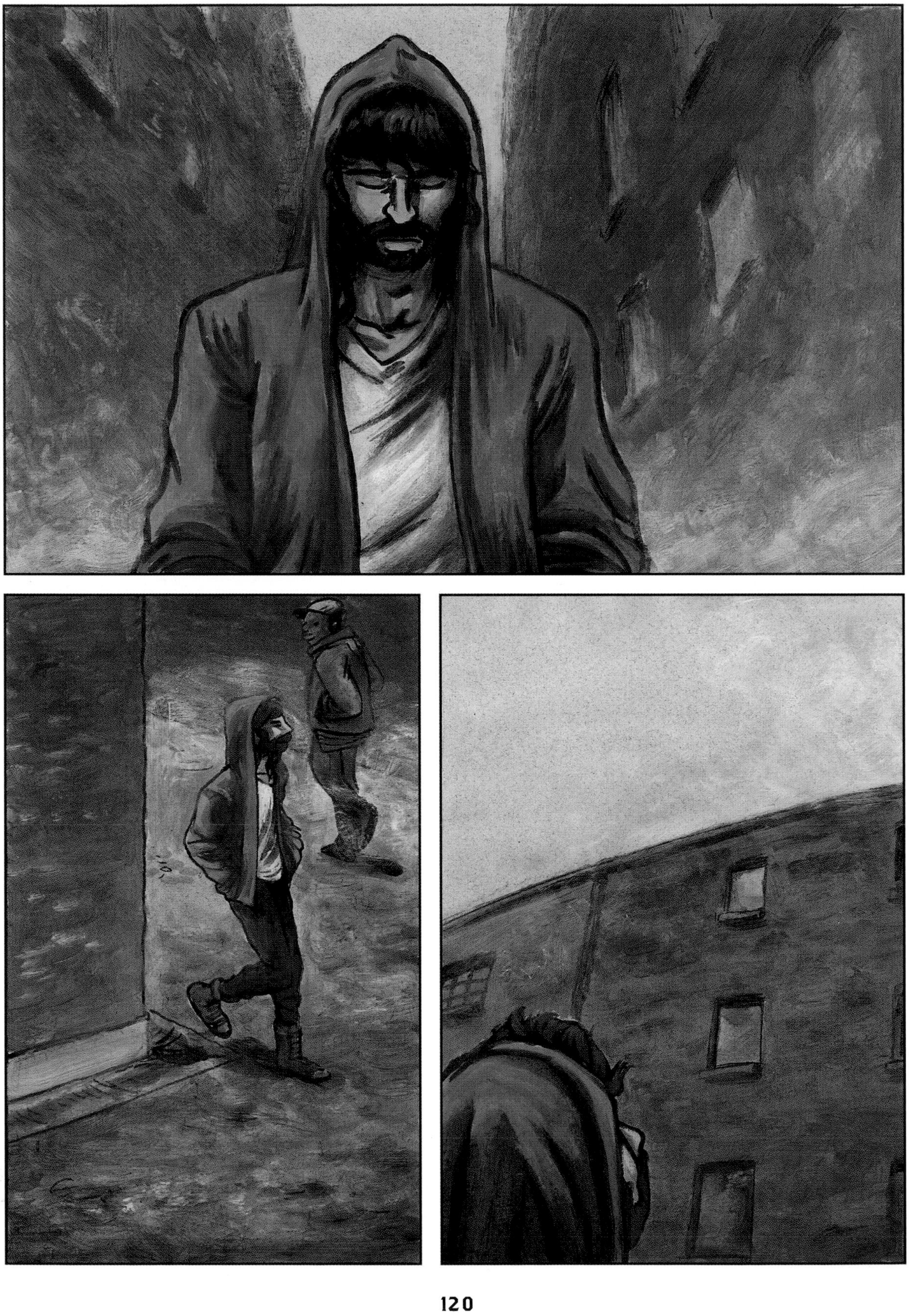

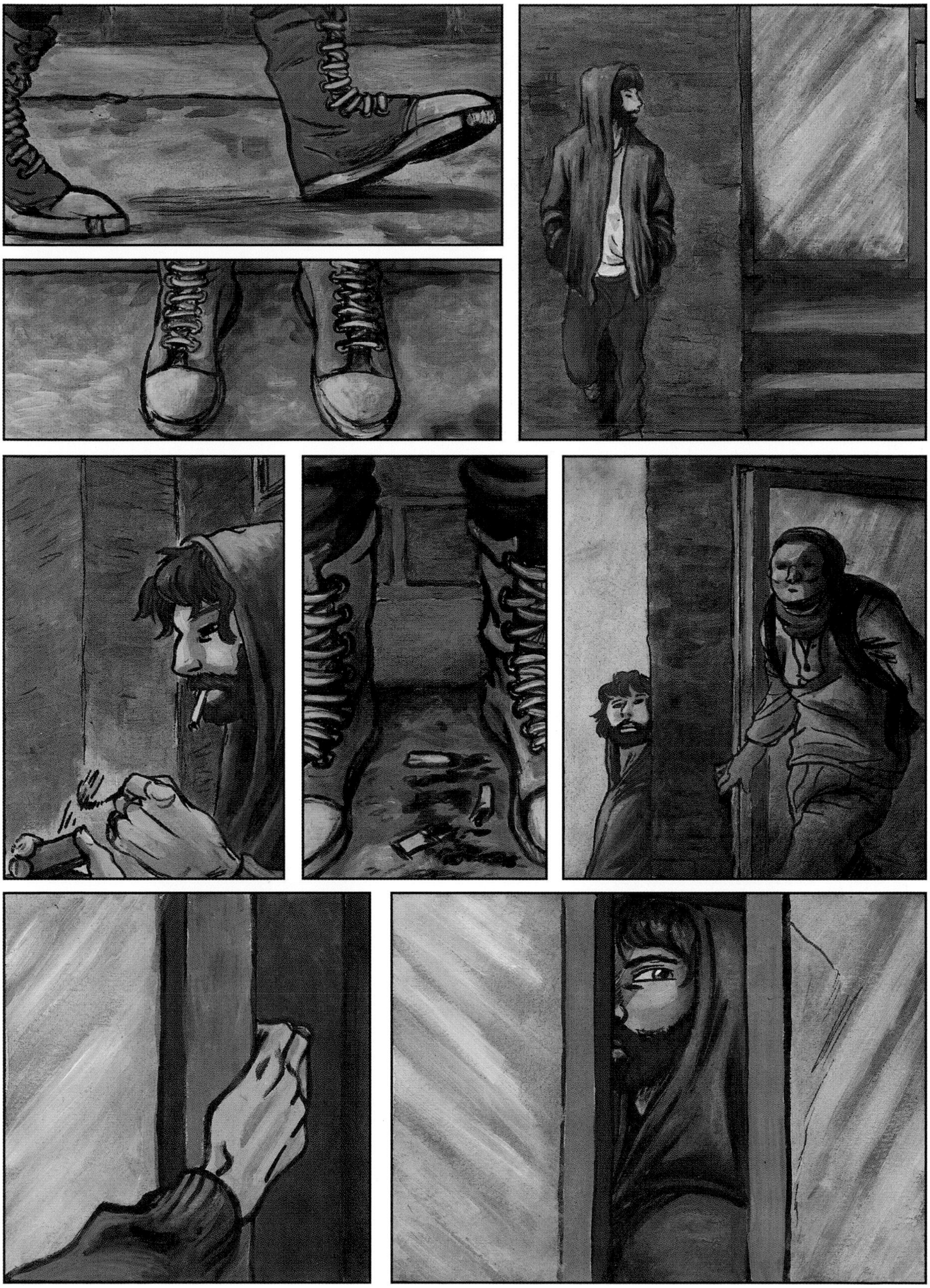

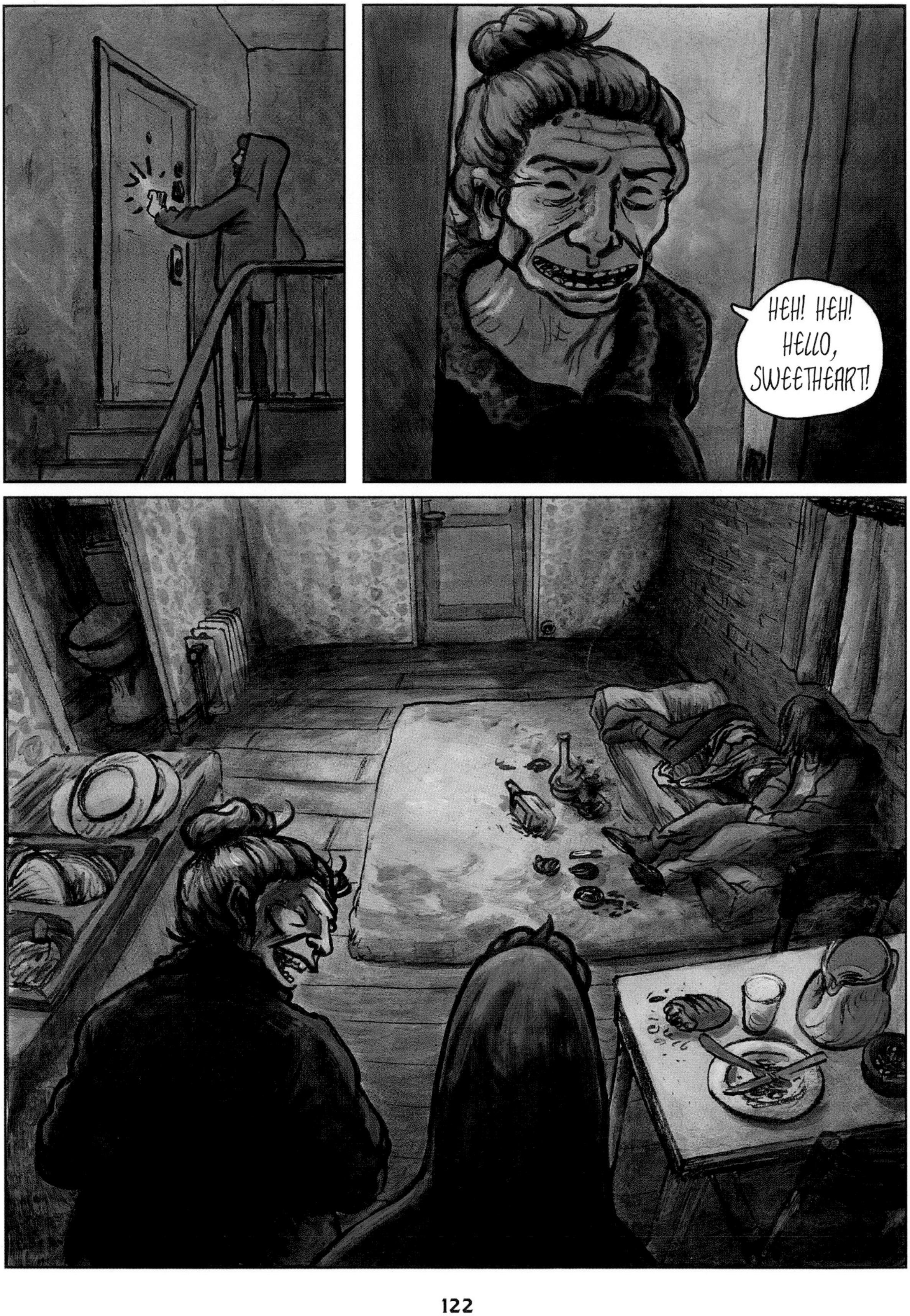
HEH! HEH! HELLO, SWEETHEART!

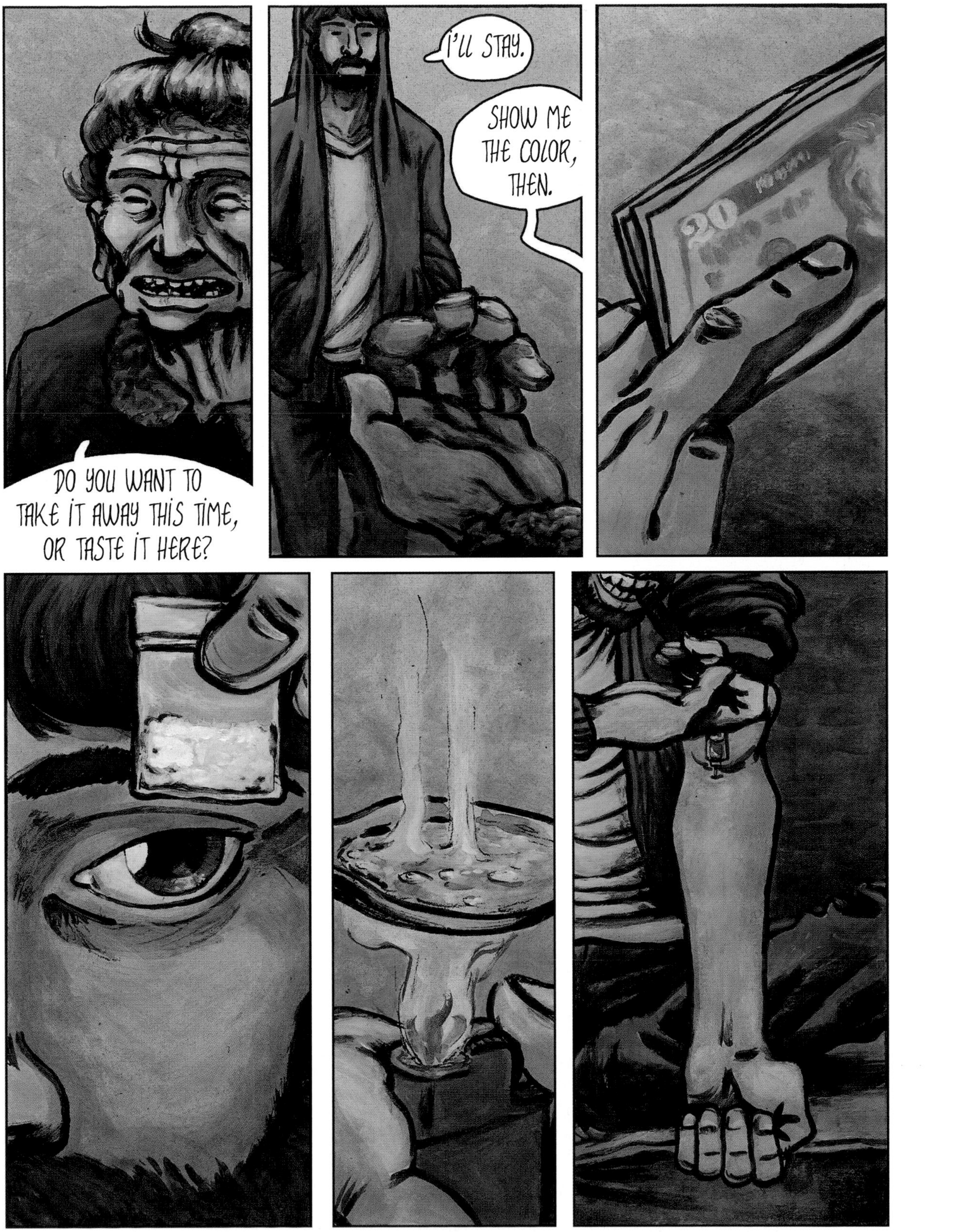
DO YOU WANT TO TAKE IT AWAY THIS TIME, OR TASTE IT HERE?
I'LL STAY.
SHOW ME THE COLOR, THEN.

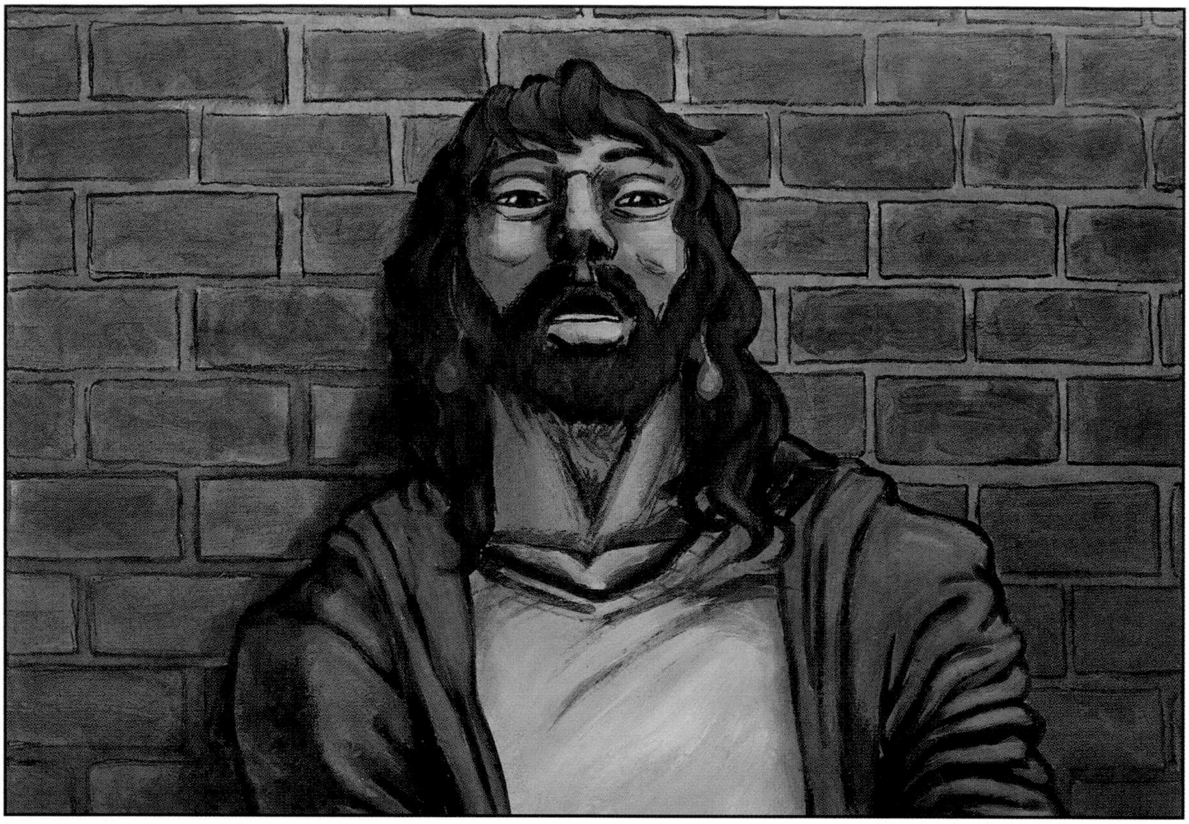

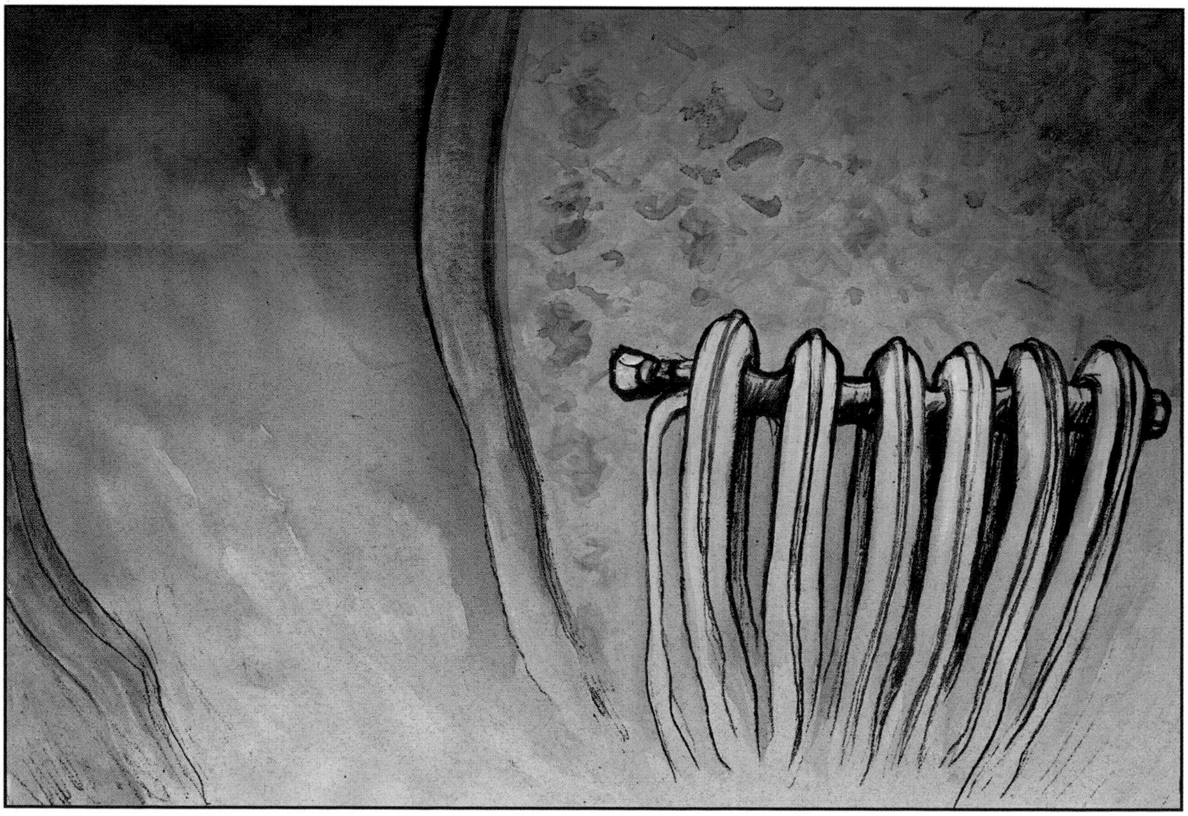

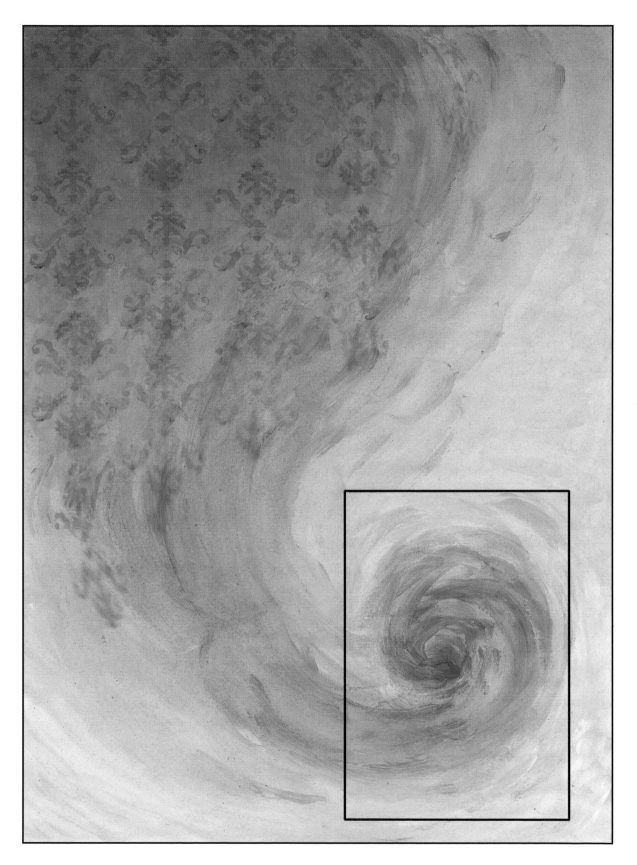

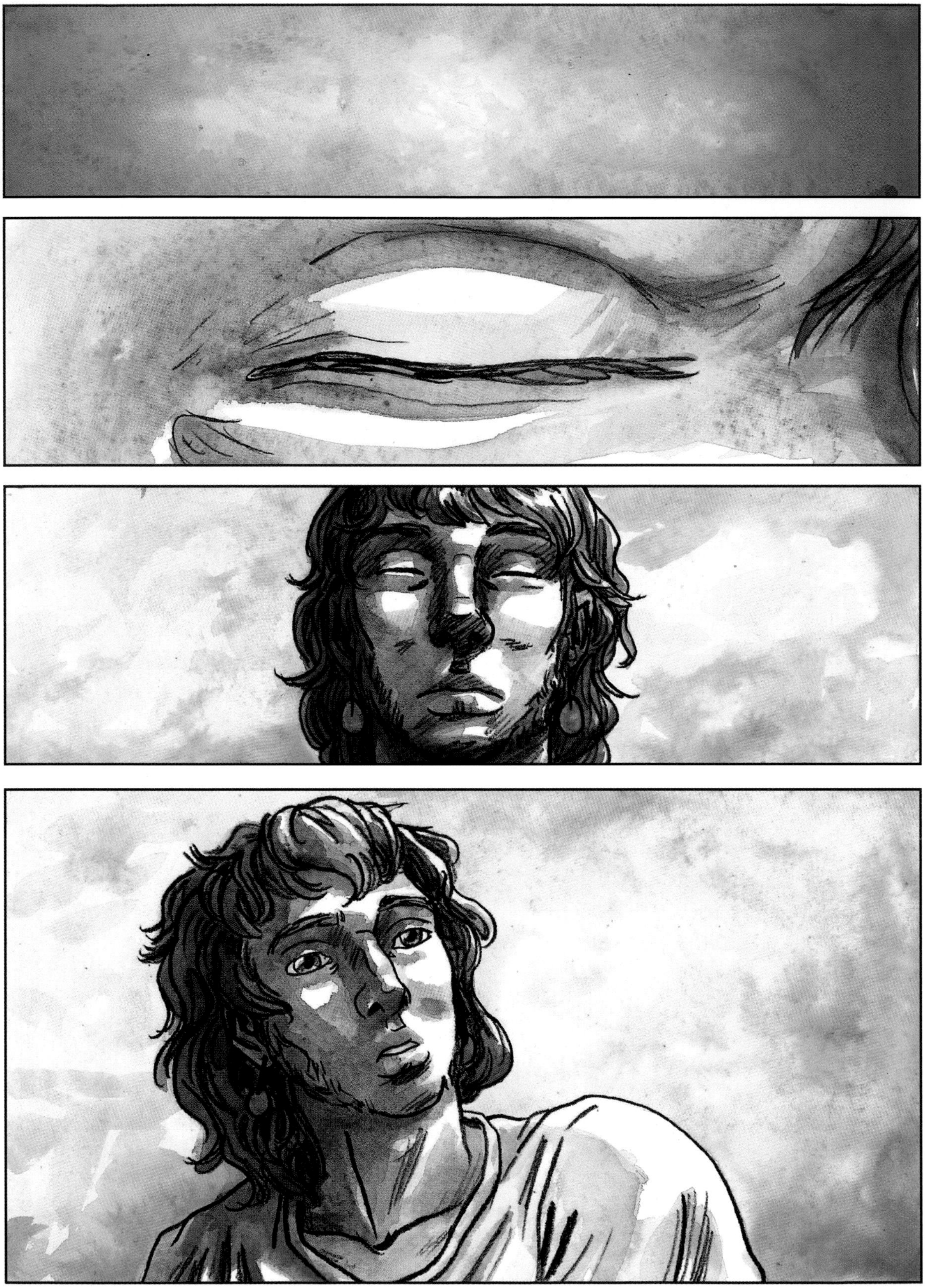

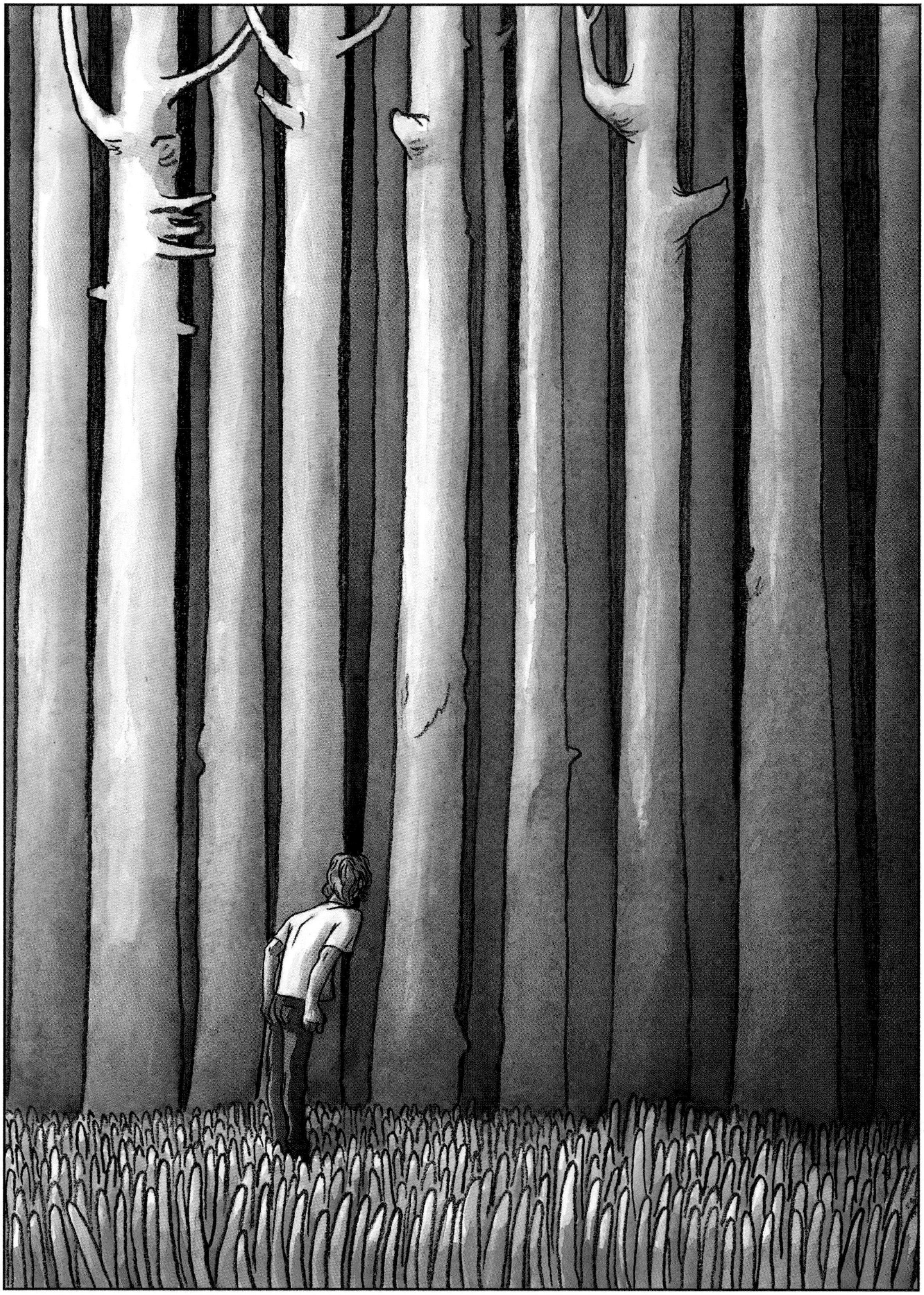

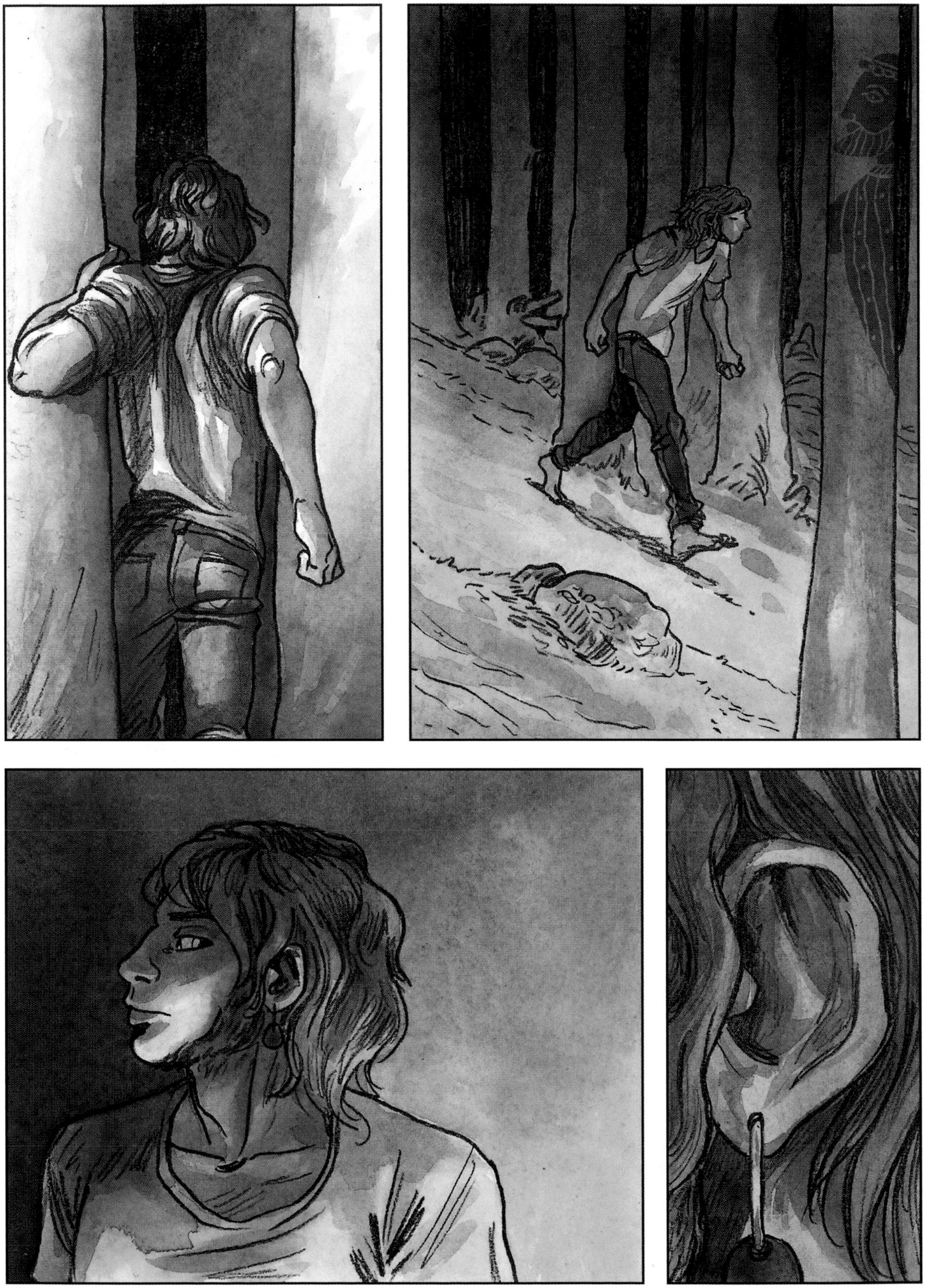

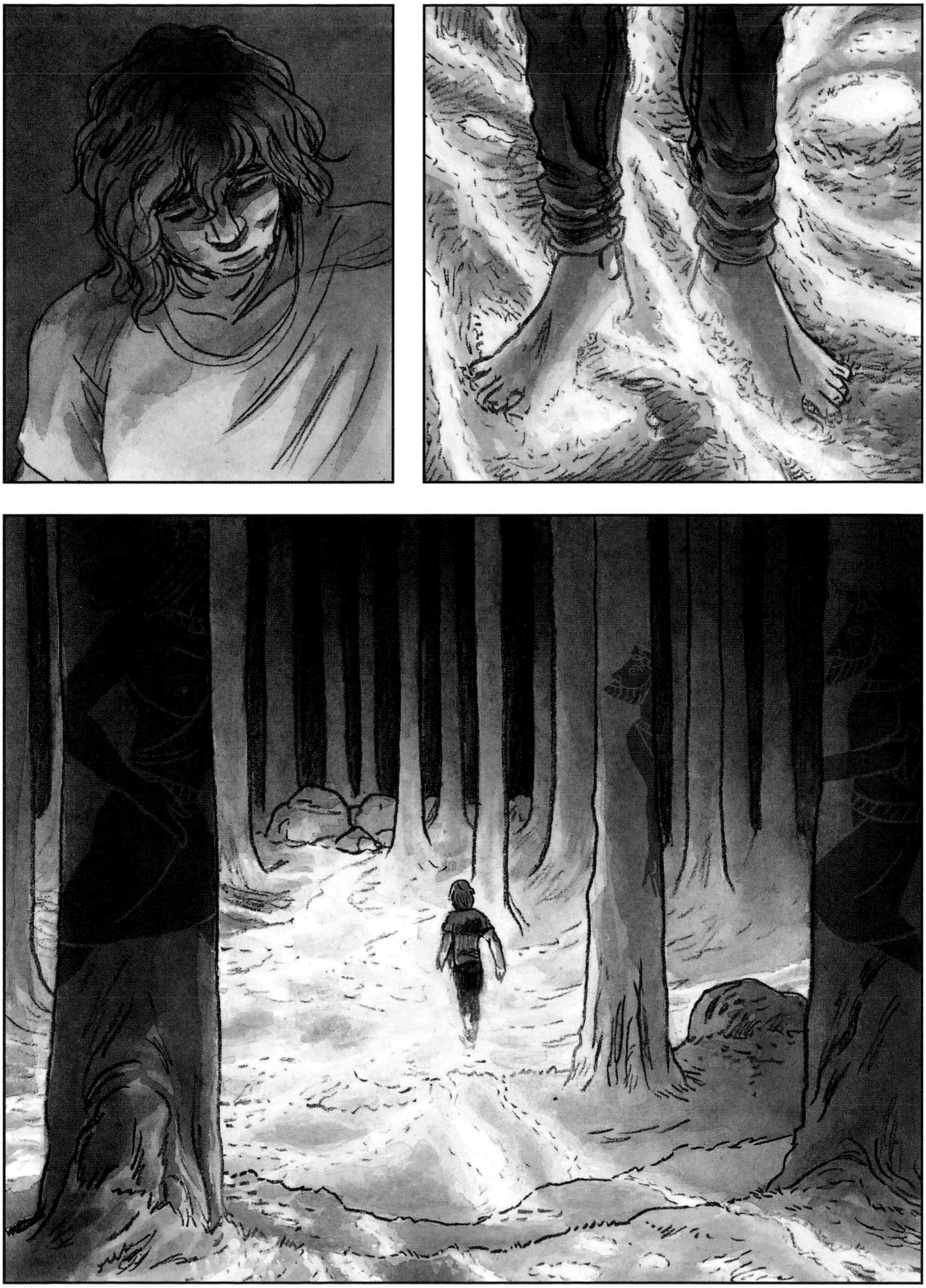

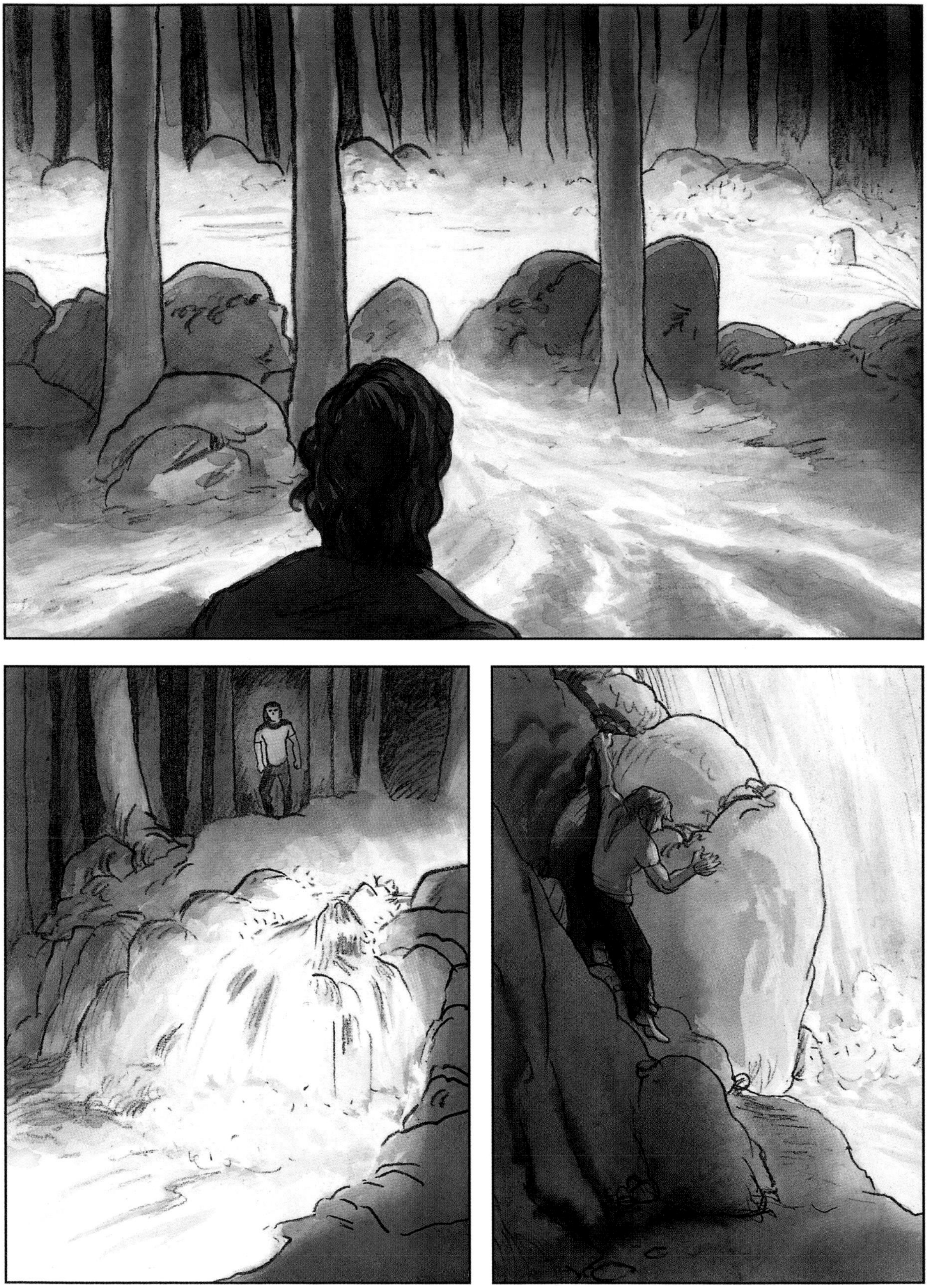

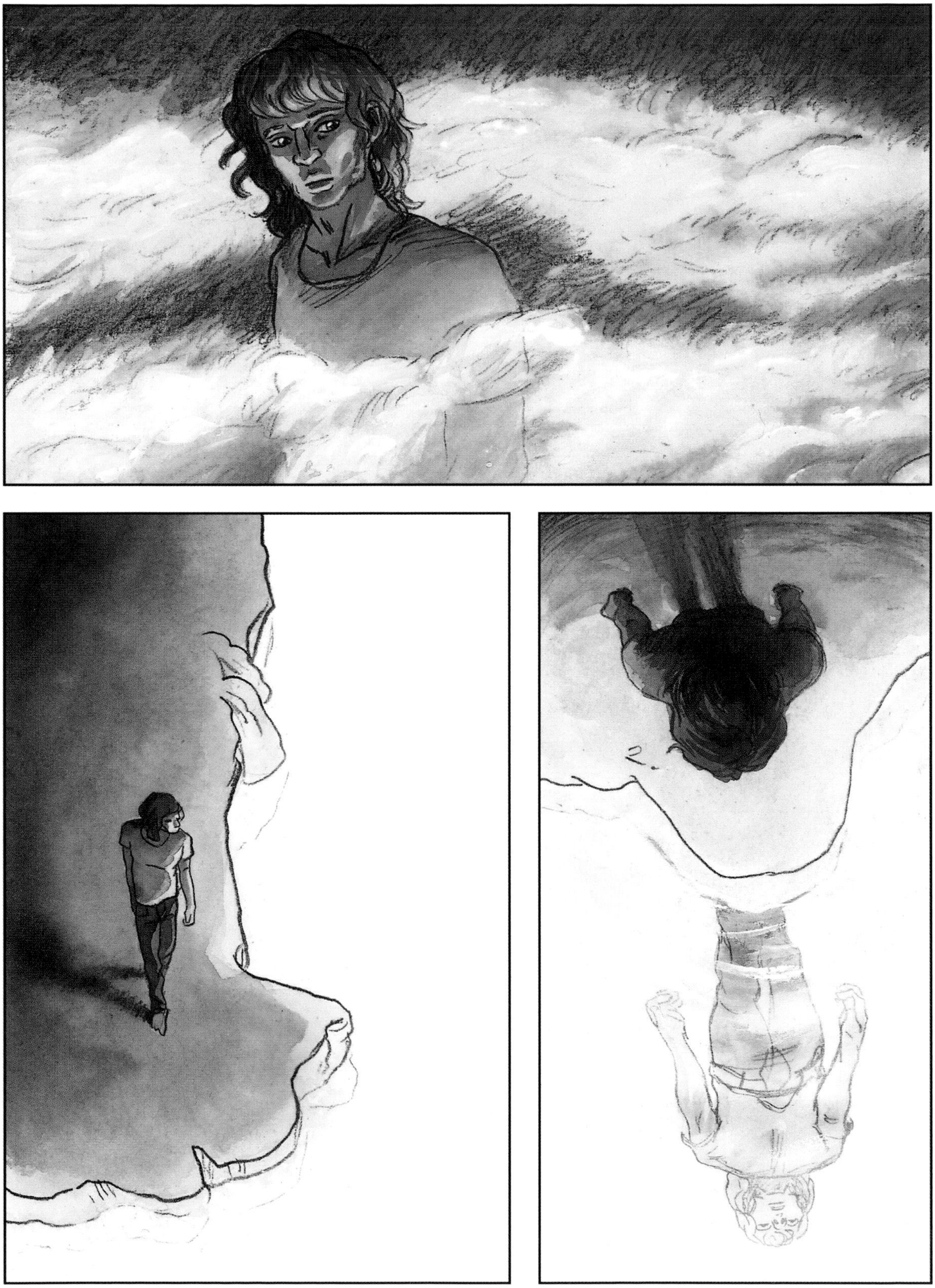

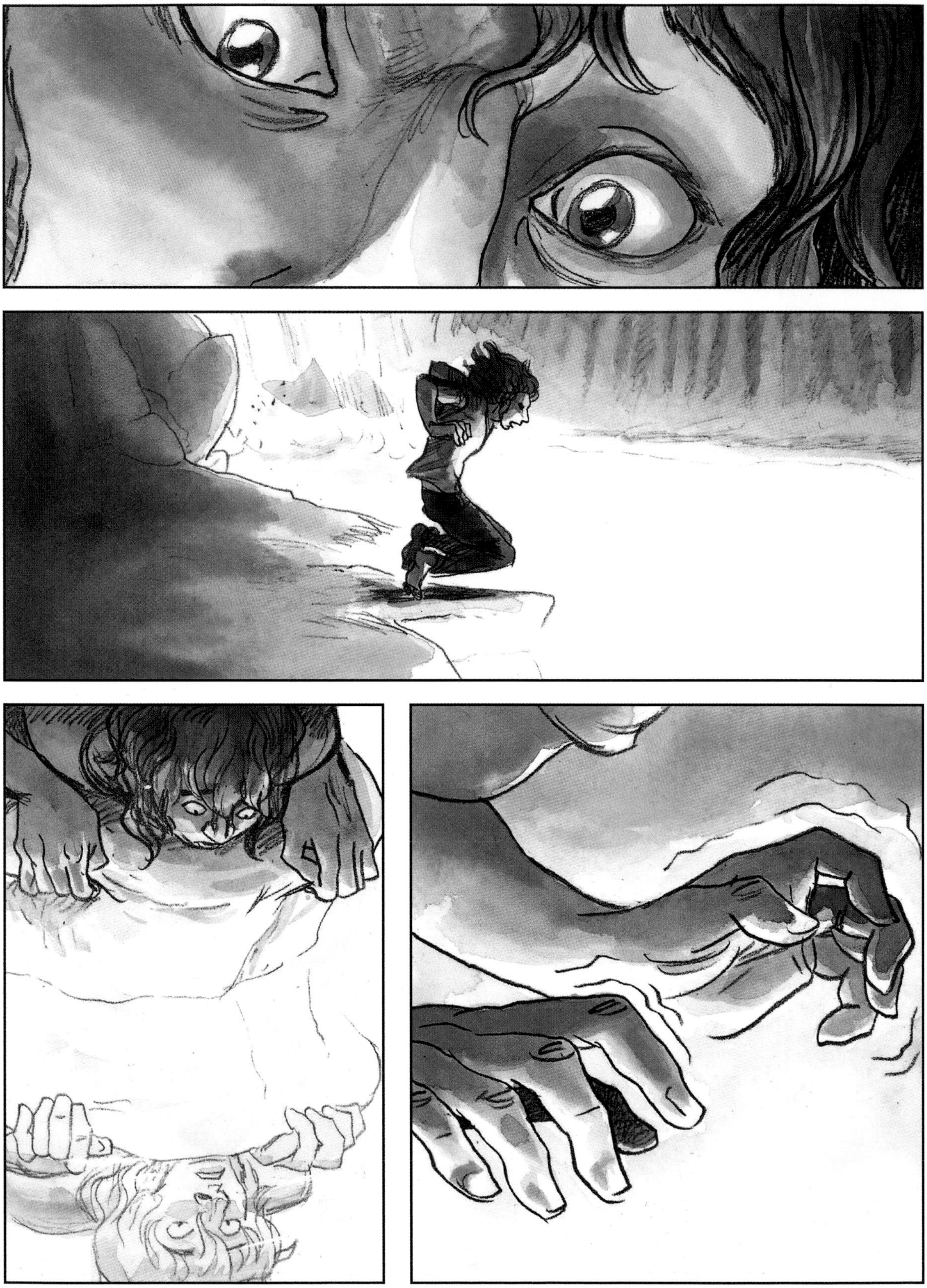

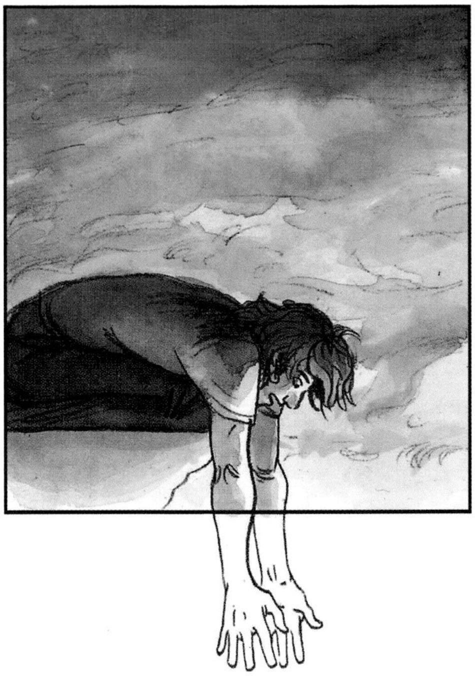

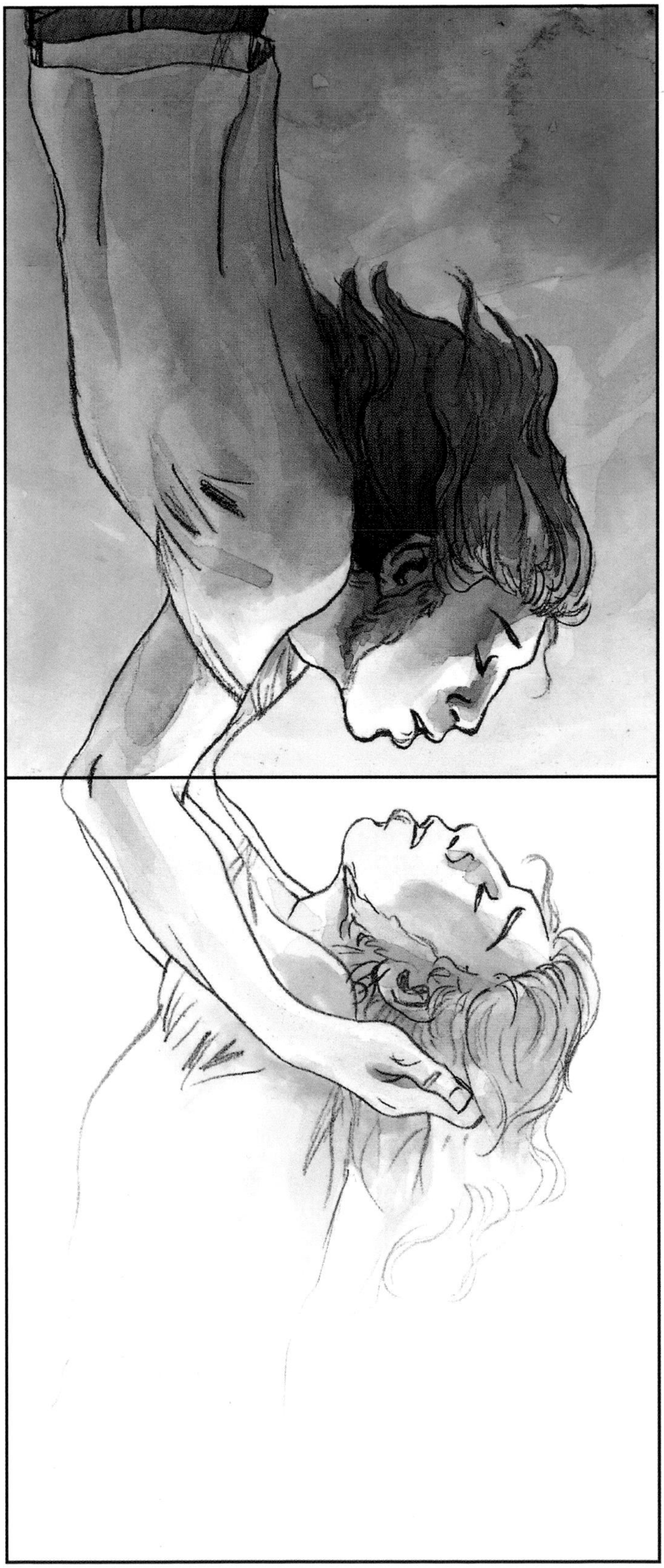

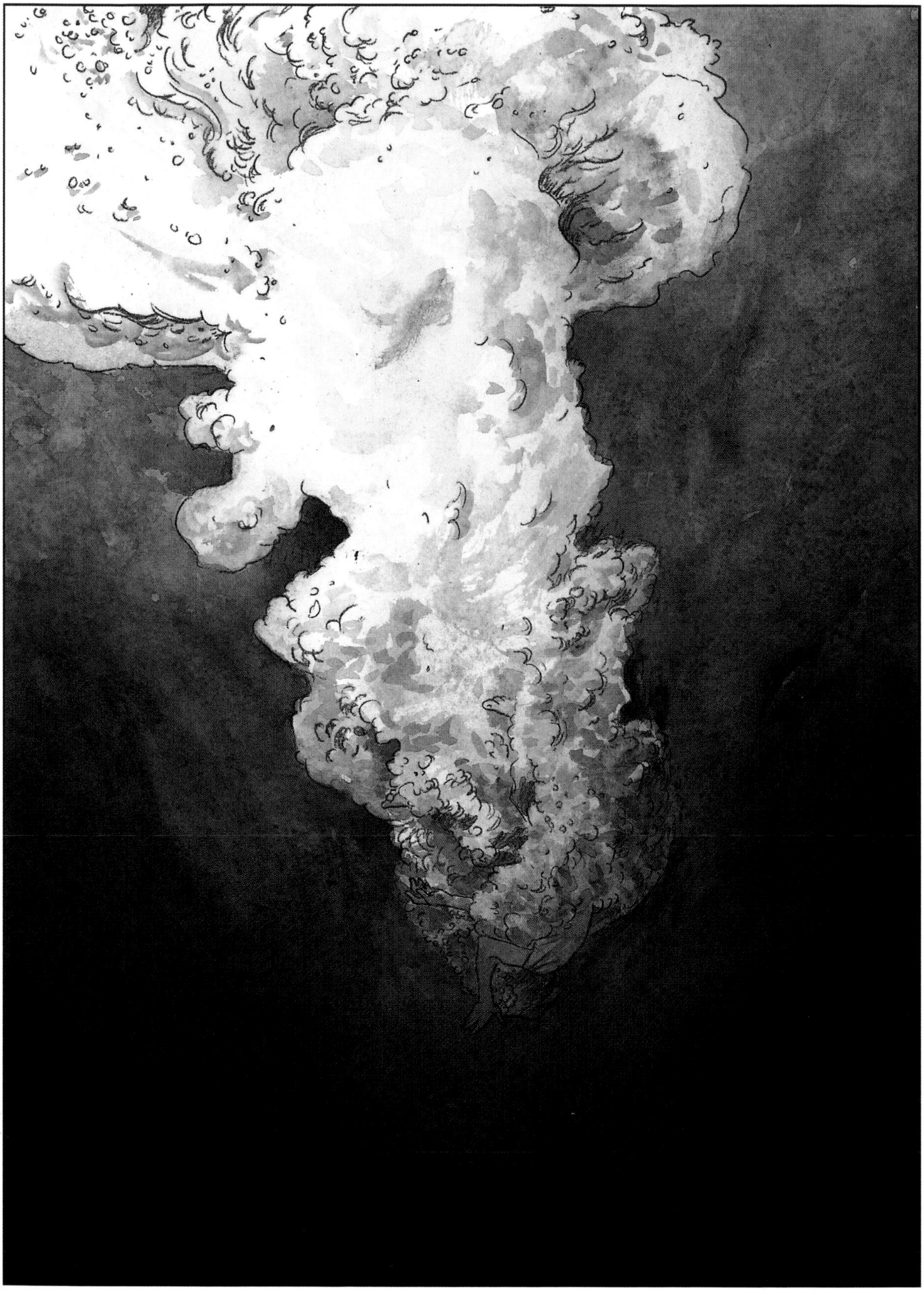

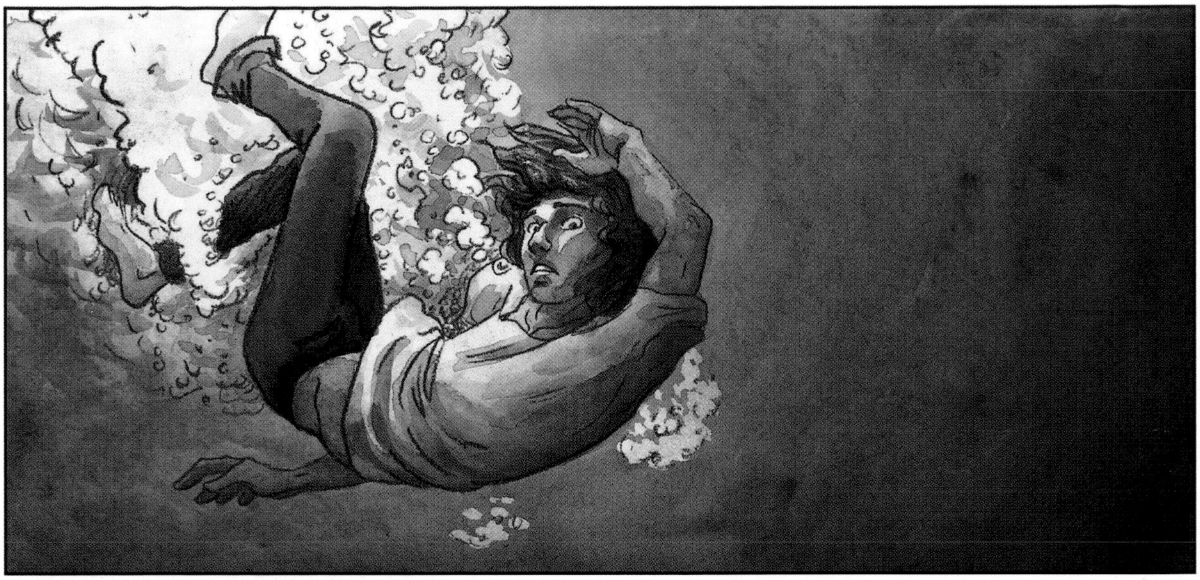

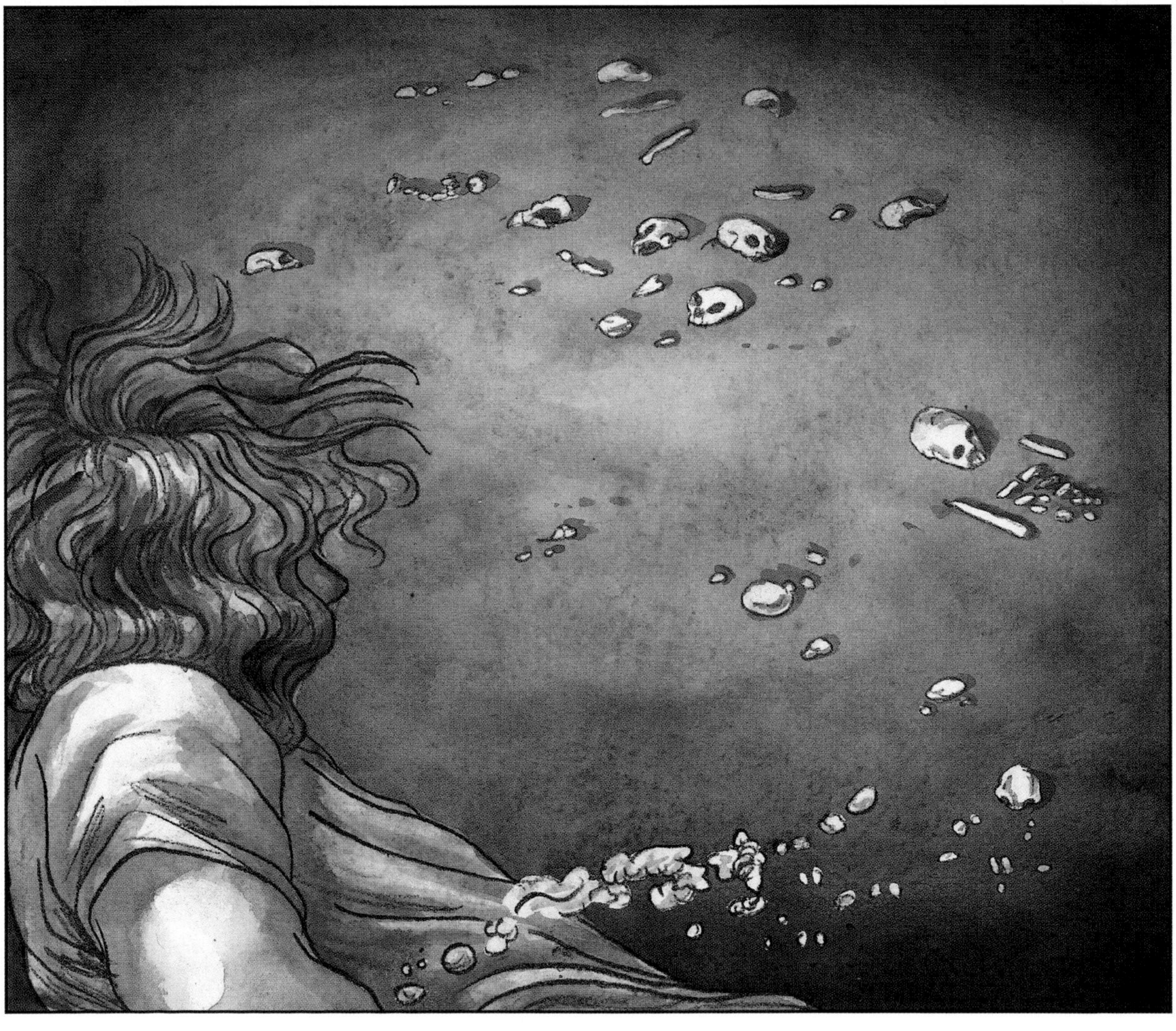

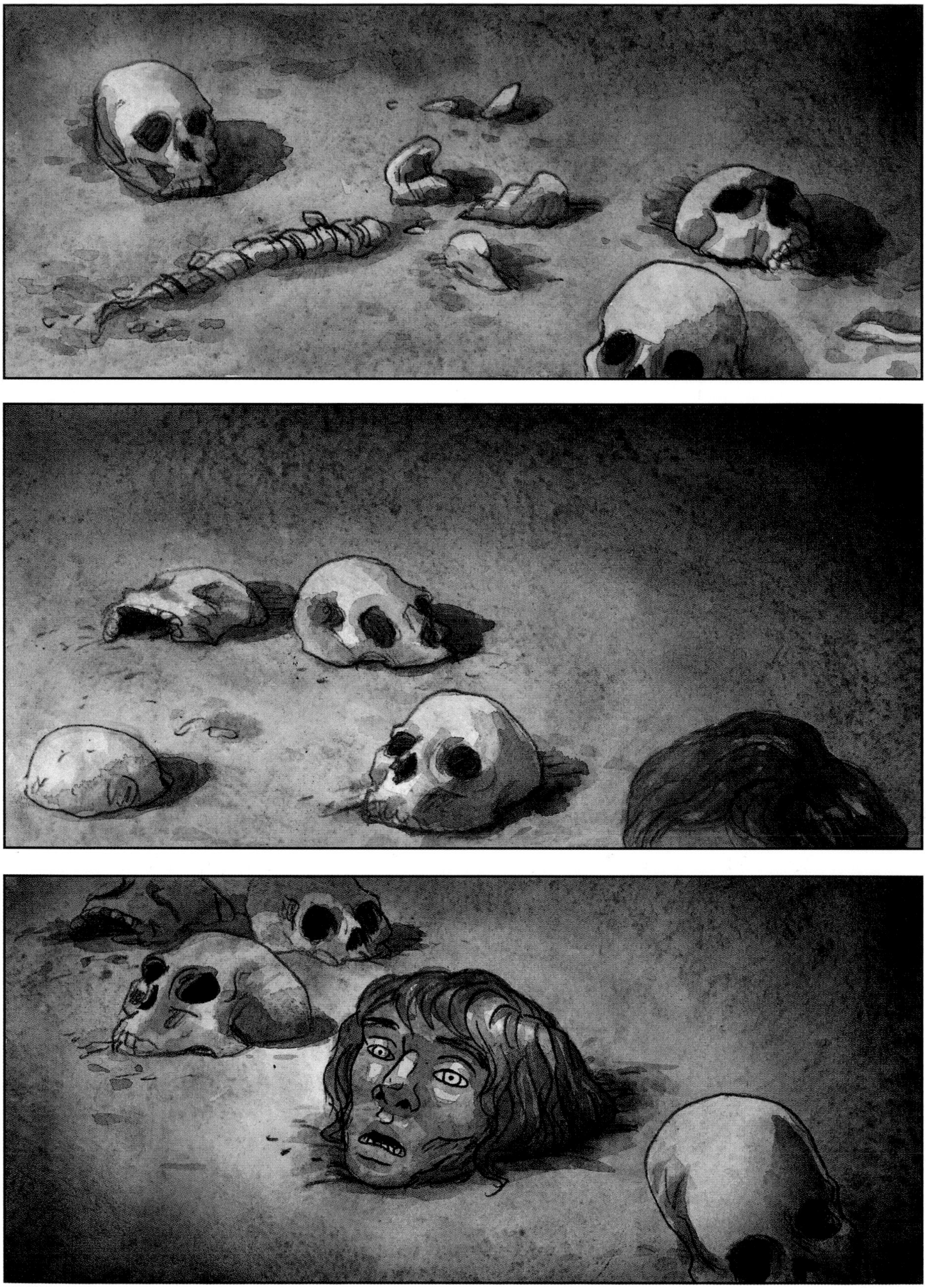

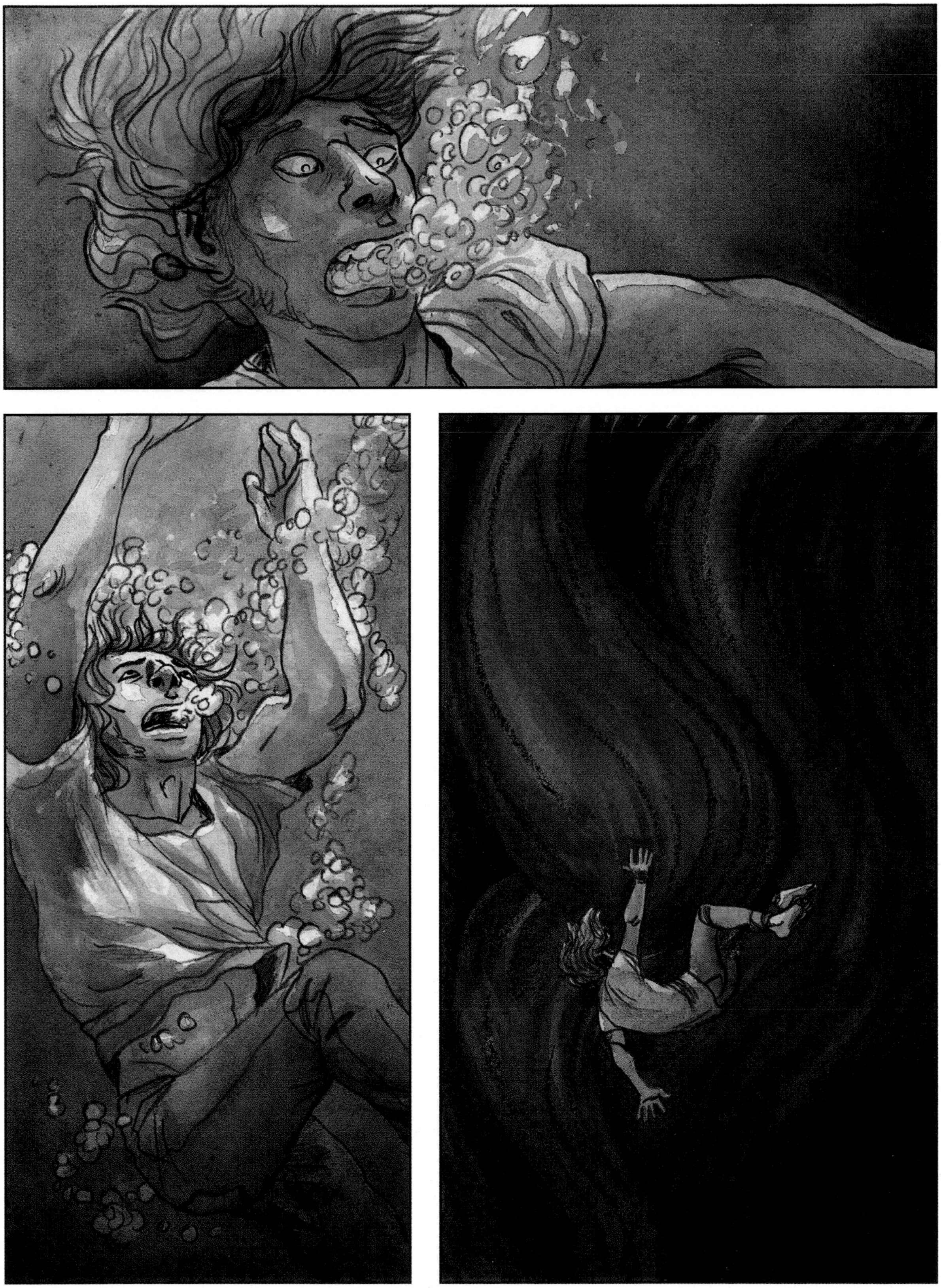

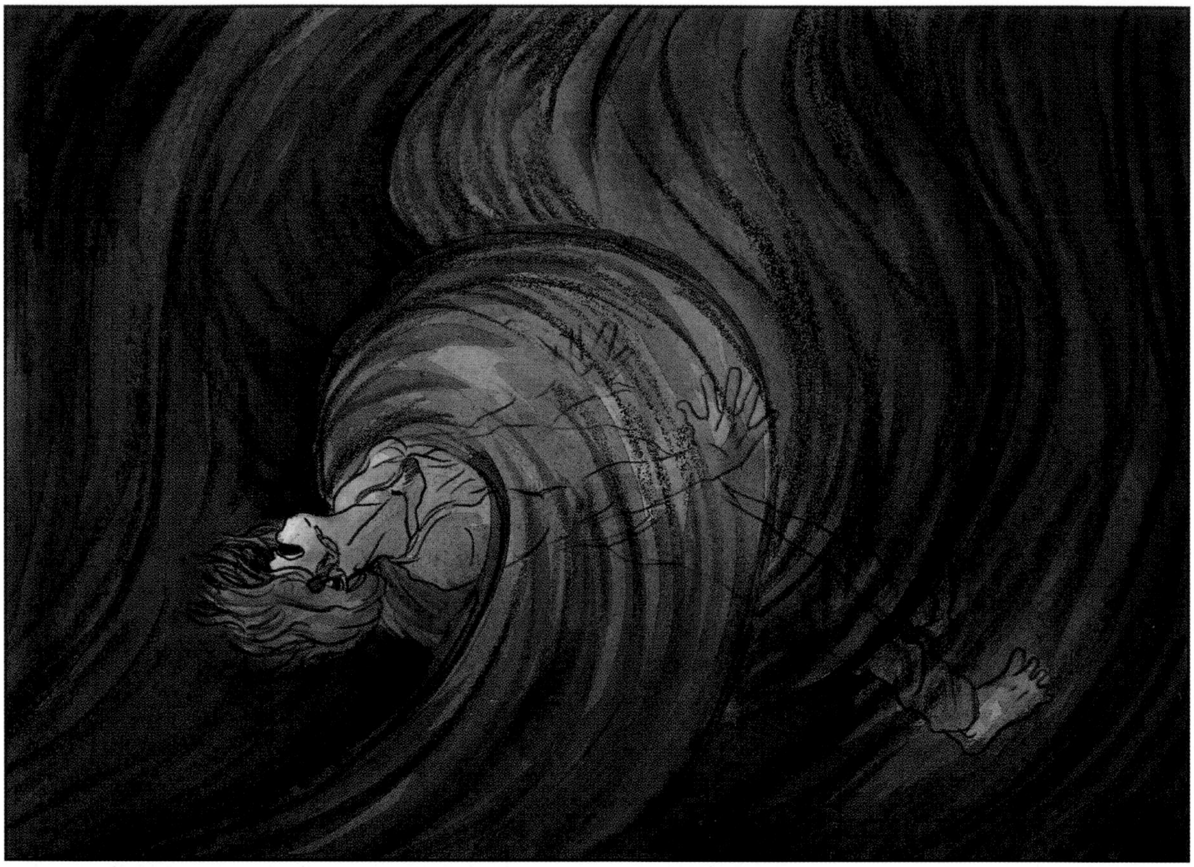

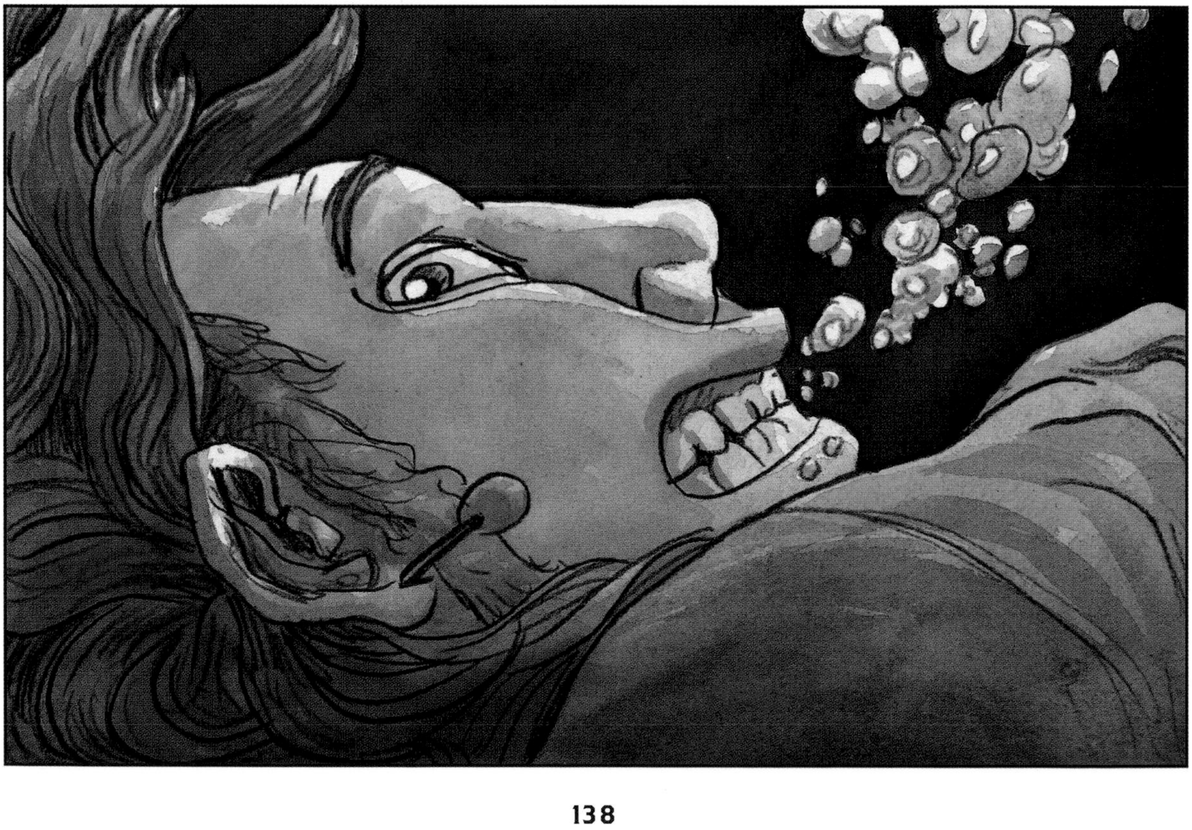

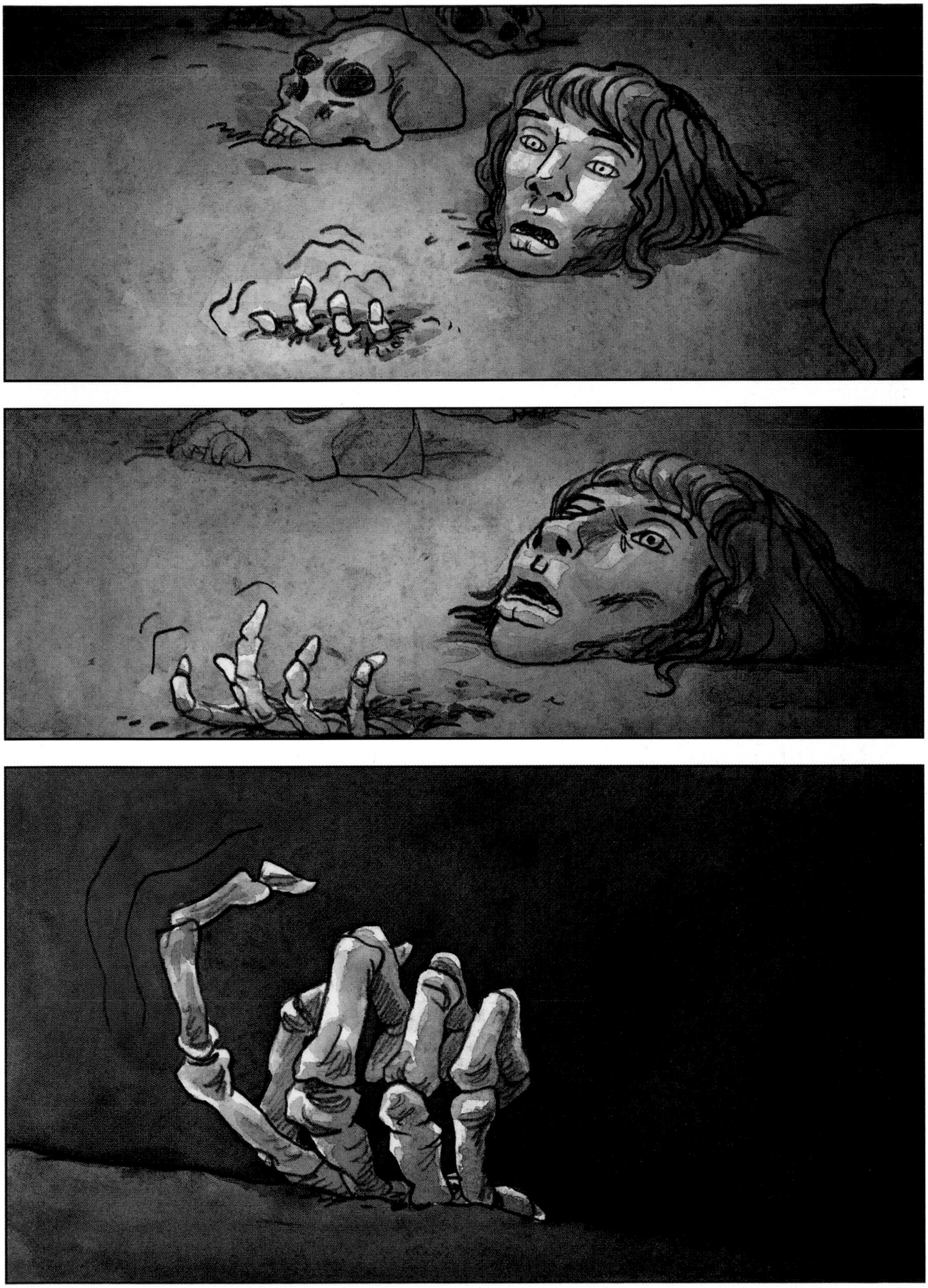

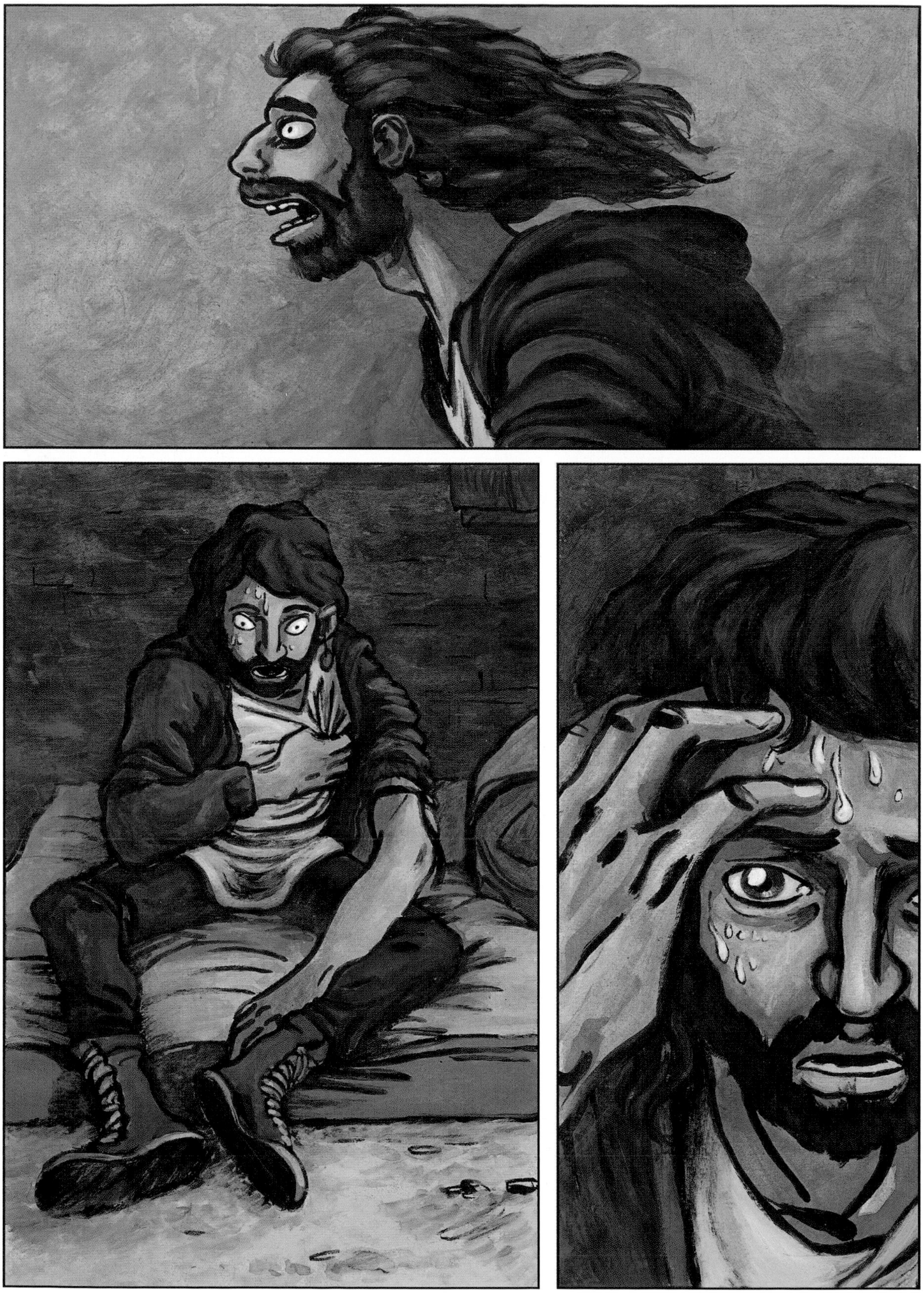

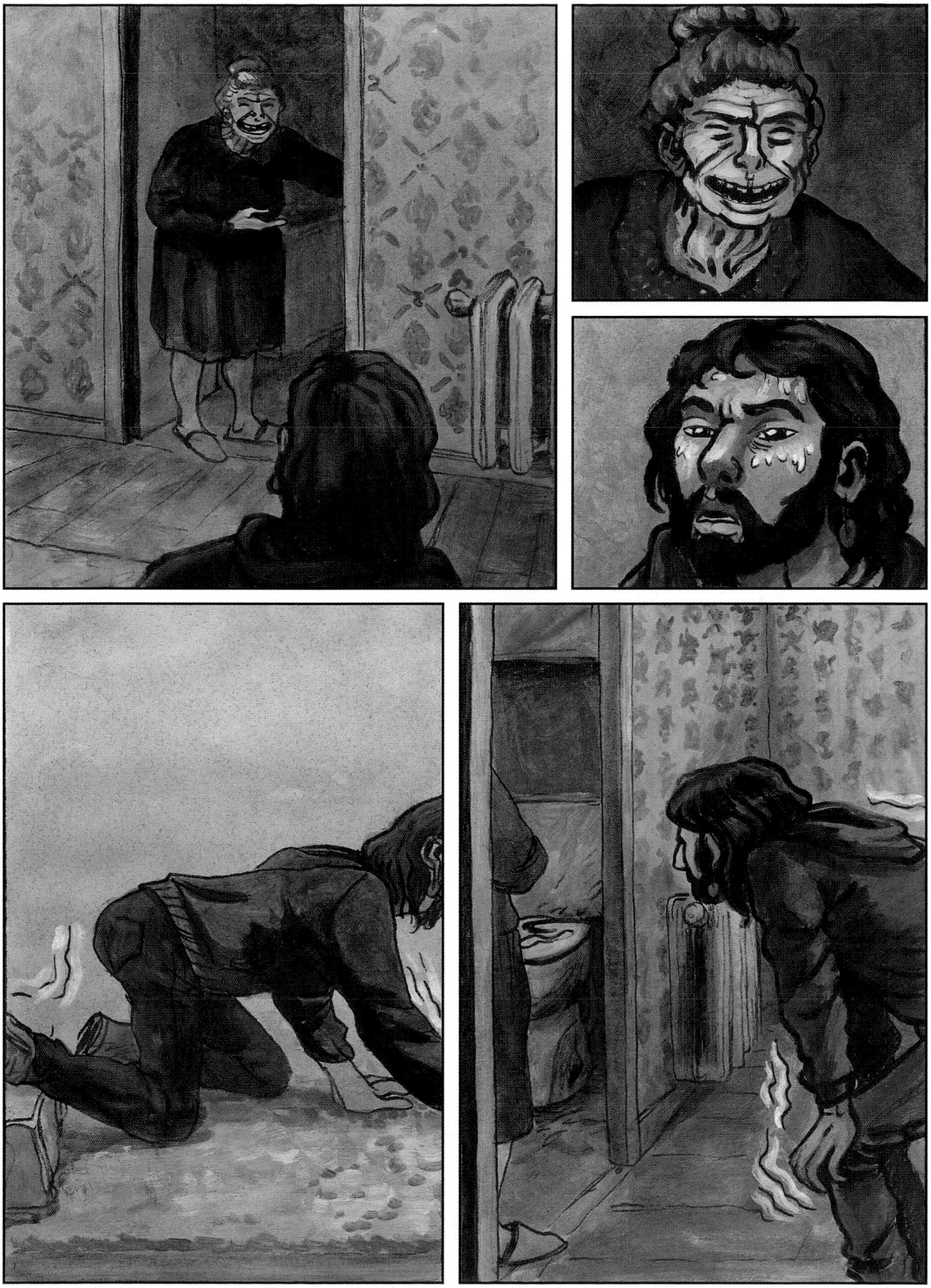

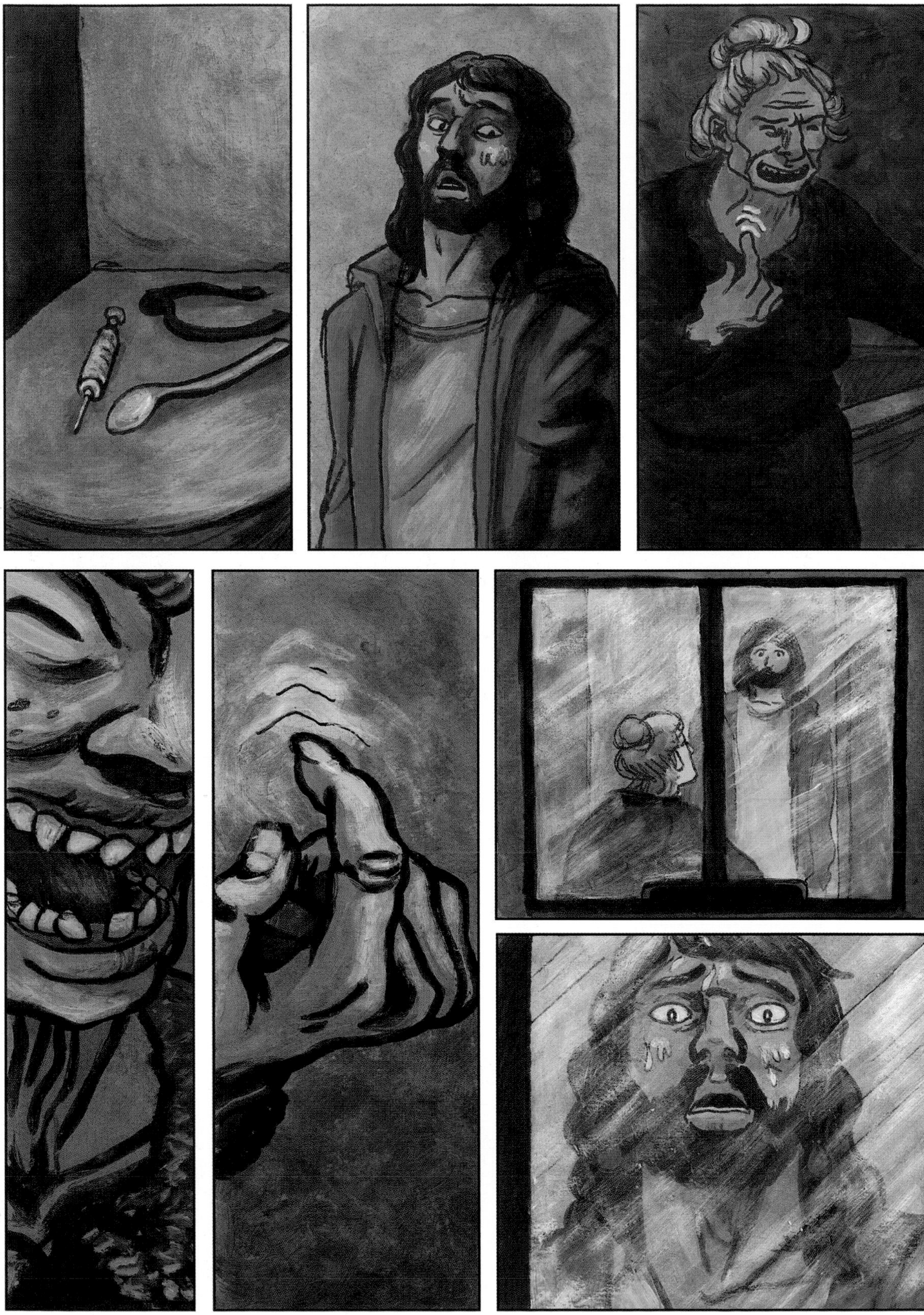

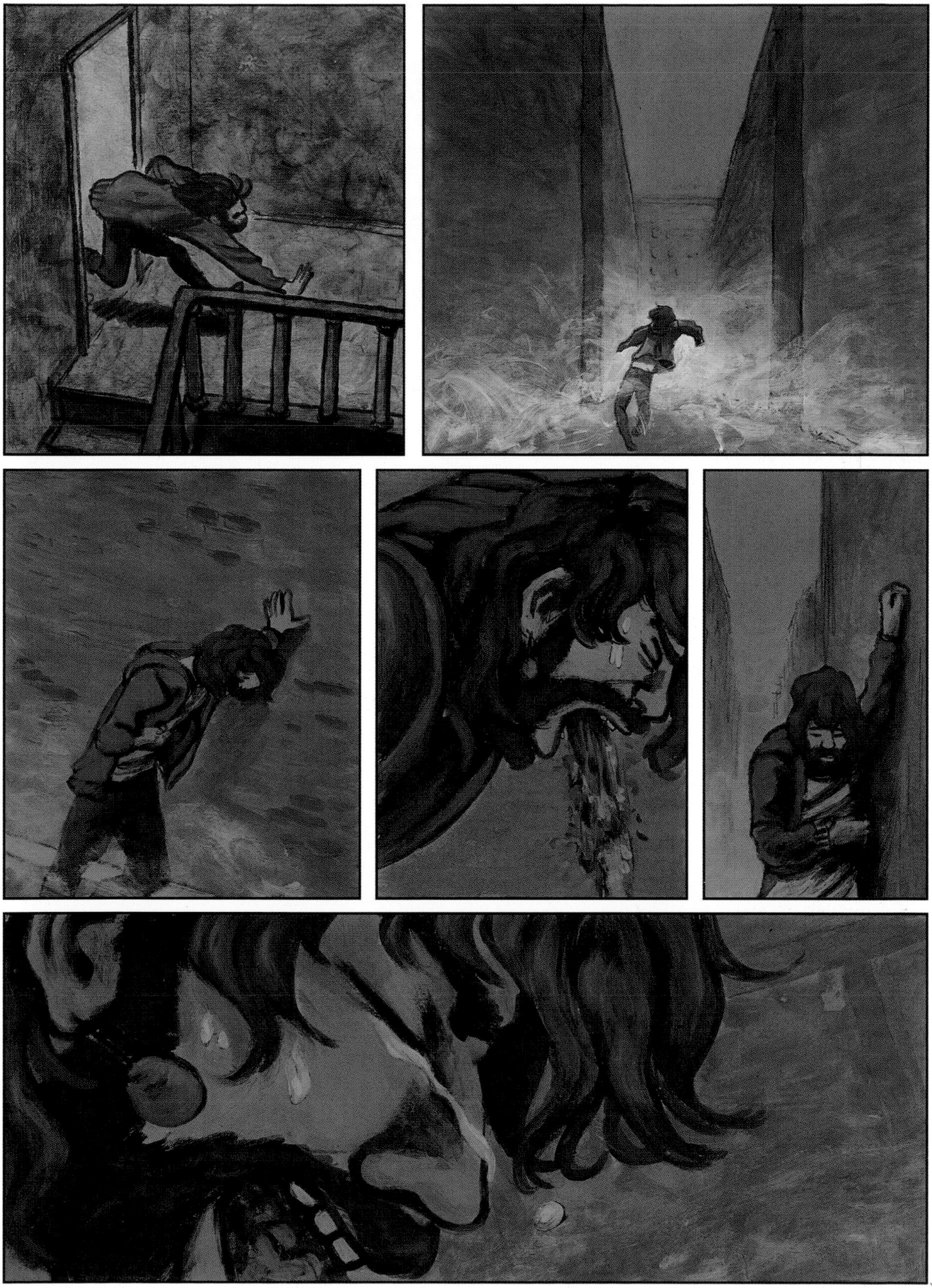

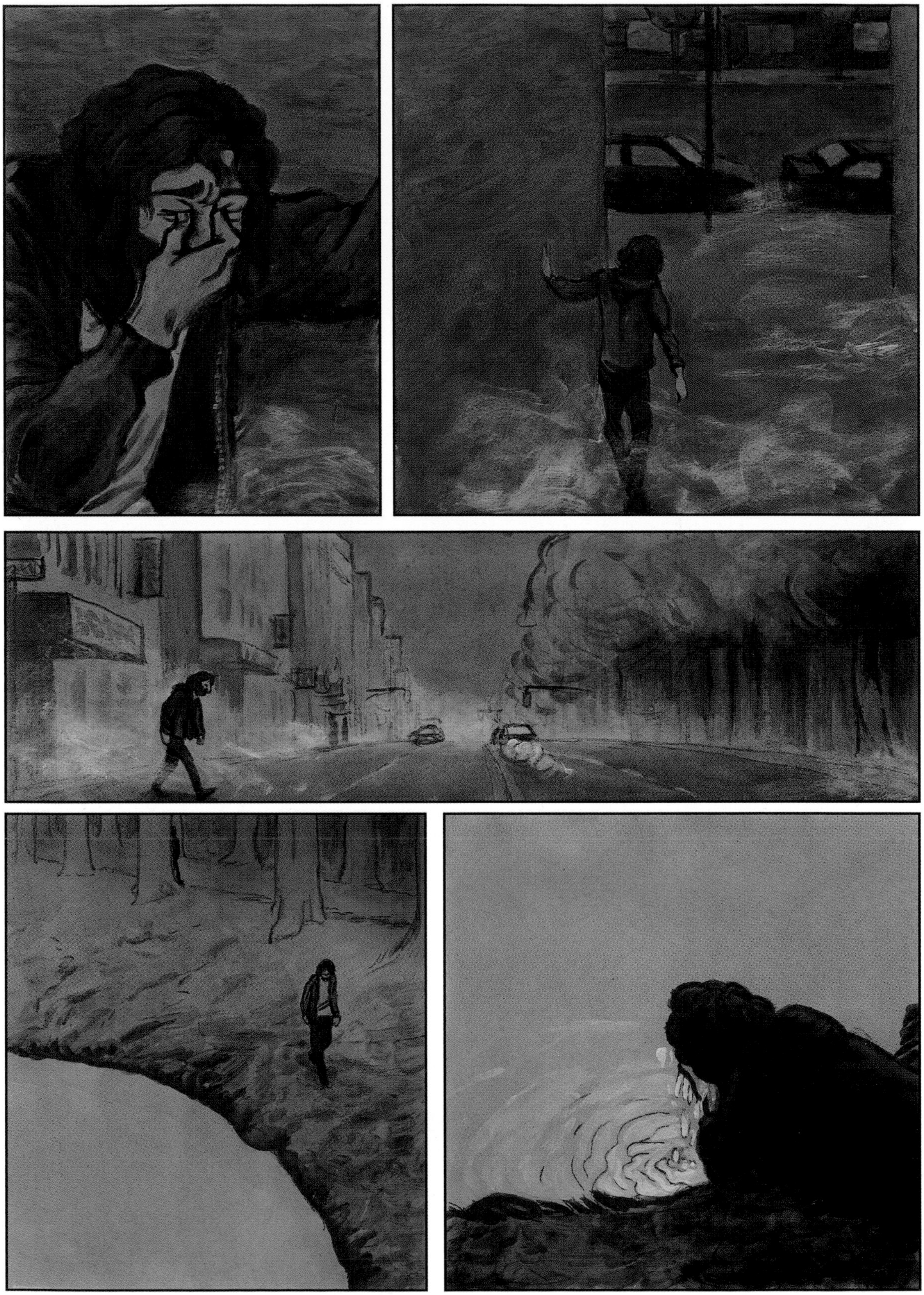

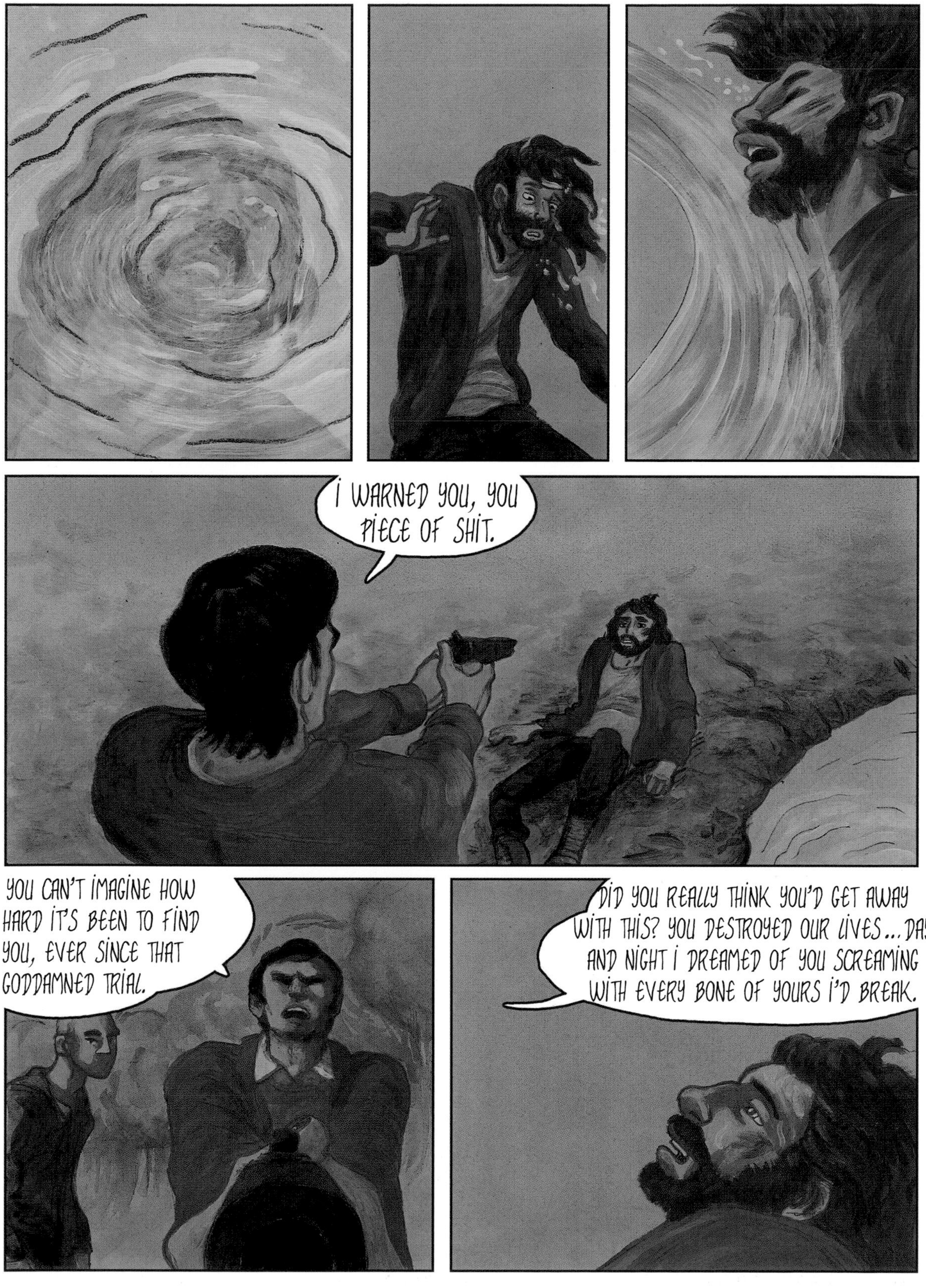
I WARNED YOU, YOU PIECE OF SHIT.
YOU CAN'T IMAGINE HOW HARD IT'S BEEN TO FIND YOU, EVER SINCE THAT GODDAMNED TRIAL.
DID YOU REALLY THINK YOU'D GET AWAY WITH THIS? YOU DESTROYED OUR LIVES... DAY AND NIGHT I DREAMED OF YOU SCREAMING WITH EVERY BONE OF YOURS I'D BREAK.

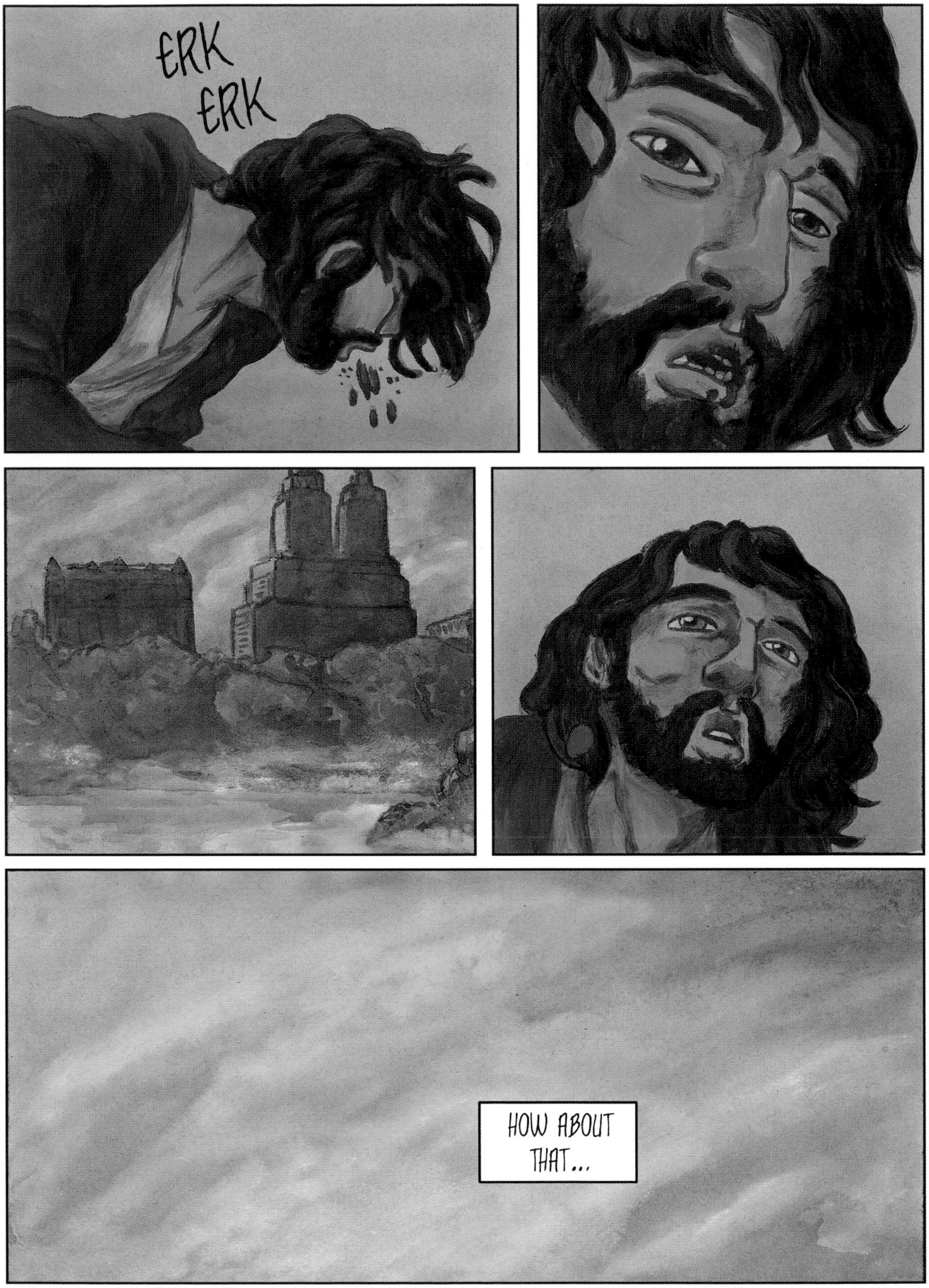
ERK
ERK
HOW ABOUT THAT...

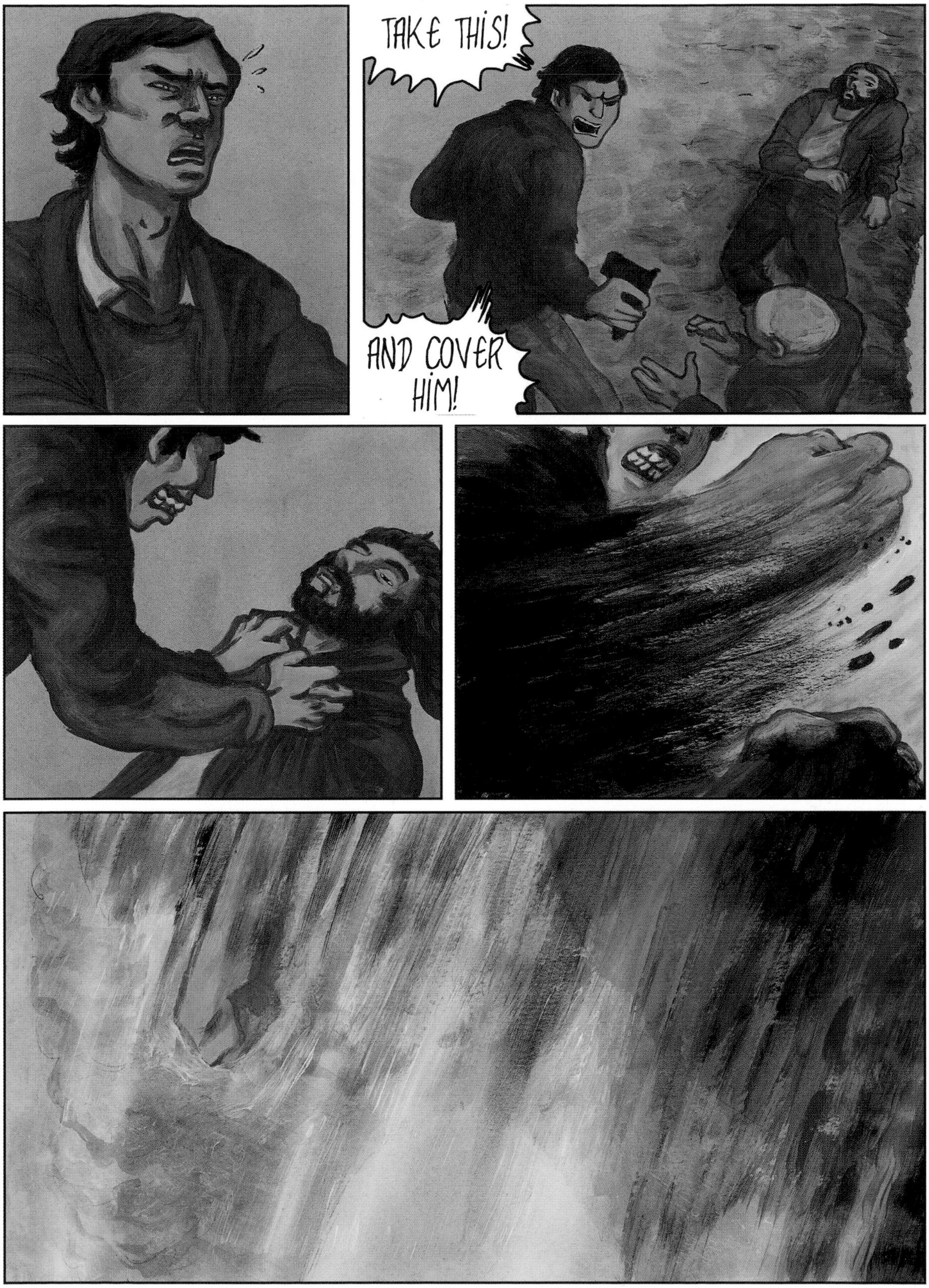
TAKE THIS!
AND COVER HIM!

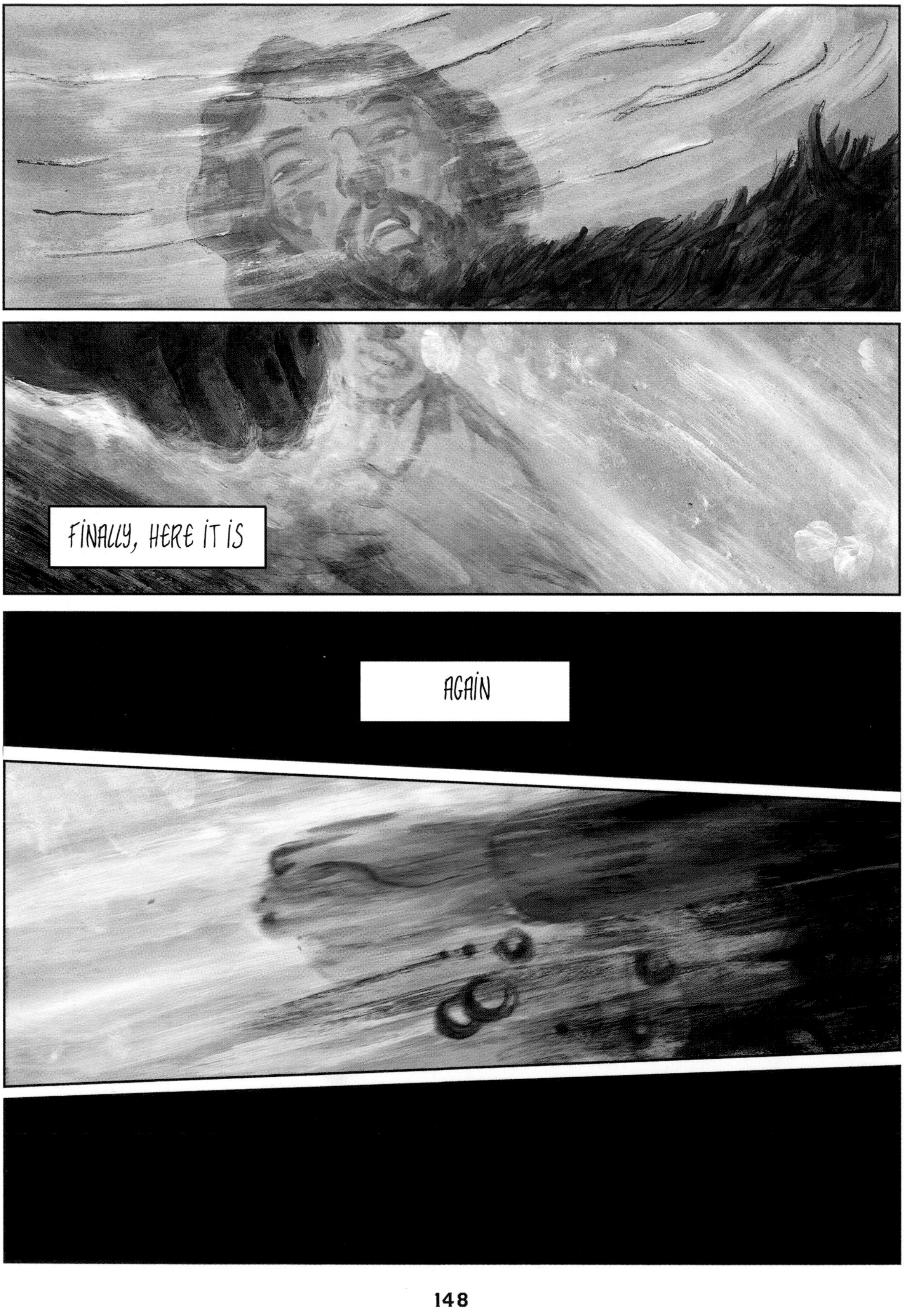
FINALLY, HERE IT IS
AGAIN

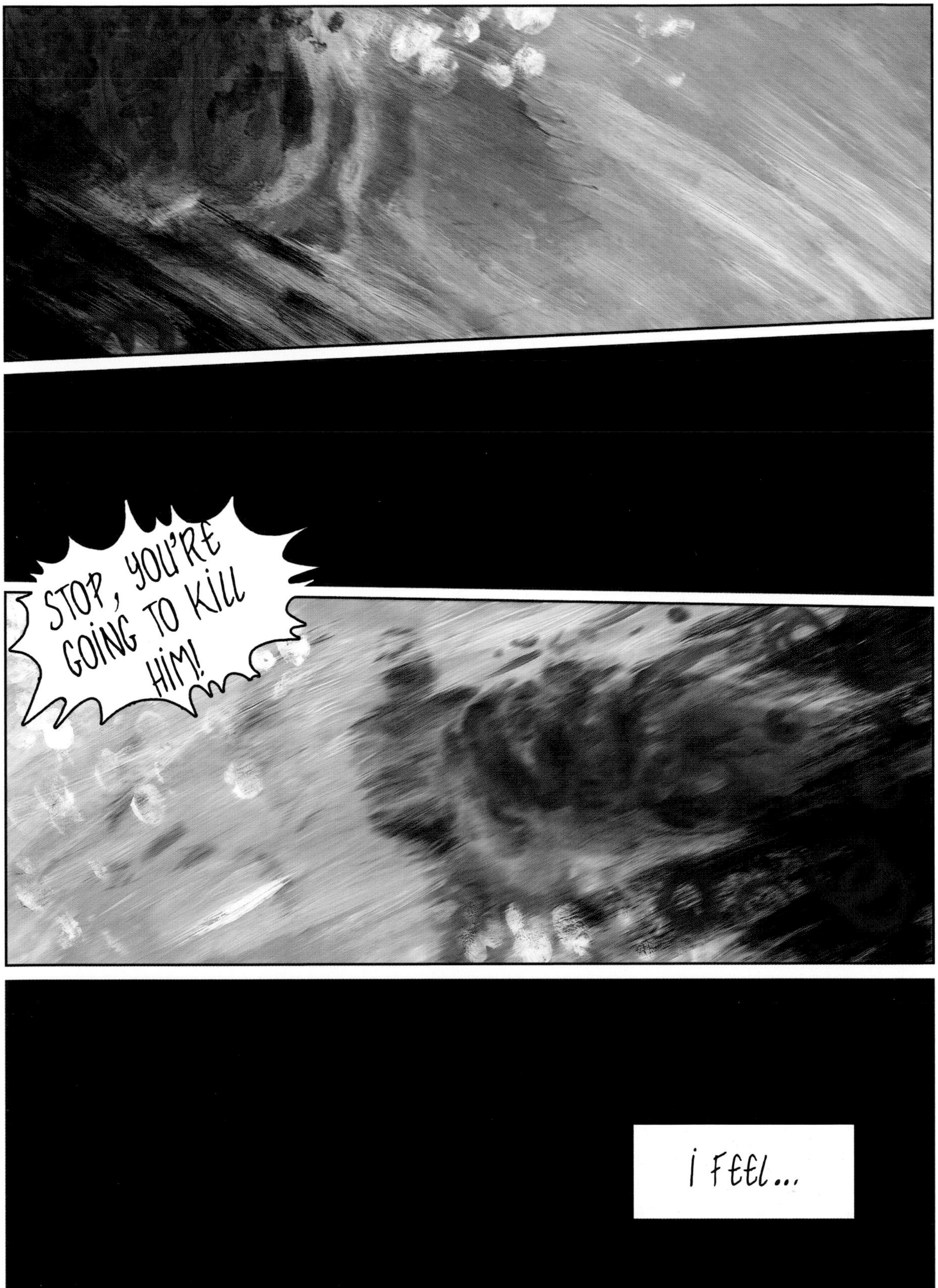
STOP, YOU'RE GOING TO KILL HIM!
I FEEL...

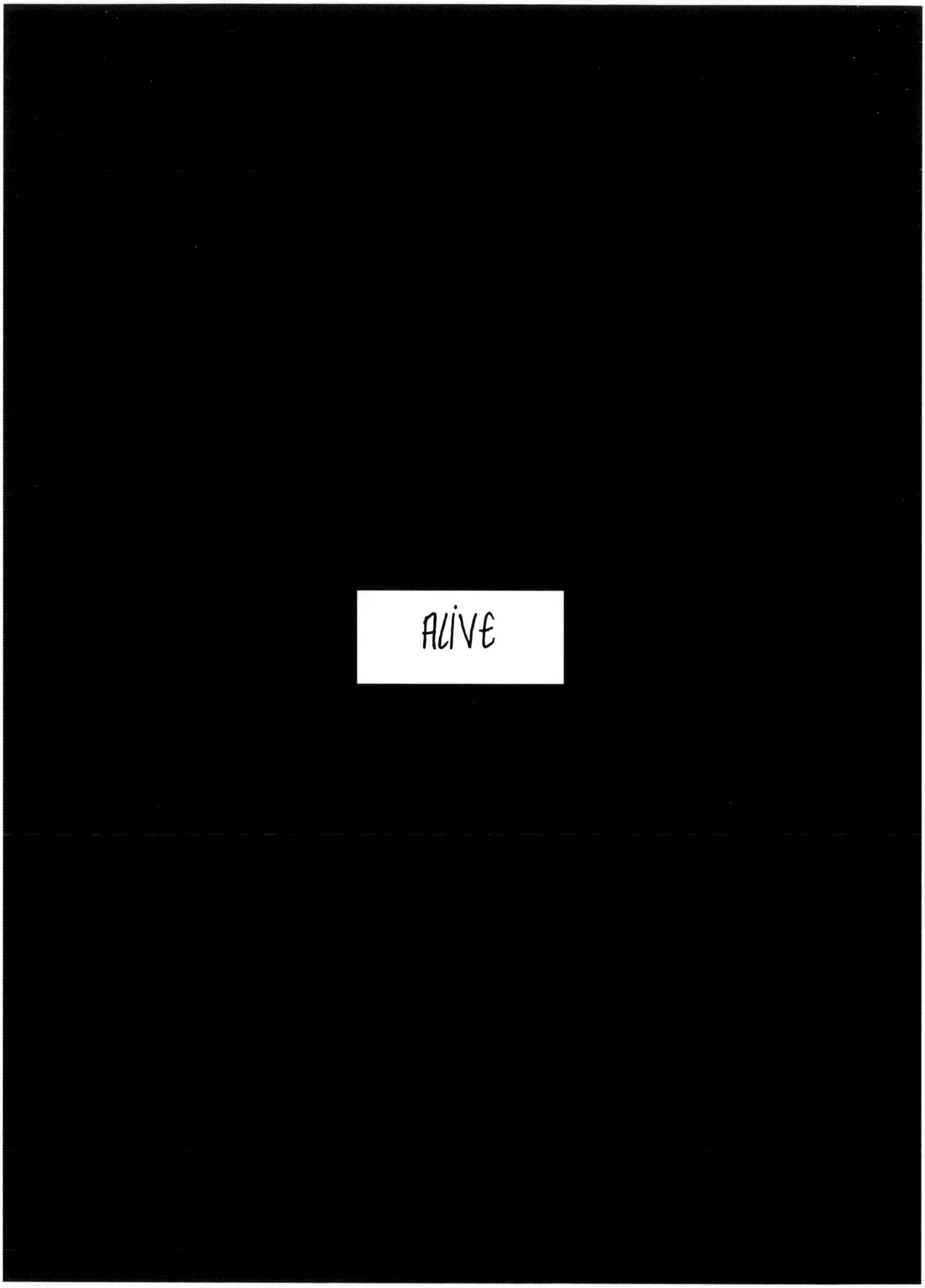
ALIVE

AFTERWORD
An Anthropological Perspective

Prohibition as a Social Norm

In the origins of civilization, mankind sought peace, and its first act was to prohibit.

"Prohibition is the first condition for social ties and the first cultural sign as well."[1] The genesis of culture, leaving behind the natural state (which Hobbes considered to be warfare) and the concept of the social contract, is the point where anthropology, ethnology, sociology, and theology interact... an endless source of philosophical inquiry.

Social customs and norms are created through the interaction of groups of individuals, and it has always been such. The goals of living in society can be described this way:

> To consider equality and the natural independence of individuals; to understand why they have renounced this independence to form civil societies and justify the existence of these societies by demonstrating, in the natural state, the "lack" that calls for their founding; to indicate the reasons that legitimize authority and that transform obedience to laws into an obligation of the conscience.[2]

The passage from nature to culture resides on a prohibition that must be respected: that against incest. The alternative means that social order crumbles. Myths and rites have been developed to transmit stories that speak of this danger.

> The prohibition of incest has neither a purely cultural nor a purely natural origin; nor is it a combination of composite elements partially borrowed from nature and partially from culture. It is the fundamental

act thanks to which, through which, and especially by, which the passage from nature to culture is accomplished.[3]

According to anthropologist Claude Lévi-Strauss, culture organizes that which nature has left to chance, especially concerning the sexual instinct. Since sexuality is perceived as being too close to animal instincts, escaping the finality of the group (the mastery over the individual, as the well-known expression "majority rule" suggests), the direction of sexuality is quickly taken over by collective forces, subordinated to alliances between men and women for procreation. Anything that encroaches on the order of society (free sexuality, incest, suicide, murder…) is portrayed tragically by myth and rites, then religion. The most compelling and well-known case is that of Oedipus: parricide, incest, epidemic, exile (social suicide). In all cultures and civilizations, myths respond to the same structure that organizes the body of knowledge.

> [T]he imitation of a transhuman model, the repetition of an exemplary scene and the breaking of profane time through a crack that opens onto Great Time, these are the essential notes of "mythic behavior."[4]

This serves as model and justification for maintaining the prohibition within the social group. The heart of its theater is desire and sacrifice. "Man's advantage over the lower animals being this, that he is the most imitative creature in the world."[5] In the Other, in what he is and what he has, our desire is born, and our identity takes form. The Other is a model but a rival as well, a mediator and an obstacle on the road leading to the object of desire. René Girard, our great theorist of mimetic desire, tells us this:

> Only mimetic desire can be *free*, can be *genuine* desire, human desire, because it *must* choose a model more than the object itself. Mimetic desire is what makes us human, what makes possible for us the breakout from routinely animalistic appetites, and constructs our own, albeit inevitably unstable, identities. It is this very mobility of desire, its mimetic nature, and this very instability of our identities, that makes us capable of *adaptation*, that gives the possibility to learn and to *evolve*.[6]

On a greater scale, that means that no culture invents itself but only replicates itself. Still, in the sphere of mimetic desire, crises are all but inevitable and lead to violence within communities, given the exacerbation of individual desires we have spoken of. Indeed, in the first century of our era,

Aristotle already noted that, "Envy is pain at the sight of such good fortune."[7] The outbreak of crises may also flow from the kind of model guiding us, whether it has a conscious influence or not. As Girard says,

> There are two arch-models: Satan and Christ. Freedom is an act of conversion to one or the other. Otherwise, it is a total illusion. […] We are free because we can truly convert ourselves at any time. In other words, we can refuse to join the mimetic unanimity. As we already explained, conversion means to become aware that we are persecutors. It means choosing Christ or a Christlike individual as a model for our desires. It also means seeing oneself as being in the process of imitating from the very beginning. Conversion is the discovery that we have always, without being aware of it, been imitating the wrong kind of models who lead us into the vicious circle of scandals and perpetual frustration.[8]

We do need to make a comment here. To keep from descending into a hasty Manichean conclusion, we should remember that a great number of myths, of sacred and religious texts, show that gods are just as—if not more—lustful and combative as demons.[9]

Skandalon

With the exasperation of mimetic desires, and the predominance of conflicts, the unity of the group is shattered. What should we do then? And who is the guilty party?

> Christ announces before his Passion that he will become a *skandalon* for everybody and for his disciples as well, for they will also play a part in his Passion. The word *skandalon* means a "mimetic stumbling-block," something that triggers mimetic rivalry. […] Although *skandalon* and Satan are fundamentally the same thing, the two terms emphasize different aspects of the same phenomenon. In the case of *skandalon*, the emphasis is on the early phases of the mimetic cycle, mimetic rivalry between two individuals who are obstacles to each other; whereas Satan refers to the whole mimetic mechanism. […] Both Jesus and Satan prompt imitation. Imitation is the road to our freedom, because we are free to imitate Christ in his incomparable wisdom in a benevolent and obedient way, or on the contrary, to imitate Satan, meaning to imitate God in a spirit of rivalry. *Skandalon* becomes the inability to walk away from mimetic rivalry, an inability that turns rivalry into an addiction, servitude, because we kneel in front of those who are

important for us, without seeing what is at stake. The proliferation of scandals, meaning of mimetic rivalry, is what produces disorder and instability in society, but this instability is put to an end by the scapegoat resolution, which produces order. Satan casts out Satan, meaning that the scapegoat mechanism produces a false transcendence that stabilizes society, through a satanic principle, and the order cannot but be only temporary, and it is bound to revert, sooner or later, into the disorder of scandals.[10]

That is the warning all myths issue. In the anguish of collective anger, reconciliation—surviving the crisis—is achieved by designating a scapegoat. This being is recognized by all as the only one responsible who must be sacrificed.

> The victim […] is a substitute for all the members of the community, offered up by the members themselves. The sacrifice serves to protect the entire community from *its own* violence; it prompts the entire community to choose victims outside itself.[11]

Only by this gesture of sacrifice can harmony and order be restored and even reinforced. Is the individual who has been killed the scapegoat? But the scapegoat, by definition, is innocent! The many different possibilities do not allow us to establish a definitive position, but that matters little. For the victimizing mechanism to work, society must believe in its right: the scapegoat is responsible for the evils within. An instance of predestination or random chance, the sacrifice requires either a being from the outside, above or below, king or slave, or one who can be a *pharmakon*, both poison and cure.

> [T]he surrogate victim—or, more simply, the final victim—inevitably appears as a being who submits to violence without provoking a reprisal; a supernatural being who sews violence to reap peace; a mysterious savior who visits affliction on mankind in order to subsequently restore it to good health.[12]

Therein lies the ambivalence of myths. The incarnation of a shared evil—the one, the monster, the demon, through whose sacrifice order is restored—becomes the pacifier, the savior, god. A terrible "union of opposites" where good and evil are but two aspects of the same reality.[13]

To incarnate such a symbol, what better than to designate a personality who already symbolizes everything we wish to attribute to him, and that we seek to expiate … When Dionysus caught fire, it wasn't to offer the crowd some kind of cathartic resolution. He danced for dancing's sake. But the crowd is always hungry for scandal.

—Julie Maroh

Endnotes

1. René Girard, *Evolution and Conversion: Dialogues on the Origins of Culture*, with Pierpaolo Antonello and Joao Cezar de Castro Rocha, p. 110.

2. Jean-Fabien Spitz, *État de nature et contrat social*.

3. Claude Lévi-Strauss, *Nature, culture et société*.

4. Mircea Eliade, *Myths, Dreams and Mysteries*, chapter 1.

5. Aristotle, *The Poetics*, chapter 4.

6. René Girard, *Evolution and Conversion*, p. 58.

7. Aristotle, *Rhetoric*, Book Two, chapter 10.

8. René Girard, *Evolution and Conversion*, p. 223.

9. For more on the subject, see the works of Sylvain Lévi, most notably his *La Doctrine du sacrifice dans les Brahmanas*.

10. René Girard, *Evolution and Conversion*, pp. 223–224.

11. René Girard, translated by Patrick Gregory, *Violence and the Sacred*, p. 8.

12. ibid, p. 86.

13. To read further about this theme and the others discussed here, explore René Girard's writings, especially those mentioned above.

ACKNOWLEDGMENTS

For their unconditional support, my thanks go to all those close to me.

To Glénat Editions, and the team in Angoulême.

Thanks to those who lent me their shoulder and part of their table:
Sophie Yanow, Lisa Mandel, Baptiste Amsallem, Dwam, Didier Garguilo,
the Turbo Zero Tattoo Shop, Marie di Monti & Benoît Preteseille, Marianne,
Zviane & Luc Bossé, the Atelier 7070.

Thanks to Antoine who posed so docilely!

Special thanks to Paul Herman, Philippe Hauri, Benoit Hamet,
Marie Tijou, Sarah Glidden, Jeremy Sorese, Mokë, Amruta Patil, Anaël
Seghezzi, Aude Samama, Juliette Paupiette, Maya Mihindou, CAäT.

For the creation of this book, the author received a residence at the
Maison des Auteurs d'Angoulême.

JULIE MAROH is an author and illustrator originally from northern France. She studied comic art at the Institute Saint-Luc in Brussels and lithography and engraving at the Royal Academy of Arts in Brussels. Her graphic novel *Blue Is the Warmest Color*, a *New York Times* bestseller and the basis for the Palme d'Or-winning feature film of the same name, has been translated into eleven languages to date.

juliemaroh.com

DAVID HOMEL, born and raised in Chicago, is a Governor General Literary Award-winning translator and writer. His most recent translations include *Kuessipan* by Naomi Fontaine, *The World is Moving around Me: A Memoir of the Haiti Earthquake* by Dany Laferriere (both Arsenal Pulp), and his own novels include *Midway* and, most recently, *The Fledglings* (both Cormorant Books). He lives in Montreal.